SHIFT OMNIBUS

BY HUGH HOWEY

Shift Omnibus

Copyright © 2013 by Hugh Howey

This work contains material previously published as:
First Shift, Second Shift, and Third Shift

Cover illustration by Hugh Howey
Interior design and layout by Hugh Howey

ISBN-13: 978-1-481983-556
ISBN-10: 1-48198355-5

www.hughhowey.com

Give feedback on the book at:
hughhowey@gmail.com
Twitter: @hughhowey

Second Edition

Printed in the U.S.A

For those who find themselves well and truly alone.

First Shift
Legacy

In 2007, the Center for Automation in Nanobiotech (CAN) outlined the hardware and software platforms that would one day allow robots smaller than human cells to make medical diagnoses, conduct repairs, and even self-propagate.

That same year, CBS re-aired a program about the effects of propranolol on sufferers of extreme trauma. A simple pill, it had been discovered, could wipe out the memory of any traumatic event.

At almost the same moment in humanity's broad history, mankind had discovered the means for bringing about its utter downfall. And the ability to forget it ever happened.

• Prologue •

Troy returned to the living and found himself inside of a tomb. He awoke to a world of confinement, a thick sheet of frosted glass pressed near to his face.

Dark shapes stirred on the other side of the icy murk. He tried to lift his arms, to beat on the glass, but his muscles were too weak. He attempted to scream—but could only cough. The taste in his mouth was foul. His ears rang with the clank of heavy locks opening, the hiss of air, the squeak of hinges long dormant.

The lights overhead were bright, the hands on him warm. They helped him sit while he continued to cough, his breath clouding the chill air. Someone had water. Pills to take. The water was cool, the pills bitter. Troy fought down a few gulps. He was unable to hold the glass without help, hands trembling, memories flooding back, scenes from long nightmares. The feeling of deep time and yesterdays mingled. He shivered.

A paper gown. The sting of tape removed. A tug on his arm, a tube pulled from his groin. Two men dressed in white helped him out of the coffin. Steam rose all around him, air condensing and dispersing.

Sitting up and blinking against the glare, exercising lids long shut, Troy looked down the rows of coffins full of the living that stretched toward the distant and curved walls. The ceiling felt low; the suffocating press of dirt stacked high above. And the years. So many had passed. Anyone he cared about would be gone.

Everything was gone.

The pills stung his throat. He tried to swallow. Memories faded like dreams upon waking, and he felt his grip loosen on everything he'd known.

He collapsed backwards—but the men in the white coveralls saw this coming. They caught him and lowered him to the ground, a paper gown rustling on shivering skin.

Memories flooded back; recollections rained down like bombs and were then gone.

The pills would only do so much. It would take time to destroy the past.

Troy began to sob into his palms, a sympathetic hand resting on his head. The two men in white allowed him this moment. They didn't rush the process. Here was a courtesy passed from one waking soul to the next, something all the men sleeping in their coffins would one day rise to discover.

And eventually... forget.

2049 · Washington, D.C.

The tall glass trophy cabinets had once served as bookshelves. There were hints. Hardware on the shelves dated back centuries, while the hinges and the tiny locks on the glass doors went back mere decades. The framing around the glass was cherry, but the cases had been built of oak. Someone had attempted to remedy this with a few coats of stain, but the grain didn't match. The color wasn't perfect. To trained eyes, details such as these were glaring.

Congressman Donald Keene gathered these clues without meaning to. He simply saw that long ago there had been a great purge, a making of space. At some point in the past, the Senator's waiting room had been stripped of its obligatory law books until only a handful remained. These tomes sat silently in the dim corners of the glass cabinets. They were shut-in, their spines laced with cracks, old leather flaking off like sunburnt skin.

A handful of Keene's fellow freshmen filled the waiting room, pacing and stirring, their terms of service newly begun. Like Donald, they were young and still hopelessly optimistic. They were bringing change to Capitol Hill. They hoped to deliver where their similarly naïve predecessors had not.

While they waited their turns to meet with the great Senator Thurman from their home state of Georgia, they chatted nervously amongst themselves. They were a gaggle of priests, Donald imagined, all lined up to meet the Pope, to kiss his ring. He let out a heavy breath and focused on the contents of the case, lost himself in the treasures behind the glass while a fellow representative from Georgia prattled on about his district's Centers for Disease Control and Prevention.

"—and they have this detailed guide on their website, this response and readiness manual in case of, okay, get this, a zombie invasion. Can you believe that? Fucking zombies. Like even the CDC thinks something could go wrong and suddenly we'd all be *eating* each other—"

Donald stifled a smile, fearful it's reflection would be caught in the glass. He turned and looked over a collection of photographs on the walls, one each of the Senator with the last four presidents. It was the same pose and handshake in each shot, the same staged background of windless flags and fancy oversized seals. The Senator hardly seemed to change as the presidents came and went. His hair started white and stayed white; he seemed perfectly unfazed by the passing of decades..

Seeing the photographs side by side devalued each of them somehow. They looked staged. Phony. It was as if this collection of the world's most powerful men had each begged for the opportunity to stand and pose with a cardboard cutout, a roadside attraction.

Donald laughed, and the congressman from Atlanta joined him.

"I know, right? Zombies. It's hilarious. But think about it, okay? Why would the CDC even *have* this field manual unless—?"

Donald wanted to correct his fellow congressman, to tell him what he'd really been laughing about. Look at the smiles, he wanted to say. They were on the faces of the *presidents*. The Senator looked like he'd rather be anyplace else. It looked as if each in this succession of commanders in chief knew who the more powerful man was, who would be there long after they had come and gone.

"—it's advice like, everyone should have a baseball bat with their flashlights and candles, right? Just in case. You know, for bashing brains."

Donald pulled out his phone and checked the time. He glanced at the door leading off the waiting room and wondered how much longer he'd have to wait. Putting the phone away, he turned back to the cabinet and studied a shelf where a military uniform had been carefully arranged like a delicate work of origami. The left breast of the jacket featured a wall of medals; the sleeves were folded over and pinned to highlight the gold braids sewn along the cuffs. In front of the uniform, a collection of decorative coins rested in a custom wooden rack, tokens of appreciation from men and women serving overseas.

The two arrangements spoke volumes: the uniform from the past and the coins from those currently deployed,– bookends on a pair of wars. One that the Senator had fought in as a youth. The other, a war he had battled to prevent as an older and wiser man.

"—yeah, it sounds crazy, I know, but do you know what rabies does to a dog? I mean, what it *really* does, the biological—?"

Donald leaned in closer to study the decorative coins. The number and slogan on each one represented a deployed group. Or was it a battalion? He couldn't remember. His sister Charlotte would know. She was over there somewhere, out in the field.

"Hey, aren't you even a little nervous about this?"

Donald realized the question had been aimed at him. He turned and faced the talkative Congressman. He must've been in his mid-thirties, probably Donald's age. In him, Donald could see his own thinning hair, his own beginnings of a gut, that uncomfortable slide to middle age.

"Am I nervous about zombies?" Donald laughed. "No. Can't say that I am."

The congressman stepped up beside Donald, his eyes drifting toward the imposing uniform that stood propped up as if a warrior's chest remained inside. "No," the man said. "About meeting *him*."

The door to the reception area opened, bleeps from the phones on the other side leaking out.

"Congressman Keene?"

An elderly receptionist stood in the doorway, her white blouse and black skirt highlighting a thin and athletic frame.

"Senator Thurman will see you now," she said.

Donald patted the congressman from Atlanta on the shoulder as he stepped past.

"Hey, good luck," the gentleman stammered after him.

Donald smiled. He fought the temptation to turn and tell the man that he knew the Senator well enough, that he had been bounced on his knee back when he was a child. Only—Donald was too busy hiding his own nerves to bother.

He stepped through the deeply paneled door of rich hardwoods and entered the Senator's inner sanctum. This wasn't like passing through a foyer to pick up a man's daughter for a date. This was different. This was the pressure of meeting as colleagues when Donald still felt like that same young child.

"Through here," the receptionist said. She guided Donald between pairs of wide and busy desks, a dozen phones chirping in short bursts. Young men and women in suits and crisp blouses double-fisted receivers. Their bored expressions suggested that this was a normal workload for a weekday morning.

Donald reached out a hand as he passed one of the desks, brushing the wood with his fingertips. Mahogany. The aides here had desks nicer than his own. And the decor: the plush carpet, the broad and ancient crown molding, the antique tile ceiling, the dangling light fixtures that may have been actual crystal.

At the end of the buzzing and bleeping room, a paneled door opened and disgorged Congressman Mick Webb, just finished with his meeting. Mick didn't notice Donald, was too absorbed by the open folder he held in front of him.

Donald stopped and waited for his colleague and old college acquaintance to approach. "So," he asked "How did it go?"

Mick looked up and snapped the folder shut. He tucked it under his arm and nodded. "Yeah, yeah. It went great." He smiled. "Sorry if we ran long. The old man couldn't get enough of me."

Donald laughed. He believed that. Mick had swept into office with ease. He had the charisma and confidence that went along with being tall and handsome. Donald used to joke that if his friend wasn't shit with names, he'd be president someday. "No problem," Donald said. He jabbed a thumb over his shoulder. "I was making new friends."

Mick smiled. "I bet."

"Yeah, well, I'll see you back at the ranch."

"Sure thing." Mick slapped him on the arm with the folder and headed for the exit. Donald caught the glare from the Senator's receptionist and hurried over. She waved him through to the dimly lit office and pulled the door shut behind him.

"Congressman Keene."

Senator Paul Thurman stood from behind his desk and stretched out a hand. He flashed a familiar smile, one Donald had come to recognize as much from photos and TV as from his childhood. Despite Thurman's age—he had to be pushing seventy if he wasn't already there—the Senator was trim and fit. His oxford shirt hugged a military frame; a thick neck bulged out of his knotted tie; his white hair remained as crisp and orderly as an enlisted man's.

Donald crossed the dark room and shook the senator's hand.

"Good to see you, sir."

"Please, sit." Thurman released Donald's hand and gestured to one of the chairs across from his desk. Donald lowered himself into the bright red leather, the gold grommets along the arm like sturdy rivets in a steel beam.

"How's Helen?"

"Helen?" Donald straightened his tie. "She's great. She's back in Savannah. She really enjoyed seeing you at the reception."

"She's a beautiful woman, your wife."

"Thank you, sir." Donald fought to relax, which didn't help. The office had the pall of dusk, even with the overhead lights on. The clouds outside had turned nasty—low and dark. If it rained, he would have to take the underpass back to his office. He hated being down there. They could carpet it and hang those little chandeliers at intervals, but he could still tell he was below ground. The tunnels in Washington made him feel like a rat scurrying through a sewer. It always seemed like the roof was about to cave in.

"How's the job treating you so far?"

"The job's good. Busy, but good."

He started to ask the Senator how Anna was doing, but the door behind him opened before he could. The receptionist entered and delivered two bottles of water. Donald thanked her, twisted the cap off, and saw that it had been pre-opened.

"I hope you're not too busy to work on something for me." Senator Thurman raised an eyebrow. Donald took a sip of water and wondered if that was a skill one could master, that eyebrow lift. It made him want to jump to attention and salute.

"I'm sure I can make the time," he said. "After all the stumping you did for me? I doubt I would've made it past the primaries." He fiddled with the water bottle in his lap.

"You and Mick Webb go back, right? Both Bulldogs."

It took Donald a moment to realize the Senator was referring to their college mascot. He hadn't spent a lot of time at Georgia following sports. "Yessir. Go Dawgs."

He hoped that was right.

The Senator smiled. He leaned forward so that his face caught the soft light raining down on his desk. Donald watched as shadows caught in wrinkles otherwise easy to miss. Thurman's lean face and square chin made him look younger head-on than he probably did in profile. Here was a man who got places by approaching others directly rather than in ambush.

"You studied architecture at Georgia."

Donald nodded. It was easy to forget that he knew Thurman better than the Senator knew him. One of them grabbed far more newspaper headlines than the other.

"That's right. For my undergrad. I went into planning for my master's. I figured I could do more good governing people than I could drawing boxes to put them in."

He winced to hear himself deliver the line. It was a pat phrase from grad school, something he should have left behind with crushing beer cans on his forehead and ogling asses in skirts. He wondered for the dozenth time why he and the other congressional newcomers had been summoned. When he first got the invite, he figured it was a social visit.

Then Mick had bragged about his own appointment, and Donald figured it was some kind of formality or tradition. But now he wondered if this was a power play, a chance to butter up the Representatives from Georgia for those times when Thurman would need a particular vote in the lower and *lesser* house.

"Tell me, Donny, how good are you at keeping secrets?"

Donald's blood ran cold. He forced himself to laugh off the sudden flush of nerves.

"I got elected, didn't I?"

Senator Thurman smiled. "And so you probably learned the best lesson there is about secrets." He picked up and raised his water bottle in salute. "*Denial.*"

Donald nodded and took a sip of his own water. He wasn't sure where this was going, but he already felt uneasy. He sensed some of the backroom dealings coming on that he'd promised his constituents he'd root out if elected.

The Senator leaned back in his chair.

"Denial is the secret sauce in this town," he said. "It's the flavor that holds all the other ingredients together. Here's what I tell the newly elected: the truth is going to get out—it always does—but it's going to blend in with all the *lies.*" The Senator twirled a hand in the air. "You have to deny each lie and every truth with the same vinegar. Let those websites and blowhards who bitch about cover-ups confuse the public *for* you."

"Uh, yessir." Donald didn't know what else to say.

The Senator lifted an eyebrow again. He remained frozen for a pause, and then asked, out of nowhere: "Do you believe in aliens, Donny?"

Donald nearly lost the water out of his nose. He covered his mouth with his hand, coughed, had to wipe his chin. The Senator didn't budge.

"Aliens?" Donald shook his head and wiped his wet palm on his thigh. "No sir. I mean, not the abducting kind. Why?"

He wondered if this was some kind of debriefing. Why had the Senator asked him if he could keep a secret? Was this a security initiation? The Senator remained silent.

"They're not real," Donald finally said. He watched for any twitch or hint. "Are they?"

The old man cracked a smile. "That's the thing," he said. "If they are or they aren't, the chatter out there would be the same. Would you be surprised if I told you they're very much real?"

"Hell, yeah, I'd be surprised."

"Good." The Senator slid a folder across the desk. Donald eyed it and held up a hand.

"Wait. Are they real or aren't they? What're you trying to tell me?"

Senator Thurman laughed. "Of course they're not real." He took his hand off the folder and propped his elbows on the desk. "Have you seen how much NASA wants from us so they can fly to Mars and back? We're not getting to another star. Ever. And nobody's coming here. Hell, why would they?"

Donald didn't know *what* to think, which was a far cry from how he'd felt less than a minute ago. He saw what the Senator meant, how truth and lies seemed black and white, but mixed together, they made everything gray and confusing. He glanced down at the folder. It looked similar to the one Mick had been carrying. It reminded him of the government's fondness for all things outdated.

"This is denial, right?" He studied the Senator. "That's what you're doing right now. You're trying to throw me off."

"No. This is me telling you to stop watching so many science fiction flicks. In fact, why do you think those eggheads are always dreaming of colonizing some other planet? You have any idea what would be involved? It's ludicrous. Not cost-effective."

Donald shrugged. He didn't think it was ludicrous. He twisted the cap back onto his water. "It's in our nature to dream of open space," he said. "To find room to spread out in. Isn't that how we ended up here?"

"Here? In America?" The Senator laughed. "We didn't come here and find open space. We got a bunch of people sick, killed them, and *made* space." Thurman pointed at the folder. "Which brings me to this. I've got something I'd like you to work on."

Donald placed his bottle on the leather inlay of the formidable desk and took the folder.

"Is this something coming through committee?"

He tried to temper his hopes. It was alluring to think of co-authoring a bill his first year in office. He opened the folder and tilted it toward the window. Outside, storms were gathering.

"No, nothing like that. This is about CAD-FAC."

Donald nodded. *Of course.* The preamble about secrets and conspiracies suddenly made perfect sense, as did the gathering of Georgia congressmen outside. This was about the Containment and Disposal Facility, nicknamed CAD-FAC, at the heart of the Senator's new energy bill, the complex that would one day house most of the world's spent nuclear fuel. Or, according to the websites Thurman had alluded to, it was going to be the next Area 51, or the site where a new-and-improved superbomb was being built, or a secure holding facility for Libertarians who had purchased one too many guns. Take your pick. There was enough noise out there to hide *any* truth.

"Yeah," Donald said, deflated. "I've been getting some entertaining calls from my district." He didn't dare mention the one about the Lizard People. "I want you to know, sir, that privately I'm behind the facility one hundred percent." He looked up at the Senator. "I'm glad I didn't have to vote on it publicly, of course, but it was about time someone offered up their backyard, right?"

"Precisely. For the common good." Senator Thurman took a long pull from his water, leaned back in his chair and cleared his throat. "You're a sharp young man, Donny. Not everyone sees what a boon to our state this'll be. A real life-saver." He smiled. "I'm sorry, you *are* still going by Donny, right? Or is it Donald, now?"

"Either's fine," Donald lied. He no longer enjoyed being called Donny, but changing names in the middle of one's life was practically impossible. He returned to the folder and flipped the cover letter over. There was a drawing underneath, a drawing that struck him as being out of place. It was...too familiar. Familiar, and yet it didn't belong there—it was from another life.

"Have you seen the economic reports?" Thurman asked. "Do you know how many jobs this bill created overnight?" He snapped his fingers.

"Forty thousand, just like that. And that's only from Georgia. A lot will be from your district, a lot of shipping, a lot of stevedores. Of course, now that it's passed, our less nimble colleagues are grumbling that *they* should've had a chance to bid—"

"I drew this," Donald interrupted, pulling out the sheet of paper. He showed it to Thurman as if the Senator would be surprised to see that it had snuck into the folder. Donald wondered if this was the Senator's daughter's doing, some kind of a joke or a hello and a wink from Anna.

Thurman nodded. "Yes, well, it needs more detail, wouldn't you say?"

Donald studied the architectural illustration and wondered what sort of test this was. He remembered the drawing. It was a last-minute project for his biotecture class his senior year. There was nothing unusual or amazing about it, just a large cylindrical building a hundred or so stories tall ringed with glass and concrete, balconies burgeoning with gardens, one side cutaway to reveal interspersed levels for housing, working, and shopping. The structure was spare where he remembered other classmates being bold, utilitarian where he could've taken risks. Green tufts jutted up from the flat roof, a horrible cliché, a nod to carbon neutrality.

In sum, it was drab and boring. Donald couldn't imagine a design so bare rising from the deserts of Dubai alongside the great new breed of self-sustaining skyscrapers. He certainly couldn't see what the Senator wanted with it.

"More detail," he murmured, repeating the Senator's words. He flipped through the rest of the folder, looking for hints, for context.

"Wait." Donald studied a list of requirements written up as if by a prospective client. "This looks like a design proposal." Words he had forgotten he'd ever learned caught his eye: *interior traffic flow, block plan, HVAC, hydroponics*—

"You'll have to lose the sunlight." Senator Thurman's chair squeaked as he leaned over his desk.

"I'm sorry?" Donald held the folder up. "What exactly are you wanting me to do?"

"I would suggest those lights like my wife uses." He cupped his hand into a tiny circle and pointed at the center. "She gets these tiny seeds to sprout in the winter, uses bulbs that cost me a goddamned fortune."

"You mean grow lights."

Thurman snapped his fingers. "And don't worry about the cost. Whatever you need. I'm also going to get you some help with the mechanical stuff. An engineer. An entire team."

Donald flipped through more of the folder. "What is this *for?* And why me?"

"This is what we call a *just-in-case* building. Probably'll never get used, but they won't let us store the fuel rods out there unless we put this bugger nearby. It's like this window in my basement I had to lower before our house could pass inspection. It was for...what do you call it—?"

"Egress," Donald said, the word flowing back unaided.

"Yes. Egress." He pointed to the folder. "This building is like that window, something we've gotta build so the rest will pass inspection. This will be where—in the unlikely event of an attack or a leak—where facility employees can go. A shelter. And it needs to be *perfect* or this project will be shut down faster than a tick's wink. Just because our bill passed and got signed doesn't mean we're home-free, Donny. There was that project out west that got okayed decades ago, scored funding. Eventually, it fell through."

Donald knew the one he was talking about. A containment facility buried under a mountain. The buzz on the Hill was that the Georgia project had the same chances of success. The folder suddenly tripled in weight as he considered this. He was being asked to be a part of this future failure. He would be staking his newly won office on it.

"I've got Mick Webb working on something related. Logistics and planning. You two will need to collaborate on a few things. And Anna is taking leave from her post at MIT to lend a hand."

"*Anna?*" Donald fumbled for his water, his hand shaking.

"Of course. She'll be your lead engineer on this project. There are details in there on what she'll need, space-wise."

Donald took a gulp of water and forced himself to swallow.

"There's a lot of other people I could call in, sure, but this project can't fail, you understand? It needs to be like *family.* That's why I want to use people I know, people I can trust." Senator Thurman interlocked his fingers. "If this is the only thing you were elected to do, I want you to do it right. It's why I stumped for you in the first place."

"Of course." Donald bobbed his head to hide his confusion. He had worried during the election that the Senator's endorsement stemmed from old family ties. This was somehow worse. Donald hadn't been using the Senator at all; it was the *other way around*. Studying the drawing in his lap, the newly elected congressman felt one job he was inadequately trained for melt away—only to be replaced by a *different* job that seemed equally daunting.

"Wait," he said. "I still don't get it." He studied the old drawing. "Why the grow lights?"

"Because this building I want you to design for me—it's going to go underground."

• 2 •

Troy held his breath and tried to remain calm while the doctor pumped the rubber bulb. The inflatable band swelled around his bicep until it pinched his skin. He wasn't sure if slowing his breathing and steadying his pulse affected his blood pressure, but he had a strong urge to impress the man in the white coveralls. He wanted his numbers to come back *normal*.

His arm throbbed a few beats while the needle bounced and the air hissed out.

"Eighty over fifty." The band made a ripping sound as it was torn loose. Troy rubbed the spot where his skin had been pinched.

"Is that okay?"

The doctor made a note on his clipboard. "It's low, but not outside the norm." Behind him, his assistant labeled a cup of dark gray urine before placing it inside a small fridge. Troy caught sight of a half-eaten sandwich among the samples, not even wrapped.

He looked down at his bare knees sticking out of the blue paper gown. His legs were pale and seemed smaller than he remembered. Bony.

"I still can't make a fist," he told the doctor, working his hand open and shut.

"That's perfectly normal. Your strength will return. Look into the light, please."

Troy followed the bright beam and tried not to blink.

"How long have you been doing this?" he asked the doctor.

"You're my third coming out. I've put two under." He lowered the light and smiled at Troy. "I've only been out myself for a few weeks. I can tell you that the strength will return."

Troy nodded. The doctor's assistant handed him another pill and a cup of water. Troy hesitated. He stared down at the little blue capsule nestled in his palm.

"A double dose this morning," the doctor said, "and then you'll be given one with breakfast and dinner. Please do not skip a treatment."

Troy looked up. "What happens if I don't take it?"

The doctor shook his head and frowned, but didn't say anything.

Troy popped the pill in his mouth and chased it with the water. A bitterness slid down his throat.

"One of my assistants will bring you some clothes and a fluid meal to kick-start your gut. If you have any dizziness or chills, you're to call me at once. Otherwise, we'll see you back here in six months." The doctor made a note, then chuckled. "Well, someone else will see you. My shift will be over."

"Okay." Troy shivered. The doctor looked up from his clipboard.

"You're not cold, are you? I keep it a little extra warm in here."

Troy hesitated before answering. "No, doctor. I'm not cold. Not anymore."

••••

Troy entered the lift at the end of the hall, his legs still weak, and studied an array of numbered buttons. The orders they'd given him included directions to his office, but he vaguely remembered how to get there. Much of his orientation had survived the decades of sleep. He remembered studying that same book over and over, thousands of men assigned to various shifts, tours of the facility before being put under like the women. The orientation felt like yesterday; it was older memories that seemed to be slipping away.

The doors to the lift closed automatically. His apartment was on thirty-seven; he remembered that. His office was on thirty-four. He reached for a button, intending to head straight to his desk, and instead found his hand sliding up to the very top. He still had a few minutes before he needed to be anywhere, and he felt some strange urge, some tug, to get as high as possible, to rise through the soil pressing in from all sides.

The elevator hummed into life and accelerated up the shaft. There was a whooshing sound as another car or maybe the counterweight zoomed by. The round buttons flashed as the floors passed. There was an enormous spread of them, seventy in all. The centers of many were dull from years of rubbing. This didn't seem right. It seemed like just yesterday the buttons were shiny and new. Just yesterday, *everything* was.

The elevator slowed. Troy palmed the wall for balance, his legs still uncertain.

The door dinged and slid open. Troy blinked at the bright lights in the hallway. He left the elevator and followed a short walk toward a room leaking chatter. His new boots were stiff on his feet, the generic gray coveralls itchy. He tried to imagine waking up like this nine more times, feeling this weak and disoriented. Ten shifts of six months each. Ten shifts he hadn't volunteered for. He wondered if it would get progressively easier or if it would only get worse.

The bustle in the cafeteria changed as he entered. A few heads turned his way. He saw at once that his gray coveralls weren't so generic. There was a scattering of colors seated at the tables, a large cluster of reds, quite a few yellows, no other grays.

That first meal of sticky paste he'd been given rumbled once more in his stomach. He wasn't allowed to eat anything else for six hours, which made the aroma from the canned foods overwhelming. He remembered the fare, had lived on it during orientation. Weeks and weeks of the same gruel. Now it would be months. It would be hundreds of years.

"Sir."

A young man nodded to Troy as he walked past, towards the elevators. Troy thought he recognized him but couldn't be sure. The gentleman certainly seemed to have recognized *him*. Or was it the gray coveralls that stood out?

"First shift?"

An older gentleman approached, thin, with white and wispy hair that circled his head. He held a tray in his hands, smiled at Troy. Pulling open a recycling bin, he slid the entire tray inside and dropped it with a clatter.

"Come up for the view?" the man asked.

Troy nodded. It was all men throughout the cafeteria. All men. They had explained why this was safer. He tried to remember as the man with the splotches of age on his skin crossed his arms and stood beside him. There were no introductions. Troy wondered if names meant less amid these short six-month shifts. He gazed out over the bustling tables toward the massive screen that covered the far wall.

Whirls of dust and low clouds hung over a field of scattered and mangled debris. A few metal poles bristled from the ground and sagged lifelessly, the tents and flags long vanished. Troy thought of something but couldn't name it. His stomach tightened like a fist around the paste and the bitter pill.

"This'll be my second shift," the man said.

Troy barely heard. His watering eyes drifted across the scorched hills, the gray slopes rising up toward the dark and menacing clouds. The debris scattered everywhere was rotting away. Next shift, or the one after, and it would all be gone.

"You can see further from the lounge." The man turned and gestured along the wall. Troy knew well enough what room he was referring to. This part of the building was familiar to him in ways this man could hardly guess.

"No, but thanks," he stammered. Troy waved him off. "I think I've seen enough."

Curious faces returned to their trays; the chatter resumed. It was sprinkled with the clinking of spoons and forks on metal bowls and plates. Troy turned and left without saying another word. He put that hideous view behind him—turned his back on the unspoken eeriness of it. He hurried, shivering, toward the elevator, knees weak with more than the long rest. He needed to be alone, didn't want anyone around him this time, didn't want sympathetic hands comforting him while he cried.

• 3 •

2049 • Washington, D.C.

D onald kept the thick folder tucked inside his jacket and hurried through the rain. He had chosen to get soaked crossing the square rather than face his claustrophobia in the tunnels.

Traffic hissed by on the wet asphalt. He waited for a gap, ignored the crosswalk signals, and scooted across.

In front of him, the marble steps of Rayburn, the office building for the House of Representatives, gleamed treacherously. He ascended them warily and thanked the doorman.

Inside, a Security officer stood by impassively while his badge was scanned, red unblinking eyes beeping at barcodes. He checked the folder Thurman had given him, made sure it was still dry, and wondered why such relics were still considered safer than an email or a digital copy.

His office was one floor up. He headed for the stairs, preferring them to Rayburn's ancient and slow lift. His shoes squeaked on the tile as he left the plush runner by the door.

The hallway upstairs was its usual mess. Two high schoolers from the page program hurried past, most likely fetching coffee. A TV crew stood outside of Amanda Kelly's office, camera lights bathing her and a young reporter in a daytime glow. Concerned voters and eager lobbyists were identifiable by the guest passes hanging around their necks. They were easy to distinguish from one another, these two groups. The voters wore frowns and invariably seemed lost. The lobbyists were the ones with the

Cheshire grins who navigated the halls more confidently than even the newly elected.

Donald opened the folder and pretended to read as he made his way through the chaos, hoping to avoid conversation. He squeezed behind the cameraman and ducked into his office next door.

"Mr. Keene."

Margaret, his secretary, stood up from her desk.

"Sir, you have a *visitor*."

Donald glanced around the waiting room. It was empty. He saw that the door to his office was partway open.

"I'm sorry I let her in." Margaret mimed carrying a box, her hands at her waist and her back arched. "She had a delivery. Said it was from the Senator."

Donald waved her concerns aside. Margaret was older than him, in her mid-forties, and had come highly recommended, but she did have a conspiratorial streak. Perhaps it came with the years of experience.

"It's fine," Donald assured her. He found it interesting that there were a hundred senators, two from his state, but only one was referred to as *the Senator*. "I'll see what it's about. In the meantime, I need you to free up a daily block in my schedule. An hour or two in the morning would be ideal." He flashed her the folder. "I've got something that's going to eat up quite a bit of time."

Margaret nodded and sat down in front of her computer. Donald turned toward his office.

"Oh, sir—?"

He looked back. She pointed to her head. "Your *hair*," she hissed.

He patted his head and remembered the glimpse he'd caught earlier. He ran his fingers through his hair, and drops of water leapt off him like startled fleas. Margaret frowned and lifted her shoulders in a helpless shrug. Donald gave up and pushed his office door open, expecting to find someone sitting across from his desk.

Instead, he saw someone wiggling *underneath* it.

"Hello?"

The door had bumped into something on the floor. Donald peeked around and saw a large box with a picture of a computer monitor on it. He glanced at the desk, saw the display was already set up.

"Oh, hey!"

The greeting was muffled by the hollow beneath his desk. Slender hips in a herringbone skirt wiggled back toward him. Donald knew who it was before her head emerged. He felt a flush of guilt, of anger at her being there unannounced.

"You know, you should have your cleaning lady dust under here once in a while." Anna Thurman stood up and smiled. She slapped her palms together, brushing them off before extending one his way. Donald took her hand nervously.

"Hey, stranger."

"Yeah. Hey." Rain dribbled down his cheek and neck, hiding any sudden flush of perspiration. "What's going on?" He walked around his desk to create some space between them. A new monitor stood innocently, a film of protective plastic blurring the screen.

"Dad thought you might need an extra one." Anna tucked a loose clump of auburn hair behind her ear. She still possessed the same alluring and elfin quality when they poked out like that. "I volunteered," she explained, shrugging.

"Oh." He placed the folder on his desk and thought about the drawing of the building he had briefly suspected was from her. And now, here she was. Checking his reflection in the new monitor, he saw the mess he had made of his hair. He reached up and tried to smooth it.

"Another thing," Anna said. "Your computer would be better off *on* your desk. I know it's unsightly, but the dust is gonna choke that thing to death. Dust is *murder* on these guys."

"Yeah. Okay."

He sat down and realized he could no longer see the chair across from his desk. He slid the new monitor to one side while Anna walked around and stood beside him, her arms crossed, completely relaxed. As if they'd seen each other yesterday.

"So," he said. "You're in town."

"Since last week. I was gonna stop by and see you and Helen on

Saturday, but I've been so busy getting settled into my apartment. Unboxing things, you know?"

"Yeah." He accidentally bumped the mouse, and the old monitor winked on. His computer was running. The terror of being in the same room with an ex subsided just enough for the timing of the day's events to dawn on him.

"Wait." He turned to Anna. "You were over here *installing* this while your father was asking me if I was interested in his project? What if I'd declined?"

She raised an eyebrow. Donald realized it wasn't something one learned—it was a talent that ran in the family.

"He practically gift-wrapped the election for you," she said flatly.

Donald reached for the folder and riffed the pages like a deck of cards. "The illusion of free will would've been nice. That's all."

Anna laughed. She was about to tousle his hair, he could feel it. Dropping his hand from the folder and patting his jacket pocket, he felt for his phone. It was like Helen was there with him. He felt the urge to call her.

"Was Dad at least gentle with you?"

He looked up to see that she hadn't moved. Her arms were still crossed, his hair untousled, nothing to panic about.

"What? Oh, yeah. He was fine. Like old times. In fact, it's like he hasn't aged a day."

"He doesn't really age, you know." She crossed the room and picked up large molded pieces of foam and slid them noisily into the empty box. Donald found his eyes drifting toward her skirt and forced himself to look away.

"He takes his nano treatments almost religiously. Started because of his knees. The military covered it for a while. Now he swears by them."

"I didn't know that," Donald lied. He'd heard rumors, of course. It was "Botox for the whole body," people said. Better than testosterone supplements. It cost a fortune, and you wouldn't live forever, but you could sure as hell delay the pain of aging.

Anna narrowed her eyes. "You don't think there's anything *wrong* with that, do you?"

"What? No. It's fine, I guess. I just wouldn't. Wait, why? Don't tell me you've been—?"

Anna rested her hands on her hips and cocked her head to the side. There was something oddly seductive about the defensive posture, something that whisked away the years since he'd last seen her.

"Do you think I would *need* to?" she asked him.

"No, no. It's not that—" He waved his hands. "It's just that *I* don't think I ever would."

A smirk thinned her lips. Maturity had hardened Anna's good looks, had refined her lean frame, but the fierceness from her youth remained. "You say that now," she said, "but wait until your joints start to ache and your back goes out from something as simple as turning your head too fast. Then you'll see."

"Okay. Well." He clapped his hands together. "This has been quite the day for catching up on old times."

"Yes, it has. Now, what day works best for you?" Anna interlocked the flaps on the large box and slid it toward the door with her foot. She walked around the back of the desk and stood beside him, a hand on his chair, the other reaching for his mouse.

"What *day*—?"

He watched while she changed some settings on his computer and the new monitor flashed to life. Donald could feel the pulse in his crotch, could smell her familiar perfume. The breeze she had caused by walking across the room seemed to stir all around him. This felt near enough to a caress, to a physical touch, that he wondered if he was cheating on Helen right at that very moment while Anna did little more than adjust sliders on his control panel.

"You know how to use this, right?" She slid the mouse from one screen to the other, dragging an old game of solitaire with it.

"Uh, yeah." Donald squirmed in his seat. "Um...what do you mean about a day that works best for me?"

She let go of the mouse. It felt like she had taken her hand off his thigh.

"Dad wants me to handle the mechanical spaces on the plans." She gestured toward the folder as if she knew precisely what was inside. "I'm taking a sabbatical from the Institute until this Atlanta project is up and running. I thought we'd want to meet once a week to go over things."

"Oh. Well. I'll have to get back with you on that. My schedule here is crazy. It's different every day."

He imagined what Helen would say to he and Anna getting together once a week.

"We could, you know, set up a shared space in AutoCAD," he suggested. "I can link you into my document—"

"We could do that."

"And email back and forth. Or video chat. You know?"

Anna frowned. Donald realized he was being too obvious. "Yeah, let's set up something like that," she said.

There was a flash of disappointment on her face as she turned for the box, and Donald felt the urge to apologize, but doing so would spell out the problem in neon lights: *I don't trust myself around you. We're not going to be friends. What the fuck are you doing here?*

"You really need to do something about the dust." She glanced back at his desk. "Seriously, your computer is going to choke on it."

"Okay. I will." He stood and hurried around his desk to walk her out. Anna stooped for the box.

"I can get that."

"Don't be silly." She stood with the large box pinned between one arm and her hip. She smiled and tucked her hair behind her ear. She could've been leaving his dorm room in college. There was that same awkward moment of a morning goodbye in last night's clothes.

"Okay, so you have my email?" he asked.

"You're in the blue pages now," she reminded him.

"Yeah."

"You look great, by the way." And before he could step back or defend himself, she was fixing his hair, a smile on her lips.

Donald froze. When he thawed some time later, Anna was gone, leaving him standing there alone, soaked in guilt.

• 4 •

2110 • Silo 1

Troy was going to be late. The first day of his first shift, already a blubbering mess, and he was going to be late. In his rush to get away from the cafeteria, to be alone, he had taken the non-express by accident. Now, as he tried to compose himself, the lift seemed intent on stopping at every floor on the way down to load and unload passengers.

He stood in the corner as the lift stopped again and a man wrestled a cart full of heavy boxes inside. A gentleman with a load of green onions crowded behind him and stood close to Troy for a few stops. Nobody spoke. When the man with the onions got off, the smell remained. Troy shivered, one violent quake that traveled up his back and into his arms, but he thought nothing of it. He got off on thirty-four and tried to remember why he had been upset earlier.

The central elevator shaft emptied onto a narrow hallway, which funneled him toward a security station. The floor plan was vaguely familiar and yet somehow alien. It was unnerving to note the signs of wear in the carpet and the patch of dull steel in the middle of the turnstile where thighs had rubbed against it over the years. These were years that hadn't existed for Troy. This wear and tear had shown up as if by magic, or like the damage from some sudden battle.

The lone guard on duty looked up from something he was reading and nodded in greeting. Troy placed his palm on a screen that had grown hazy from use. There was no chit-chat, no small talk, no expectation of forming a lasting relationship. The light above the console flashed green, the pedestal gave a loud click, and a little more sheen was rubbed off the revolving bar as Troy pushed through.

At the end of the hallway, Troy paused and pulled his orders out of his breast pocket. There was a note on the back from the doctor. He flipped it over and turned the little map around to face the right direction, was pretty sure he knew the way, but everything was dropping in and out of focus.

The red dash marks on the map reminded him of fire safety plans he'd seen on walls somewhere else. Following the route took him past a string of small offices. Clacking keyboards, people talking, phones ringing—the sounds of the workplace made him feel suddenly tired. It also ignited a burn of insecurity, of having taken on a job he surely couldn't perform.

"Troy?"

He stopped and looked back at the man standing in a doorway he'd passed. A glance at his map showed him he'd almost missed his office.

"That's me."

"Merriman." The gentleman didn't offer his hand. "You're late. Step inside."

Merriman turned and disappeared into the office. Troy followed, his legs sore from the walk. He recognized the man, or thought he did. Couldn't remember if it was from the orientation or some other time.

"Sorry I'm late," Troy started to explain. "I got on the wrong elevator—"

Merriman raised a hand. "That's fine. Do you need a drink?"

"They fed me."

"Of course." Merriman grabbed a clear thermos off his desk, the contents a bright blue. Troy remembered the foul taste. The older man smacked his lips and let out a breath as he lowered the thermos.

"That stuff's awful," he said.

"Yeah." Troy looked around the office, his post for the next six months. The place, he figured, had aged quite a bit. Merriman, too. If he was a little grayer from the past six months, it was hard to tell, but he had kept the place in order. Troy resolved to extend the same courtesy to the next guy.

"You remember your briefing?" Merriman shuffled some folders on his desk.

"Like it was yesterday."

Merriman glanced up, a smirk on his face. "Right. Well, there hasn't been anything exciting for the last few months. We had some mechanical issues when I started my shift but worked through those. There's a guy named Jones you'll want to use. He's been out a few weeks and is a lot sharper than the last guy. Been a lifesaver for me. He works down on sixty-eight with the power plant, but he's good just about anywhere, can fix pretty much anything."

Troy nodded. "Jones. Got it."

"Okay. Well, I left you some notes in these folders. There have been a few workers we had to deep-freeze, some who aren't fit for another shift." He looked up, a serious expression on his face. "Don't take that lightly, okay? Plenty of guys here would love to nap straight through instead of work. Don't resort to the deep freeze unless you're sure they can't handle it."

"I won't."

"Good." Merriman nodded. "I hope you have an uneventful shift. I've got to run before this stuff kicks in." He took another fierce swig, and Troy's cheeks sucked in with empathy. He walked past Troy, slapped him on the shoulder, and started to reach for the light switch. He stopped himself at the last minute and looked back, nodded, then was gone.

And just like that, Troy was in charge.

"Hey, wait!" He glanced around the office, hurried out, and caught up with Merriman, who was already turning down the main hall toward the security gate. Troy jogged to catch up.

"You leave the light on?" Merriman asked.

Troy glanced over his shoulder. "Yeah, but—"

"Good habits," Merriman said. He shook his thermos. "Form them."

A heavyset man hurried out of one of the offices and labored to catch up with them. "Merriman! You done with your shift?"

The two men shared a warm handshake. Merriman smiled and nodded. "I am. Troy here will be taking my place."

The man shrugged, didn't introduce himself. "I'm off in two weeks," he said, as if that explained his indifference.

"Look, I'm running late," Merriman said, his eyes darting toward Troy with a trace of blame. He pushed the thermos into his friend's palm. "Here. You can have what's left." He turned to go, and Troy followed along.

"No thanks!" the man called out, waving the thermos and laughing.

Merriman glanced at Troy. "I'm sorry, did you have a question?" He passed through the turnstile, and Troy followed. The guard never looked up from his tablet.

"A few, yeah. You mind if I ride down with you? I was a little...behind at orientation. Sudden promotion. Would love to clarify a few things—"

"Hey, I can't stop you. You're in charge." Merriman jabbed the call button on the express.

"So, basically, I'm just here in case something goes wrong?"

The elevator opened. Merriman turned and squinted at Troy almost as if to gauge if he was being serious.

"Your job is to *make sure* nothing goes wrong." They both stepped into the elevator. and the car raced downward.

"Right. Of course. That's what I meant."

"You've read the Order, right?"

Troy nodded. *But not for this job*, he wanted to say. He had studied to run one of the other silos, not this one that oversaw them all.

"Just follow the script. You'll get questions from the other silos now and then. I found it wise to say as little as possible. Just be quiet and listen. Keep in mind that these are mostly second and third generation survivors, so their vocabulary is already a little different. There's a cheat-sheet and a list of forbidden words in your folder."

Troy felt a bout of dizziness and nearly sagged to the ground as weight was added, the elevator slowing to a stop. He was still incredibly weak.

The door opened; he followed Merriman down a short hallway, the same one he had emerged from hours earlier. The doctor and his assistant waited in the room beyond, preparing an IV. The doctor looked curiously at Troy, as if he hadn't planned on seeing him again so soon, if ever.

"You finish your last meal?" the doctor asked, waving Merriman toward a stool.

"Every vile drop of it." Merriman unclasped the tops of his coveralls and let them flop down around his waist. He sat and held out his arm, palm up. Troy saw how pale Merriman's skin was, the loose tangle of purple lines weaving past his elbow. He tried not to watch the needle go in.

"I'm repeating my notes here," Merriman told him, "but you'll want to meet with Victor in the psych office. He's right across the hall from you. There's some strange things going on in a few of the silos, more fracturing than we thought. Try and get a handle on that for the next guy."

Troy nodded.

"We need to get you to your chamber," the doctor said. His young assistant stood by with a paper gown. The entire procedure looked very familiar. The doctor turned to Troy as if he were a stain that needed scrubbing away.

Troy backed out the door and glanced down the hall in the direction of the deep-freeze. The women and children were kept there, along with the men who couldn't make it through their shifts. "Do you mind if I—?" He felt a very real tug pulling him in that direction. Merriman and the doctor both frowned.

"It's not a good idea—" the doctor began.

"I wouldn't," Merriman said. "I made a few visits the first weeks. It's a mistake. Let it go."

Troy stared down the hallway. He wasn't exactly sure what he would find there, anyway.

"Get through the next six months," Merriman said. "It goes by fast. It all goes by fast."

Troy nodded. The doctor shooed him away with his eyes while Merriman began tugging off his boots. Troy turned, gave the heavy door down the hall one last glance, then headed in the other direction for the lift.

He hoped Merriman was right. Jabbing the button to call the express, he tried to imagine his entire shift flashing by. And the one after that. And the next one. Until this insanity had run its course, little thought to what came after.

• 5 •

2049 • Washington, D.C.

Time flew by for Donald Keene. Another day came to an end, another week, and still he needed more time. It seemed the sun had just gone down when he looked up and it was past eleven.

Helen. There was a rush of panic as he fumbled for his phone. He had promised his wife he would always call before ten. He felt a guilty heat wedge around his collar. He imagined her sitting around, staring at her phone, waiting and waiting.

It didn't even ring on his end before she picked up.

"There you are," she said, her voice soft and drowsy, her tone hinting more at relief than anger.

"Sweetheart. God, I'm really sorry. I totally lost track of time."

"That's okay, baby." She yawned, and Donald had to fight the infectious urge to do the same. "You write any good laws today?"

He laughed and rubbed his face. "They don't really let me do that. Not yet. I'm mostly staying busy with this little project for the Senator—"

He stopped himself. Donald had dithered all week on the best way to tell her, what parts to keep secret. He glanced at the extra monitor on his desk. Anna's perfume was somehow frozen in the air, still lingering a week later.

Helen's voice perked up: "Oh?"

He could picture her clearly: Helen in her nightgown, his side of the bed still immaculately made, a glass of water within her reach. He missed her terribly. The guilt he felt, despite his innocence, made him miss her all the more.

"What does he have you doing? It's legal, I hope."

"What? Of course it's legal. It's...some architectural stuff, actually." Donald leaned forward to grab the finger of gold scotch left in his tumbler. "To be honest, I'd forgotten how much I love the work. I would've been a decent architect if I'd stuck with it." He took a burning sip and eyed his monitors, which had gone dark to save the screens. He was dying to get back to it. Everything fell away, disappeared, when he lost himself in the drawing.

"Sweetheart, I don't think designing a new bathroom for Mr. Thurman's office is why the taxpayers sent you to Washington."

Donald smiled and finished the drink. He could practically hear his wife grinning on the other end of the line. He set the glass back on his desk and propped up his feet. "It's nothing like that," he insisted "It's plans for that facility they're putting in outside of Atlanta. Just a minor portion of it, really. But if I don't get it just right, the whole thing could fall apart."

He eyed the open folder on his desk. His wife laughed sleepily.

"Why in the world would they have you doing something like that?" she asked. "If it's so important, wouldn't they pay someone who knows what they're doing?"

Donald laughed dismissively, however much he agreed. He couldn't help but feel like a campaign donor sent to Paris to act as ambassador, just another of Washington's quirks for assigning jobs to people who weren't qualified for them. "I'm actually quite good at this," he told his wife. "I'm starting to think I'm a better architect than congressman."

"I'm sure you're wonderful at it." His wife yawned again. "But you could've stayed *home* and been an architect. You could work late *here*."

"Yeah, I know." Donald remembered their discussions on whether or not he should run for office, if it would be worth them being apart. Now he was spending his time away doing the very thing they'd agreed he should give up. "I think this is just something they put us through our first year," he said. "Think of it like your internship. It'll get better.

And besides, I think it's a *good* sign he wants me in on this. He sees the Atlanta thing as a family project, something to keep in-house. He actually took notice of some of my work at—"

"*Family* project."

"Well, not *literally* family, more like—" This wasn't how he wanted to tell her. It was a bad start. It was what he got for putting it off, for waiting until he was exhausted and tipsy.

"Is this why you're working late? Why you're calling me after ten?"

"Baby, I lost track of the time. I was on my computer—" He looked to his tumbler, saw that it held the barest of sips, just the golden residue that had slid down the tumbler after his last pull. "This is good news for us. I'll be coming home more often because of this. I'm sure they'll need me to check out the job site, work with the foremen—"

"That *would* be good news. Your dog misses you."

Donald smiled. "I hope you *both* do."

"You know I do."

"Good." He swilled the last drops in the glass and gulped it down "And listen, I know how you're gonna feel about this, and I swear it's out of my control, but the Senator's daughter is working on this project with me. Mick Webb, too. You remember him?"

Cold silence.

"I remember the Senator's daughter," Helen said.

Donald cleared his throat. "Yeah, well, Mick is doing some of the organizational work, securing land, dealing with contractors. It's practically his district, after all. And you know neither of us would be where we are today without the Senator stumping for us—"

"What I remember is that you two used to date. And that she used to flirt with you even when I was around—"

Donald laughed. "Are you serious? Anna Thurman? C'mon, honey, that was a lifetime ago—"

"I thought you were going to come home more often, anyway. On the weekends." He heard his wife let out her breath. "Look, it's late. Why don't we both get some sleep? We can talk about this tomorrow."

"Okay. Yeah, sure. And sweetheart?"

She waited.

"Nothing's gonna come between us, okay? This is a huge opportunity for me. And it's something I'm really good at. I'd forgotten how good at it I am."

A pause.

"There's a lot you're good at," his wife said. "You're a good husband, and I know you'll be a good congressman. I just don't trust the people you're surrounding yourself with."

"But you know I wouldn't be here if it wasn't for him."

"I know."

"Okay. Look, I'll be careful. I promise."

"Okay. I'll talk to you tomorrow. Sleep tight. I love you."

She hung up, and Donald looked down at his phone, saw that he had a dozen emails waiting for him. He decided to ignore them until morning. Rubbing his eyes, he willed himself awake, to think clearly. He shook the mouse to stir his monitors. They could afford to nap, to go dark a while, but not him.

A wireframe apartment sat in the middle of his new screen. Donald zoomed out and watched the apartment sink away and a hallway appear, then dozens of identical wedge-shaped living quarters squeeze in from the edges. The building specs called for a bunker that could house ten thousand people for at least a year—utter overkill. Donald approached the task as he would any design project. He imagined himself in their place, a toxic spill, a leak or some horrible fallout, a terrorist attack, something that might send all the facility workers underground where they would have to stay for weeks or months until the area was cleared.

The view pulled back further until another floor appeared above and below, empty floors he would eventually fill with storerooms, hallways, more apartments. Entire other floors and mechanical spaces had been left empty for Anna—

"Donny?"

His door opened—the knock came after. Donald's arm jerked so hard his mouse went skidding off the pad and across his desk. He sat up straight, peered over his monitors, and saw Mick Webb grinning at him from the doorway. Mick had his jacket tucked under one arm, tie hanging loose, a peppery stubble on his dark skin. He laughed at Donald's harried expression and sauntered across the room. Donald fumbled for the mouse and quickly minimized the AutoCAD window.

"Shit, man, you haven't taken up day-trading, have you?"

"Day-trading?" Donald leaned back in his chair.

"Yeah. What's with the new setup?" Mick walked around behind his desk and rested a hand on the back of his chair. An abandoned game of FreeCell sat embarrassingly on the smaller of the two screens.

"Oh, the extra monitor." He minimized the card game and turned in his seat. "I like having a handful of programs up at the same time."

"I can see that." Mick gestured at the empty monitors, the wallpaper of cherry blossoms framing the Jefferson Memorial.

Donald laughed and rubbed his face. He could feel his own stubble, had forgotten to eat dinner. The project had only begun a week ago, and he was already a wreck.

"I'm heading out for a drink," Mick told him. "You wanna come?"

"No, I've got a little more to do here."

Mick clasped his shoulder and squeezed until it hurt. "I hate to break it to you, man, but you're gonna have to start over. You bury an ace like that, there's no coming back. C'mon, let's get a drink."

"I can't." Donald twisted out from his friend's grasp and turned to face him. "I wasn't sitting here playing solitaire, man, I was working on those plans for Atlanta. I'm not supposed to let anyone see them. It's top secret."

For emphasis, he reached out and closed the folder on his desk. The Senator had told him there would be a division of labor and that the walls of that divide needed to be a mile high.

"Ohhh. *Top secret.*" Mick waggled both hands in the air. "I'm working on the same project, asshole." He waved at the monitor. "And you're doing the plans? What gives? My GPA was higher than yours." He leaned over the desk and stared at the taskbar. "AutoCAD? Cool. C'mon, let's see it."

"Yeah, right."

"Come the fuck on. Don't be a child about this."

Donald laughed. "Look, even the people on my team aren't going to see the entire plan. And neither will I."

"That's ridiculous."

"No, it's how shit like this gets done. You don't see me prying into your part in all this."

Mick waved a hand dismissively. "Whatever. Grab your coat. Let's go."

"Fine, sure." Donald patted his cheeks with his palms, trying to wake up. "I'll work better in the morning."

"Working on a Saturday. Thurman must love you."

"Let's hope so. Just give me a couple of minutes to shut this down."

Mick laughed. "Go ahead. I'm not looking." He walked over to the door while Donald finished up.

When Donald stood to go, his desk phone rang. His secretary wasn't there, so it was someone with his direct line. Donald reached for it and held up a finger to Mick.

"Helen—?"

Someone cleared their throat on the other end. A deep and rough voice apologized. "Sorry, no."

"Oh." Donald glanced up at Mick, who was tapping his watch. "Hello, sir."

"You boys going out?" Senator Thurman asked.

Donald turned toward the window. "Excuse me?"

"You and Mick. It's a Friday night. Are you hitting the town?"

"Uh, just the one drink, sir."

What Donald wanted to know was how the hell the Senator knew Mick was there.

"Good. Tell Mick I need to see him first thing Monday morning. My office. You, too. We need to discuss your first trip down to the job site."

"Oh. Okay."

Donald waited, wondering if that was all.

"You boys will be working closely on this moving forward."

"Good. Of course."

"As we discussed last week, there won't be any need to share details about what you're working on with other project members. The same goes for Mick."

"Yes sir. Absolutely. I remember our talk."

"Excellent. You boys have a good time. Oh, and if Mick starts blabbing, you have my permission to kill him on the spot."

There was a breath of silence, and then the hearty laugh of a man whose lungs sounded much younger than his years.

"Ah." Donald watched Mick, who had taken out the plug from a decanter to take a sniff. "Okay, sir. I'll be sure to do that."

"Great. See you Monday."

The Senator hung up abruptly. As Donald returned the phone to its cradle and grabbed his coat, his new monitor remained quietly perched on his desk, watching him blankly.

T roy's beat-up plastic meal tray slid down the line behind the splattered sheet of glass. Once his badge was scanned, a measured portion of canned string beans fell out of a tube and formed a steaming pile on his plate. A perfectly round cut of turkey plopped from the next tube, the ridges still visible from the tin. Mashed potatoes spat out at the end of the line like a spit wad from a child's straw. Gravy followed with a squirt.

Behind the serving line stood a heavy-set man in white coveralls, hands clasped behind his back. He didn't seem interested in the food. He concentrated on the workers as they lined up for their meals.

When Troy's tray reached the end of the line, a younger man in pale green coveralls and probably not out of his twenties arranged silverware and napkins by the plate. A glass of water was added from a tightly packed tray nearby. The final step was like a ritualized handshake, one Troy remembered from the months of orientation: a small plastic shot glass was handed over, a pill rattling in the bottom, a blurry blue shape barely visible through the translucent cup.

Troy shuffled into place.

"Hello, sir."

A young grin. Perfect teeth. Everyone called him sir, even those much older. It was discomfiting no matter who it came from.

The pill rattled in the plastic. Troy took the cup and tossed it down. He swallowed it dry, grabbed his tray, and tried not to hold up the line.

Searching for a seat, he caught the heavy-set man watching him. Everyone in the facility seemed to think Troy was in charge, but he wasn't fooled. He was just another person doing a job, following a script.

He found an empty spot facing the screen. Unlike that first day, it no longer bothered him to see the scorched world outside. The view had grown oddly comforting. It created a dull ache in his chest, which was near to feeling *something*.

A mouthful of potatoes and gravy washed away the taste of the pill. Water was never up to the task, could never take away the bitterness. Eating methodically, he watched the sun set on the first week of his first shift. Twenty-five more weeks to go. It was a countable number phrased like that. It seemed shorter than half a year.

An older gentleman in blue coveralls with thinning hair sat down diagonally across from him, polite enough to not block the view. Troy recognized the man, had spoken with him once by the recycling bin. When he looked up, Troy nodded in greeting.

They ate.

The cafeteria hummed pleasantly. A few hushed conversations rose and faded. Plastic, glass, and metal beat out a rhythmless tune.

Troy glanced at the view and felt there was something he was supposed to know, something he kept forgetting. He awoke each morning with familiar shapes at the edges of his vision, could feel memories nearby, but by the time breakfast came, they were already fading. By dinner, they were lost. It left Troy with a sadness, a cold sensation, and a feeling like a hollow stomach—different from hunger—like rainy days as a child when he didn't know how to fill his time. It was the pain of a chronic boredom mixed with the discomfort of time wasted.

The gentleman across from him slid over a little and cleared his throat. "Things going okay?" he asked.

He reminded Troy of someone. Blotchy skin hung slightly loose around his weathered face. He had a drooping neck, an unsightly pinch of flesh hanging from his Adam's apple.

"Things?" Troy repeated and returned the smile.

"Anything, I suppose. Just checking in. I go by Hal." The gentleman lifted his glass. Troy did the same. It was as good as a handshake.

"Troy," he said. He supposed to some people it still mattered what they called themselves.

Hal took a long pull from his glass. His neck bobbed, the gulp loud. Self-conscious, Troy took a small sip and worked on the last of his beans and turkey.

"I've noticed some people sit facing it and some sit with their backs to it." Hal jerked his thumb over his shoulder.

Troy looked up at the screen. He chewed his food, didn't say anything.

"I reckon those who sit and watch, they're trying to remember something."

Troy swallowed and forced himself to shrug.

"And those of us who don't want to watch," he continued. "I figure we're trying our best to forget."

Troy knew they shouldn't be having this conversation, but now it had begun, and he wanted to see where it would lead.

"It's the bad stuff," Hal said, staring off toward the elevators. "Have you noticed that? It's just the bad stuff that slips away. All the unimportant things, we remember well."

Troy jabbed his beans, even though he didn't plan on eating them.

It makes you wonder, don't it? Why we all feel so rotten inside?"

Hal finished up his food, nodded a goodbye and got up to leave. Troy was left alone. He found himself staring at the screen, a dull ache inside that he couldn't name. It was the time of evening just before the hills disappeared, before they darkened and faded into the cloud-filled sky.

• 7 •

Donald was glad he had decided to walk to his meeting with the Senator. The rain from the week before had finally let up, and the traffic in Dupont Circle was at a crawl. Heading up Connecticut and leaning into a stiffening breeze, Donald wondered why his meeting with the Senator had been moved to Kramer's Bookshop of all places. There were a dozen superior coffee houses much closer to the office.

He crossed a side street and hurried up the short flight of stone steps to the bookshop. The front door to Kramer's was one of those ancient wooden affairs older establishments hung like a boast, like a testament to their endurance. Hinges squeaked and actual bells jangled overhead as he pushed open the door, and a young woman straightening books on a center table of bestsellers glanced up and smiled hello.

The café, Donald saw, was packed with men and women in business suits sipping from white porcelain cups. There was no sign of the Senator. Donald started to check his phone, see if he was too early, when a Secret Service agent caught his eye.

The agent stood broad-shouldered at the end of an aisle of books in the small corner of Kramer's that acted as the cafés bookshop. Donald laughed at how conspicuously hidden the man was: the earpiece, the bulge by his ribs, the sunglasses indoors. Donald headed the agent's way, the wooden boards underfoot groaning with age.

The agent's gaze shifted his way, but it was hard to tell if he was looking at Donald or toward the front door.

"I'm here to see Senator Thurman," Donald said, his voice cracking a little. "I have an appointment."

The agent turned his head to the side. Donald followed the gesture and peered down an aisle of books to see Thurman browsing through the stacks at the far end.

"Ah. Thanks." He stepped between the towering shelves of old books, the light dimming and the smell of coffee replaced with the tang of mildew mixed with leather.

"What do you think of this one?"

Senator Thurman held out a book as Donald approached. No greeting, just a question.

Donald checked the title embossed in gold on the thick leather cover. "Never heard of it," he admitted.

Senator Thurman laughed. "Of course not. It's over a hundred years old—and it's French. I mean, what do you think of the *binding*?" He handed Donald the book.

Donald was surprised by how heavy the volume was. He cracked it open and flipped through a few pages. It felt like a law book, had that same dense heft, but he could see by the whitespace between lines of dialog that it was a novel. As he turned a few pages, he admired how thin the individual sheets were. Where the pages met at the spine, they had been stitched together with tiny ropes of blue and gold thread. He had friends who still swore by physical books—not for decoration, but to actually read. Studying the one in his hand, Donald could understood their nostalgic affection.

"The binding looks great," he said, brushing it with the pads of his fingers. "It's a beautiful book." He handed the novel back to the Senator. "Is this how you shop for a good read? You mostly go by the cover?"

Thurman tucked the book under his arm and pulled another from the shelf. "It's just a sample for another project I'm working on." He turned and narrowed his eyes at Donald. It was an uncomfortable gaze. He felt like prey.

"How's your sister doing?" Thurman asked.

The question caught Donald off guard. A lump formed in his throat at the mention of her.

"Charlotte? She's...she's fine, I guess. She redeployed. I'm sure you heard."

"I did." Thurman slotted the book in his hand back into a gap and weighed the one Donald had appraised. "I was proud of her for re-upping. She does her country proud."

Donald thought about what it cost a family to do a country proud.

"Yeah," he said. "I mean, I know my parents were really looking forward to having her home, but she was having trouble adjusting to the pace back here. It...I don't think she'll be able to really *relax* until the war's over. You know?"

"I do. And she may not find peace even then."

That wasn't what Donald wanted to hear. He watched the Senator trace his finger down an ornate spine adorned with ridges, bumps, and recessed lettering. The old man's eyes seemed to focus beyond the rows of books.

"I can drop her a line if you want. Sometimes a soldier just needs to hear that it's okay to see someone."

"If you mean a shrink, she won't do it." Donald recalled the changes in his sister around the time of her sessions. "We already tried."

Thurman's lips pursed into a thin, wrinkled line, his worry revealed in hidden signs of age. "I'll talk to her. I'm familiar enough with the hubris of youth, believe me. I used to have the same attitude when I was younger. I thought I didn't need any help, that I could do everything on my own." He turned to face Donald. "The profession's come a long way. They have pills now that can help her with the battle fatigue."

Donald shook his head. "No. She was on those for a while. They made her too forgetful. And they caused a—" He hesitated, didn't want to talk about it. "—a *tic*."

He wanted to say tremors, but that sounded too severe. And while he appreciated the Senator's concern—this feeling like the man was family—he felt uncomfortable discussing his sister's problems. He remembered the last time she was home, the disagreement they'd had while going through his and Helen's photographs from Mexico. He had asked her if she remembered Cozumel from when they were kids, and Charlotte had insisted she'd never been. The disagreement had turned into an argument, and he had lied and said his tears were ones of frustration. Parts of his sister's life had been erased, and the only way the doctors could explain it was to say that it must've been something she *wanted* to forget. And what could be wrong with that?

Thurman rested a hand on Donald's arm. "Trust me on this," he said quietly. "I'll talk to her. I know what she's going through."

Donald bobbed his head. "Yeah. Okay. I appreciate it." He almost added that it wouldn't do any good, could possibly cause harm, but the gesture was a nice one. And it would come from someone his sister looked up to, rather than from family.

"And, hey, Donny, she's piloting drones." Thurman studied him, seemed to be picking up on his worry. "It's not like she's in any physical danger."

Donald rubbed the spine of a shelved book. "Not physical, no."

The conversation fell silent, and Donald let out a heavy breath. He could hear the chatter from the café, the clink of a spoon stirring in some sugar, the clang of bells against the old wooden door, the squeal and hiss of milk being steamed.

He had seen videos of what Charlotte did, camera feeds from the drones and then from the missiles as they were guided into their targets. The video quality was amazing. You could see people turning to look up toward the heavens in surprise, could see the last moments of their lives, could cycle through the video frame by frame and decide—after the fact— if this had been your man or not. He knew what his sister did, what she dealt with.

"I spoke with Mick earlier," Thurman said, seeming to sense that he'd brought up a sore topic. "You two are going to head down to Atlanta and see how the excavation is going."

Donald snapped to. "Of course. Yeah, it'll be good to get the lay of the land. I got a nice head start on my plans last week, gradually filling in the dimensions you set out. You do realize how deep this thing goes, right?"

"That's why they're already digging the foundations. The outer walls should be getting a pour over the next few weeks." Senator Thurman patted Donald's shoulder and nodded toward the end of the aisle, signaling that they were finished looking through books.

"Wait. They're already *digging?*" Donald walked alongside Thurman. "I've only got an outline ready. I hope they're saving mine for last."

"The entire complex is being worked on at the same time. All they're pouring are the outer walls and foundations, the dimensions of which are fixed. We'll fill each structure from the bottom up, the floors craned down completely furnished before we pour the slabs between. But look, this is why I need you boys to go check things out. It sounds like a damned nightmare down there with the staging. I've got a hundred crews from a dozen countries working on top of one another while materials pile up everywhere. I can't be in ten places at once, so I need you to get a read on things and report back."

When they reached the Secret Service agent at the end of the aisle, the Senator handed him the old book with the French embossing. The man in the dark shades nodded and headed toward the counter.

"While you're down there," Thurman said, "I want you to meet up with Charlie Rhodes. He's handling delivery of most of the building materials. See if he needs anything."

"*Charles* Rhodes? As in the governor of Oklahoma?"

"That's right. We served together. And hey, I'm working on transitioning you and Mick into some of the higher levels of this project. Our leadership team is still short a few dozen members. So keep up the good work. You've impressed some important people with what you've put together so far, and Anna seems confident you'll be able to stay ahead of schedule. She says the two of you make a great team."

Donald nodded. He felt a blush of pride—and also the inevitability of extra responsibilities, more bites out of his ever-dwindling time. Helen wouldn't like hearing that his involvement with the project might grow. In fact, Mick and Anna might be the only people he could share the news with, the only ones he could talk to. Every detail about the build seemed to require convoluted layers of clearance. He couldn't tell if it was the fear of nuclear waste, the threat of a terrorist attack, or the likelihood that the project would fall through.

The agent returned and took up a position beside the Senator, shopping bag in hand. He looked over at Donald and seemed to study him through those impenetrable sunglasses. Not for the first time, Donald felt watched.

Senator Thurman shook Donald's hand and said to keep him posted. Another agent materialized from nowhere and formed up on Thurman's flank. They marched the Senator through the jangling door, and Donald only relaxed once they were out of view.

• 8 •

The Book of the Order lay open on his desk, the pages curling up from a spine stitched to last. Troy studied the upcoming procedure once again, his first official act as head of Operation Fifty, and it brought to mind a ribbon-cutting ceremony, a grand display where the man with the shears took credit for the hard work of others.

The Order, he had decided, was more recipe book than operations manual. The shrinks who had written it had accounted for everything, every quirk of human nature. And like the field of psychology, or any field that involved human nature, the parts that made no sense usually served some deeper purpose.

It made Troy wonder what *his* purpose was. How necessary his position. He had studied for a much different job, was meant to be head of a single silo, not all of them. He had been promoted at the last minute, and that made him feel arbitrary, as if anyone could be slotted into his place.

Of course, even if his office was mostly titular, perhaps it served some symbolic purpose. Maybe he wasn't there to lead so much as to provide an illusion to the others that *they were being led*.

Troy skipped back two paragraphs in the Order. His eyes had passed over every word, but none of them had registered. Everything about his new life made him prone to distraction, made him think too much. It had all been perfectly arranged—all the levels and tasks and job descriptions—but for what? For maximum *apathy*?

Glancing up, he could see Victor sitting at his desk in the Office for Psychological Services across the hall. It would be easy enough to walk over there and ask. They, more than any one architect, had designed this place. He could ask them how they had done it, how they had managed to make everyone feel so empty inside.

Sheltering the women and the children played some part; Troy was sure of that. The women and children of Silo 1 had been gifted with a long sleep while the men stayed and took shifts. It removed the passion from the plans, forestalled the chance that the men might fight among themselves.

And then there was the routine, the mind-numbing routine. It was the castration of thought, the daily grind of an office worker who drooled at the clock, punched out, watched TV until sleep overtook him, slapped an alarm three times, did it again. It was made worse by the absence of weekends. There were no free days. It was six months on and *decades* off.

It made him envious of the rest of the facility, all the other silos, where hallways must echo with the laughter of children, the voices of women, the passion and happiness missing from this bunker at the heart of it all. Here, all he saw was stupor, dozens of communal rooms with movies playing in loops on flat-panel TVs, dozens of unblinking eyes in comfortable chairs. No one was truly awake. No one was truly alive. They must have wanted it that way.

Checking the clock on his computer, Troy saw that it was time to go. Another day behind him. Another day closer to the end of his shift. He closed his copy of the Order, locked it away in his desk, and headed for the communications room down the hall.

A pair of heads looked up from the radio stations as he walked in, all frowns and lowered brows. Troy took a deep breath, pulled himself together. This was an office. It was a job. And he was the man in charge. He just had to keep his shit together. He was there to cut a ribbon.

Saul, one of the lead radio techs, took off his headset and rose to greet him. Troy vaguely knew Saul; they lived on the same executive wing and saw each other in the gym from time to time. While they shook hands,

Saul's wide and handsome face tickled some deeper memory, an itch Troy had learned to ignore. Maybe this was someone he had met at his orientation, from before his long sleep.

Saul introduced him to the other tech, who waved and kept his headset on. The name faded immediately. It didn't matter. An extra headset was pulled from a rack. Troy accepted it and lowered it around his neck, keeping the muffs off his ears so he could still hear. Saul found the silvery jack at the end of the headset and ran his fingers across an array of fifty numbered receptacles. The layout and the room reminded Troy of ancient photographs of phone operators back before they were replaced with computers and automated voices.

The mental image of a bygone day mixed and fizzed with his nerves and the shivers brought on by the pills, and Troy felt a sudden bout of giggles bubble beneath the surface. The laughter nearly burst out of him, but he managed to hold it together. It wouldn't be a good sign for the head of overall operations to lurch into hysterics when he was about to gauge the fitness of a future silo head.

"—and you'll just run through the set questions," Saul was telling him. He held out a plastic card to Troy, who was pretty sure he didn't need it but took it anyway. He'd been memorizing the routine for most of the day. Besides, he was sure it didn't matter what he said. The task of gauging a candidate's fitness was better left to the machines and the computers, all the sensors embedded in a distant headset.

"Okay. There's the call." Saul pointed to a single flashing light on a panel studded with flashing lights. "I'm patching you through,"

Troy adjusted the muffs around his ears as the tech made the connection. He heard a few beeps before the line clicked over. Someone was breathing heavily on the other end. Troy reminded himself that this young man would be far more nervous than he was. After all, he had to *answer* the questions—Troy simply had to ask them.

He glanced down at the card in his hand, his mind suddenly blank, thankful that he'd been given the thing.

"Name?" he asked the young man.

"Marcus Dent, sir."

There was a quiet confidence in his young voice, the sound of a chest thrust out with pride. Troy remembered feeling that once, a long time ago. And then he thought of the world Marcus Dent had been born into, a legacy *he* would only ever know from books.

"Tell me about your training," Troy said. reading the lines. He tried to keep his voice even, deep, full of command, even though the computers were designed to do that for him. Saul made a hoop with his finger and thumb, letting him know he was getting good data from the boy's headset. Troy wondered if his was similarly equipped. Could anyone in that room—or any other room—tell how nervous he was?

"Well, sir, I shadowed under Deputy Willis before transferring to IT Security. That was a year ago. I've been studying the Order for six weeks. I feel ready, sir."

Shadowing. Troy forgot it was called that. He had meant to bring the latest vocabulary card with him.

"What is your primary duty to the...silo?" He had nearly said *facility*.

"To maintain the Order, sir."

"And what do you protect above all?"

He kept his voice flat. The best readings would come from not imparting too much emotion into the man being measured.

"Life and Legacy," Marcus recited.

Troy had a difficult time seeing the next question. It was obscured by an unexpected blur of tears. His hand trembled. He lowered the shaking card to his side before anyone noticed.

"And what does it take to protect the things we hold dear?" he asked. His voice sounded like someone else's. He ground his teeth together to keep them from chattering. Something was wrong with him. Powerfully wrong.

"Sacrifice," Marcus said, steady as a rock.

Troy blinked rapidly to clear his vision, and Saul held up his hand to let him know he could continue, that the measures were coming through. Now they needed baselines so the biometrics could tease out the boy's sincerity toward the first questions.

"Tell me, Marcus, do you have a girlfriend?"

He didn't know why that was the first thing that came to mind. Maybe it was the envy that other silos didn't freeze their women, didn't freeze anyone at all. Nobody in the comm room seemed to react or care. The formal portion of the test was over.

"Oh, yessir," Marcus said, and Troy heard the boy's breathing change, could imagine his body relaxing. "We've applied to be married, sir. Just waiting to hear back."

"Well, I don't think you'll have to wait too much longer. What's her name?"

"Melanie, sir. She works here in IT."

"That's great." Troy wiped at his eyes. The shivers passed. Saul waved his finger in a circle over his head, letting him know he could wrap it up. They had enough.

"Marcus Dent," he said, "welcome to Operation Fifty of the World Order."

"Thank you, sir." The young man's voice lifted an octave.

There was a pause, then the sound of a deep breath taken and held.

"Sir? Is it okay if I ask a question?"

Troy looked to the others. There were shrugs and not much else. He considered the role this young man had just assumed, knew well the sensation of being promoted to new responsibilities, that mix of fear, eagerness, and confusion.

"Sure, son. One question." He figured he was in charge. He could make a few rules of his own.

Marcus cleared his throat., and Troy pictured this shadow and his silo Head sitting in a distant room together, the master studying his student.

"I lost my grandmother a few years ago," Marcus said. "She used to let slip little things about the world before. Not in a forbidden way, but just as a product of her dementia. The doctors said she was resistant to her medication."

Troy didn't like the sound of this, that third-generation survivors were gleaning anything about the past. Marcus may be newly cleared for such things, but others weren't.

"What's your question?" Troy asked.

"The Legacy, sir. I've done some reading in it as well, not neglecting my studies of the Order and the Pact, of course, and there's something I have to know."

Another deep breath.

"Is everything in the Legacy true?"

Troy thought about this. He considered the great collection of books that contained the world's history—a carefully edited history. In his mind, he could see the leather spines and the gilded pages, the rows and rows of books they had been shown during their orientation.

He nodded and found himself once again needing to wipe his eyes.

"Yes," he told Marcus, his voice dry and flat. "It's true."

Someone in the room sniffled. Troy knew the ceremony had gone on long enough.

"Everything in there is absolutely true."

He didn't add that not every *true thing* was written in the Legacy. Much had been left out. And there were other things he suspected that *none* of them knew, that had been edited out of books and brains alike.

The Legacy was the allowed truth, he wanted to say, the truth that was carried from each generation to the next. But the lies, he thought to himself, were what they carried there in Silo 1, in that drug-hazed asylum charged somehow with humanity's survival.

• 9 •

2049 • Fulton County, Georgia

The front-end loader let out a throaty blat as it struggled up the hill, a charcoal geyser streaming from its exhaust pipe. When it reached the top, a load of dirt avalanched out of its toothy bucket, and Donald saw that the loader wasn't climbing the hill so much as creating it.

Hills of fresh dirt were taking shape like this all over the site. Between them—through temporary gaps left open like an ordered maze—burdened dump trucks carried away soil and rock from the cavernous pits being hollowed from the earth. These gaps, Donald knew from the topo plans, would one day be pushed closed, leaving little more than a shallow crease where each hill met its neighbor.

Standing on one of these growing mounds, Donald watched the ballet of heavy machinery while Mick Webb spoke with a contractor about the delays. In their white shirts and flapping ties, the two congressmen seemed out of place. The men in hardhats with the leather faces, calloused hands, and busted knuckles belonged there. He and Mick, blazers tucked under their arms, sweat stains spreading in the humid Georgia heat, were somehow—nominally, at least—supposed to be in charge of that ungodly commotion.

Another loader released a mound of soil as Donald shifted his gaze toward downtown Atlanta. Past the massive clearing of rising hills and over the treetops still stripped bare from fading winter rose the glass and steel spires of the old Southern city. An entire corner of sparsely populated Fulton County had been cleared. Remnants of a golf course were still visible at one end where the machines had yet to disturb the land.

Down by the main parking lot, a staging zone the size of several football fields held thousands of shipping containers packed with building supplies, more than Donald thought necessary. But he was learning by the hour that this was the way of government projects, where public expectations were as high as the spending limits. Everything was done in excess or not at all. The plans he had been ordered to draw up practically begged for proportions of insanity, and his building wasn't even a necessary component of the facility. It was only there for the worst case scenario.

Between Donald and the field of shipping containers stood a sprawling city of trailers; a few functioned as offices, but most of them served as housing. This was where the thousands of men and women working on the construction could ditch their hard hats, clock off, and take their well-earned rest.

Flags flew over many of the trailers, the workforce as multinational as an Olympic village. Spent nuclear fuel rods from the world over would one day end up buried beneath the pristine soil of Fulton County. It meant that the world had a stake in the project's success. The logistical nightmare this ensured didn't seem to concern the back-room dealers. He and Mick were finding that many of the early construction delays could be traced to language barriers, as neighboring work crews couldn't communicate with one another and had evidently given up trying. Everyone simply worked on their set of plans, heads down, ignoring the rest.

Beside this temporary city of tin cans sat the vast parking lot he and Mick had trudged up from. He could see their rental car down there, the only quiet and electric thing in sight. Small and silver, it seemed to cower among the belching dump trucks and loaders on all sides. The overmatched car looked precisely how Donald felt, both on that little hill at the construction site and back at the Hill in Washington.

"Two months behind."

Mick smacked him on the arm with his clipboard. "Hey, did you hear me? Two months behind already, and they just broke ground six months ago. How is that even possible?"

Donald shrugged as they left the frowning foremen and trudged down the hill toward the parking lot. "Maybe it's because they have elected officials pretending to do jobs that belong to the private sector," he offered.

Mick laughed and squeezed his shoulder. "Jesus, Donny, you sound like a goddamned Republican!"

"Yeah? Well, I feel like we're in over our heads, here." He waved his arm at the depression in the hills they were skirting, a deep bowl scooped out of the earth. Several mixer trucks were pouring concrete into the wide hole at its center. More trucks waited in line behind them, their butts spinning impatiently.

"You do realize," Donald said, "that one of these holes is going to hold the building they let *me* draw up? Doesn't that scare you? All this money? All these people. It sure as hell scares me."

Mick's fingers dug painfully into Donald's neck. "Take it easy. Don't go getting all philosophical on me."

"I'm being serious," Donald said. "Billions of taxpayer dollars are gonna nestle in the dirt out there in the shape that *I* drew up. It seemed so...*abstract* before."

"Christ, this isn't about you or your plans." He popped Donald with the clipboard and used it to point toward the container field. Through a fog of dust, a large man in a cowboy hat waved them over. "Besides," Mick said, as they angled away from the parking lot, "what're the chances anyone even uses your little bunker? This is about energy independence. It's about the death of coal. You know, it feels like the rest of us are building a nice big house over here, and you're over in a corner stressing about where you're gonna hang the fire extinguisher—"

"*Little bunker?*" Donald held his blazer up over his mouth as a cloud of dust blew across them. "Do you know how many floors *deep* this thing is gonna be? If you set it on the ground, it'd be the tallest building in the world—!"

Mick laughed. "Not for long it wouldn't. Not if you designed it."

The man in the cowboy hat drew closer. He smiled widely as he kicked through the packed dirt to meet them, and Donald finally recognized him from TV: Charles Rhodes, the governor of Oklahoma.

"You Senator Thawman's boys?"

Governor Rhodes smiled. He had the authentic drawl to go with the authentic hat, the authentic boots, and the authentic buckle. He rested his hands on his wide hips, a clipboard in one of them.

Mick nodded. "Yessir. I'm Congressman Webb. This is Congressman Keene."

The two men shook hands. Donald was next. "Governor," he said.

"Got your delivery." He pointed the clipboard toward the staging area. "Just shy of a hundred containers. Should have somethin' rollin' in about every week. Need one of you to sign right here."

Mick reached out and took the clipboard. Donald saw an opportunity to ask something about Senator Thurman, something he figured an old war buddy would know.

"Why do some people call him Thawman?" he asked.

Mick flipped through the delivery report, a breeze pinning back the pages for him.

"I've heard others call him that when he wasn't around," Donald explained, "but I've been too scared to ask."

Mick looked up from the report with a grin. "It's because he was an ice-cold killer in the war, right?"

Donald cringed. Governor Rhodes laughed.

"Unrelated," he said. "True, but unrelated."

The Governor glanced back and forth between them. Mick passed the clipboard to Donald, tapped a page that dealt with the emergency housing facility. Donald looked over the materials list.

"You boys familiar with his anti-cryo bill?" Governor Rhodes asked. He handed Donald a pen, seemed to expect him to just sign the thing and not look over it too closely.

Mick shook his head and shielded his eyes against the Georgia sun. "Anti-cryo?" he asked.

"Yeah. Aw, hell, this probably dates back before you squirts were even born. Senator Thawman penned the bill that put down that cryo fad. Made it illegal to take advantage of rich folk and turn them into ice cubes. It went to the big court, where they voted five–four, and suddenly tens of thousands of popsicles with more money than sense were thawed out and buried proper. These were people who'd frozen themselves in the hopes that doctors from the future would discover some medical procedure for extracting their rich heads from their own rich asses!"

The Governor laughed at his own joke, and Mick joined him. A line on the delivery report caught Donald's eye. He turned the clipboard around and showed the Governor. "Uh, this shows two thousand spools of fiber-optic. I'm pretty sure my plans call for forty spools."

"Lemme see." Governor Rhodes took the clipboard and procured another pen from his pocket. He clicked the top of it three times, then scratched out the quantity. He wrote in a new number to the side.

"Wait, will the price reflect that?"

"Price is the same," he said. "Just sign the bottom."

"But—"

"Son, this is why hammers cost the Pentagon their weight in gold. It's government accounting. Just a signature, please."

"But that's *fifty times* more fiber than we'll need," Donald complained, even as he found himself scribbling his name. He passed the clipboard to Mick, who signed for the rest of the goods.

"Oh, that's all right." Rhodes took the clipboard and pinched the brim of his hat. "I'm sure they'll find a use for it somewhere."

"Hey, you know," Mick said, "I remember that cryo bill. From law school. There were lawsuits, weren't there? Didn't a group of families bring murder charges against the Feds?"

The governor smiled. "Yeah, but it didn't get far. Hard to prove you killed people who'd already been pronounced dead. And then there were Thawman's bad business investments. Those turned out to be a lifesaver."

Rhodes tucked his thumb in his belt and stuck out his chest.

"Turned out he'd sunk a fortune into one of these cryo companies before digging deeper and reconsidering the...*ethical* considerations.

Old Thawman may have lost most of his money, but it ended up savin'
his ass in Washington. Made him look like some kinda saint, suffering a
loss like that. Only defense better woulda been if he'd unplugged his dear
momma with all them others."

Mick and the Governor laughed. Donald didn't see what was so funny.

"All right, now, you boys take care. The good state of Oklahoma'll
have another load for ya in a few weeks."

"Sounds good," Mick said, grasping and pumping that huge
Midwestern paw.

Donald shook the Governor's hand as well, and he and Mick trudged
off toward their rental. Overhead, against the bright blue Southern sky,
vapor trails like stretched ropes of white yarn revealed the flight lines
of the numerous jets departing the busy hub of Atlanta International.
And as the throaty noise of the construction site faded, the chants from
the anti-nuke protestors could be heard outside the tall mesh of security
fences beyond. They passed through the security gate and into the
parking lot, the guard waving them along.

"Hey, you mind if I drop you off at the airport a little early?" Donald
asked "It'd be nice to get a jump on traffic and get down to Savannah with
some daylight."

"That's right," Mick said with a grin. "You've got a hot date tonight."

Donald laughed.

"Sure, man. Abandon me and go have a good time with your wife."

"Thanks."

Mick fished out the keys to the rental. "But you know, I was really
hoping you'd invite me to come along. I could join you two for dinner,
crash at your place, hit some bars like old times."

"Not a chance," Donald said.

Mick slapped the back of Donald's neck and squeezed. "Yeah, well,
happy anniversary anyway."

Donald winced as his friend pinched his neck. "Thanks," he said. "I'll
be sure to give Helen your regards."

• 10 •

2110 • Silo 1

Troy played a hand of solitaire while Silo 12 collapsed. There was something about the game that he found blissfully numbing. The repetition held off the waves of depression even better than the pills. The lack of skill required moved beyond distraction and into the realm of complete mindlessness. The truth was, the player won or lost the very moment the computer shuffled the deck. The rest was simply a process of finding out.

For a computer game, it was absurdly low-tech. Instead of cards, there was just a grid of letters and numbers with an asterisk, ampersand, percent, or plus sign to designate the suit. It bothered Troy not to know which symbol stood for hearts or clubs or diamonds. Even though it was arbitrary, even though it didn't really matter, it frustrated him to not know.

He had stumbled upon the game by accident while digging through some folders. It took a bit of experimenting to learn how to flip the draw deck with the spacebar and place the cards with the arrow keys, but he had plenty of time to work things like this out. Besides meeting with department heads, going over Merriman's notes, and refreshing himself on the Order, all he had was time. Time to collapse in his office bathroom and cry until snot ran down his chin, time to sit under a scalding shower and shiver, time to hide pills in his cheek and squirrel them away for when the hurt was the worst, time to wonder why the drugs weren't working like they used to, even when he doubled the dosage on his own.

Perhaps the game's numbing powers were the reason it existed at all, why someone had spent the effort to create it, and why subsequent heads had kept it secreted away. He had seen it on Merriman's face during that elevator ride at the end of his shift. The chemicals only cut through the worst of the pain, that indefinable ache. But lesser wounds resurfaced. The bouts of sudden sadness had to be coming from somewhere.

The last few cards fell into place while his mind wandered. The computer had shuffled for a win, and Troy got all the credit for verifying it. The screen flashed *Good Job!* in large block letters. It was strangely satisfying to be told this by a homemade game—told that he had done a good job. There was a sense of completion, of having *done* something with his day.

He left the message flashing and glanced around his office for something else to do. There were amendments to be made in the Order, announcements to write up for the Heads of the other silos, and he needed to make sure the vocabulary in these memos adhered to the ever-changing standards.

He got it wrong himself, often calling them bunkers instead of silos. It was difficult for those who had lived in the time of the Legacy. An old vocabulary, a way of seeing the world, persisted despite the medication. He felt envious of the men and women in the other silos, those who were born and who would die in their own little worlds, who would fall in and out of love, who would keep their hurts in memory, feel them, learn from them, be changed by them. He was jealous of these people even more than he envied the women of his silo who remained in their long-sleep lifeboats—

There was a knock on his open door. Troy looked up and saw Randall, who worked across the hall in the psych office, standing in the doorway. Troy waved him inside with one hand and minimized the game with the other. He fidgeted with the copy of the Order on his desk, trying to look busy.

"I've got that beliefs report you wanted." Randall waved a folder.

"Oh, good. Good." Troy took the folder. Always with the folders. He was reminded of the two groups that had built that place: the politicians and the doctors. Both were stuck in a prior era, a time of paperwork. Or it was possible that neither group trusted any data they couldn't shred or burn?

"The head of Silo 6 has a new replacement picked out and processed. He wants to schedule a talk with you, make the induction formal."

"Oh. Okay." Troy flipped through the folder and saw typed transcripts from the communication room about each of the silos. He looked forward to another induction ceremony. Any task he had already done once before filled him with less dread.

"Also, the population report on Silo 32 is a little troubling." Randall came around his desk. He licked his thumb before sorting through the reports, and Troy glanced at his monitor to make sure he'd minimized the game. "They're getting close to the maximum and fast. Doc Haines thinks it might be a bad batch of birth control implants. The Head of 32, a Biggers, here we go—" Randall pulled out the report. "He denies this, says no one with an active implant has gotten pregnant. He thinks the lottery is being gamed or that there's something wrong with our computers."

"Hmm." Troy took the report and looked it over. Silo 32 had crept above nine thousand inhabitants, and the median age had fallen into the low twenties. "Let's set up a call for first thing in the morning. I don't buy the lottery being gamed. They shouldn't even be running the lottery, right? Until they have more space?"

"That's what I said."

"And all the population accounts for every silo are run from the same computer." Troy tried to not make this sound like a question, but it was. He couldn't remember.

"Yup," Randall confirmed.

"Which means we're being lied to. I mean, this doesn't happen overnight, right? Biggers had to see this coming, which means he knew about it earlier, so either he's complicit, or he's lost control over there."

"Exactly."

"Okay. What do we know about Biggers's second?"

"His shadow?" Randall hesitated. "I'd have to pull that file, but I know he's been in place for a while. He was there before we started our shifts."

"Good. I'll speak with him tomorrow. Alone."

"You think we should replace Biggers?"

Troy nodded grimly. The Order was clear on problems that defied explanation: *Start at the top. Assume the explanation was a lie.* Because of the rules, he and Randall were talking about a man being put out of commission as if he were broken machinery.

"Okay, one more thing—"

The thunder of boots down the hallway interrupted the thought. Randall and Troy looked up as Saul bolted into the room, his eyes wide with fear.

"Sirs—"

"Saul. What's going on?"

The communications officer looked like he'd seen a thousand ghosts.

"We need you in the comm room, sir. Right now."

Troy pushed away from his desk. Randall was right behind him.

"What is it?" Troy asked.

Saul hurried down the hallway. "It's Silo 12, sir."

The three of them ran past a man on a ladder who was replacing a long light bulb that had gone dim, the large rectangular plastic cover above him hanging open like a doorway to the heavens. Troy found himself breathing hard as he struggled to keep up.

"What *about* Silo 12?" he huffed.

Saul flashed a look over his shoulder, his face screwed up with worry. "I think we're losing it, sir."

"What, like contact? You can't reach them?"

"No. Losing *it*, sir. The *silo*. The whole damn thing."

2049 • Savannah, Georgia

Donald wasn't one for napkins, but he obeyed decorum by shaking the folded cloth loose and draping it in his lap. Each of the napkins at the other settings around the table had been bent into a decorative pyramid that stood upright amid the silverware. He didn't remember the Corner Diner having cloth napkins when he was in high school. Didn't they used to have those paper napkin dispensers that were all dented up from years of abuse? And those little salt and pepper shakers with the silver caps, even those had gotten fancier. A dish of what he assumed was sea salt sat near the flower arrangement, and if you wanted pepper, you had to wait for someone to come around and crack it on your food for you.

He started to mention this to his wife, and saw that she was still gazing past him at the other booth. Donald turned in his seat, the original vinyl that had survived outdatedness and returned to chic squeaking beneath him. He glanced over at the older couple sitting in the booth where he and Helen had sat on their first date.

"I swear I asked them to reserve it for us," Donald said.

His wife's gaze drifted back to him.

"I think they might've gotten confused when I described which one it was." He stirred the air with his finger. "Or maybe I got turned around when I was on the phone."

She waved her hand. "Sweetie, forget about it. We could be eating grilled cheese at home and I'd be thrilled. I was just staring off into space."

Helen unfolded her own napkin with delicate care, almost as if she were studying the folds, seeing how to piece it back together, how to return a disassembled thing to its original state. The waiter came over in a bustle and filled their glasses with water, careless drips spotting the white tablecloth. He apologized for the wait, and then left them to wait some more.

"This place sure has changed," he said.

"Yeah. It's more grown-up."

They both reached for their waters at the same time. Donald smiled and held his glass up. "Fifteen years to the day that your father made the mistake of extending your curfew."

Helen smiled and tapped her glass against his. "To fifteen more," she said.

They took sips.

"If this place keeps up, we won't be able to afford to eat here in fifteen years."

Helen laughed. Donald could imagine the crystal blushing at the sound. She had barely changed since that first date. Or maybe it was because the changes were so subtle. It wasn't like coming to a restaurant every five years and seeing the leaps all at once. It was how siblings aged rather than distant cousins.

"You fly back in the morning?" Helen asked.

"Yeah, but to Boston. I have a meeting with the Senator."

"Why Boston?"

He waved his hand. "He's having one of those nano treatments of his. I think he stays locked up in there for a week or so at a time. He still somehow gets his work done—"

"Yeah, by having his minions go out of *their* way—"

"We're not his minions," Donald said, laughing.

"—to come kiss his ring and leave gifts of myrrh."

"C'mon, it's not like that."

"I just worry that you're pushing yourself too hard. How much of your free time are you spending on this project of his?"

A lot, he wanted to say. He wanted to tell his wife how grueling the hours were, but he knew what she would say. "It's not as time-consuming as you'd think."

"Really? Because it seems like it's the only thing I hear you talking about. I don't even know what else it is you do."

Their waiter came by with a platter full of drinks and said it would be just a moment longer. Helen studied the menu.

"I'll be done with my portion of the plans in another few months," he told her. "And then I won't bore you with it anymore."

"Honey, you don't bore me. I just don't want him taking advantage of you. This isn't what you signed up for. You decided *not* to become an architect, remember? Otherwise, you could've stayed home."

"Baby, I want you to know—" He dropped his voice. "This project we're working on is—"

"It's really important, I know. You've told me, and I believe you. And then in your moments of self-doubt, you admit that your part in the entire scheme of things is superfluous anyway and will never be used."

Donald forgot they'd had that conversation.

"I'll just be glad when it's done," she said. "They can truck the fuel rods through our *neighborhood* for all I care. Just bury the whole thing and smooth the dirt over and stop talking about it."

This was something else. Donald thought about the phone calls and emails he'd been getting from the district, all the headlines and fear mongering over the route the spent rods would take from the port as the trucks skirted Atlanta. Every time Helen heard a peep about the project, all she could likely think of was him wasting his time on it rather than doing his real job. Or the fact that he could've stayed in Savannah and done the same work.

Helen cleared her throat. "So—" She hesitated. "Was Anna at the job site today?"

She peered over the lip of her glass, and Donald realized, in that moment, what his wife was *really* thinking when the CAD-FAC project and the fuel rods came up. It was the insecurity of him working with *her*, of being so far away from home.

"No." He shook his head. "No, we don't really see each other. We send plans back and forth. Mick and I went, just the two of us. He's coordinating a lot of the materials and crews—"

The waiter arrived, pulled his black folio from his apron, and clicked his pen. "Can I start you off with drinks?"

Donald ordered two glasses of the house Merlot. Helen declined the offer of an appetizer.

"Every time I bring her up," she said, once their waiter had angled off toward the bar, "you mention Mick. Stop changing the subject."

"Please, Helen, can we not talk about her?" Donald folded his hands together on the table. "I've seen her once since we started working on this. I set it up so that we didn't have to meet, because I knew you wouldn't like it. I have no feelings for her, honey. Absolutely none. Please. This is our night."

"Is working with her giving you second thoughts?"

"Second thoughts about what? About taking on this job? Or about being an architect?"

"About...*anything*." She glanced at the other booth, the booth he should've reserved.

"No. God, no. Honey, why would you even say something like that?"

The waiter came back with their wine. He flipped open his black notebook and eyed the two of them. "Have we decided?"

Helen opened her menu and looked from the waiter to Donald. "I'm going to get my usual," she said. She pointed to what had once been a simple grilled cheese sandwich with fries that now involved fried green heirloom tomatoes, Gruyère cheese, a honey-maple glaze, and matchstick frites with tartar.

"And for you, sir?"

Donald looked over the menu. The conversation had him flustered, but he felt the pressure to choose and to choose swiftly.

"I think I'm going to try something different," he said, picking his words poorly.

· 12 ·
2110 · Silo 1

S ilo 12 was collapsing, and by the time Troy and the others arrived, the communication room was awash in overlapping radio chatter and the stench of sweat. Four men crowded around a comm station normally manned by a single operator. The men looked precisely how Troy felt: panicked, out of their depth, ready to curl up and hide somewhere. It had a calming effect on him. Their panic was his strength. He could fake this. He could hold it together.

Two of the men wore sleepshirts, suggesting that the late shift had been woken up and called in. Troy wondered how long Silo 12 had been in trouble before they finally came and got *him.*

"What's the latest?" Saul asked an older gentleman, who held a headphone to one ear.

The gentleman turned, his bald head shining in the overhead light, sweat in the wrinkles of his brow, his white eyebrows high with concern. "I can't get anyone to answer the server," he said.

"Give us *just* the feeds from 12," Troy said, pointing to one of the other three workers. A man he had met just a week or so ago pulled off his headset and flipped a switch. The speakers in the room buzzed with overlapping shouts and orders. The others stopped what they were doing and listened.

One of the other men, in his thirties, cycled through dozens of video feeds. It was chaos everywhere. There was a shot of a spiral staircase crammed with people pushing and shoving. A head disappeared, someone falling down, presumably being trampled as the rest moved on. Eyes were wide in fear, jaws clenched or shouting.

"Let's see the server room," Troy said.

The man at the controls typed something on his keypad. The crush of people disappeared and was replaced with a calm view of perfectly still cabinets. The server casings and the grating on the floor throbbed from the blinking overhead lights of an unanswered call.

"What happened?" Troy asked. He felt unusually calm.

"Still trying to determine that, sir."

A folder was pressed into his hands. A handful of people gathered in the hallway, peering in. News was spreading, a crowd gathering. Troy felt a trickle of sweat run down the back of his neck, but still that eerie calmness, that resignation to this statistical inevitability.

A desperate voice from one of the radios cut through the rest, the panic palpable:

"—they're coming through. Dammit, they're bashing down the door. They're gonna get through—"

Everyone in the comm room held their breath, all the jitters and activity ceasing as they listened and waited. Troy was pretty sure he knew which door the panicked man was talking about. A lone door stood between the cafeteria and the airlock. It should have been made stronger. A lot of things should have been made stronger.

"—I'm on my own up here, guys. They're gonna get through. Holy shit, they're gonna get through—"

"Is that a deputy?" Troy asked. He flipped through the folder. There were status updates from Silo 12's IT Head. No alarms. Two years since the last cleaning. The fear index was pegged at an eight the last time it'd been measured. A little high, but not too low.

"Yeah, I think that's a deputy," Saul said.

The man at the video feed looked back at Troy. "Sir, we're gonna have a mass exodus."

"Their radios are locked down, right?"

Saul nodded. "We shut down the repeaters. They can talk among themselves, but that's it."

Troy fought the urge to turn and meet the curious faces peering in from the hallway. "Good," he said. The priority in this situation was to contain the outbreak: don't let it spread to neighboring cells. This was a cancer. Excise it. Don't mourn the loss.

The radio crackled:

"—they're almost in, they're almost in, they're almost in—"

Troy tried to imagine the stampede, the crush of people, how the panic had spread. The Order was clear on not intervening, but his conscience was muddled. He held out a hand toward the radioman.

"Let me speak to him," Troy said.

Heads swiveled his way. A crowd that thrived on protocol sat stunned. After a pause, the receiver was pressed into his palm. Troy didn't hesitate. He squeezed the mic.

"Deputy?"

"Hello? Sheriff?"

The video operator cycled through the feeds, then waved his hand and pointed to one of the monitors. The floor number "72" sat in the corner of the screen, and a man in silver coveralls lay slumped over a desk. There was a gun in his hand, a pool of blood around a keyboard.

"That's the Sheriff?" Troy asked.

The operator wiped his forehead and nodded.

"Sheriff? What do I do?"

Troy clicked the mic. "The sheriff is dead," he told the deputy, surprised by the steadiness of his own voice. He held the transmit button and pondered this stranger's fate. It dawned on him that most of these silo dwellers thought they were alone. They had no idea about each other, about their true purpose. And now Troy had made contact, a disembodied voice from the clouds.

One of the video feeds clicked over to the deputy, who was gripping a handset, the cord spiraling to a radio mounted on the wall. The floor number in the corner read: "1."

"You need to lock yourself in the holding cell," Troy radioed, seeing that the least obvious solution was the best. It was a temporary solution, at least. "Make sure you have every set of keys."

He watched the man on the video screen. The entire room, and those in the hallway, watched the man on the video screen.

The door to the upper security office was just visible in the warped bubble of the camera's view. The edges of the door seemed to bulge outward because of the lens. And then the center of the door bulged *inward* because of the mob. They were beating the door down. The deputy didn't respond. He dropped the microphone and hurried around the desk. His hands shook so violently as he reached for the keys that the grainy camera was able to capture it.

The door cracked along the center. Someone in the comm room drew in an audible breath. Troy wanted to launch into the statistics. He had studied and trained to be on the *other* end of this, to lead a small group of people in the event of a catastrophe, not to lead them *all*.

Maybe that's why he was so calm. He was watching a horror that he should have been in the middle of, that he should have lived and died through.

The deputy finally secured the keys. He ran across the room and out of sight. Troy imagined him fumbling with the lock on the cell as the door burst in, an angry mob forcing their way through the splintered gap in the wood. It was a solid door, strong, but not strong enough. It was impossible to tell if the deputy had made it to safety. Not that it mattered. It was temporary. It was all temporary. If they opened the doors, if they made it out, the deputy would suffer a fate far worse than being trampled.

"The inner airlock door is open, sir. They're trying to get out."

Troy nodded. The trouble had probably started in IT, had spread from there. Maybe the Head—but more likely his shadow. Someone with override codes. Here was the curse: a person had to be in charge, had to guard the secrets. Some wouldn't be able to. It was statistically predictable. He reminded himself that it was inevitable, the cards already shuffled, the game just waiting to play out.

"Sir, we've got a breach. The outer door, sir."

"Fire the canisters now," Troy said.

Saul radioed the control room down the hall and relayed the message. The view of the airlock filled with a white fog.

"Secure the server room," Troy added. "Lock it down."

He had this portion of the Order memorized.

"Make sure we have a recent backup just in case. And put them on our power."

"Yessir."

Those in the room who had something to do seemed less anxious than the others, who were left shifting about nervously while they watched and listened.

"Where's my outside view?" Troy asked.

The mist-filled scene of people pushing on one another's backs through a white cloud was replaced with an expansive shot of the outside, of a claustrophobic crowd scampering across a dry land, of people collapsing to their knees, clawing at their faces and their throats, a billowing fog rising up from the teeming ramp.

No one in the comm room moved or said a word. There was a soft cry from the hallway. Troy shouldn't have allowed them to stay and watch.

"Okay," he said. "Shut it down."

The view of the outside went black. There was no point in watching the crowd fight their way back in, no reason to witness the frightened men and women dying on the hills.

"I want to know why it happened." Troy turned and studied those in the room. "I want to know, and I want to know what we do to prevent this next time." He handed the folder and the microphone back to the men at their stations. "Don't tell the other silo Heads just yet. Not until we have answers for the questions they'll have."

Saul raised his hand. "What about the people still inside 12?"

"The only difference between the people in Silo 12 and the people in Silo 13 is that there won't be future generations growing up in Silo 12. That's it. Everyone in all the silos will eventually die. We all die, Saul. Even us. Today was just their day." He nodded to the dark monitor and tried not to picture what was really going on over there. "We knew this would happen, and it won't be the last. Let's concentrate on the others. Learn from it."

There were nods around the room.

"Individual reports by the end of this shift," Troy said, feeling for the first time that he was actually in charge of something. "And if anyone from 12's IT staff can be raised, debrief them as much as you can. I want to know who, why, and how."

Several of the exhausted people in the room stiffened before trying to look busy. The gathering in the hallway shrank back as they realized the show was over and the boss was heading their way.

The boss.

Troy felt the fullness of his position for the first time, the heavy weight of responsibility. There were murmurs and sidelong glances as he headed back toward his office. There were nods of sympathy and approval, men thankful that they occupied lower posts. Troy strode past them all.

More will try to escape, Troy thought. For all their careful engineering, there was no way to make a thing infallible. The best they could do is plan ahead, stockpile spares, not mourn the dark and lifeless cylinder as it was discarded and others were turned to with hope.

Back in his office, he closed the door and leaned back against it for a moment. His shoulders stuck to his coveralls with the light sweat worked up from the swift walk. He took a few deep breaths before crossing to his desk and resting his hand on his copy of the Order. The fear persisted that they'd gotten it all wrong. How could a room full of doctors plan for everything? Would it really get easier as the generations went along, as people forgot and the whispers from the original survivors faded?

Troy wasn't so sure. He looked over at his wall of schematics, that large blueprint showing all the silos spread out amid the hills, fifty circles spaced out like stars on an old flag he had once served.

A powerful tremor coursed through Troy's body: his shoulders, elbows, and hands twitched. He gripped the edge of his desk until it passed. Opening the top drawer, he picked up a red marker and crossed to the large schematic, the shivers still wracking his chest.

Before he could consider the permanence of what he was about to do, before he could consider that this mark of his would be on display for every future shift, before he could consider that this may become a trend, an act taken by his replacements, he drew a bold 'X' through Silo 12.

The marker squealed as it was dragged violently across the paper. It seemed to cry out. Troy blinked away the blurry vision of the red X and sagged to his knees. He bent forward until his forehead rested against the tall spread of papers, old plans rustling and crinkling as his chest shook with heavy sobs.

With his hands in his lap, shoulders bent with the weight of another job he'd been pressured into, Troy cried. He bawled as silently as he could so those across the hall wouldn't hear.

• 13 •

2049 • RYT Hospital, Dwayne Medical Center

D onald had toured the Pentagon once, had been to the White House twice, went in and out of the Capitol building a dozen times a week, but nothing he'd seen in D.C. prepared him for the security around RYT's Dwayne Medical Center. The lengthy checks hardly made the hour-long meeting with the Senator seem worthwhile.

By the time he passed through the full body scanners leading into the nanobiotech wing, he'd been stripped, given a pair of green medical scrubs to wear, had a blood sample taken, and had allowed every sort of scanner and bright light to probe his eyes and record—so they said—the infrared capillary pattern of his face.

Heavy doors and sturdy men blocked every corridor as they made their way deeper and deeper into the NBT wing. When Donald spotted the Secret Service agents—who had been allowed to keep their dark suits and shades—he knew he was getting close. A nurse scanned him through a final set of stainless steel doors. The nanobiotic chamber awaited him inside.

Donald eyed the massive machine warily. He'd only ever seen them on TV dramas, and this one loomed even larger in person. It looked like a small submarine that had been marooned on the upper floors of the RYT. Hoses and wires led away from the curved and flawless white exterior in bundles. Studded along the length were several small glass windows that brought to mind the portholes of a ship.

"And you're sure it's safe for me to go in?" He turned to the nurse. "Because I can always wait and visit him later."

The nurse smiled. She couldn't be out of her twenties, had her brown hair wrapped in a knot on the back of her head, was pretty in an uncomplicated way. "It's perfectly safe," she assured him. "His nanos won't interact with your body. We often treat multiple patients in a single chamber."

She led him to the end of the machine, and spun open the locking wheel at the end. A hatch opened with a sticky, ripping sound from the rubber seals and let out a slight gasp of air from the difference in pressure.

"If it's so safe, then why are the walls so *thick*?"

A soft laugh. "You'll be fine." She waved him toward the hatch. "There'll be a slight delay and a little buzz after I seal this door, and then the inner one will unlock. Just spin the wheel and push to open."

"I'm a little claustrophobic," Donald admitted.

God, listen to himself. He was an adult. Why couldn't he just say he didn't want to go in and have that be enough? Why was he allowing himself to be pressured into this?

"Just step inside please, Mr. Keene."

The nurse placed her hand on the small of Donald's back. Somehow, the pressure of a young and pretty woman watching was stronger than his abject terror of the oversized capsule packed with its invisible machines. He wilted and found himself ducking through the small hatch, his throat constricting with fear.

The door behind him thumped shut, leaving him in a small curved space hardly big enough for two. The locks behind him clanked into the jamb. There were tiny silver benches set into the arching walls on either side of him. He tried to stand up, but his head brushed the ceiling. Donald reached for the handle on the inner door and walked through.

An angry hum filled the chamber. The hair on the back of his neck stood on end, and the air felt charged with electricity. He looked for an intercom, some way to communicate with the Senator through the door so he didn't have to go in any further. It felt like he couldn't breathe; he needed to get *out*. There was no wheel on the outer door. Everything had been taken out of his control—

The inner locks clanked. Donald lunged for the door and tried the handle. Holding his breath, he opened the hatch and escaped the small airlock for the larger chamber in the center of the capsule.

"Donald!" Senator Thurman looked up from a thick book. He was sprawled out on one of the benches running the length of the long cylinder. A notepad and pen sat on a small table; a plastic tray held the remnants of dinner.

"Hello, sir," he said, barely parting his lips.

"Don't just stand there, get in. You're letting the buggers out."

Against his every impulse, Donald stepped through and pushed the door shut, and Senator Thurman laughed. "You might as well breathe, son. They could crawl right through your skin if they wanted to."

Donald let out his held breath and shivered. It may have been his imagination, but he thought he felt little pinpricks all over his skin, bites like Savannah's no-see-ems on summer days.

"You can't feel 'em," Senator Thurman said. "It's all in your head. They know the difference between you and me."

Donald glanced down and realized he was scratching his arm.

"Have a seat." Thurman gestured to the bench opposite his. He had the same color scrubs on and a few days' growth on his chin. Donald noticed the far end of the capsule opened onto a small bathroom, a showerhead with a flexible hose clipped to the wall. Thurman swung his bare feet off the bench and grabbed a half-empty bottle of water, took a sip. Donald obeyed and sat down, a nervous sweat tickling his scalp. A stack of folded blankets and a few pillows sat at the end of the bench. He saw how the frames folded open into cots but couldn't imagine being able to sleep in this tight coffin.

"You wanted to see me, sir?" He tried to keep his voice from cracking. The air tasted metallic, a hint of the machines on his tongue.

"Drink?" The Senator opened a small fridge below the bench and pulled out a bottle of water.

"Thanks." Donald accepted the water but didn't open it, just enjoyed the cool against his palm. "Mick said he filled you in." He wanted to add that this meeting felt unnecessary.

Thurman nodded. "He did. Met with him yesterday. He's a solid boy." The Senator smiled and shook his head. "The irony is, this class we just swore in? Probably the best bunch the Hill has seen in a very long time."

"The irony?"

Thurman waved his hand, shooing the question away. "You know what I love about this treatment?"

Practically living forever? Donald nearly blurted.

"It gives you time to think. A few days in here, nothing with batteries allowed, just a few books to read and something to write on, it really clears your head."

Donald kept his opinions to himself. He didn't want to admit how uncomfortable the procedure made him, how terrifying it was to be in that room right then. Knowing that tiny machines were coursing through the Senator's body, picking through his individual cells and making repairs, repelled him. Supposedly, your urine turned the color of charcoal once all the machines shut down. He trembled at the thought.

"Isn't that nice?" Thurman asked. He took in a deep breath and let it out. "The quiet?"

Donald didn't answer. He realized he was holding his breath again.

Thurman looked down at the book in his lap, then lifted his gaze to study Donald.

"Did you know your grandfather taught me how to play golf?"

Donald laughed. "Yeah. I've seen the pictures of you two together." He flashed back to his grandmother flipping through old albums. She had this outmoded obsession with printing the pictures from her computer and stuffing them in books. Said they became more real once they were displayed like that.

"You and your sister have always felt like family to me," the Senator said.

"Well, I appreciate that, sir." The Senator had definitely been locked up too long. He remembered a night in college when Mick had gotten sloshed and "opened up to him." It was uncomfortable. A small vent in the corner of the pod circulated some air, but it still felt warm in there.

"I want you in on this project," Thurman said. "All the way in."

Donald swallowed. "Sir. I'm fully committed, I promise."

Thurman raised his hand and shook his head. "No, not like—" He dropped his hand to his lap, glanced at the door. "You know, I used to think you couldn't hide anything anymore. Not in this age. It's all out there, you know?" He waggled his fingers in the air. "Hell, you ran for office and squeezed through that mess. You know what it's like."

Donald nodded. "Yeah, I had a few things I had to own up to."

The Senator cupped his hands into a bowl. "It's like trying to hold water and not letting a single drop through."

Donald nodded.

"A president can't even get a blow job anymore without the world finding out."

Donald's confused squint had Thurman waving at the air. "Before your time. But here's the thing, here's what I've found, both overseas and in Washington. It's the *unimportant* drips that leak through. The peccadilloes. Embarrassments, not life and death stuff. You want to invade a foreign country? Look at D-Day. Hell, look at Pearl Harbor. Or 9/11. Not a problem."

"I'm sorry, sir, I don't see what—"

Thurman's hand flew out, his fingers thudding shut as he pinched the air. Donald thought for a moment that he meant for him to keep quiet, but then the Senator leaned forward and held the pinched pads of his fingers for Donald to see, as if he had snatched a mosquito.

"Look," he said.

Donald leaned closer, but he still couldn't make anything out. He shook his head. "I don't see, sir—"

"That's right. And you wouldn't see it coming, either. That's what they've been working on, those snakes."

Senator Thurman released the invisible pinch and studied the pad of his thumb for a moment. He blew a puff of air across it. "Anything these puppies can stitch, they can *unstitch*."

He peered across the pod at Donald. "You know why we went into Iran the first time? It wasn't about nukes, I'll tell you that. I crawled through every hole that's ever been dug in those dunes over there, and those rats had a bigger prize they were chasing than nukes. You see, they've figured out how to attack us without being *seen*, without having to blow themselves up, and with *zero* repercussions."

Donald was sure he didn't have the clearance to hear any of this.

"Well, the Iranians didn't figure it out for themselves so much as steal what Israel was working on." He smiled at Donald. "So, of course, we had to start playing catch-up."

"I don't understa—"

"These critters in here are programmed for my DNA, Donny. Think about that. Have you ever had your ancestry tested?" He looked Donald up and down like he was surveying a mottled mutt. "What are you, anyway? Scottish?"

"Maybe Irish, sir. I honestly couldn't tell you." He didn't want to admit that it was unimportant to him; it seemed like a topic close to Thurman's heart..

"Well, these buggers can tell. If they ever get them perfected, that is. They could tell you what clan you came from. And that's what the Iranians are working on: a weapon you can't see, that you can't stop, and if it decides you're Jewish, even a *quarter* Jew—" Thurman drew his thumb across his own neck.

"I thought we were wrong about that. We never found any NBs in Iran."

"That's because they self-destructed. *Remotely.* Poof." The old man's eyes widened.

Donald laughed. "You sound like one of those conspiracy theorists—"

Senator Thurman leaned back and rested his head against the wall. "Donny, the conspiracy theorists sound like *us*."

Donald waited for the Senator to laugh. Or smile. Neither came.

"What does this have to do with me?" he asked. "Or our project?"

Thurman closed his eyes, his head tilted back against the wall behind him. "You know why Florida has such pretty sunrises?"

Donald wanted to scream. He wanted to beat on the door until they hauled him out of there in a straightjacket. Instead, he took a sip of water.

Thurman cracked an eye. Studied him again.

"It's because the sand from Africa blows clear across the Atlantic."

Donald nodded. He saw what the Senator was getting at. He'd heard the same fear-mongering on the twenty-four-hour news programs, how toxins and tiny machines can circle the globe, just like seeds and pollens have done for millennia.

"It's coming, Donny. I know it is. I've got eyes and ears everywhere, even in here. I asked you to meet me here because I want you to have a seat at the *after* party."

"Sir?"

"You and Helen both."

Donald scratched his arm and glanced at the door.

"It's just a contingency plan for now, you understand? There are plans in place for anything. Mountains for the president to crawl inside of, but we need something else."

Donald remembered the congressman from Atlanta prattling on about zombies and the CDC. This sounded like more of that nonsense.

"I'm happy to serve on any committee you think's important—"

"Good." The Senator took the book from his lap and handed it to Donald. "Read this," Thurman said.

Donald checked the cover. It was familiar, but instead of French script, it read: *The Order*. He opened the heavy tome to a random page and started skimming.

"That's your bible from now on, son. When I was in the war, I met boys no higher than your knee who had the entire Qur'an memorized, every stinkin' verse. You need to do better."

"Memorize?"

"As near as you can. And don't worry, you've got a couple of years."

Donald raised his eyebrows in surprise, then shut the book and studied the spine. "Good. I'll need it." He wanted to know if there would be a raise involved or a ton of committee meetings. This sounded ludicrous, but he wasn't about to refuse the old man, not with his reelection coming up every two years.

"All right. Welcome." Thurman leaned forward and held out his hand. Donald tried to get his palm deep into the Senator's. It made the older man's grip hurt a lot less. "You're free to go."

"Thank you, sir."

He stood and exhaled in relief. Cradling the book, he moved to the airlock door.

"Oh, and Donny?"

He turned back. "Yessir?"

"The National Convention is in a couple of years. I want you to go ahead and pencil it into your schedule. And make sure Helen is there."

Donald felt goose bumps run down his arms. Did that mean a real possibility of promotion? Maybe a speech on the big stage?

"Absolutely, sir." He knew he was smiling.

"Oh, and I'm afraid I haven't been completely honest with you about the critters in here."

"Sir?" Donald swallowed. His smile melted. He had one hand on the hatch's wheel. His mind resumed playing tricks on him, the taste on his tongue metallic, the pricks everywhere on his skin.

"Some of the buggers in here are very much for you."

Senator Thurman stared at Donald for a beat, and then he started laughing.

Donald turned, sweat glassy on his brow as he worked the wheel in the door with a free hand. It wasn't until he secured the airlock, the seals deadening the Senator's laughter, that he could breathe again.

The air around him buzzed, a jolt of static to kill any strays. Donald blew out his breath, harder than usual, and unsteadily walked away.

The shrinks kept Troy's door locked and delivered his meals while he went through the Silo 12 reports alone. He spread the pages across his keyboard—safely away from the edge of his desk. This way, when stray tears fell, they didn't smudge the paper.

For some reason, Troy couldn't stop crying. The shrinks with the strict meal plans had taken him off his meds the last two days, long enough to compile his findings with Troy sober, free from the forgetfulness the pills brought about. He had a deadline. After he put his final notes together, they would get him something to cut through the pain.

Images of the dying interfered with his thoughts, the picture of the outside, of people suffocating and falling to their knees. Troy remembered giving the order. What he regretted most was making someone else push the button.

Coming off his meds had brought back other random haunts. He began to remember his father, events from before his orientation. And it worried him that the billions who had been wiped out could be felt as an ache in his gut while the few thousand of Silo 12 who had scrambled to their deaths made him want to curl up and die.

The reports on his keyboard told a story of a shadow who had lost his nerve, an IT Head who couldn't see the darkness rising at her feet, and an honest enough Security chief who had chosen poorly. All it took was for a lot of seemingly decent people to put the wrong person in power, and then pay for their innocent choice.

The keycodes for each video feed sat in the margins. It reminded him of an old book he had once known; the references had a similar style.

Jason 2:17 brought up a slice of the IT shadow's feed. Troy followed the action on his monitor. A young man, probably in his late teens or early twenties, sat on a server room floor. His back was to the camera, the corners of a plastic tray visible in his lap. He was bent over a meal, the bony knots of his spine casting dots of shadow down the back of his coveralls.

Troy watched. He glanced at the report to check the timecode. He didn't want to miss it.

In the video, Jason's right elbow worked back and forth. He looked to be eating. The moment was coming. Troy willed himself not to blink, could feel tears coat his eyes from the effort.

A noise startled Jason. The young IT shadow glanced to the side, his profile visible for a moment, an angular and gaunt face from weeks of privation. He grabbed the tray from his lap; it was the first time Troy could spot the rolled-up sleeve. And there, as he fought with the cuff to roll it back down, were the dark parallel lines across his forearm, and nothing on his tray that called for a knife.

The rest of the clip was of Jason speaking to the IT Head, her demeanor motherly and tender, a touch on his shoulder, a squeeze of his elbow. Troy could imagine her voice. He had spoken to her once or twice to take down a report. In a few more weeks, they would've scheduled a time to speak with Jason and induct him formally.

The clip ended with Jason descending back into the space beneath the server room floor, a shadow swallowing a shadow. The Head of IT— the *true* Head of Silo 12—stood alone for a moment, hand on her chin. She looked so *alive*. Troy had a childlike impulse to reach out and brush his fingers across the monitor, to acknowledge this ghost, to apologize for letting her down.

Instead, he saw something the reports had missed. He watched her body twitch toward the hatch, stop, freeze for a moment, then turn away.

Troy clicked the slider at the bottom of the video to see it again. There she was rubbing her shadow's shoulder, talking to him, Jason nodding.

She squeezed his elbow, was concerned about him. He was assuring her everything was fine.

Once he was gone, once she was alone, the doubts and fears overtook her. Troy couldn't know it for sure, but he could *sense* it. She knew a darkness was brewing beneath her feet, and here was her chance to destroy it. It was a mask of concern, a twitch in that direction, reconsidering, turning away.

Troy paused the video and made some notes, jotted down the times. The shrinks would have to verify his findings. Shuffling the papers, he wondered if there was anything he needed to see again. A decent woman had been murdered because she could not bring herself to do the same, to kill in order to protect. And a Security chief had let loose a monster who had mastered the art of concealing his pain, a young man who had learned how to manipulate others, who wanted *out*.

He typed up his conclusions. It was a dangerous age for shadowing, he noted in his report. Here was a boy between his teens and twenties, an age deep in doubts and shallow in control. Troy asked in his report if anyone at that age could ever be ready. He made mention of the first head of IT he had inducted, the question the boy had asked after hearing tales from his demented grandmother. Was it right to expose anyone to these truths? Could men at such a fragile age be expected to endure such blows without shattering?

What he didn't add, what he asked himself, was if anyone at *any* age could ever be ready.

There was precedence, he typed, for limiting certain positions of authority by age. And while this would lead to shorter terms—which meant subjecting more unfortunate souls to the abuse of being locked up and shown their Legacy—wasn't it better to go through a damnable process more often rather than take risks such as these?

He knew this report would matter little. There was no planning for insanity. With enough revolutions and elections, enough transfers of power, eventually a madman would take the reins. It was inevitable. These were the odds they had planned for. This was why they had built so many.

He rose from his desk and walked to the door, slapped it soundly with the flat of his palm. In the corner of his office, a printer hummed and shot four pages out of its mouth. Troy took them; they were still warm as he slid them into the folder, these reports on the newly dead and still dying. He could feel the life and warmth draining from those printed pages. Soon, they would be as cool as the air around them.

A key rattled in his lock before the door opened.

"Done already?" Victor asked. The gray-haired psychiatrist stood across from his desk, keys jangling as they returned to his pocket. He held a small plastic cup in his hand.

Troy handed him the folder. "The signs were there," he told the doctor, "but they weren't acted upon."

Victor took the folder with one hand and held out the plastic cup with the other.

Troy typed a few commands on his computer and wiped his copy of the videos. The cameras were of no use for predicting and preventing these kinds of problems. There were too many to watch all at once. You couldn't get enough people to sit and monitor an entire populace. They were there to sort through the wreckage, the aftermath.

"Looks good," Victor said, flipping through the folder. The plastic cup sat on Troy's desk, two pills inside. They had increased the dosage to what he had taken at the start of his shift, a little extra to cut through the extra pain.

"Would you like me to fetch you some water?"

Troy shook his head. He hesitated. Looking up from the cup, he asked Victor a question.

"How long do you think it'll take? Silo 12, I mean. Before all of those people are gone."

Victor shrugged. "Not long, I imagine. Days."

Troy nodded. Victor watched him carefully. Troy tilted his head back and rattled the pills past his trembling lips. There was the bitter taste on his tongue. He made a show of swallowing.

"I'm sorry that it was your shift," Victor said. "I know this wasn't the job you signed up for."

Troy nodded. "I'm actually glad it was mine," he said after a moment. "I'd hate for it to have been anyone else's."

Victor rubbed the folder with one hand. "You'll be given a commendation in my report."

"Thank you," Troy said. He didn't know what the fuck for.

With a wave of the folder, Victor finally turned to leave and go back to his desk across the hall where he could sit and glance up occasionally at Troy.

And in that brief moment it took for Victor to walk over, with his back turned, Troy spat the pills into the palm of his hand.

Shaking his mouse with one hand, waking up his monitor so he could boot a game of solitaire, Troy smiled across the hallway at Victor, who smiled back. And in his other hand, still sticky from the outer coating dissolved by his saliva, the two pills nestled in his palm. Troy was tired of forgetting. He had decided to remember.

• 15 •

2049 • Savannah, Georgia

Donald sped down highway 17, a flashing red light on his dash warning him as he exceeded the local speed limit. He didn't care about being pulled over, didn't care about being wired a ticket or his insurance rates creeping up. It all seemed trivial. The fact that there were circuits riding along in his car keeping track of everything he did paled in comparison to the suspicion that machines in his *blood* were doing the same.

The tires squealed as he spiraled down his exit ramp too fast. He merged onto Berwick Boulevard, the overhead lights strobing through the windshield as he flew beneath them. Glancing down at his lap, he watched the gold inlay text on the book throb with the rhythm of the passing lights.

Order. Order. Order.

He had read enough to worry, to wonder what he'd gotten himself mixed up in. Helen had been right to warn him, had been wrong about the scale of the danger.

Turning into his neighborhood, Donald remembered a conversation from long before—he remembered her begging him not to run for office, that it would change him, that he couldn't fix anything up there, but that he could sure as hell come home broken.

How right had she been?

He pulled up to the house and had to leave the car by the curb. Her Jeep was in the middle of the driveway. One more habit formed in his absence, a reminder that he didn't live there anymore, didn't have a real home.

Leaving his bags in the trunk, he took just the book and his keys. The book was heavy enough.

The motion light came on as he neared the stoop. He saw a form by the window, heard frantic scratching on the other side. Helen opened the door, and Karma rushed out, tail whacking the side of the jamb, tongue lolling, so much bigger in just the few weeks that he'd been away.

Donald crouched down and rubbed her head, let the dog lick his cheek.

"Good girl," he said. He tried to sound happy. The cool emptiness in his chest intensified from being home. The things that should have felt comforting only made him feel worse.

"Hey, honey." He smiled up at his wife.

"You're early."

Helen wrapped her arms around his neck as he stood. Karma sat down and whined at them, tail swishing on the concrete. Helen's kiss tasted like coffee.

"I took an earlier flight."

He glanced over his shoulder at the dark streets of his neighborhood. As if anyone needed to follow him.

"Where're your bags?"

"I'll get 'em in the morning. C'mon, Karma. Let's go inside." He steered his dog through the door.

"Is everything okay?" Helen asked.

Donald went to the kitchen. He set the book down on the island and fished in the cabinet for a glass. Helen watched him with concern as he pulled a bottle of brandy out of the cabinet.

"Baby. What's going on?"

"Maybe nothing," he said. "Lunatics—" He poured three fingers of brandy, looked to Helen and raised the bottle to see if she wanted any. She shook her head. "Then again," he continued, "maybe there's something to it—" He took more than a sip. His other hand hadn't left the neck of the bottle.

"Baby, you're acting strange. Come sit down. Take off your coat."

He nodded and let her help him remove his jacket. He slid his tie off, saw the worry on her face, knew it to be a reflection of his own.

"What would you do if you thought it all might end?" he asked his wife. "What would you do?"

"If what? You mean us? Oh, you mean life. Honey, did someone pass away? Tell me what's going on."

"No, not someone. Everyone. Everything."

He tucked the bottle under his arm, grabbed his drink and the book, and went to the living room. Helen and Karma followed. Karma was already on the sofa waiting for him to sit down before he got there, oblivious to anything he was saying, just thrilled for the pack to be reunited.

"It sounds like you've had a very long day," Helen said, trying to find excuses for him.

Donald sat on the sofa and put the bottle and book on the coffee table. He pulled his drink away from Karma's curious nose.

"I have something I have to tell you," he said.

Helen stood in the middle of the room, her arms crossed. "That'd be a nice change." She smiled to let him know she was joking. Donald nodded.

"I know, I know," he said. His eyes fell to the book. "This isn't about that project. And honestly, do you think I enjoy keeping my life from you?"

Helen crossed to the recliner next to the sofa and sat down. "What is this about?" she asked.

"I've been told it's okay to tell you about a...promotion. Well, more of an assignment than a promotion. Not an assignment, really, more like being on the National Guard. Just in case—"

Helen reached over and squeezed his knee. "Take it easy," she whispered. Her eyebrows were lowered, confusion and worry lurking in the shadows there.

Donald took a deep breath. He was still revved up from running the conversation over in his head, from driving too fast. In the weeks since his meeting with Thurman he had been reading too much into the book—

and too much into that conversation. He couldn't tell if he was piecing something together, or just falling apart.

"How much have you followed what's going on in Iran?" he asked, scratching his arm. "And Korea?"

She shrugged. "I see blurbs online."

"Mmm." He took a burning gulp of the brandy, smacked his lips, and tried to relax and enjoy the numbing chill as it traveled through his body. "They're working on ways to take everything out," he said.

"Who? *We* are?" Helen's voice rose. "We're thinking of taking *them* out?"

"No, no—"

"Are you sure I'm allowed to hear this—?"

"No, sweetheart, they're designing weapons to take *us* out. Weapons that can't be stopped, that can't be defended against."

Helen leaned forward, her hands clasped, elbows on her knees. "Is this stuff you're learning in Washington? Classified stuff?"

He waved his hand. "Beyond classified. Look, you know why we went into Iran—"

"I know why they *said* we went in—"

"It wasn't bullshit," he said, cutting her off. "Well, maybe it was. Maybe they hadn't figured it out yet, hadn't mastered how—"

"Honey, slow down."

"Yeah." He took another deep breath. He had an image in mind of a large mountain out west, a concrete road disappearing straight into the rock, thick vault doors standing open as files of politicians crowded inside with their families.

"I met with the Senator a few weeks ago." He stared down into the ginger-colored liquor in his glass.

"In Boston," Helen said.

He nodded. "Right. Well, he wants us to be on this alert team—"

"You and Mick."

He turned toward his wife. "No, us."

"*Us?*" Helen placed a hand on her chest. "What do you mean, us? You and me?"

"Now listen—"

"You're volunteering *me* for one of his—?"

"Sweetheart, I had no idea what this was all about." He set his glass on the coffee table and grabbed the book. "He gave me this to read."

Helen frowned. "What is that?"

"It's like an instruction manual for the—well, for the *after*. I think."

Helen got up from the recliner and stepped between him and the coffee table. She nudged Karma out of the way, the dog grunting at being disturbed. Sitting down beside him, she put a hand on his back, her eyes shiny with worry.

"Donny, were you drinking on the plane?"

"No." He pulled away. "Just please listen to me. It doesn't matter *who* has them, it only matters *when*. Don't you see? This is the ultimate threat. A world-ender. I've been reading about the possibilities on this website—"

"A website," she said, voice flat with skepticism.

"Yeah. Listen. Remember those treatments the Senator takes? These nanos are like synthetic life. Imagine if someone turned them into a virus that didn't care about its host, that didn't need *us* in order to spread. They could be out there already—" He tapped his chest, glanced around the room suspiciously, took a deep breath. "They could be in every one of us right now, little timer circuits waiting for the right moment—"

"Sweetheart—"

"Very bad people are working on this, trying to make this happen." He reached for his glass. "We can't sit back and let them strike first. So we're gonna do it." There were ripples in the liquor. His hand was shaking. "God, baby, I'm pretty sure we're gonna do it before *they* can—"

"You're scaring me, honey—"

"Good." Another burning sip. He held the glass with both hands to keep it steady. "We should be scared."

"Do you want me to call Dr. Martin?"

"Who?" He tried to make room between them, bumped up against the armrest. "My sister's doctor? The *shrink*?"

She nodded gravely.

"Listen to what I'm telling you," he said, holding up a finger. "These tiny machines are *real*." His mind was racing. He was going to babble and convince her of nothing but his paranoia.

"Look," he said. "We use them in medicine, right?"

Helen nodded. She was giving him a chance, a slim one. But he could tell she really wanted to go call someone. Her mother, a doctor, *his* mother.

"It's like when we discovered radiation, okay? The first thing we thought was that this would be a cure, a medical discovery. X-rays, but then people were taking drops of radium like an elixir—"

"They poisoned themselves," Helen said. "Thinking they were doing something good." She seemed to relax a little. "Is this what you're worried about? That the nanos are going to mutate and turn on us? Are you still freaked out from being inside that machine?"

"No, nothing like that. I'm talking about how we looked for medicinal uses first, then ended up building the bomb. This is the *same thing*." He paused, hoping she would get it. "I'm starting to think we're building them, too. Tiny machines, just like the ones in the nanobaths that stitch up people's skin and joints. Only *these* would tear people apart."

Helen didn't react. Didn't say a word. Donald realized he sounded crazy, that every bit of this was already online and in podcasts that radiated out from lonely basements on lonely airwaves. The Senator had been right. Mix truth and lies and you couldn't tell them apart. The book on his coffee table and a zombie survival guide would be treated the same way.

"I'm telling you they're real," he said, unable to stop himself. "They'll be able to reproduce. They'll be invisible. There won't be any warning when they're set loose, just dust in the breeze, okay? Reproducing and reproducing, this invisible war will wage itself all around us while we're turned to mush."

Helen fell silent. He realized she was waiting for him to finish, and then she would call her mom and ask what to do. She would call Dr. Martin and get his advice.

Donald started to complain, could feel the anger welling up, and knew that anything he said would confirm her fears rather than convince her of his own.

"Is there anything else?" she whispered. She was looking for permission to leave and make her phone calls, to talk to someone rational.

Donald felt numb. Helpless and alone.

"The National Convention is going to be held in Atlanta." He wiped at the bottoms of his eyes, tried to make it look like weariness, like the strain of travel. "The DNC hasn't announced it yet, but I heard from Mick before I got on the flight." He turned to Helen. "The Senator wants us both there, is already planning something big."

"Of course, baby." She rested her hand on his thigh and looked at him like he was her patient.

"And I'm going to ask that I spend more time down here, maybe do some of my work from home on weekends, keep a closer eye on the project."

"That'd be great." She rested her other hand on his arm.

"I want us to be good to each other," he said. "For whatever time we have left—"

"Shh, baby, it's okay." She wrapped her arm around his back and shushed him again, trying to soothe him. "I love you," she said.

He wiped at his eyes again.

"We'll get through this," she told him.

Donald bobbed his head. "I know," he said. "I know we will."

The dog grunted and nuzzled her head into Helen's lap, could sense something was wrong. Donald scratched the pup's neck. He looked up at his wife, tears in his eyes. "I know we'll get through this," he said, trying to calm himself. "But what about everyone *else*?"

• 16 •

2110 · Silo 1

Troy needed to see a doctor. Ulcers had formed in both sides of his mouth, down between his gums and the insides of his cheeks. He could feel them like little wads of tender cotton embedded in his flesh. In the morning, he kept the pill tucked down on the left side. At supper, on the right. On either side, it would burn and dry out his mouth with the bitter bite of the medicine, but he would endure it.

He rarely employed napkins during meals, a bad habit he had formed long ago. They went into his lap to be polite and then onto his plate when he was finished. Now he had a different routine. One quick small bite of something, wipe his mouth, spit out the burning blue capsule, take a huge gulp of water, swish it around.

The hard part was not checking to see if anyone was watching while he spat it out. He sat with his back to the wallscreen, imagining eyes drilling through the side of his head, but he kept his gaze in front of him and chewed his food.

He remembered to use his napkin occasionally, to wipe with both hands, always with both hands, pinching across his mouth, staying consistent. He smiled at the man across from him and made sure the pill didn't fall out. The man's gaze drifted over Troy's shoulder as he stared at the view of the outside world on the screen.

Troy didn't turn to look. There was still the same draw to the top of the Silo, the same compulsion to be as high as possible, to escape the suffocating depths, but he no longer felt any desire to see outside. Something had changed.

He spotted Hal at the next table over—recognized his bald and splotchy scalp. The old man was sitting with his back to Troy. Troy waited for him to turn and catch his eye, but Hal never looked around.

He finished his corn and worked on his beets. It had been long enough since spitting out his pill to risk a glance toward the serving line. Tubes spat food; plates rattled on trays; one of the doctors from Victor's office stood beyond the glass serving line, arms crossed, a wan smile on his face. He was scanning the men in line and looking out over the tables. Why? What was there to keep an eye on? Troy wanted to know. He had dozens of burning questions like this. Answers sometimes presented themselves, but they skittered away if he trained his thoughts on them.

The beets were awful.

He ate the last of them while the gentleman across the table stood with his tray. It wasn't long before someone took his place. Troy looked up and down the row of adjoining tables. The vast majority of the workers sat on the *other* side so they could see out. Only a handful sat like Hal and himself. It was strange that he'd never noticed this before.

In the past weeks, it seemed patterns were becoming easier to spot, even as other faculties slipped and stumbled. He cut into a rubbery hunk of canned ham, his knife screeching against his plate, and wondered when he'd get some real sleep. He couldn't ask the doctors for anything to help, couldn't show them his gums. They might find out he was off his meds. The insomnia was awful. He might doze off for a minute or two, but deep sleep eluded him. And instead of remembering anything concrete, all he had were these dull aches, these bouts of terrible sadness, and the inescapable feeling that something was deeply wrong.

He caught one of the doctors watching him. Troy looked down the table and saw men shoulder to shoulder on the other side, eyeing the view. It wasn't long ago that he wanted to sit and stare, mesmerized by the gray hills on the screen. And now he felt sick when he caught even a glimpse; the view brought him close to tears.

He stood with his tray, then worried he was being obvious. The napkin fell from his lap and landed on the floor, and something skittered away from his foot.

Troy's heart skipped a beat. He bent and snatched the napkin, hurried down the line, looking for the pill. He bumped into a chair that had been pulled back from the table, felt all the room's eyes on him.

The pill. He found it and scooped it up with his napkin, the tray teetering dangerously in his palm. He stood and composed himself. A trickle of sweat itched his scalp and ran down the back of his neck. Everyone knew.

Troy turned and walked toward the water fountain, not daring to glance up at the cameras or over at the doctors. He was losing it. Growing paranoid. And there was just over a month left on this shift. A month that would test every inch of will he had left.

Trying to walk naturally with so many eyes on him was impossible. He rested the edge of his tray on the water fountain, stepped on the lever with his foot, and topped up his glass. This was why he had gotten up: he was thirsty. He felt like announcing the fact out loud.

Returning to the tables, Troy squeezed between two other workers and sat down facing the screen. He balled up his napkin, felt the pill hidden within its folds, and tucked it between his thighs. He sat there, sipping his water, facing the screen like everyone else, like he was supposed to, but he didn't dare look.

· 17 ·

T he fat raindrops on the canopy outside De'Angelos restaurant sounded like rhythmless fingers tapping on a drum. The traffic on L Street hissed through puddles gathering against the curb, and the asphalt that flashed between the cars gleamed shiny and black from the streetlights. Donald shook two pills out of a plastic vial and into his palm. Two years on the meds. Two years completely free of anxiety, gloriously numb.

He glanced at the label and thought of his sister, then popped them in his mouth and swallowed. He was sick of the rain, preferred the cleanliness of the snow. Winter had been too warm again.

Keeping out of the foot traffic flowing through the front doors, he cradled his cell phone against his ear and listened patiently while his wife urged Karma to pee.

"Maybe she doesn't need to go," he suggested. He dropped the vial into his coat pocket and cupped his hand over the phone as the lady beside him wrestled with her umbrella, water flicking everywhere.

Helen continued to cajole Karma with words the poor dog didn't understand. This was typical of Helen and Donald's conversations of late. There was nothing real to say to one another.

"But she hasn't been since *lunch*," Helen insisted.

"She didn't go somewhere in the house, did she?"

"She's four years old."

Donald forgot. Lately, time felt locked in a bubble. He wondered if his medication was causing that or if it was the workload. Whenever anything seemed...off anymore, he always assumed it must be the medication. Before, it could have been the vagaries of life; it could have been anything. Somehow, it felt worse to have something concrete and new to pin it on.

There was shouting across the street, two homeless men yelling at each other in the rain, squabbling over a bag of tin cans. More umbrellas were shaken and more fancy dresses flowed into the restaurant. Here was a city charged with governing all the others, and it couldn't even take care of itself. These things used to worry him more. He patted the capsule in his jacket pocket, a comforting twitch he'd developed.

"She won't go," his wife said exhaustedly.

"Baby, I'm sorry I'm up here and you have all that to take care of. But look, I really need to get inside. We're trying to wrap up final revisions on these plans tonight."

"How is everything going with that? Are you almost done?"

A file of taxis drove by, hunting for fares, fat tires rolling across sheets of water like hissing snakes. Donald watched as one of them slowed to a stop, brakes squealing from the wet. He didn't recognize the man stepping out, coat held up over his head. It wasn't Mick.

"Huh? Oh, it's going great. Yeah, we're basically done, maybe a few tweaks here and there. The outer shells are poured, and the lower floors are in—"

"I meant, are you almost done working with *her?*"

He turned away from the traffic to hear better. "Who, Anna? Yeah. Look, I've told you. We've only consulted here and there. Most of it's done electronically."

"And Mick is there?"

"Yup."

Another cab slowed as it passed by. Donald turned, but the car didn't stop.

"Okay. Well, don't work too late. Call me tomorrow."

"I will. I love you."

"Love you—Oh! Good girl! That's a good girl, Karma—!"

"I'll talk to you tomorr—"

But the line was already dead. Donald glanced at his phone before putting it away, shivered once from the cool evening and from the moisture in the air. He pressed through the crowd outside the door and made his way to the table.

"Everything okay?" Anna asked. She sat alone at a table with three settings. A wide-necked sweater had been pulled down to expose one shoulder. She pinched her second glass of wine by its delicate stem, a pink half-moon of lipstick on its rim. Her auburn hair was tied up in a bun, the freckles across her nose almost invisible behind a thin veil of makeup. She looked, impossibly, more alluring than she had in college.

"Yeah, everything's fine." Donald twisted his wedding ring with his thumb—a habit. "Have you heard from Mick?" He reached into his pocket and pulled out his cell, checked his texts. He thought of firing off another, but there were already four unanswered messages sitting there.

"Nope. Wasn't he flying in from Texas this morning? Maybe his flight was delayed."

Donald saw that his glass, which he'd left near empty when he made the call outside, had been topped up. He knew Helen would disapprove of him sitting there alone with Anna, even though nothing was going to happen. Nothing ever would.

"We could always do this another time," he suggested. "I'd hate for Mick to be left out."

She set down her glass and studied the menu. "Might as well eat while we're here. Be a little late to find something else. Besides, Mick's logistics are independent of our design. We can send him our materials report later."

Anna leaned to the side and reached for something in her purse, her sweater falling dangerously open. Donald looked away quickly, a flush of heat on the back of his neck. She pulled out her tablet and placed it on top of his manila folder, the screen flashing to life.

"I think the bottom third of the design is solid." She spun the tablet for him to see. "I'd like to sign off on it so they can start layering the next few floors in."

"Well, a lot of these are yours," he said, thinking of all the mechanical spaces at the bottom. "I trust your judgment."

He picked the tablet up, relieved that their conversation hadn't veered away from work. He felt like a fool for thinking Anna had anything else in mind. They had been exchanging emails and updating each other's plans for over two years and there had never been a hint of impropriety. He warned himself not to let the setting, the music, the white tablecloths, fool him.

"There *is* one last-minute change you're not going to like," she said. "The central shaft needs to be modified a little. But I think we can still work with the same general plan. It won't affect the floors at all."

He scrolled through the familiar files until he spotted the difference. The emergency stairwell had been moved from the side of the central shaft to the very middle. The shaft itself seemed smaller, or maybe it was because all the other gear they'd filled it with was gone. Now there was empty space, the discs turned to doughnuts. He looked up from the tablet and saw their waiter approaching.

"What, no lift?" He wanted to make sure he was seeing this right. He asked the waiter for a water and said he'd need more time with the menu.

The waiter bowed and left. Anna placed her napkin on the table and slid over to the adjacent chair. "The board said they had their reasons."

"The medical board?" Donald exhaled. He had grown sick of their meddling and their suggestions, but he had given up fighting with them. He never won. "Shouldn't they be more worried about people falling over these railings and breaking their necks?"

Anna laughed. "You know they're not into that kind of medicine. All they can think about is what these workers might go through, emotionally, if they're ever trapped in there for a few weeks. They wanted the plan to be simpler. More...*open*."

"More open." Donald chuckled and reached for his glass of wine. "And what do they mean, trapped for a few weeks?"

Anna shrugged. "You're the elected official. I figure you should know more about this government silliness than I do. I'm just a consultant. I'm just getting paid to lay out the pipes."

She finished her wine, and the waiter returned with Donald's water and to take their orders. Anna raised her eyebrow, a familiar twitch that begged a question: *Are you ready?* It used to mean much more, Donald thought, as he glanced at the menu.

"How about you pick for me?" he finally said, giving up.

Anna ordered, and the waiter jotted down her selections.

"So now they want a single stairwell, huh?" Donald imagined the concrete needed for this, then thought of a spiral design made of metal. Stronger and cheaper. "We can keep the service lift, right? Why couldn't we slide this over and put it in right here?"

He showed her the tablet.

"No. No lifts. Keep everything simple and open. That's what they said."

He didn't like this. Even if the facility would never be used, it should be built as if it might. Why else bother? He'd seen a partial list of supplies they were going to stockpile inside. Lugging them by stair seemed impossible, unless they planned to stock the floors before the prebuilt sections were craned inside. That was more Mick's department. It was one of many reasons he wished his friend were there.

"You know, this is why I didn't go into architecture." He scrolled through their plans and saw all the places where his design had been altered. "I remember the first class we had where we had to go out and meet with mock clients, and they always wanted either the impossible or the downright stupid—or both. And that's when I knew it wasn't for me."

"So you went into politics." Anna laughed.

"Yeah. Good point." Donald smiled, saw the irony. "But hey, it worked for your father."

"My dad went into politics because he didn't know what else to do. He got out of the army, sank too much money into busted venture after busted venture, then figured he'd serve his country some other way."

She studied him a long moment.

"This is *his* legacy, you know." She leaned forward and rested her elbows on the table, bent a graceful finger at the tablet. "This is one of those things they said would never get done, and *he's* doing it."

Donald put the tablet down and leaned back in his chair. "He keeps telling me the same thing," he said. "That this is our legacy, this project. I told him I feel too young to be working on my crowning achievement."

Anna smiled. They both took sips of wine. A basket of bread was dropped off, but neither of them reached for it.

"Speaking of legacies and leaving things behind," Anna asked, "is there a reason you and Helen decided not to have kids?"

Donald placed his glass back on the table. Anna lifted the bottle, but he waved her off. "Well, it's not that we don't want them. We just both went directly from grad school to our careers, you know? We kept thinking—"

"That you'll have forever, right? That you'll always have time. There's no hurry."

"No. It's not that—" He rubbed the tablecloth with the pads of his fingers and felt the slick and expensive fabric slide over the other tablecloth hidden below. When they were finished with their meals and out the door, he figured this top layer would be folded back and carried off with their crumbs, a new layer revealed beneath. Like skin. Or the generations. He took a sip of wine, the tannins numbing his lips.

"I think that's it exactly," Anna insisted. "Every generation is waiting longer and longer to pull the trigger. My mom was almost forty when she had me, and that's getting more and more common."

She tucked a loose strand of hair behind her ear.

"Maybe we all think we might be the first generation that simply doesn't die, that lives forever." She raised her eyebrows. "Now we all *expect* to hit a hundred and thirty, maybe longer, like it's our right. And so this is my theory—" She leaned closer. Donald was already uncomfortable with where the conversation was going. "Children *used* to be our legacy, right? They were our chance to cheat death, to pass these little bits of ourselves along. But now we hope it can simply be *us*."

"You mean like cloning? That's why it's illegal."

"I don't mean cloning—and besides, just because it's illegal, you and I both know people do it." She took a sip of her wine and nodded at a family in a distant booth. "Look. He has daddy's *everything*."

Donald followed her gaze and watched the kid for a moment, then realized she was just making a point.

"Or how about *my* father?" she asked. "Those nano baths, all the stem-cell vitamins he takes. He truly thinks he's gonna live forever. You know he bought a load of stock in one of those cryo firms years back?"

Donald laughed. "I heard. And I heard it didn't work out so well. Besides, they've been trying stuff like that for years—"

"And they keep getting closer," she said. "All they ever needed was a way to stitch up the cells damaged from the freezing, and now that's not so crazy a dream, right?"

"Well, I hope the people who dream such things get whatever it is they're looking for, but you're wrong about us. Helen and I talk about having kids all the time. I know people having their first kid in their fifties. We've got time."

"Mmm." She finished what was in her glass and reached for the bottle. "You think that," she said. "Everyone thinks they've got all the time left in the world." She leveled her cool gray eyes at him. "But they never stop to ask just how much time that is."

••••

After dinner, they waited under the awning for Anna's car service. Donald declined to share a ride, saying he needed to get back to the office and would just take a cab. The rain hitting the awning had changed, had grown somber.

Her ride pulled up, a shiny black Lincoln, just as Donald's phone began vibrating. He fumbled in his jacket pocket while she leaned in for a hug and kissed his cheek. He felt a flush of heat despite the cool air, saw that it was Mick calling, and picked up..

"Hey, you just land, or what?" Donald asked.

A pause.

"Land?" Mick sounded confused. There was noise in the background. The driver hurried around the Lincoln to get the door for Anna. "I took a redeye," Mick said. "My flight got in early this morning. I'm just walking out of a movie and saw your texts. What's up?"

Anna turned and waved. Donald waved back.

"You're getting out of a movie? We just wrapped up our meeting at De'Angelo's. You missed it. Anna said she emailed you like three times—"

He glanced up at the car as Anna drew her leg inside. Just a glimpse of her red heels, and then the driver pushed the door shut. The rain on the tinted glass stood out like jewels.

"Huh. I must've missed them. Probably went to junk mail. Not a big deal. We'll catch up. Anyway, I just got out of this trippy movie. If you and I were still in our getting-high days, I would totally force you to blast one with me right now and go to the midnight showing. My mind is totally bent—"

Donald watched the driver hurry around the car to get out of the rain. Anna's window lowered a crack. One last wave, and the car pulled out into light traffic.

"Yeah, well, those days are long gone, my friend." Donald said distractedly. Thunder grumbled in the distance. An umbrella opened with a pop as a gentleman prepared to brave the storm. "Besides," Donald told Mick, "some things are better off back in the past. Where they belong."

• 18 •

2110 • Silo 1

The exercise room on level twelve smelled of sweat, of having been recently used. A line of iron weights sat in a jumble in one corner, and a forgotten towel had been left draped over the bar of the bench press, over a hundred pounds of iron discs still in place.

Troy eyed the mess as he worked the last bolt free from the side of the exercise bike. When the cover plate came off, washers and nuts rained down from recessed holes and bounced across the tile. Troy scrambled for them and pushed the hardware into a tidy pile. He peered inside the bike's innards and saw a large cog, its jagged teeth conspicuously empty.

The chain that did all the work hung slack around the cog's axle. Troy was surprised to see it there, would think the thing ran on belts. This seemed too fragile. Not a good choice for the length of time it would be expected to serve. It was strange, in fact, to think that this machine was already fifty years old—and that it needed to last centuries more.

He wiped his forehead. Sweat was still beading up from the handful of miles he'd gotten in before the machine broke. Fishing around in the toolbox Jones had loaned him, he found the flathead screwdriver and began levering the chain back onto the cog.

Chains on cogs. *Chains on cogs.* He laughed to himself. Wasn't that the way?

"Excuse me, sir?"

Troy turned to find Jones, his chief mechanic for another week, standing in the gym's doorway.

"Almost done," Troy said. "You need your tools back?"

"Nossir. Dr. Henson is looking for you." He raised his hand, had one of those clunky radios in it.

Troy grabbed an old rag out of the toolbox and wiped the grease from his fingers. It felt good to be working with his hands, getting dirty. It was a welcome distraction, something to do besides checking the blisters in his mouth with a mirror or hanging out in his office or apartment waiting to cry again for no reason.

He left the bike and took the radio from Jones. Troy felt a wave of envy for the older man. He would love to wake up in the morning, put on those blue denim coveralls with the patches on the knees, grab his trusty toolbox, and work down a list of repairs. Anything other than sitting around while he waited for something much bigger to break.

Squeezing the button on the side of the radio, he held it up to his mouth.

"This is Troy," he said.

The name sounded strange. In recent weeks, he hadn't liked saying his own name, didn't like hearing it. He wondered what Dr. Henson and the shrinks would say about that.

The radio crackled. "Sir? I hate to disturb you—"

"No, that's fine. What is it?" Troy walked back to the exercise bike and grabbed his towel from the handlebars. He wiped his forehead and saw Jones hungrily eyeing the disassembled bike and scattering of tools. When he lifted his brows questioningly, Troy waved his consent.

"We've got a gentleman in our office who's not responding to treatment," Dr. Henson said.

A blast of static, and then Dr. Henson continued: "It looks like another deep-freeze. I'll need you to sign the waiver."

Jones glanced up from the bike and frowned. Troy rubbed the back of his neck with the towel. He remembered Merriman saying to be careful handing these out. There were plenty of good men who would just as soon sleep through all this mess than serve out their shifts.

"You're sure?" he asked.

"We've tried everything. He's been restrained. Security is taking him down the express right now. Can you meet us down here? You'll have to sign off before he can be put away."

"Sure, sure." Troy rubbed his face with his towel, could smell the detergent in the clean cloth cut through the odor of sweat in the room and the tinge of grease from the open bike. Jones grabbed one of the pedals with his thick hands and gave it a turn. The chain was back on the cog, the machine operational again.

"I'll be right down," Troy said before releasing the mic and handing the radio back to the mechanic. Some things were a pleasure to fix. Others weren't.

••••

The express had already passed when Troy reached the lifts; he could see the floor display racing down. He pressed the call button for the other one and tried to imagine the sad scene playing out below. Whoever it was had his sympathies.

He shook violently, blamed it on the cool air in the hallway and his damp skin. A ping-pong ball clocked back and forth in the rec room around the corner, sneakers squeaking as players chased the next shot. From the same room, a television was playing a movie, the sound of a woman's voice.

Looking down at his feet, Troy felt self-conscious about his shorts and tee shirt. The only authority he really felt was lent by his coveralls, but there was no time to ride up and change.

The lift beeped and opened, and the conversation inside fell quiet. Troy nodded a greeting, and two men in yellow said hello. The three of them rode in silence for a few levels until the men got off on forty-four, a general living level. Before the doors could close, Troy saw a bright ball skitter across the hallway, two men racing after it. There were shouts and laughter followed by guilty silence when they noticed Troy.

The metal doors squeezed shut on the brief glimpse of lower and more normal lives.

With a shudder, the lift sank deeper into the earth. Troy could feel the dirt and concrete squeezing in from all sides, piling up above. Sweat from nerves mixed with that from his exercise. He was coming out of the other side of the medication, he thought. Every morning, he could feel some semblance of his old self returning, and it lasted longer and longer into the day.

The fifties went by. The lift never stopped on the fifties. Emergency supplies he hoped would never be needed filled the corridors beyond. He remembered parts of the orientation, back when everyone had been awake. He remembered the code names they came up with for everything, the way new labels obscured the past. There was something here nagging him, but he couldn't place it.

Next were the mechanical spaces and the general storerooms, followed by the two levels that housed the reactor. Finally, the most important storage of all: the Legacy, the men and women asleep in their shiny coffins, the survivors from the *before*.

There was a jolt as the lift slowed and the doors chimed open. Troy immediately heard a commotion in the doctor's office, Henson barking commands to his assistant. He hurried down the hallway in his gym attire, sweat cooling on his skin.

When he entered the ready room, he saw an elderly man being restrained on a gurney by two men from Security. It was Hal—Troy recognized him from the cafeteria, remembered speaking with him the first day of his shift and several times since. The doctor and his assistant fumbled through cabinets and drawers, gathering supplies.

"*My name is Carlton!*" Hal roared, his thin arms flailing while unbuckled restraints dangled from the table and swayed from the commotion. Troy assumed they would've had him under control to get him down the lift, wondered if he had broken free when he had come to. Henson and his assistant found what they needed and gathered by the gurney. Hal's eyes widened at the sight of the needle; the fluid inside was a blue the color of open sky.

Dr. Henson looked up and saw Troy standing there in his exercise clothes, paralyzed and watching the scene. Hal screamed once more that his name was Carlton and continued to kick at the air, his heavy boots slamming against the table. The two Security men jerked with effort as they held him down.

"A hand?" Henson grunted, teeth clenched as he began to wrestle with one of Hal's arms.

Troy hurried to the gurney and grabbed one of Hal's legs. He stood shoulder to shoulder with the Security officers and wrestled with a boot while trying not to get kicked. Hal's legs felt like a bird's inside the baggy coveralls, but they kicked like a mule's. One of the officers managed to work a strap across his thighs. Troy leaned his weight on Hal's shin while a second strap was pulled tight.

"What's wrong with him?" he asked. His concerns about himself swiftly subsided in the presence of true madness. Or was this where he was heading?

"Meds aren't taking," Henson said.

Or he's not taking them, Troy thought.

The medical assistant used his teeth to pull the cap off the sky-colored syringe. Hal's wrist was pinned. The needle disappeared into his trembling arm, the plunger moving the bright blue liquid into his pale and blotchy flesh.

Troy cringed at the sight of the needle being stabbed into Hal's jerking arm—but the power in the old man's legs faded immediately. Everyone seemed to take deep breaths as he wilted into unconsciousness, his head drifting to the side, one last incomprehensible scream fading into a moan, and then a deep and breathy exhalation.

"What the hell?" Troy wiped his forehead with the back of his arm. He was dripping with sweat, partly from the exertion but mostly from the scene before him, from feeling a man go under like that, sensing the life and will drain from his kicking boots as he was forced asleep. His own body shook with a sudden and violent tremor, gone before he knew it was coming. The doctor glanced up and frowned.

"I apologize for that," Henson said. He glared at the officers, directing his blame.

"We had him no problem," one of them said, shrugging.

Henson turned to Troy. His jowls sagged with disappointment. "I hate to ask you to sign off on this—"

Troy wiped his face with the front of his shirt and nodded. The losses had been accounted for—individual losses as well as silos, spares stocked accordingly—but they all stung.

"Of course," he said. This was his job, right? Sign this. Say these words. Follow the script. It was a joke. They were all reading lines from a play none of them could remember. But he was beginning to. He could feel it.

Henson shuffled through a drawer of forms while his assistant unbuckled Hal's coveralls. The men from Security asked if they were needed, checked the restraints a final time, and were waved away. One of them laughed out loud over something the other said as their boots faded toward the lift,

Troy, meanwhile, lost himself in Hal's slack face, the slight rise and fall of his old and narrow chest. *Here* was the reward for remembering, he thought. This man had woken up from the routine of the asylum. He hadn't gone crazy; he'd had a sudden bout of *clarity*. He'd cracked open his eyes and seen through the mist.

A clipboard was procured from a peg on the wall, the right form shoved into its metal jaws. Troy was handed a pen. He scratched his name, passed the clipboard back and watched the two doctors work; he wondered if they felt any of what he felt. What if they were all playing the same part? What if each and every one of them was concealing the same doubts, none of them talking because they all felt so completely alone?

"Could you get that one for me?"

The medical assistant was down on his knees, twisting a knob on the base of the table. Troy saw that it was on wheels. The assistant nodded toward Troy's feet.

"Of course." Troy crouched down to free the wheel. He was a part in this. It was his signature on the form. It was him twisting the knob that would free the table and allow it to roll down the hall.

With Hal under, the restraints were loosened, his coveralls peeled off with care. Troy volunteered with the boots, unknotting the laces and setting them aside. There was no need for a paper gown—his modesty was no longer a concern. An IV needle was inserted and taped down; Troy knew it would plug into the cryopod. He knew what it felt like to have ice crawl through his veins.

They pushed the gurney down the hall and to the reinforced steel doors of the deep-freeze. Troy studied the doors. They seemed familiar. He seemed to remember speccing something similar for a project once, but that was for a room full of machines. No, computers.

The keypad on the wall chirped as the doctor entered his code. There was the heavy *thunk* of rods withdrawing into the thick jamb.

"The empties are at the end," Henson said, nodding into the distance.

Rows and rows of gleaming and sealed beds filled the freezing chamber. His eyes fell to the readout screens on the bases of each pod. There were green lights solid with life, no space needed for a pulse or heartbeat, first names only, no way to connect these strangers to their past lives.

Cassie, Catherine, Gabriella, Gretchen.

Made-up names.

Gwynn. Halley. Heather.

Everyone in order. No shifts for them. Nothing for the men to fight over. It would all be done in an instant. Step inside the lifeboat, dream a moment, step out onto dry land.

Another Heather. Duplicates without last names. Troy wondered how that would work. He steered blindly between the rows, the doctor and his assistant chatting about the procedure, when a name caught his peripheral vision and a fierce tremor vibrated through his limbs.

Helen. And another: *Helen.*

Troy lost his grip on the gurney and nearly fell. The wheels squealed to a stop.

"Sir?"

Two Helens. But before him, on a crisp display showing the frozen temps of a deep, deep slumber, another:

Helena.

Troy staggered away from the gurney and Hal's naked body. The echo of the old man's feeble screams came back to him, insisting he was someone named Carlton. Troy ran his hands along the curved top of the cryopod.

She was *here.*

"Sir? We really need to keep moving—"

Troy ignored the doctor. He rubbed the glass shield, the cold inside leaching into his hand.

"Sir—"

A spiderweb of frost covered the glass. He wiped the frozen film of condensation away so he could see inside.

"We need to get this man installed—"

Closed eyes lay inside that cold and dark place. Blades of ice clung to her lashes. It was a familiar face, but this was not his wife.

"Sir!"

Troy stumbled, hands slapping at the cold coffin for balance, bile rising in his throat with remembrance. He heard himself gag, felt his limbs twitch, his knees buckle. He hit the ground between two of the pods and shook violently, spit on his lips, strong memories wrestling with the last residue of the drugs still in his veins.

The two men in white shouted at each other. Footsteps slapped frosted steel and faded toward the distant and heavy door. Inhuman gurgles hit Troy's ears and sounded faintly as though they came from him.

Who was he? What was he doing there? What were any of them doing?

This was not Helen. His name was not Troy.

Footsteps stomped toward him in a hurry. The name was on his tongue as the needle bit his flesh.

Donny.

But that wasn't right, either.

And then the darkness took him, tightening down around anything from his past that his mind deemed too awful to bear.

• 19 •

Some mash-up of music festival, family reunion, and state fair had descended on the southernmost corner of Fulton County. For the past two weeks, Donald had watched while colorful tents sprang up over a brand-new nuclear containment facility. Fifty state flags flew over fifty depressions in the earth. Stages had been erected, an endless parade of supplies flowing over the rolling hills, golf carts and four-wheelers forming convoys of food, Tupperware containers, baskets of vegetables—some even pulled small enclosed trailers loaded with livestock.

Farmers' markets had been staked out in winding corridors of tents and booths, chickens clucking and pigs snorting, children petting rabbits, dogs on leashes. Owners of the latter guided dozens of breeds through the crowds. Tails wagged happily, and wet noses sniffed the air.

On Georgia's main stage, a local rock band performed a sound check. When they fell quiet to adjust levels, Donald could hear the twangs of bluegrass spilling over from the general direction of North Carolina's delegation. In the opposite direction, someone was giving a speech on Florida's stage while the convoys moved supplies over the rise, and families spread blankets and picnicked on the banks of sweeping bowls. The hills, Donald saw, formed stadium seating, as if they'd been designed for the task.

What he couldn't figure out was where they were putting all those supplies. The tents seemed to keep gobbling them up with no end in sight. The four-wheelers with their little boxed trailers had been rumbling up and down the slopes the entire two weeks he'd been there helping prep for the national convention.

Mick rumbled to a stop beside him, sitting atop one of the ubiquitous ATVs. He grinned at Donald and goosed the throttle while still holding the brakes. The Honda lurched, tires growling against the dirt.

"Wanna go for a ride to South Carolina?" he yelled over the engine. He shifted forward on the seat to make room.

"You got enough gas to make it there?" Donald held his friend's shoulder and stepped on the second set of pegs, threw his leg over the seat.

"It's just over that hill, you idiot."

Donald resisted the urge to assure Mick he'd been joking. He held on to the metal rack behind him as Mick shifted through the gears. His friend stuck to the dusty highway between the tents until they reached the grass, then angled toward the South Carolina delegation, the tops of the buildings of downtown Atlanta visible off to one side.

Mick turned his head as the Honda climbed the hill. "When is Helen getting here?" he yelled.

Donald leaned forward. He loved the feel of the crisp October morning air. It reminded him of Savannah that time of year, the chill of a sunrise on the beach. He had just been thinking of Helen when Mick asked about her.

"Tomorrow," he shouted. "She's coming on a bus with the delegates from Savannah."

They crested the hill, and Mick throttled back and steered along the ridgeline. They passed a loaded-down four-wheeler heading in the opposite direction. The network of ridges formed an interlocked maze of highways high above each containment facility's sunken bowl.

Peering into the distance, Donald watched the ballet of scooting ATVs weave across the landscape. One day, he imagined, the flat roads on top of the hills would rumble with much larger trucks bearing hazardous waste and radiation warnings.

And yet, seeing the flags waving over the Florida delegation to one side and the Georgia stage to the other, and noting the way the slopes would carry record crowds and afford everyone a perfect view of each stage, Donald couldn't help but think that all the happy accidents had some larger purpose. It was as if the facility had been planned from the beginning to serve the 2052 National Convention, as if it had been built with more than its original goal in mind.

••••

A large blue flag with a white tree and crescent moon swayed lazily over the South Carolina stage. Mick parked the four wheeler in a sea of ATVs ringing the large hospitality tent.

Following Mick through the parked vehicles, Donald saw that they were heading toward a smaller tent, which was swallowing a ton of traffic.

"What kind of errand are we on?" he asked.

Not that it mattered. In recent days they'd done a little of everything around the facility: running bags of ice to various state headquarters, meeting with congressmen and senators to see if they needed anything, making sure all the volunteers and delegates were settling into their trailers okay, whatever the Senator needed.

"Oh, we're just taking a little tour," Mick said cryptically. He waved Donald into the small tent where workers were filing through in one direction with their arms loaded and coming out the other side empty-handed.

The inside of the small tent was lit up with flood-lights, the ground packed hard from the traffic, the grass matted flat. A concrete ramp led deep into the earth, workers with volunteer badges trudging up one side. Mick jumped into the line heading down.

Donald knew where they were going. He recognized the ramp. He hurried up beside Mick.

"This is one of the rod storage facilities." He couldn't hide the excitement in his voice, didn't even try. He'd been dying to see the other design, either on paper or in person. All he was privy to was his bunker project; the rest of the facility remained shrouded in mystery. "Can we just go *in*?"

As if to answer, Mick started down the ramp, blending with the others.

"I begged for a tour the other day," Donald hissed, "but Thurman spouted all this national security crap—"

Mick laughed. Halfway down the slope, the roof of the tent seemed to recede into the darkness above, the concrete walls on either side funneling the workers toward the gaping steel doors.

"You're not going to see inside one of those other facilities," Mick told him. He put his hand on Donald's back and ushered him through the industrial-looking and familiar entrance chamber. The foot traffic ground to a halt as people took turns entering or leaving through the small hatch ahead. Donald felt turned around.

"Wait." Donald caught glimpses through the hatch. "What the hell? This is my design."

They shuffled forward. Mick made room for the people coming out. He had a hand on Donald's shoulder, guiding him along.

"What're we doing here?" Donald asked. He could've sworn his own bunker design was in the bowl set aside for Tennessee. Then again, they'd been making so many last-minute changes the past weeks, maybe he'd been mixed up.

"Anna told me you wimped out and skipped the tour of this place."

"That's bullshit." Donald stopped at the oval hatch. He recognized every rivet. "Why would she say that? I was right here. I cut the damn ribbon."

Mick pushed at his back. "Go. You're holding up the line."

"I don't want to go." He waved the people out. The workers behind Mick shifted in place, heavy Tupperware containers in their hands. "I saw the top floor last time," he said. "That was enough."

His friend clasped his neck with one hand and gripped his wrist with the other. As his head was bent forward, Donald had to move along to avoid falling on his face. He tried to reach for the jamb of the interior door, but Mick had his wrist.

"I want you to see what you *built*," his friend said.

Donald stumbled through to the security office. He and Mick stepped aside to let the congestion they'd caused ease past.

"I've been looking at this damn thing every day for three years," Donald said. He patted his pocket for his pills, wondered if it was too soon to take another. What he didn't tell Mick was that he'd forced himself to envision his design being *above* ground the entire time he'd worked on it, more a skyscraper than a buried straw. No way could he share that with his best friend, tell him how terrified he felt right then with no more than ten meters of dirt and concrete over his head. He seriously doubted Anna had used the phrase "wimped out," but that's exactly what he had done after cutting the ribbon. While the Senator led dignitaries through the complex, Donald had hurried up to find a patch of grass with nothing but bright blue sky above.

"This is really fucking important," Mick said. He snapped his fingers in front of Donald. Two lines of workers filed past. Beyond them, a man sat in a small cubicle, a brush in one hand and a can of paint in the other. He was applying a coat of flat gray to a set of steel bars. A technician behind him worked to wire something into the wall, some kind of massive screen. Not everything looked like it was being finished precisely the way Donald had drawn it.

"Donny, listen to me. I'm serious. Today is the last day we can have this talk, okay? I need you to see what you built." Mick's permanent and mischievous grin was gone, his eyebrows tilted. He looked, if anything, sad. "Will you please come inside?" he asked.

Taking a full breath and fighting the urge to rush out to the hills and fresh air, away from the stifling crowds, Donald found himself agreeing. It was the look on Mick's face, the feeling that he needed to tell Donald about a loved one who had just passed away, something deathly serious.

Mick patted his shoulder in gratitude as Donald nodded.

"This way."

Mick led him toward the central shaft. They passed through the cafeteria, which was being used. It made sense. Workers sat at tables and ate off plastic trays, taking a break. The smell of food drifted from the kitchens beyond. Donald laughed. He never thought they'd be used at all. Again, it felt like the convention had given this place a purpose. It made him happy. He thought of the entire complex devoid of life one day, all the workers milling about outside storing away nuclear rods, while this massive building that would have touched the clouds had it been above ground, would sit perfectly empty.

Down a short hallway, the tile gave way to metal grating, and a broad cylinder dove straight through the heart of the facility. Anna had been right. It really was worth seeing.

They reached the railing of the central shaft, and Donald paused to peer over. The vast height made him forget for a moment that he was underground. On the other side of the landing, a conveyor lift rattled on its gears while a never ending series of flat loading trays spun empty over the top. It reminded Donald of the buckets on a waterwheel. The trays flopped over before descending back down through the building.

The men and women from outside deposited each of their containers onto one of the empty trays before turning and heading back out. Donald looked for Mick and saw him disappearing down the staircase.

He hurried after, his fear of being buried alive chasing him.

"Hey!"

His shoes slapped the freshly painted stairs, the diamond plating keeping him from skidding off in his haste. He caught up with Mick as they made a full circuit of the thick inner post. Tupperware containers full of emergency supplies—supplies Donald figured would rot, unused— drifted eerily downward beyond the rail.

"I don't want to go any deeper than this," he insisted.

"Two levels down," Mick called back up. "C'mon, man, I want you to see."

Donald numbly obeyed. It would've been worse to make his way out alone.

At the first landing they came to, a worker stood by the conveyor with some type of gun. As the next container passed by, he shot its side with a flash of red, the scanner buzzing. The worker leaned on the railing, waiting for the next one while the container continued its ratcheting plummet.

"Did I miss something?" Donald asked. "Are we still fighting deadlines? What's with all the supplies?"

Mick shook his head. "Deadlines, lifelines," he said.

At least, that's what Donald thought his friend said. Mick seemed lost in thought.

They spiraled down another level to the next landing, ten more meters of reinforced concrete between, thirty-three feet of wasted depth. Donald knew the floor. And not just from the plans he'd drawn. He and Mick had toured a floor like this in the factory where it had been built.

"I've been here before," he told Mick.

Mick nodded. He waved Donald down the hallway until it made a turn. Mick picked one of the doors, seemingly at random, and opened it for Donald. Most of the floors had been pre-fabbed and furnished before being craned into place. If that wasn't that exact floor the two of them had toured, it had been one of the many just like it.

Once Donald was inside, Mick flicked on the apartment's overhead lights and closed the door. Donald was surprised to see that the bed was made. Stacks of linen were piled up in a chair. Mick grabbed the linens and moved them to the floor. He sat down and nodded toward the foot of the bed.

Donald ignored him and poked his head into the small bathroom. "This is actually pretty cool to see," he told his friend. He reached out and turned the knob on the sink, expecting nothing. When clear water gurgled out, he found himself laughing.

"I knew you'd dig it once you saw it," Mick said quietly.

Donald caught sight of himself in the mirror, the joy still on his face. He tended to forget how the corners of his eyes wrinkled up when he smiled. He touched his hair, sprinkles of gray even though he had another five years before he was over that proverbial hill. His job was aging him prematurely. He had feared it might.

"Amazing that we built this, huh?"

Mick was still waiting for him to sit. Donald turned and joined his friend in the tight quarters. He wondered if it was the work they'd been elected to perform that had aged them both or if it had been this one project, this all-consuming build.

"I appreciate you forcing me down here." He almost added that he would love to see the rest, but he figured that would be pushing it. Besides, the crews back in the Georgia tents were probably looking for them already.

"Look," Mick said, "there's something I want to tell you."

Donald looked at his friend, who seemed to be searching for the words. He glanced at the door. Mick was silent. Donald finally relented and sat at the foot of the bed.

"What's up?" he asked.

But he thought he knew. The Senator had included Mick in his other project, the one that had driven Donald to seek help from the doctor. Donald thought of the thick book he had largely memorized. Mick had done the same. And he'd brought him there not just to let him see what they'd accomplished, but to find a spot of perfect privacy, a place where secrets could be divulged. He patted his pocket where he kept his pills, the ones that kept his thoughts from running off to dangerous places.

"Hey," Donald said, "I don't want you saying anything you're not supposed to—"

Mick looked up, eyes wide with surprise.

"You don't need to say *anything*, Mick. Assume I know what *you* know."

Mick shook his head sadly. "You don't," he said.

"Well, assume it anyway. I don't want to know anything."

"I *need* you to know."

"I'd rather not—"

"It's not a secret, man. It's just...I want you to know that I love you like a brother. I always have."

The two of them sat in silence. Donald glanced toward the door. The moment was uncomfortable, but it somehow filled his heart to hear Mick say it.

"Look—" Donald started.

"I know I'm always hard on you," Mick said. "And hell, I'm sorry. I really do look up to you. And Helen—" Mick turned to the side and scratched at his cheek. "I'm happy for the two of you."

Donald reached across the narrow space and squeezed his friend's arm.

"You're a good friend, Mick. I'm glad we've had this time together, the last few years, running for office, building this—"

Mick nodded. "Yeah. Me too. But listen, I didn't bring you down here to get all sappy like this." He reached for his cheek again, and Donald saw that he was wiping at his eyes. "I had a talk with Thurman last night. He—a few months ago, he offered me a spot on a team, a top team, and I told him last night that I'd rather you take it."

"What? A committee?" Donald couldn't imagine his friend giving up an appointment, *any* kind of appointment. "Which one?"

Mick shook his head. "No, something else."

"What?" Donald asked.

"Look," Mick said, "when you find out about it, and you understand what's going on, I want you to think of me right here." Mick glanced around the room. There were a few breaths of complete silence punctuated by drips of water from the bathroom sink. "If I could choose anywhere to be, *anywhere* in the coming years, it would be right down here with the first group."

"Okay. Yeah, I'm not sure what you mean—"

"You will. Just remember this, all right? That I love you like a brother and that everything happens for a reason. I wouldn't have wanted it any other way. For you or for Helen."

"Okay." Donald smiled. He couldn't tell if Mick was fucking with him or if his friend had consumed a few too many Bloody Marys from the hospitality tent that morning.

"All right." Mick stood abruptly. He certainly moved as though he were sober. "Let's get the hell out of here. This place gives me the creeps."

Mick threw open the door and flicked off the lights.

"Wimping out, eh?" Donald called after his friend.

Mick shook his head and the two of them headed back down the hallway. Behind them, they left the small, random apartment in darkness, its little sink dripping. And Donald tried to sort out how he'd gotten turned around, how the Tennessee tent where he'd cut the ribbon had become the one from South Carolina. He almost had it, his subconscious flashing to a delivery of goods, to fifty times more fiber optic than needed, but the connection was lost.

Meanwhile, containers loaded with supplies rumbled down the mammoth shaft. And empty trays rattled up.

• 20 •

2110 • Silo 1

Troy woke up in a fog, groggy and disoriented, his head pulsing. He lifted his hands and groped in front of his face, expecting to find the chill of icy glass, the press of domed steel, the doom of a deep-freeze. His hands found only empty air. The clock beside his bed showed it was a little after three in the morning. The PM light was unlit.

He sat up and saw that he had on a pair of gym shorts. He couldn't remember changing the night before, couldn't remember going to bed. Planting his feet on the floor, he rested his elbows on his knees, sunk his head into his palms, and sat there a moment. His entire body ached.

After a few minutes slipped by, he dressed himself in the dark, buckling up his coveralls. Light would be bad for his headache. It wasn't a theory he needed to test.

The hallway outside was still dimmed for the evening, just bright enough to grope one's way to the shared bathrooms. Troy stole down the hall and headed for the lift.

He hit the "Up" button, hesitated, wasn't sure if that was right. Something tugged at him. He pressed the "Down" button as well.

It was too early to go into his office, not unless he wanted to fiddle on the computer. He wasn't hungry, but he could go up and watch the sun rise. The late shift would be up there drinking coffee. Or he could hit the rec room and go for a jog. That would mean going back to his room to change.

The lift arrived with a beep while he was still deciding. Both lights went off, the up and the down. He could take this lift anywhere.

Troy stepped inside. He didn't know where he wanted to go.

The elevator closed. It waited on him patiently. Eventually, he figured, it would whisk off to heed some other call, pick up a person with purpose, someone with a destination. He could stand there and do nothing and let that other soul decide.

Running his finger across the buttons, he tried to remember what was on each level. There was a lot he'd memorized, but not everything he knew felt accessible. He had a sudden urge to head for one of the lounges and watch TV, just let the hours slide past until he finally needed to be somewhere. This was how the shift was supposed to go. Waiting and then doing. Sleeping and then waiting. Make it to dinner and then make it to bed. The end was always in sight. There was nothing to rebel against, just a routine.

The elevator shook into motion. Troy jerked his hand away from the buttons and took a step back. It didn't show where they were going but it felt like it had started downwards.

Only a few floors passed before the lift lurched to a halt. The doors opened on a lower apartment level. A familiar face from the cafeteria, a man in reactor red, smiled as he stepped inside.

"Morning," he said.

Troy nodded.

The man turned and jabbed one of the lower buttons, one of the reactor levels. He studied the otherwise blank array, turned, and gave Troy a quizzical look.

"You feeling okay, sir?"

"Hmm? Oh, yeah."

Troy leaned forward and pressed sixty-eight. The man's concern for his well-being must've had him thinking of the doctor, even though Henson wouldn't be on shift for several hours. But there was something else nagging him, something he felt he needed to see, a dream slipping away.

"Must not have taken the first time," he explained, glancing at the button.

"Mmm."

The silence lasted one or two floors.

"How much longer you got?" the reactor mechanic asked.

"Me? Just another couple of weeks. How about you?"

"I just got on a week ago. But this is my second shift."

"Oh?"

The lights counted downward in floors but upward in number. Troy didn't like this; he felt like the lowest level should be level 1. They should count *up*.

"Is the second shift easier?" he asked. The question came out unbidden. It was as though the part of him dying to know was more awake than the part of him praying for silence.

The mechanic considered this.

"I wouldn't say it's easier. How about...less uncomfortable?" He laughed quietly. Troy felt their arrival in his knees, gravity tugging on him. The door beeped open.

"Have a good one," the mechanic said. They hadn't shared their names. "In case I don't see you again."

Troy raised his palm. "Next time," he said. The man stepped out, and the doors winked shut on the halls to the power plant. With a hum, the elevator continued its descent.

The doors dinged on the medical level. Troy stepped out and heard voices down the corridor. He crept quietly across the tile, and the voices became louder. One was female. It wasn't a conversation; it must have been an old movie. Troy peeked into the main office and saw a man lounging on a gurney, his back turned, a TV set up in the corner. Troy slinked past so as not to disturb him.

The hallway split in two directions. He imagined the layout, could picture the pie-shaped storerooms, the rows of deep-freeze coffins, the tubes and pipes that led from the walls to the bases, from the bases into the people inside.

He stopped at one of the heavy doors and tried his code. The light changed from red to green. He dropped his hand, didn't need to enter this room, didn't feel the urge, just wanted to see if it would work. The urge was elsewhere.

He meandered down the hall past a few more doors. Wasn't he just here? Had he ever left? His arm throbbed. He rolled back his sleeve and saw a spot of blood, a circle of redness around a pinprick scab.

If something bad had happened, he couldn't remember. That part of him had been choked off.

He tried his code on this other pad, this other door, and waited for the light to turn green. This time, he pushed the button that opened the door. He didn't know what it was, but there was something inside that he needed to see.

• 21 •

Light rains on the morning of the Convention left the man-made hills soggy, the new grass slick, but did little to erode the general festivities. Parking lots had been emptied of construction vehicles and mud-caked pickups. Now they held hundreds of idling buses and a handful of sleek black limos, the latter splattered with mud.

The lot where temporary trailers had served as offices and living quarters for construction crews had been handed over to the staffers, volunteers, delegates, and dignitaries who had labored for weeks to bring that day to fruition. The area was dotted with welcoming tents that served as the headquarters for the event coordinators. Throngs of new arrivals filed from the buses and made their way through the CAD-FAC's security station. Massive fences bristled with coils of razor wire that seemed outsized and ridiculous for the convention but made sense for the storing of nuclear material. These barriers and gates held at bay an odd union of protestors: those on the Right who disagreed with the facility's current purpose and those on the Left who feared its future one.

There had never been a National Convention with such energy, such crowds. Downtown Atlanta loomed far beyond the treetops, but the city seemed far removed from the sudden bustle in lower Fulton County.

Donald shivered beneath his umbrella at the top of a knoll and gazed out over the sea of people gathering across the hills, heading toward whichever stage flew their state's flag, umbrellas bobbing and jostling like water bugs.

Somewhere, a marching band blared a practice tune and stomped another hill into mud. There was a sense in the air that the world was about to change—a woman was about to win nomination for president, only the second such nomination in Donald's lifetime. And if the pollsters could be believed, this one had more than a chance. Unless the war in Iran took a sudden turn, a milestone would be reached, a final glass ceiling shattered. And it would happen right there in those grand divots in the earth.

More buses churned through the lot and let off their passengers, and Donald pulled out his phone and checked the time. He still had an error icon, the network choked to death from the overwhelming demand. He was surprised, with so much other careful planning, that the committee hadn't accounted for this and erected a temporary tower or two.

"Congressman Keene?"

Donald startled and turned to find Anna walking along the ridgeline toward him. He glanced down toward the Georgia stage but didn't see her ride. He was surprised she would just walk up. And yet, it was like her to do things the difficult way.

"I couldn't tell if that was you," she said, smiling. "Everyone has the same umbrella."

"Yeah, it's me." He took a deep breath, found his chest still felt constricted with nerves whenever he saw her, as though any conversation could get him into trouble.

Anna stepped close as if she expected him to share his umbrella. He moved it to his other hand to give her more space, the drizzle peppering his exposed arm. He scanned the bus lot and searched impossibly for any sign of Helen. She should have been there by now.

"This is gonna be a mess," Anna said.

"It's supposed to clear up."

Someone on the North Carolina stage checked her microphone with a squawk of feedback.

"We'll see."

Anna wrapped her coat tighter against the early morning breeze. "Isn't Helen coming?"

"Yeah. Senator Thurman insisted. She's not gonna be happy when she sees how many people are here. She hates crowds. She won't be happy about the mud, either."

Anna laughed. "I wouldn't worry about the conditions of the grounds after this."

Donald thought about all the loads of radioactive waste that would be trucked in. "Yeah." He saw her point.

He peered down the hill toward the Georgia stage. It would be the site of the first national gathering of delegates later that day, all the most important people under one tent. Behind the stage and among the smoking food tents, the only sign of the underground containment facility was a small concrete tower rising up from the ground, a bristle of antennas sprouting from the top. Donald thought of how much work it would take to haul away all the flags and soaked buntings before the first of the spent fuel rods could finally be brought in.

"It's weird to think of a few thousand people from the state of Tennessee stomping around on top of something *we* designed," Anna said. Her arm brushed against Donald's. He stood perfectly still, wondering if it had been an accident. "I wish you'd seen more of the place."

Donald shivered, more from fighting to remain still than from the cold and moist morning air. He hadn't told anyone about Mick's tour the day before. It felt too sacred. He would probably tell Helen about it and no one else. "It's crazy how much time went into something nobody will ever use," he said.

Anna murmured her agreement. Her arm was still touching his. There was still no sign of Helen. Donald felt irrationally that he would somehow spot her among the crowds. He usually could. He remembered the high balcony of a place they'd stayed in during their honeymoon in Hawaii. Even from up there, he could spot her taking her early morning walks along the foam line, looking for seashells. There might be a few hundred strollers out on the beach, and yet his eyes would be immediately drawn to her.

"I guess the only way they were going to build any of this was if we gave them the right kind of insurance," Donald said, repeating what the Senator had told him. But it still didn't feel right.

"People want to feel safe," Anna said. "They want to know, if the worst happens, they'll have someone—*something*—to fall back on."

Again, Anna rested against his arm. Definitely not an accident. Donald felt himself withdraw and knew she would sense it, too.

"I was really hoping to tour one of the *other* bunkers," he said, changing the subject. "It'd be interesting to see what the other teams came up with. Apparently, though, I don't have the clearance."

Anna laughed. "I tried the same thing. I'm dying to see our competition. But I can understand them being sensitive. There's a lot of eyes on this joint." She leaned into him once more, ignoring the space he'd made.

"Don't you feel that?" she asked. "Like there's some huge bull's-eye over this place? I mean, even with the fences and walls down there, you can bet the whole world is gonna be keeping an eye on what happens here."

Donald nodded. He knew she wasn't talking about the convention but about what the place would be used for afterward.

"Hey, it looks like I've got to get back down there."

He turned to follow her gaze, saw Senator Thurman climbing the hill on foot, a massive black golf umbrella shedding the rain around him. The man seemed impervious to the mud and grime in a way no one else was, the same way he seemed oblivious to the passing of time.

Anna reached over and squeezed Donald's arm. "Congrats again. It was fun working together on this."

"Same," he said. "We make a good team."

She smiled. He wondered for a moment if she would lean over and kiss his cheek. It would feel natural in that moment. But it came and went. Anna left his protective cover and headed off toward the Senator.

Thurman lifted his umbrella, kissed his daughter's cheek and watched her descend the hill. He hiked up to join Donald.

They stood beside each other a pause, the rain dripping off their umbrellas with a muted patter.

"Sir," Donald finally said. He felt newly comfortable in the man's presence. The last two weeks had been like summer camp, where being around the same people almost every hour of the day brought a level of familiarity and intimacy that knowing them casually for years could never match. There was something about forced confinement that brought people together. Beyond the obvious, physical ways.

"Damn rain" was Thurman's reply.

"You can't control everything," Donald said.

The Senator grunted as if he disagreed. "Helen not here yet?"

"No sir." Donald fished in his pocket and felt for his phone. "I'll message her again in a bit. Not sure if my texts are getting through or not—the networks are absolutely crushed. I'm pretty sure this many people descending on this corner of the county is unprecedented."

"Well, this will be an unprecedented day," Thurman said. "Nothing like it ever before."

"It was mostly your doing, sir. I mean, not just building this place, but choosing not to run. This country could've been yours for the taking this year."

The Senator laughed. "That's true most years, Donny. But I've learned to set my sights higher than that."

Donald shivered again. He couldn't remember the last time the Senator had called him that. Maybe that first meeting in his office, more than two years ago? The old man seemed unusually tense.

"When Helen gets here, I want you to come down to the state tent and see me, okay?"

Donald pulled out his phone and checked the time. "You know I'm supposed to be at the Tennessee tent in an hour, right?"

"There's been a change of plans. I want you to stay close to home. Mick is going to cover for you over there, which means I need you with me."

"Are you sure? I was supposed to meet with—"

"I know. This is a good thing, trust me. I want you and Helen near the Georgia stage with me. And look—"

The Senator turned to face him. Donald peeled his eyes away from the last of the unloading buses. The rain had picked up a little.

"You've contributed more to this day than you know," Thurman said.

"Sir?"

"The world is going to change today, Donny."

Donald wondered if the Senator had been skipping his nanobath treatments. His eyes seemed dilated and focused on something in the distance. He appeared older, somehow.

"I'm not sure I understand—"

"You will. Oh, and a surprise visitor is coming. She should be here any moment." He smiled. "The national anthem starts at noon. There'll be a flyover from the 141st after that. I want you nearby when that happens."

Donald nodded. He had learned when to stop asking questions and just do what the Senator expected of him.

"Yes sir," he said, shivering against the cold.

Senator Thurman left. Turning his back to the stage, Donald scanned the last of the buses and wondered where in the world Helen was.

· 22 ·

2110 · Silo 1

Troy walked down the line of cryopods as if he knew where he was going. It was just like the way his hand had drifted to the button that had brought him to that floor. There were made-up names on each of the panels. He knew this somehow. He remembered coming up with his name. It had something to do with his wife, some way to honor her, or some kind of secret and forbidden link so that he might one day remember.

This all lay in the past, deep in the mist, a dream forgotten. Before his shift there had been an orientation. There were familiar books to read and re-read. That's when he had chosen his name.

A bitter explosion on his tongue brought him to a halt. It was the taste of a pill dissolving. Troy stuck out his tongue and scraped it with his fingers, but there was nothing there. He could feel the ulcers on his gums against his teeth but couldn't recall how they'd formed.

He walked on. Something wasn't right. These memories weren't supposed to return. He pictured himself on a gurney, screaming, someone strapping him down, stabbing him with needles. That wasn't him. He was holding that man's boots.

Troy stopped at one of the pods and checked the name. Helen. His gut lurched and groped for its medicine. He didn't want to remember. That was a secret ingredient: the *not wanting to remember*. Those were the parts that slipped away, the parts the drugs wrapped their tentacles

·141·

around and pulled beneath the surface. But now, there was some small part of him that was dying to know. It was a nagging doubt, a feeling of having left some important piece of himself behind. It was willing to drown the rest of him for the answers.

The frost on the glass wiped away with a squeak. He didn't recognize the person inside and moved on to the next pod, a scene from before orientation returning.

Troy recalled halls packed with people crying, grown men sobbing, pills that dried their eyes. Fearsome clouds rose on a videoscreen. Women were put away for safety. Like a lifeboat, women and children first.

Troy remembered. It wasn't an accident. He remembered a talk in another pod, a bigger pod with another man there, a talk about the coming end of the world, about making *room*, about ending it all before it ended on its own.

A controlled explosion. Bombs were sometimes used to put out fires.

He wiped another frost-covered sheet of glass. The sleeping form in the next chamber had eyelashes that glittered with ice. She was a stranger. He moved on, but it was coming back to him. His arm throbbed. The shakes were gone.

Troy remembered a calamity, but it was all for show. The real threat was in the air, invisible. The bombs were to get people to move, to make them afraid, to get them crying and forgetting. People had spilled like marbles down a bowl. Not a bowl, a *funnel*. Someone explained why they were spared. He remembered a white fog, walking through a white fog. The death was already in them. Troy remembered a taste on his tongue metallic.

The ice on the next pane was already disturbed, had been wiped away by someone recently. Beads of condensation stood like tiny lenses warping the light. He rubbed the glass and knew what had happened. He saw the woman inside with the auburn hair that she sometimes kept in a bun. This was not his wife. This was someone who wanted that, wanted *him* like that.

"Hello?"

Troy turned toward the voice. The night shift doctor was heading his way, weaving between the pods, coming for him. Troy clasped his hand over the soreness on his arm. He didn't want to be taken again. They couldn't make him forget.

"Sir, you shouldn't be in here."

Troy didn't answer. The doctor stopped at the foot of the pod. Inside, a woman who wasn't his wife lay in slumber. Wasn't his wife, but had wanted to be.

"Why don't you come with me?" the doctor asked.

"I'd like to stay," Troy said. He felt a bizarre calmness. All the pain had been ripped away. This was more forceful than forgetting. He remembered everything. His soul had been cut free.

"I can't have you in here, sir. Come with me. You'll freeze in here."

Troy glanced down. He had forgotten to put on shoes. He curled his toes away from the floor...then allowed them to settle.

"Sir? Please." The young doctor gestured down the aisle. Troy let go of his arm and saw that things were handled as needed. No kicking meant no straps. No shivering meant no needles.

He heard the squeak of hurrying boots out in the hallway. A large man from Security appeared by the open vault door, visibly winded. Troy caught a glimpse of the doctor waving the man down. They were trying not to scare him. They didn't know that he couldn't be scared anymore.

"You'll put me away for good," Troy said. It was something between a statement and a question. It was a realization. He wondered if he was like Hal—like *Carlton*—if the pills would never take again. He glanced toward the far end of the room, knew the empties were kept there. This was where he would be buried.

"Nice and easy," the doctor said.

He led Troy toward the exit; he would embalm him with that bright blue sky. The pods slid by as the two of them walked in silence.

The man from Security took deep breaths as he filled the doorway, his great chest heaving against his coveralls. There was a squeak from more boots as he was joined by another. Troy saw that his shift was over. Two weeks to go. He'd nearly made it.

The doctor waved the large men out of the way, seemed to hope they wouldn't be needed. They took up positions to either side, seemed to think otherwise. Troy was led down the hallway, hope guiding him and fear flanking him.

"You *know*, don't you?" Troy asked the doctor, turning to study him. "You remember everything."

The doctor didn't turn to face him. He simply nodded.

This felt like a betrayal. It wasn't fair.

"Why are you allowed to remember?" Troy asked. He wanted to know why those dispensing the medicine didn't have to take some of their own.

The doctor waved him into his office. His assistant was there, wearing a sleepshirt and hanging an IV bag bulging with blue liquid.

"Some of us remember," the doctor said, "because we know this isn't a bad thing we've done." He frowned as he helped Troy onto the gurney. He seemed truly sad about Troy's condition. "We're doing good work, here," he said. "We're saving the world, not ending it. And the medicine only touches our regrets." He glanced up. "Some of us don't have any."

The doorway was stuffed with Security. It overflowed. The assistant unbuckled Troy's coveralls. Troy watched numbly.

"It would take a different kind of drug to touch what *we* know," the doctor said. He pulled a clipboard from the wall. A sheet of paper was fed into its jaws. There was a pause, and then a pen was pressed into Troy's palm.

Troy laughed as he signed off on himself.

"Then why me?" he asked. "Why am I here?" He had always wanted to ask this of someone who might know. These were the prayers of youth, but now with a chance of some reply.

The doctor smiled and took the clipboard. He was probably in his late twenties, had come on shift just a few weeks ago. Troy was a few years shy of forty. And yet this man had all the wisdom, all the answers.

"It's good to have people like you in charge," the doctor said, and he seemed to genuinely mean it. The clipboard was returned to its peg. One of the Security men yawned and covered his mouth. Troy watched as his coveralls were unsnapped and flopped to his waist. A fingernail makes a distinct click when it taps against a needle.

"I'd like to think about this," Troy said. He felt a sudden panic wash over him. He knew this needed to happen, but wanted just a few more minutes alone with his thoughts, to savor this brief bout of comprehension. He wanted to sleep, certainly, but not quite yet.

The men in the doorway stirred as they sensed Troy's doubts, could see the fear in his eyes.

"I wish there was some other way," the doctor said sadly. He rested a hand on Troy's shoulder, guided him back against the table. The men from Security stepped closer.

There was a prick on his arm, a deep bite without warning. He looked down and saw the silver barb slide into his vein, the bright blue liquid pumped inside.

"I don't want—" he said.

There were hands on his shins, his knees, weight on his shoulders. The heaviness against his chest was from something else.

A burning rush flowed through his body, chased immediately by numbness. They weren't putting him to sleep. *They were killing him.* Troy knew this as suddenly and swiftly as he knew that his wife was dead, that some other person had tried to take her place. He would go into a coffin *for good* this time. And all the dirt piled over his head would finally serve some purpose.

Darkness squeezed in around his vision. He closed his eyes, tried to yell for it to stop, but nothing came out. He wanted to kick and fight it, but more than mere hands had a hold of him, now. He was sinking.

His last thoughts were of his beautiful wife, but the thoughts made little sense—they were the dreamworld invading.

She's in Tennessee, he thought. He didn't know why or how he knew this. But she was there—and waiting. She was already dead and had a spot hollowed out by her side just for him.

Troy had just one more question, one name he hoped to grope for and seize before he went under, some part of himself to take with him to those depths. It was on the tip of his tongue like a bitter pill, so close that he could taste it—

But then he forgot.

• 23 •

2052 • Above Silo 1

The rain finally let up just as warring announcements and battling tunes filled the currents of air above the teeming hills. While the main stage was prepped for the evening's gala, it sounded to Donald as though the real action was taking place at all the other states. Opening bands ripped into their sets as the buzz of ATVs subsided to a trickle.

It felt vaguely claustrophobic to be down in the bottom of the bowl by the Georgia stage. Donald felt an unquenchable urge for height, to be up on the ridge where he could see what was going on. It left him imagining the sight of thousands of guests arrayed across each of the hills, picturing the political fervor in the air everywhere, the gelling of like-minded families celebrating the promise of something new.

As much as Donald wanted to celebrate new beginnings with them, he was mostly looking forward to the *end*. He couldn't wait for the convention to wrap up. The weeks had worn on him. He was looking forward to a real bed, to some privacy, his computer, reliable cell phone service, dinners out, and, most of all: time alone with his wife.

Fishing his cell phone out of his pocket, he checked his messages for the umpteenth time. They were minutes away from the anthem, and then the flyover from the 141st. He had also heard someone mention fireworks to start the convention off with a bang.

His phone showed that the last half-dozen messages still hadn't gone through. The network was still clogged, an error message popping up that he'd never seen before. At least some of the earlier ones looked like they'd been sent. He scanned the wet banks for her, hoping to see her making her way down, a smile he could spot from any distance.

Someone stepped up beside him. Donald looked away from the hills to see that Anna had joined him by the stage.

"Here we go," she said quietly, scanning the crowd.

She looked and sounded nervous. Maybe it was for her father, who had done so much to arrange the main stage and make sure everyone was in the right place. Glancing back, he saw that people were taking their seats, chairs wiped down from the morning drizzle, not nearly as many people as it seemed before. They must be either working in the tents or off to the other stages. This was the quiet brewing before the—

"*There* she is."

Anna waved her arms. Donald felt his heart swell up into his neck as he turned and followed Anna's gaze. His relief was mixed with the panic of Helen seeing him there with her, the two of them waiting side by side.

Shuffling down the hill was certainly someone familiar. A young woman in a pressed blue uniform, a hat tucked under one arm, a dark head of hair wrapped up in a crisp bun.

"Charlotte?" Donald shielded his eyes from the glare of the noonday sun filtering through wispy clouds. He gaped in disbelief. All other events and concerns melted away as his sister spotted them and waved back.

"She sure as hell cut this close," Anna muttered.

Donald hurried over to his four-wheeler and turned the key. He hit the ignition, gave the handle some gas, and raced across the wet grass to meet her.

Charlotte beamed as he hit the brakes at the base of the hill. He killed the engine.

"Hey, Donny."

His sister leaned into him before he could dismount. She threw her arms around his neck and squeezed.

He returned her embrace, worried about denting the creases of her neat uniform. "What the hell are you doing here?" he asked.

She let go and took a step back, smoothed the front of her shirt. The Air Force dress hat disappeared back under her arm, every motion like an ingrained and precise habit.

"Are you surprised?" she asked. "I thought the Senator would've let it slip by now."

"Hell, no. Well, he said something about a visitor but not who. I thought you were in Iran. Did he swing this?"

She nodded, and Donald felt his cheeks cramping from smiling so hard. Every time he saw her, there came a relief from discovering that she was still the same person. The sharp chin and splash of freckles across her nose, the shine in her eyes that had not yet dulled from the horrible things she'd seen. She had just turned thirty, had been half a world away with no family on her birthday, but she was frozen in his mind as the young teen who had enlisted.

"I think I'm supposed to be on the stage for this thing tonight," she said.

"Of course." Donald smiled. "I'm sure they'll want you on camera. You know, to show support for the troops."

Charlotte frowned. "Oh, God, I'm one of *those* people, aren't I?"

He laughed. "I'm sure they'll have someone from the Army, Navy, and Marines there with you."

"Oh, God. And I'm the *girl*."

They laughed together, and one of the bands beyond the hills finished their set. Donald scooted forward and told his sister to hop on, his chest suddenly less constricted. There had been a shift in the weather, these breaking clouds, the quieting stages, and now the arrival of family.

He cranked the engine and raced through the least muddy path on the way back to the stage, his sister holding on tight behind him. They pulled up beside Anna, his sister hopping off and into her arms. While they chatted, Donald killed the ignition and checked his phone for messages. Finally, one had gotten through.

Helen: *In Tennessee. where r u?*

There was a jarring moment as his brain tried to make sense of the message. It was from Helen. What the hell was she doing in *Tennessee?*

Another stage fell silent. It took only a heartbeat or two for Donald to realize that she wasn't hundreds of miles away. She was just over the hill. None of his messages about meeting at the Georgia stage had gone through.

"Hey, I'll be right back."

He cranked the ATV. Anna grabbed his wrist.

"Where are you going?" she asked.

He smiled. "Tennessee. Helen just texted me."

Anna glanced up at the clouds. His sister was inspecting her hat. On the stage, a young girl was being ushered up to the mic. She was flanked by a color guard, and the seats facing the stage were filling up, necks stretched with anticipation.

Before he could react or put the ATV in gear, Anna reached across, twisted the key, and pulled it out of the ignition.

"Not now," she said.

Donald felt a flash of rage. He reached for her hands, for the key, but it disappeared behind her back.

"Wait," she hissed.

Charlotte had turned toward the stage. Senator Thurman stood with a microphone in hand, the young girl, maybe sixteen, beside him. The hills had grown deathly quiet. Donald realized what a racket the ATV had been making. The girl was about to sing.

Ladies and gentlemen, fellow Democrats—

There was a pause. Donald got off the four-wheeler, took a last glance at his phone, then tucked it away.

—and our handful of Independents.

Laughter from the crowd. Donald set off at a jog across the flat at the bottom of the bowl. His shoes squished in the wet grass and the thin layer of mud. Senator Thurman's voice continued to roar through the microphone:

Today is the dawn of a new era, a new time.

He was out of shape, his shoes growing heavy with mud.

As we gather in this place of future independence—

By the time the ground sloped upward, he was already winded.

—I'm reminded of the words from one of our enemies. A Republican.

Distant laughter, but Donald paid no heed. He was concentrating on the climb.

It was Ronald Reagan who once said that freedom must be fought for, that peace must be earned. As we listen to this anthem, written a long time ago as bombs dropped and a new country was forged, let's consider the price paid for our freedom and ask ourselves if any cost could be too great to ensure that these liberties never slip away.

A third of the way up—and Donald had to stop and catch his breath. His calves were going to give out before his lungs did. He regretted puttering around on the ATV the past weeks while some of the others slogged it on foot. He promised himself he'd get in better shape.

He started back up the hill, and a voice like ringing crystal filled the bowl. It spilled in synchrony over the looming rise. He turned toward the stage below where the national anthem was being sung by the sweetest of young voices—

And he saw Anna hurrying up the hill after him, a scowl of worry on her face.

Donald knew he was in trouble. He wondered if he was dishonoring the anthem by scurrying up the hill. Everyone had assigned places for the anthem and he was ignoring his. He turned his back on Anna and set off with renewed resolve.

—o'er the ramparts we watched—

He laughed, out of breath, wondering if these mounds of earth could be considered ramparts. It was easy to see the bowls for what they'd become in the last weeks, individual states full of people, goods, and livestock, fifty state fairs bustling at once, all for this shining day, all to be gone once the facility was up and running..

—and the rockets' red glare, the bombs bursting in air—

He reached the top of the hill and sucked in deep lungfuls of crisp, clean air. On the stage below, flags swayed idly in a soft breeze. A large screen showed a video of the girl singing about *proof* and *still being there.*

A hand seized his wrist.

"Come back," Anna hissed.

He was panting. Anna was also out of breath, her knees covered in mud and grass stains. She must've slipped on the way up.

"Helen doesn't know where I am," he said.

—bannerrr yet waaaaave—

Applause stirred before the end, a compliment. The jets streaking in from the distance caught his eye even before he heard their rumble. A diamond pattern with wingtips nearly touching.

"Get the fuck back down here," Anna yelled. She yanked on his arm.

Donald twisted his wrist away. He was mesmerized by the sight of the jets approaching.

—o'er the laaand of the freeeeeee—

That sweet and youthful voice lifted up from fifty holes in the earth and crashed into the thunderous roar of the powerful jets, those soaring and graceful angels of death.

"Let go," Donald demanded, as Anna grabbed him and scrambled to pull him back down the hill.

—and the hooome of the...braaaaave...

The air shook from the grumble of the perfectly timed fly-by. Afterburners screamed as the jets peeled apart and curved upward into the white clouds.

Anna was practically wrestling him, arms wrapped around his shoulders. Donald snapped out of a trance induced by the passing jets, the beautiful rendition of the anthem amplified across half a county, the struggle to spot his wife in the bowl below.

"Goddamnit, Donny, we've got to get *down—*"

The first flash came before she could get her hands over his eyes. A bright spot in the corner of his vision in the direction of downtown Atlanta. It was a daytime strike of lightning. Donald turned toward it, expecting thunder. The flash of light had become a blinding glow. Anna's arms were around his waist, jerking him backward. His sister was there, panting, covering her eyes, screaming, *What the fuck?*

Another flash of light, starbursts in one's vision. Sirens spilled out of all the speakers. It was the recorded sound of air raid klaxons.

Donald felt half blinded. Even when the mushroom clouds rose up from the earth—impossibly large to be so distant—it still took a heartbeat to realize what was happening.

They pulled him down the hill. Applause had turned to screams audible over the rise and fall of the blaring siren. Donald could hardly see. He stumbled backward and nearly fell as the three of them slipped and slid down the bowl, the wet grass funneling them toward the stage. The puffy tops of the swelling clouds rose up higher and higher, staying in sight even as the rest of the hills and the trees disappeared from view.

"Wait!" he yelled.

There was something he was forgetting. He couldn't remember what. He had an image of his ATV sitting up on the ridge. He was leaving it behind. How did he get up there? What was happening?

"Go. Go. Go," Anna was saying.

His sister was cussing. She was frightened and confused, just like him. He had never known his sister to be either one.

"The main tent!"

Donald spun around, his heels slipping in the grass, hands wet with rain and studded with mud and grass. When had he fallen?

The three of them tumbled down the last of the slope as the sound of distant thunder finally reached them. The clouds overhead seemed to race away from the blasts, pushed aside by an unnatural wind. The undersides of the clouds strobed and flashed as if more strikes of lightning were hitting, more bombs detonating. Down by the stage, people weren't running to escape the bowl—they were instead running into the tents, guided by volunteers with waving arms, the markets and food stalls clearing out, the rows of wooden chairs now a heaped and upturned tangle, a dog still tied to a post, barking.

Some people still seemed to be aware, to have their faculties intact. Anna was one of them. Donald saw the Senator by a smaller tent coordinating the flow of traffic. Where was everyone going? Donald felt empty as he was ushered along with the others. It took long moments for his brain to process what he'd seen. Nuclear blasts. The live view of what had forever been resigned to grainy wartime video. Real bombs going off in the real air. Nearby. He had seen them. Why wasn't he completely blind? Was that even what happened?

The raw fear of death overtook him. Donald knew, in some recess of his mind, that they were all dead. The end of all things was coming. There was no outrunning it. No hiding. Paragraphs from a book he'd read came to mind, thousands of memorized paragraphs. He patted his pants for his pills, but they weren't there. Looking over his shoulder, he fought to remember what he'd left behind—

Anna and his sister pulled him past the Senator, who wore a hard scowl of determination, who frowned at his daughter. The tent flap brushed Donald's face, the darkness within interspersed with a few hanging lights. The spots in his vision from the blasts made themselves known in the blackness. There was a crush of people, but not as many as there should have been. Where were the crowds? It didn't make sense until he found himself shuffling downward.

A concrete ramp, bodies on all sides, shoulders jostling, people wheezing, yelling for one another, hands outstretched as the flowing crush drove loved ones away, husband and wife separated, some people crying, some perfectly poised—

Husband and wife.

Helen!

Donald yelled her name over the crowd. He turned and tried to swim against the flowing torrent of the frightened mob. Anna and his sister pulled on him. People fighting to get below pushed from above. Donald was forced downwards, into the depths. He wanted to go under with his wife. He wanted to drown with her.

"Helen!"

Oh, God, he remembered.

He remembered what he had left behind.

Panic subsided and fear took its place. He could see. His vision had cleared. But he could not fight the push of the inevitable.

Donald remembered a conversation with the Senator about how it would all end. There was an electricity in the air, the taste of dead metal on his tongue, a white mist rising around him. He remembered most of a book. He knew what this was, what was happening.

His world was gone.

A new one swallowed him.

• 24 •

Silo 1

Troy startled awake from a series of terrible dreams. The world was on fire, and the people who had been sent to extinguish it were all asleep. Asleep and frozen stiff, smoking matches still in their hands, wisps and gray curls of evil deeds.

He had been buried, was enveloped in darkness, could feel the tight walls of his small coffin hemming him in.

Dark shapes moved beyond the frosted glass, the men with their shovels trying to free him.

Troy's eyelids seemed to rip and crack as he fought to open them fully. There was crust in the corners of them, melting frost coursing down his cheek. He tried to lift his arms to wipe it away, but they responded feebly. An IV tugged at his wrist as he managed to raise one hand. He was aware of his catheter. Every inch of his body tingled as he emerged from the numbness and into the cold.

The lid popped with a hiss of air. There was a crack of light to his side that grew as the shadows folded away.

A doctor and his assistant reached in to tend to him. Troy tried to speak but could only cough. They helped him up, brought him the bitter drink. Swallowing took effort. His hands were so weak, arms trembling, that they had to help him with the cup. The taste on his tongue was metallic. It tasted like death.

"Easy," they said when he tried to drink too fast. Tubes and IVs were carefully removed by expert hands, pressure applied, gauze taped to frigid skin. There was a paper gown.

"What year?" he asked, his voice a dry rasp.

"It's early," the doctor said, a different doctor. Troy blinked against the harsh lights, didn't recognize either man tending to him. The sea of coffins around him remained a hazy blur.

"Take your time," the assistant said, tilting the cup.

Troy managed a few sips. He felt worse than last time. It had been longer. The cold was deep within his bones. He remembered that his name wasn't Troy. He was supposed to be dead. Part of him regretted being disturbed. Another part hoped he had slept through the worst of it.

"Sir, we're sorry to wake you, but we need your help."

"Your report—"

Two men were talking at once.

"Another silo is having problems, sir. Silo 18—"

Pills were produced. Troy waved them away. He no longer wished to take them.

The doctor hesitated; the two capsules rested in his palm. He turned to consult with someone else, a third man. Troy tried to blink the world into focus. Something was said. Fingers curled around the pills, filling him with relief.

They helped him up, had a wheelchair waiting. A man stood behind it, his hair as stark white as his coveralls, his square jaw and iron frame familiar. Troy recognized him. This was the man who woke the freezing.

Another sip of water as he leaned against the pod, knees trembling from the weak and cold.

"What *about* Silo 18?" Troy whispered the question as the cup was lowered.

The doctor frowned and said nothing. The man behind the wheelchair studied him intently.

"I know you," Troy said.

The man in white nodded. The wheelchair was waiting for Troy. Troy felt his stomach twist as dormant parts of him stirred.

"You're the Thaw Man," he said, even though this didn't sound quite right.

The paper gown was warm. It rustled as his arms were guided through the sleeves. The men working on him were nervous. They chattered back and forth, one of them saying a silo was falling, the other that they needed his help. Troy cared only about the man in white. They helped him toward the wheelchair.

"Is it over?" he asked. He watched the colorless man, his vision clearing, his voice growing stronger. He dearly hoped that he had slept through it all.

The Thaw Man shook his head sadly. Troy was lowered into the chair.

"I'm afraid, son," a familiar voice said, "that it's only begun."

Second Shift

Order

• Silo 18 •

In the year of the Great Uprising

Now they lay me in the deep,
I pray the 'Lo my soul to keep.
To keep me safe inside the earth.

And if I die before I wake,
I pray the 'Lo my soul to take.
To take and grant another birth.

-Sasha Sway, age 11

Deathdays were birthdays. That's what they said to ease their pain, those who were left behind. An old man dies and a lottery is won. Children weep while hopeful parents cry tears of joy. Deathdays were birthdays, and no one knew this better than Mission Jones.

Tomorrow was his seventeenth. Tomorrow, he would grow a year older. It would also mark seventeen years since his mother died.

The cycle of life was everywhere—it wrapped around all things like the great spiral staircase—but nowhere was it more evident, nowhere could it be seen so clearly that a life given was one taken away. And so Mission approached his birthday without joy, with a heavy load on his young back, thinking on death and celebrating nothing.

Three steps below him and matching his pace, Mission could hear his friend Cam wheezing from his half of the load. When Dispatch assigned them a tandem, the two boys had flipped a coin, heads for heads, and Cam had lost. That left Mission with a clear view of the stairs. It also gave him rights to set the pace, and dark thoughts made for an angry one.

Traffic was light on the stairwell that morning. The children were not yet up and heading to school, those of them who still went anymore. A few bleary-eyed shopkeepers staggered toward work. There were service workers with grease stains on their bellies and patches sewn into their knees coming off late shifts. One man descended bearing more than a non-porter should, but Mission was in no mood to set down his burden and weigh another's. It was enough to glare at the gentleman, to let him know that he'd been seen.

"Three more to go," he huffed to Cam as they passed the twenty-fourth. His porter's strap was digging into his shoulders, the load a great one. Heavier still was its destination. Mission hadn't been back to the farms in near on four months, hadn't seen his father in just as long. His brother, of course, he saw at the Nest now and then, but it'd still been a few weeks. To arrive so near to his birthday would be awkward, but there was no helping it. He trusted his father to do as he always had and ignore the occasion altogether, to ignore that he was getting any older.

Past the twenty-fourth they entered another gap between the levels full of graffiti. The noxious odor of home-mixed paint hung in the air. Recent work dribbled in places, parts of it done the night before. Bold letters wrapped across the curving wall of concrete far beyond the stairway railing that read:

This is our 'Lo.

The slang for silo felt dated, even though the paint was not yet dry. Nobody said that anymore. Not for years. Farther up and much older:

Clean this, Mother-

The rest was obscured in a slap of censoring paint. As if anyone could read it and not fill in the blank on their own. It was the first half that was a killing offense, anyway. The second was just a word.

Down with the Up Top!

Mission laughed at this one. He pointed it out to Cam. Probably painted by some kid born above the mids and full of self-loathing, some kid who couldn't abide their own good fortune. Mission knew the kind. They were *his* kind. He studied all this graffiti painted over last year's graffiti and all the many years before. It was here between the levels, where the steel girders stretched out from the stairwell to the cement beyond, that such slogans went back generations. Atop the angry words were pockmarks, scars, and burns of old wars. Atop these wounds lay ever more angry scribbles, on and on.

The End is Coming . . .

Mission marched past this one, unable to argue. The end *was* coming. He could feel it in his bones. He could hear it in the wheezing rattle of the silo with its loose bolts and its rusty joints, could see it in the way people walked of late with their shoulders up around their ears, their belongings clutched to their chests. The end was coming for certain.

His father would laugh and disagree, of course. Mission could hear his old man's voice from all the levels away, could hear his father telling him how people had thought the same thing long before he and his brother were born, that it was the hubris of each generation to think this anew, to think that their time was special, that all things would come to an end with them. His father said it was *hope* that made people feel this, not dread. People talked of the end coming with barely concealed smiles. Their prayer was that when they went, they wouldn't go alone. Their hope was that no one would have the good fortune to come after.

Thoughts such as these made Mission's neck itch. He held the hauling strap with one hand and adjusted the 'chief around his neck with the other. It was a nervous habit, hiding his neck when he thought about the end of things. But that had been two birthdays ago.

"You doing okay up there?" Cam asked.

"I'm fine," Mission called back, realizing he'd slowed. He gripped his strap with both hands and concentrated on his pace, on his job. There was a metronome in his head from his shadowing days, a tick-tock, tick-tock for tandem hauls. Two porters with good timing could fall into a rhythm and wind their way up a dozen flights, never feeling a heavy load. Mission and Cam weren't there yet. Now and then one of them would have to shuffle his feet or adjust his pace to match the other. Otherwise, their load might sway dangerously.

Their load.

Mission's grandfather came to mind, though Mission had never known the man. He had died in the uprising of '78, had left behind a son to take over the farm and a daughter to become a chipper. Mission's aunt had quit that job a few years back; she no longer banged out spots of rust and primed and painted raw steel like she used to. Nobody did. Nobody bothered. But his father was still farming that same plot of soil, that same plot generations of Jones boys had farmed, forever insisting that things would go on, that they would never change.

"That word means something else, you know," his father had told him once, when Mission had spoken of revolution. "It also means to go around and around. To revolve. One revolution, and you get right back to where you started."

This was the sort of thing Mission's father liked to say when the priests came to bury a man beneath his corn. His dad would pack the dirt with a shovel, say that's how things go, and plant a seed in the neat depression his thumb made.

A few weeks later, Mission had told his friends this other meaning of revolution. He had pretended to come up with it himself. It was just the sort of pseudo-intellectual nonsense they regaled each other with late at night on dark landings while they inhaled potato glue out of plastic bags.

His best friend Rodny had been the only one unimpressed. "Nothing changes until we *make* it change," he had said with a serious look in his eye.

Mission wondered what his best friend was doing now. He hadn't seen Rodny in months. Whatever he was shadowing for on thirty-four kept him from getting out much.

He thought back to better days, growing up in the Nest with friends tight as a fist. He remembered thinking they would all stay together and grow old in the Up Top. They would live along the same hallways, watch their eventual kids play the way they had.

But all had gone their separate ways. It was hard to remember who had done it first, who had shaken off the shadowing expected by their parents, but eventually most of them had. Like a group decision never discussed, like a dozen private revolutions. They had left home to choose a new fate. Sons of plumbers took up farming. Daughters of the cafe learned to sew. None of them bothered to ask how many of their parents had done the same. Everything felt new and unique, and so it had to be.

Mission remembered being angry when he left home. He remembered a fight with his father, throwing down his shovel, promising he'd never dig a trench again. He'd learned in the Nest that he could be anything he wanted, that he was in charge of his own fate. And so when he grew miserable, he assumed it was the farms that made him feel that way; he assumed it was his family.

He thought about his mother, about family he had never known, and a ring of fire burned around his neck, the remnants of a rope's embrace.

He and Cam had flipped a dime back in Dispatch, heads for heads, and now Mission could feel a man's shoulders pressed against his own. When he lifted his gaze to survey the steps ahead, the back of his skull met the crown of the dead man's through the plastic bag—birthdays and deathdays pressed tight, two halves of a single coin.

Mission carried them both, that load meant for two. He took the stairs a pair at a time, a brutal pace, up toward the farm of his youth.

$\cdot 26 \cdot$

The coroner's office was on the farm's lower level, tucked away at the end of those dark and damp halls that wound their way beneath the roots. The ceiling was low in that half level. Pipes hung visible from above and rattled angrily as pumps kicked on and moved nutrients to distant and thirsty roots. Water dripped from dozens of small leaks into buckets and pots. A recently emptied pot banged metallic with each strike. Another overflowed. The floors were slick, the walls damp like sweaty skin.

Inside her office, the boys lifted the body onto a slab of dented metal, and the coroner signed Mission's work log. She tipped them for the speedy delivery, and when Cam saw the extra chits, his grumpiness over the pace dissolved. Back in the hallway, he bid Mission good day and splashed toward the exit to find some vice to pair with the bonus.

Mission watched him go, feeling much more than a year older than his friend. Cam hadn't been told of the evening's plans, the midnight rendezvous of porters. This seemed to set them apart, his being privy to adult and dangerous things. It made him envy Cam for what the boy didn't know.

Not wanting to arrive at the farms deadheading and have his father lecture him on laziness, Mission stopped by the maintenance room to see if anything needed carrying up. Winters was on duty, a dark man with a white beard and a knack with pumps. He regarded Mission suspiciously and claimed he hadn't the budget for portering. Mission explained he was going up anyway and that he was glad to take anything.

"In that case," Winters said. He hoisted a monstrous water pump onto his workbench.

"Just the thing," Mission told him, smiling.

Winters narrowed his eyes as if Mission had worked a bolt loose.

The pump wouldn't fit inside his porter's pack, but the haul straps on the outside of the pack looped nicely across the jutting pipes and sharp fittings. Winters helped him get his arms through the straps and the pump secured to his back. He thanked the old man, which drew another worried frown, and set off and up the half level. Back at the stairwell, the odor of mildew from the wet halls faded, replaced by the smell of loam and freshly tilled soil, scents of home that yanked Mission back in time.

The landing on nineteen was crowded as a jam of people attempted to squeeze inside the farms for the day's food. Standing apart from them was a mother in farmer green cradling a wailing child. She had the stains on her knees of a picker and the agitated look of one sent out of the grow plots to soothe her noisy brood. As Mission crowded past, he heard between the baby's cries the words of a familiar nursery rhyme. The mother rocked the child frightfully close to the railing, the infant's eyes wide with what looked to Mission like unadulterated fear.

He worked his way through the crowd, and the cries from the infant receded amid the general din. It occurred to Mission how few kids he saw anymore. It wasn't like when he was young. There had been an explosion of newborns after the violence the last generation had wrought, but now it was just the trickle of natural deaths and the handful of lottery winners. It meant fewer babies crying and fewer parents rejoicing.

With much cajoling and claiming the passage of a porter, he eventually made it through the doors and into the main hall. Using his 'chief, Mission wiped the sweat from his lips. He'd forgotten to top up his canteen a level below, and his mouth was dry. The reasons for pushing so swift a pace felt silly now. It was as if his looming birthday were some deadline to beat, and so the sooner he visited and got away the better. But now in the wash of sights and sounds from his childhood, his dark and angry thoughts melted. It was home, and Mission hated how good it felt to be there.

There were a few hellos and waves as he worked his way toward the gates. Some porters he knew were loading sacks of fruits and vegetables to haul up to the cafeteria. He saw his aunt working one of the vending stalls outside the security gate. After giving up chipping, she now performed the questionably legal act of vending, something she'd never shadowed for. Mission did his best not to catch her eye; he didn't want to get sucked into a lecture or have his hair mussed and his 'chief straightened.

Beyond the stalls, a handful of younger kids clustered in the far corner where it was dark, probably dealing seeds, not looking nearly as inconspicuous as they likely thought. The entire scene in the entrance hall was one of a second bazaar, of farmers selling direct, of people crowding in from distant levels to get food they feared would never make it to their shops and stores. It was fear begetting fear, crowds becoming throngs, and it was easy to see how mobs were next.

Working the main security gate was Frankie, a tall and skinny kid Mission had grown up with. Mission wiped his forehead with the front of his undershirt, which was already cool and damp with sweat. "Hey, Frankie," he called out.

"Mission." A nod and a smile. No hard feelings from another kid who'd jumped shadows long ago. Frankie's father worked in security, down in IT. Frankie had wanted to become a farmer, which Mission never understood. Their teacher, Mrs. Crowe, had been delighted and had encouraged Frankie to follow his dreams. And now Mission found it ironic that Frankie had ended up working security for the farms. It was as if he couldn't escape what he'd been born to do.

Mission smiled and nodded at Frankie's hair. "Did someone splash you with grow quick?"

Frankie tugged on his locks, which were nearly down to his shoulders. "I know, right? My mother threatens to come up here and knife it in my sleep."

"Tell her I'll hold you down while she does it," Mission said, laughing. "Buzz me through?"

There was a wider gate to the side for wheelbarrows and trolleys. Mission didn't feel like squeezing through the turnstiles with the massive pump strapped to his back. Frankie hit a button, and the gate buzzed. Mission pushed his way through.

"Whatcha haulin'?" Frankie asked.

"Water pump from Winters. How've you been?"

Frankie scanned the crowds beyond the gate. "Hold on a sec," he said, looking for someone. Two farmers swiped their work badges and marched through the turnstiles, jabbering away. Sweat dripped from Mission's nose. Frankie waved over someone in green and asked if they could cover for him while he went to the bathroom.

"C'mon," Frankie told Mission. "Walk me."

The two old friends headed down the main hall toward the bright aura of distant grow lights. The smells were intoxicating and familiar. Mission wondered what those same smells meant to Frankie, who had grown up six levels down near the fetid stink of the water plant. Perhaps this reeked to him the way the plant did to Mission. Perhaps the water plant brought back fond memories, instead.

"Things are going nuts around here," Frankie whispered once they were away from the gates.

Mission nodded. "Yeah, I saw a few more stalls had sprouted up. More of them every day, huh?"

Frankie held Mission's arm and slowed their pace so they'd have more time to talk. There was the smell of fresh bread from one of the offices. It was too far from the bakery for warm bread, but such was the new way of things. Probably ground the flour somewhere deep in the farms.

"You've seen what they're doing up in the cafe, right?" Frankie asked.

"I took a load up that way a few weeks ago," Mission said. He tucked his thumbs under his shoulder straps and wiggled the heavy pump higher onto his hips. "I saw they were building something by the wallscreens. Didn't see what."

"They're starting sprouts up there," Frankie said. "Corn, too, supposedly." They stopped by the public restrooms. The sound of a loud flush on the other side of the wall flicked a switch inside Mission's bladder and made him need to go.

"I guess that'll mean fewer runs for us between here and there,"

Mission said, thinking like a porter. He tapped the wall with the toe of his boot. "Roker'll be pissed when he hears."

Frankie bit his lip and narrowed his eyes. "Yeah, but wasn't Roker the one who started growin' his own beans down in Dispatch?"

Mission wiggled his shoulders. His arms were going numb. He wasn't used to standing still with a load—he was used to moving. "That's different," he argued. He tried to remember why it was different. "That's for climbing food."

Frankie shook his head. "Yeah, but ain't that hypercritical of him?"

"You mean hypocritical?"

"Whatever, man. All I'm saying is everyone has an excuse. We're doing it because they're doing it and someone else started it. So what if we're doing it a little more than they are? That's the attitude, man. But then we get in a twist when the next group does it a little more. It's like a ratchet, the way these things work."

Mission glanced down the hall toward the glow of distant lights. "I dunno," he said. "The mayor seems to be letting things slide lately."

Frankie laughed. "You really think the mayor's in charge? The mayor's scared, man. Scared and *old*." Frankie glanced back down the hall to make sure nobody was coming. The nervousness and paranoia had been in him since his youth. It'd been amusing when he was younger; now it was sad and a little worrisome. "You remember when we talked about being in charge one day?" Frankie asked. "How things would be different?"

"It doesn't work like that," Mission said. "By the time we're in charge, we'll be old like them and won't care anymore. And then *our* kids can hate us for pulling the same crap."

Frankie laughed, and the tension in his wiry frame seemed to subside. "I bet you're right."

"Yeah, well, I need to go before my arms fall off." He shrugged the pump higher up his back.

Frankie slapped his shoulder. "Yeah. Good seeing you, man."

"Same." Mission nodded and turned to go.

"Oh, hey, Mish."

He stopped and looked back.

"You gonna see the Crow anytime soon?"

"I'll pass that way tomorrow," he said, assuming he'd live through the night.

Frankie smiled. "Tell her I said hey, wouldja?"

"I will," Mission promised.

One more name to add to the list. If only he could charge his friends for all the messages he ran for them, he'd have way more than the three-hundred eighty-four chits already saved up. Half a chit for every hello he passed to the Crow, and he'd have his own apartment by now. He wouldn't need to stay in the waystations. He could ask Jenine to marry him. But messages from friends weighed far less than dark thoughts, so Mission didn't mind them taking up space. They crowded out the other. And Lord knew, Mission hauled his fair share of the heavier kind.

• 27 •

It would've made more sense and been kinder on Mission's back to drop off the pump before visiting his father, but the whole point of hauling it up was so his old man would see him with the load. And so he headed into the planting halls and toward the same growing station his grandfather had worked and supposedly his great-grandfather, too. Past the beans and the blueberry vines, beyond the squash and the lurking potatoes. In a spot of corn that looked ready for harvest, he found his old man on his hands and knees looking how Mission would always remember him. With a small spade working the soil, his hands picked at weeds like a habit, the way a girl might curl her fingers in her hair over and over without even knowing she was doing it.

"Father."

His old man turned his head to the side, sweat glistening on his brow under the heat of the grow lights. There was a flash of a smile before it melted. Mission's half-brother Riley appeared behind a back row of corn, a little twelve-year-old mimic of his dad, hands covered in dirt. He was quicker to call out a greeting, shouting "Mission!" as he hurried to his feet.

"The corn looks good," Mission said. He rested a hand on the railing, the weight of the pump settling against his back, and reached out to bend a leaf with his thumb. Moist. The ears were a few weeks from harvest, and the smell took him right back. He saw a midge running up the stalk and killed the parasite with a deft pinch.

"Wadja bring me?" his little brother squealed.

Mission laughed and tussled his brother's dark hair, a gift from the boy's mother. "Sorry, bro. They loaded me down this time." He turned slightly so Riley could see, but also for his father. His brother stepped onto the lowest rail and leaned over for a better look.

"Why dontcha set that down for a while?" his father asked. He slapped his hands together to keep the precious dirt on the proper side of the fence, then reached out and shook Mission's hand. "You're looking good."

"You too, Dad." Mission would've thrust his chest out and stood taller if it didn't mean toppling back on his rear from the pump. "So what's this I hear about the cafe starting in their own sprouts?"

His father grumbled and shook his head. "Corn, too, from what I hear. More goddamn up-sourcing." He jabbed a finger at Mission's chest. "This affects you lads, you know."

His father meant the porters, and there was a tone of having told him so. There was always that tone. Riley tugged on Mission's coveralls and asked to hold his porter knife. Mission slid the blade from its sheath and handed it over while he studied his father, a heavy silence brewing. His dad looked older. His skin was the color of oiled wood, an unhealthy darkness from working too long under the grow lights. It was called a "tan," and you could spot a farmer two landings away because of it, could pick them out by their skin like burnt toast.

Mission could feel the intense heat radiating from the bulbs overhead, and the anger he felt when he was away from home melted into a hollow sadness. The spot of air his mother had left empty could be felt. It was a reminder to Mission of what his being born had cost. More was the pity that he felt for his old man with his damaged skin and dark spots on his nose from years of abuse. These were the signs of all those in green who toiled among the dead. And this was where his father would have Mission work as well, if it were up to him.

While his father studied him and Riley played with the knife, Mission flashed back to his first solid memory as a boy. Wielding a small spade that had in those days seemed to him a giant shovel, he had been playing between the rows of corn, turning over scoops of soil, mimicking his father, when without warning his old man had grabbed his wrist.

"Don't dig there," his father had said with an edge to his voice. This was back before Mission had witnessed his first funeral, before he had seen for himself what went beneath the seeds. After that day, he learned to spot the mounds where the soil was dark from being disturbed. He learned to study the way those same mounds gradually sank and leveled out as the worms carried off what lay beneath.

"They've got you doing the heavy lifting, I see," his father said, breaking the quiet. He assumed the load Mission had begged for was instead assigned by Dispatch. Mission didn't correct him.

"They let us carry what we can handle," he said. "The older porters get mail delivery. We each haul what we can."

"I remember when I first stepped out of the shadows," his dad said. He squinted and wiped his brow, nodded down the line. "Got stuck with potatoes while my caster went back to plucking blueberries. Two for the basket and one for him."

Not this again. Mission watched as Riley tested the tip of the knife with the pad of his finger. He reached to take back the blade, but his brother twisted away from him.

"The older porters get mail duty because they *can* get mail duty," his father explained.

"You don't know what you're talking about," Mission said. The sadness was gone, the anger back. "The old ports have bad knees is why we get the loads. Besides, my bonus pay is judged by the pound and the time I make, so I don't mind."

"Oh, yes." His father waved at Mission's feet. "They pay you in bonuses and you pay them with your knees."

Mission could feel his cheeks tighten, could sense the burn of the whelp around his neck.

"All I'm saying, son, is that the older you get and the more seniority, you'll earn your own choice of rows to hoe. That's all. I want you to watch out for yourself."

"I'm watching out for myself, Dad." He nearly added: *It isn't like I have anyone else.*

Riley climbed up, sat on the top rail, and flashed his teeth at his own reflection in the knife. The kid already had that band of spots across his nose, those freckles, the start of a tan. Damaged flesh from damaged flesh, father like son. And Mission could easily picture Riley years hence on the other side of that rail, could see his half-brother all grown up with a kid of his own, and it made Mission thankful that he'd wormed his way out of the farms and into a job he didn't take home every night beneath his fingernails.

"Are you joining us for lunch?" his father asked, sensing perhaps that he was pushing Mission away. A change in subjects was as near to an apology as the old man dared.

"If you don't mind," Mission said. He felt a twinge of guilt that his father expected to feed him, but he appreciated not having to ask. "I'll have to run afterward, though. I've got a . . . delivery tonight."

His father frowned. "You'll have time to see Allie though, right? She's forever asking about you. The boys here are lined up to marry that girl if you keep her waiting."

Mission wiped his face to hide his expression. Allie was a great friend—his first and briefest romance—but to marry her would be to marry the farms, to return home, to live among the dead. "Probably not this time," he said. And he felt bad for admitting it.

"Okay. Well, go drop that off. Don't squander your bonus sitting here jawing with us." The disappointment in the old man's voice was hotter than the lights and not so easy to shade. "We'll see you in the feeding hall in half an hour?" He reached out, took his son's hand one more time, and gave it a squeeze. "It's good to see you, Son."

"Same." Mission shook his father's hand, then clapped his palms together over the grow pit to knock loose any dirt. Riley reluctantly gave the knife back, and Mission slipped it into its sheath. He fastened the clasp around the handle, thinking on how he might need it that night. He pondered for a moment if he should warn his father, thought of telling him and Riley both to stay inside until morning, to not dare go out.

But he held his tongue, patted his brother on the shoulder, and made his way to the pump room. As he walked through rows of planters and pickers, he thought about farmers selling their own vegetables in makeshift stalls. He thought about the cafe growing its own sprouts. He thought of the plans recently discovered to move something heavy from one landing to another without involving the porters.

Everyone was trying to do it all in case the violence returned. Mission could feel it brewing, the suspicion and the distrust, the walls being built. Everyone was trying to get a little less reliant on the others, preparing for the inevitable, hunkering down.

He loosened the straps on his pack as he approached the pump room, and a dangerous thought occurred to him, a revelation: Everyone was trying to get to where they didn't *need* one another. And how exactly was that supposed to help them all get along?

· 28 ·

After the best meal he'd had in ages—as fresh as it was free—
Mission hurried down four flights toward Sanitation to see
Jenine. He felt light as a feather downbound and with the load
off. With just his empty porter's pack on his back, his canteen jouncing
on one hip, his knife on the other, he skipped down the steps side-style
with one hand on the rail. At times like these, descending after a long
slog up, it felt as though he could leap over the rail and float unharmed
to Mechanical like a mote of dust. He apologized to those he overtook,
saying "porter, ma'am" and "porter, sir" by the book, even though he
wasn't carrying anything official.

Weightless as a bird, with his heart thrumming like one was trapped
in his ribcage, it occurred to him that maybe it wasn't the descent that
had him feeling giddy. Everyone expected him to grow up a farmer, to
settle down with the girl who loved him, but Mission wanted the opposite
of what was easily attainable. He wondered if this was a punishment of
sorts, a slow strangulation, his thirst for distant things. Did he love the
chase? Or was it that staying on the move made it more difficult for the
past to catch up to him?

He arrived at Sanitation, a rumble of footfalls on steel treads, and
pushed through doors in need of oil. Sanitation was one of the levels
laid out in a spiral; a single hallway coiled its way from the landing and
did three circuits before dead ending into the waste plant. Fresh water
emerged near the landing and was piped out to the rest of the Up Top,

while gray water and black water—euphemisms both—were pumped into the waste room. The gray came from showers, sinks, and drains, the black from toilets.

Such were the romantic and decidedly un-sexy conversations Mission had with the girl of his dreams that he could name the plant's every phase of operation as he wound his way toward the waste room. If needed, he could also bore a porter to tears with rumors of who had said what about whom throughout the plant. This was the mark of deep infatuation, he thought: the desire to watch a woman talk just to see her lips move, to be around her.

The noise along the curving hallway grew louder the deeper he went. It started out as a background hum near the control rooms and offices, and just when he'd gotten used to this residual noise, another layer piled on top, more machines macerating, filtering, straining, and pumping. Mission never appreciated how loud the combined buzzing was until he left the plant with his hearing rattled and his throat sore from yelling over it all.

Inside the waste room, he spotted familiar faces all around the processing vats. Knowing who he was looking for, one of the workers pointed down the long row of low steel cylinders that held the gray and black water. Jenine was on top of one of the cylinders, which was almost as big around as his dad's apartment and crisscrossed with pipes and valves. Crouched down, she worked a series of large valves while an older woman filled a glass vial with murky fluid and held it up to the light. Mission waited patiently. This was where the water eventually came from that his father was always cursing. He remembered his old man sitting around the dinner table, shaking his fist at the floor, grumbling about the supply of water, how it was more than he needed for his crops one day, never enough the next.

Jenine eventually felt his presence. She turned, smiled, and lifted a finger, asking him to wait a moment, then finished opening and closing the valves. The woman testing the waste water glanced up at the two of them, frowned at Mission, and carefully dispensed a dark dye into the tube before shaking it, a thumb unhygienically used to cork the end. These were dark arts, Mission thought, whatever they did to make shower water and urine safe to drink. Dark and noisy arts. But at least he had grown used to the smell, which wasn't the foulness one would expect but rather something chemical, something caustic.

Jenine yelled to her supervisor that she was taking her break, wiped her palms on the seat of her pants, and hopped down. She led Mission away from the rows and rows of containers before digging the foam inserts out of her ears.

"Hey, Mish!" she yelled, as she pulled him into the hallway. She clasped his neck and kissed him on the cheek. By the time he thought to hug her back or return the gesture, it was already over, leaving him scrambling awkwardly at the air and feeling a fool.

She led him down two doors to the break room, which stank of microwaved soup and sweaty coveralls. It smelled almost exactly like the break room in Dispatch, fifty levels down, in fact. Mission wondered if every break room smelled just like this.

Jenine grabbed a dented metal cup from a pile of them by the sink and filled it with water. "Whadja bring me?" she asked, glancing at his shoulder.

Mission shook his head and turned to show her his empty pack. "I'm sorry," he said, feeling like an ass.

She waved her hand and took a long pull on the tin cup. "It's fine." She refilled the cup from the sink, and Mission noticed that she waited for the faucet to stop dripping into the vessel, even tapped it twice with her fist to get the last drop, before pulling it away. Every profession had its quirks and habits, he supposed. Like how a porter never passed a landing without checking for a signal 'chief, nor missed a rumor whispered on the stairs.

"Sorry if I made it sound like it's your duty to shower me with gifts." She winked at him, and Mission laughed.

"Don't be sorry," he said. "I like bringing you stuff. I was just weighed down with a tandem haul this time." He swung his arms and twisted at the waist to stretch his spine. "They've been pouring it on us. But this is what I've been told to expect our first year."

"Tell me about it." Jenine leaned back against the counter and waved Mission toward the jumbled pile of cups. "I thought shadowing was bad, but first year is even worse."

He accepted her offer and filled a cup with water. He reminded himself to top up his thermos before he left as well.

"It's almost enough to make you miss school, isn't it?" she asked.

Mission laughed. "Oh, hell yeah it is."

"Here's to better days." She held her cup up.

Mission tinked his against hers, careful not to splash any water. "To better days."

They watched each other over the lips of their cups while they drank. And in that breathless pause, in the time it took to swallow once, twice, three times, Mission felt an incredible rush of happiness that just as quickly plummeted away. It was like a memory of something that had not yet happened, a vivid image of him and Jenine sitting at a small table in a small apartment, and then a sense of the space between them brought on by their occupations. In this imaginary future, he would find himself leaving for another week of runs before he got his next day off. And so the same dread he felt right then in that break room, the desire to maximize their time together, to sip rather than gulp, would surely haunt him in a future he could only dream about. He swallowed and peered into his cup, searching for the courage to tell her how he felt.

"Speaking of better days," Jenine said, "have you been by the Nest lately?"

Mission shook his head. He finished his water with another long pull and filled it halfway back up. "I will tomorrow." He turned and studied his friend and had a sudden sense of how grown up they had become, standing around like that, both with jobs, sipping water from dented cups, swapping memories of the long ago. "You?"

She nodded. "I was up last weekend. A few of us are trying to go more regularly, help with the kids, though there aren't as many of them around as there used to be."

"A few of you? Did Rodny go?"

He braced himself for her reply. An old rumor had spread that the two of them had been spending time together, back before Rodny was swallowed up by his work. Jenine was going to tell him that yes, she and Rodny were in love, had made it official, had registered with the Pact. She was going to tell him and break his heart—

"I haven't seen Rod in a while. I was going to ask you. Whatever they have him doing in IT, they don't seem to let him out much."

Mission shrugged and feigned indifference. In fact, he had grown concerned. The last two times he'd been through the thirties and stopped to see his friend, he'd been told Rodny was "unavailable." Even when Mission insisted he didn't mind waiting, they'd told him it wouldn't happen. Mission worried his old friend was becoming a recluse or a workaholic, one more piece of his childhood wrested away. He used to laugh when Rodny boasted he'd be Mayor or a department head one day. It didn't seem so funny anymore.

"I have to get back," Jenine said. "I only get a ten." She grabbed a small towel from a hanger over the sink and rubbed the cup inside and out. She set it back on the pile and held her hand out for Mission's. "You got another delivery today, or are you done?"

"I'm done." He finished his water and let her have the cup. "I'm crashing in the waystation on nineteen. I might do a run up-top before heading down to see the Crow tomorrow."

"So what're you doing tonight?" She waved her consent as Mission held up his thermos questioningly. "You wanna hang out? Me and some friends are going up to twenty-three to drop paint bombs."

"I can't tonight." His metal thermos sang as it was filled, and he felt doubly bad for not bringing her anything. "I've got this thing later."

"What thing? I thought you were gonna sack out."

"I meant that I have to get up early. And haven't you gotten a little old for paint bombs?"

Jenine smiled. "There's this place on twenty-three where if you release at just the right spot, the bomb goes almost a hundred levels down before splatting at one-twenty-two."

Mission shifted his weight to his other foot. "Yeah, I've seen it." He wanted to tell her that he walked through that spot on one-twenty-two all the time, that people he knew down there complained, that Sharen, another porter, had nearly been hit by a paint bomb dropped from the

Mids a few weeks ago. Instead, he told Jenine about the time something had whistled by his head in the dead of night as he worked his way through the eighties. "Maybe it's not such a good idea," he told her.

Jenine's smile melted. She didn't say anything, didn't have to— the silence was enough. It was as if she were beginning to understand something even better than Mission did: he was no longer just of the Up Top. He was a child of the entire silo, now. It meant more than being a target everywhere he went. It meant having no one to conspire with anymore, no one to pick out targets with in whispers.

"Well, you've gotta get up early tomorrow, anyway."

"Yeah." He brushed his hair off his forehead. All the barbers he passed in a typical week, never enough time to stop. He would look like Frankie soon enough. "Hey, it was good seeing you."

"Same. For sure. Take care of yourself, Mish. Watch your steps."

Mission smiled. And this time, when she leaned in to touch his neck and kiss his cheek, he was ready to reciprocate. "You know I will," he said, kissing her lightly on the cheek. "You watch your steps as well."

L
ater that night, Mission could still feel the soft touch of her hand on his neck and the press of her lips to his cheek. In the quiet and deathly darkness of the silo's nighttime, he could hear Jenine whispering for him to be safe.

The lights had been dimmed so man and silo might sleep. It was those wee hours when children were long hushed with sing-song lullabies and only those with trouble in mind crept about. Mission held very still in that darkness and waited. He thought on love and other forbidden things. And somewhere in the dark, there came the chirp of rope wound tight and sliding against metal, the bird-like sound fibers made as they gripped steel and strained under some great burden.

A gang of porters huddled with him on the stairway. Mission pressed his cheek against the silo's untrembling inner post, the cool steel touching him where Jenine's lips had. He lost himself in his thoughts, controlling his breathing like he'd been shadowed how. And he listened for the rope. He knew well the sounds they made, could feel the burn on his neck, that raised weal healed over by the years, a mark glanced at by others but rarely mentioned aloud. And again in that thick gray of the dim-time there came a chirp like some caged bird flexing its beak.

He waited for the signal. He thought on rope, his own life, and secret love—all these forbidden things. There was a book in Dispatch down on seventy-four that kept accounts. In the main waystation for all the porters, a massive ledger fashioned out of a fortune in paper was kept under lock and key. On this year's wage of pulp was a careful tally of certain types of deliveries, handwritten so the information couldn't slip off into wires. Only a handful of porters knew for certain it existed—to the rest the book was legend.

Mission had heard that they kept track of certain kinds of pipe in this ledger, but he didn't know why. Brass, too, and various types of fluids coming out of Chemical. Any of these or too much rope, and you were put on the watching list. Porters were the lords of rumor. They knew where everything went. And their whisperings gathered like condensation in Dispatch Main where they were written down.

Mission listened to the rope creak and sing in the darkness. He knew what it felt like to have a length of it cinched tightly around his neck. And it seemed strange to him—it seemed wrong—that if you ordered enough to hang yourself, nobody cared. Enough to span a few levels, and eyebrows were raised.

He adjusted his handkerchief and thought on this in the dim-time. A man may take his own life, he supposed, as long as he didn't take another's job.

"Ready yourself," came the whisper from above.

Mission tightened the grip on his knife and concentrated on the task at hand. His eyes strained to see in the wan light. The steady breathing of his neighbors was occasionally heard. They would be squeezing their own knives or their empty and angry fists.

The knives came with the job—they were as much a part of porting as the inverted hearts that grew on practiced calves. A porter's knife for slicing open delivered goods, for cutting fruit to eat on the climb, and for keeping peace as its owner strayed from all the heights and depths, taking the silo's dangers two at a time. It was said that a porter's knife shadowed for a thousand jobs, that its caster was its owner, its home a good sheath. Here waited but another job for Mission's gleaming shadow. With the flick of a wrist, it would quiet the neck of that singing bird. It would part a rope that groaned under a darkened and illicit strain.

Up the stairwell two full turns, on a dim landing, a group of farmers argued in soft voices as they handled the other end of that rope, as they performed a porter's job in the dark of night that they might save a hundred chits or two. Beyond the rail across from Mission, a black shape slid past. The rope was invisible in the inky void. He would have to lean out and grope for the chirping bird's neck. He felt a ring of heat by his collar, and the hilt of his blade felt unsure in his sweating palm.

"Not yet," Morgan whispered, and Mission felt his old caster's hand on his shoulder, holding him back, still treating him like a shadow even now. Mission cleared his mind. Another soft chirp, the sound of line taking the strain of a heavy generator, and a dense patch of gray drifted through the black. The men above shouted in whispers as they handled the load, as they did in green the work of men in blue.

While the patch of gray inched past, Mission thought of the night's danger and marveled at the fear in his heart. He possessed a sudden care for a life he had once labored to end, a life that never should've been. He thought of his mother and wondered what she was like, beyond her disobedience. That was all he knew of her. He knew the implant in her hip had failed, as one in ten thousand might. And instead of reporting the malfunction—and the pregnancy—she had hid him in loose clothes until it was past the time the Pact allowed a child to be treated as a cyst.

"Ready yourself," Morgan hissed.

The gray mass of the generator crept down and out of sight. Mission clutched his knife and thought of how he should've been cut out of her and discarded. But past a certain date, and one life was traded for another. Such was the Pact. Born behind bars, Mission had been allowed free while his mother had been sent outside. In the middle of the night, she must've watched as they cleaned the blood from his wailing flesh. By the morning, she was cleaning for them all.

"Now," Morgan commanded, and Mission startled. Soft and well-worn boots squeaked on the stairs above, the sounds of men lurching into action. Mission concentrated on his part. He pressed himself against the curved rail and reached out into the space beyond. His palm found rope as stiff as steel, and he thought of the great depths below him, how long the fall. He remembered less dangerous games with paint bombs and paper parachutes as he pressed his blade to the taut line.

There was a pop like sinew snapping, the first of the braids parting with just a touch of his sharp blade.

Mission had but a moment to think of those on the landing below, the accomplices waiting two levels down. Another pop, and the wounded bird sang at a different pitch. Men were storming up the staircase. Mission longed to join them. With the barest of sawing motions, the rope parted the rest of the way and let out a twangy cry. Mission thought he heard the heavy generator whistle as it picked up speed. There was a ferocious crash a moment later, men screaming in alarm down below, but those screams could've been coming from anywhere. The fighting had broken out above.

With one hand on the rail and another strangling his knife, Mission took the stairs three at a time. He rushed to join the melee above, this midnight lesson on breaking the Pact, on doing another's job.

Grunts and groans and slapping thuds spilled from the landing, and Mission threw himself into the scuffle, thinking not where wars come from but only on this one battle. His feet tangled briefly in forbidden rope, all those shorter strands twisted and woven into something bigger, a line long enough to tangle a thousand souls.

• Silo 1 •

A second shift.

"The mind is its own place, and in itself
Can make a heaven of hell, a hell of heaven."

- John Milton

· 30 ·

The wheelchair squeaked as its wheels went 'round and 'round. With each revolution there was a sharp peal of complaint followed by a circuit of deathly silence. Donald lost himself in this rhythmic sound. He began to anticipate each chirp, like a lonely bird crying for its mate. Chirp and silence. Chirp and silence. As he was pushed along, his breath puffed out into the air, the room harboring the same deep chill as his bones.

There were rows and rows of pods stretched out to either side. Names glowed orange on tiny screens. Made-up names. Phony names designed to sever the past from the now. Donald watched them slide by as they pushed him toward the exit. His head felt heavy, his neck inadequate for propping up his skull, the weight of remembrance replacing the wisps of dreams that coiled away and vanished like vaporous smoke.

The men in the pale blue coveralls guided him through the door and into the hallway, and Donald seemed to float along like a ghost, like a man disturbed from his grave. He was steered into a familiar room with a familiar table. Boots kicked here—he remembered from a dream. In one dream, he was the one holding the boots still, bones like a bird's struggling beneath his grip, and he was the enemy. In another dream it was *his* boots doing the kicking. He could see them at the ends of his own legs while ice burned in his veins.

The wheelchair shimmied as they removed his bare feet from the footrests. He asked how long it'd been, how long he'd been asleep.

"Seventy years," someone said. He did the math. A hundred and twenty since orientation. No wonder the wheelchair felt unsteady—it was older than he was. Its screws had worked loose over the long decades that Donald had been asleep.

They helped him stand. His feet were still numb from his hibernation, the cold fading to painful tingles. A noisy curtain was drawn. They asked him to urinate in a cup, which came as glorious relief. The sample was the color of charcoal, dead machines flushed from his system. The paper gown wasn't enough to warm him, even though he knew the cold was in his flesh, not in the room. They gave him more of the bitter drink.

"How long before his head is clear?" someone asked.

"A day," the doctor said. "Tomorrow at the earliest."

They had him sit while they took his blood. A man in white coveralls with hair just as stark stood in the doorway, frowning. "Save your strength," the man said. He nodded to the doctor to continue his work and disappeared before Donald could place him in his faltering memory. He felt dizzy and watched as his blood, blue from the cold, was taken from him.

••••

They rode a familiar elevator. The men around him talked, but their voices were drones behind a slowly parting fog. Donald felt as though he had been drugged, but he remembered that he had stopped taking their pills. He reached for his bottom lip, finger and mouth both tingling, and felt for an ulcer, that little pocket where he kept his pills unswallowed.

But the ulcer wasn't there. It would've healed in his sleep decades ago. The lift dinged, the doors parted, and Donald felt more of that dreamtime fade.

They pushed him down another hall, scuff marks on the walls the height of the wheels, black arcs where rubber had once met the paint. His eyes roamed the walls, the ceiling, the tiles, all bearing centuries of wear. Like the wheelchair, these halls never slept. Yesterday, they were almost new. Now they were heaped with abuse, a jarring eyeblink of decrepitude, a sudden crumbling into ruin. Donald remembered designing halls just like these. He remembered thinking they were making something to last for ages. The truth was there all along. The truth was in the design, staring back at him, too insane to be taken seriously.

The wheelchair slowed.

"The next one," a voice behind him said, a gruff voice, an exhausted and familiar voice. Donald was pushed past one closed door to another. One of the orderlies bustled around the wheelchair, a ring of keys jangling from his hip. A key was selected and slotted into the knob with a series of neat clicks. Hinges cried out as the door was pushed inward. The lights inside were turned on.

It was a room like a cell, musky with the scent of disuse. There was a narrow double bunk in the corner, a side table, a dresser, a bathroom. The light overhead flickered before it came on, like a tingling hand that needed a moment before forming a fist.

"Why am I here?" Donald asked, his voice cracking.

"This will be your room," the orderly said, putting away his keys. His young eyes darted up to the man steering the wheelchair as if unsure of the rightness of his answer. Another young man in pale blue hurried around and removed Donald's feet from the stirrups and placed them on carpet worn flat by the years.

Donald's last memory was of being chased by snarling dogs with leathery wings, chased up a mountain of bones. But that was a dream. What was his last *real* memory? It was the one of being put to sleep for good. He remembered a needle. He remembered dying. That felt real.

"I mean—" Donald swallowed painfully. "Why am I . . . *awake?*"

He almost said alive. The two orderlies exchanged glances as they helped him from the chair to the lower bunk. The wheelchair squeaked once as it was pushed back into the hallway. The man guiding it paused, his broad shoulders making the doorway appear small.

One of the orderlies held Donald's wrist—two fingers pressing lightly on ice-blue veins, lips silently counting. The other orderly dropped two pills into a plastic cup and fumbled with the cap on a bottle of water.

"That won't be necessary," the silhouette in the doorway said.

The orderly with the pills glanced over his shoulder, and Donald remembered that these weren't orderlies at all. They were the other kind of doctors. Doctors of the body, not of the mind.

"I remember," Donald muttered. He pictured himself inside a straw plunged deep into the dirt. There were other straws around him, concrete tombs lined with pipe and wire, things that he could draw, that he had designed.

The man in the doorway stepped inside the small room, and some of the air was displaced. "Good," he said, in that familiar voice, that old voice. The room shrank further. It became more difficult to breathe.

"You're the Thaw—" Donald whispered.

The old man with the white hair waved a hand at the two doctors. "Give us a moment," he said. The one with a grip on Donald's wrist finished his counting and nodded to the other. Unswallowed pills rattled in a paper cup as they were put away.

"I remember everything," Donald said, though he suspected this wasn't quite true. "You're the Thaw Man."

A smile was flashed, as white as his hair, wrinkles forming around his lips and eyes. The chair in the hallway squeaked as it was pushed away, off to retrieve someone else, never sleeping. The door clicked shut. Donald thought he heard a lock engage, but his teeth still chattered occasionally, and his ears were full of lead.

"Thurman," the man said, correcting him. "But I don't go by that anymore. Just as you don't go by Donald."

"But I remember," Donald said. More came back to him. He remembered his office, the one upstairs and some other office far away, some place where it still rained and the grass grew. This man had been a Senator. But of what? Donald remembered drawing this place.

"And that's a mystery we need to solve." The senator of nothing tilted his head. "For now, it's good that you do. We *need* you to remember."

Thurman leaned against the metal dresser. He looked as though he hadn't slept in days. His hair was unkempt, not quite how Donald remembered it. There were dark circles beneath his sad eyes. He seemed much . . . older, somehow.

Donald peered down at his own palms, the springs in the bed making the room feel as though it were swaying. He flashed again to the horrible sight of a man remembering his own name and wanting to be free.

"Who am I?" he asked. He had felt so certain a moment before. Had he swallowed those pills? No, he remembered them rattling back into that orderly's coat. That *doctor's* coat. This was just the waking confusion. It would pass, he told himself. This was the groggy morning after a century of vivid dreams.

"Who do you think you are?" the Thaw Man asked. He produced a folded piece of paper and waited for an answer. Recollections came back and then receded like a sea swelling in and out against a pier.

"My name is Donald Keene."

"So you do remember. And you know who I am."

Donald nodded.

"Good." The Thaw Man turned and placed the folded piece of paper on the dresser. He arranged it on its bent legs so it tented upward, toward the ceiling. "We need you to remember everything," he said. "Study this report when the fog clears, see if it jars anything loose. Once your stomach is settled, I'll have a proper meal brought down."

Donald rubbed his temples. The sea drew away from the pier.

"You've been gone for some time," the Thaw Man said. He rapped his knuckles on the door.

Donald wiggled his bare toes against the carpet. The sensation was returning to his feet. The door clicked before swinging open, and the Senator once again blocked the light spilling from the hallway. He became a shadow for a moment.

"Rest, and then we'll get our answers together. There's someone who wants to see you."

The room was sealed tight before Donald could ask what that meant. And somehow, with the door shut and him gone, there was more air to breathe in that small space. Donald took a few deep breaths. He waited for the world to change, for the snarling dogs with the bat-like wings to return, for the mountain of skulls to reappear beneath his scrambling hands and knees, that interminable climb upward to a peak that would not come. But the room was too solid for that. After a long while, he grabbed the frame of the bed and struggled to his feet. He stood there a moment, swaying.

"Get our answers," he repeated aloud. Someone wants to see him.

He shook his head, which made the world spin. As if he had any answers. All he had were questions. He remembered the orderlies who woke him saying something about a silo falling. He couldn't remember which one. Why would they wake him for that?

He moved unsteadily to the door, tried the knob, confirmed what he already knew. He went to the dresser where the piece of paper stood on its remembered folds.

"Get some rest," he said, laughing at the suggestion. As if he could sleep. He felt as though he'd been asleep forever. He picked up the piece of paper and unfolded it.

A report. Donald remembered this. It was a copy of a report. A report about a young man doing horrible things. The room twisted around him as if he stood on some great pivot, the memory of men and women trampled and dying, of giving some awful order, faces peering in at him from a hallway somewhere far in the past. Somewhere like yesterday.

Donald blinked away a curtain of tears and studied the trembling report. Hadn't he written this? He had signed it, he remembered. But that wasn't his name at the bottom. It was his handwriting, but it wasn't his name.

Troy.

Donald's legs went numb. He sought the bed—but collapsed to the floor instead. He kept saying he remembered even as more and more washed over him. Troy and Helen. Helen and Troy. He remembered his wife. He saw her disappearing over a hill, her arm raised to the sky where bombs were falling, his sister and some dark and nameless shadow pulling him back as people spilled like marbles down a slope, spilled and gathered, plunking through a funnel and into some deep hole filled with white mist.

Donald remembered. He remembered all that he had helped do to the world. There was a troubled boy in a silo full of the dead, a shadow among the servers. That boy had brought an end to silo number 12. But Donald— What had he done? There were no numbers to contain all the dead. Their skulls made a pile that reached to the heavens. And the tears that popped against the trembling report, they were tinged a pale blue.

• 31 •

A doctor brought soup and bread a few hours later, plus a tall glass of water. Donald ate hungrily while the man checked his arm. The warm soup felt good. It slid to his center and seemed to radiate its heat outward. He tore at the bread with his teeth and chased it with the water. Somehow these things were going to keep his flesh from collapsing inward. Donald ate with the desperation of so many years of fasting.

"Thank you," he said between bites. "For the food."

The doctor glanced up from checking his blood pressure. He was an older man, heavyset, with great bushy eyebrows and a fine wisp of hair clinging to his scalp like a cloud to a hilltop.

"I'm Donald," he said, introducing himself.

There was a wrinkle of confusion on the old man's brow. His gray eyes strayed toward his clipboard as if either it or his patient couldn't be trusted. The needle on the gauge jumped with Donald's pulse.

"Who're you?" Donald asked.

"I'm Doctor Henson," he finally said, though without confidence.

Donald took a long swig on his water, thankful they'd left it at room temperature. He didn't want anything cold inside him ever again. "Where're you from?"

The doctor removed the cuff from Donald's arm with a loud rip. "Level ten. But I work out of the shift office on sixty-eight." He put his tools back in his bag and made a note on the clipboard.

"No, I mean, where are you *from*. You know . . . before."

Dr. Henson patted Donald's knee and stood. The clipboard went on a hook on the outside of the door. "You might have some dizziness the next few days. Let us know if you experience any trembling, okay?"

Donald nodded. He remembered being given the same advice earlier. Or was that his last shift? Maybe the repetition was for those who had trouble remembering. He wasn't going to be one of those people. Not this time.

A shadow fell into the room. Donald looked up to see the Thaw Man in the doorway. He gripped the meal tray to keep it from sliding off his knees.

The Thaw Man nodded to Dr. Henson, but this was not their names. *Thurman*, Donald told himself. Senator Thurman. He knew this.

"Do you have a moment?" Thurman asked the doctor.

"Of course." Henson grabbed his bag and stepped outside. The door clicked shut, leaving Donald alone with his soup.

He took quiet spoonfuls, trying to make anything of the murmurs on the other side of the door. *Thurman*, he reminded himself again. And not a senator. Senator of what? Those days were gone. Donald had drawn the plans.

The report stood tented on the dresser, returned to its spot. Donald took a bite of bread and remembered the floors he'd laid out. Those floors were now real. They existed. People lived inside them, raising their children, laughing, having fights, singing in the shower. People lived in the things he'd made, in the holes he'd dug. Those people—and no more.

A few minutes passed before the knob tilted and the door swung inward. The Thaw Man entered the room alone. He pressed the door shut and frowned at Donald. "How're you feeling?"

The spoon clacked against the rim of the bowl. Donald set the utensil down and gripped the tray with both hands to keep them from shaking, to keep them from forming fists.

"You know," Donald hissed, teeth clenched together. "You know what we did."

Thurman showed his palms. "We did what had to be done."

"No. Don't give me that." Donald shook his head. The water in his glass trembled as if something dangerous approached. "The world . . ."

"We saved it."

"That's not true!" Donald's voice cracked. He tried to remember. "There is no world." He recalled the view from the top, from the cafeteria. He remembered the hills a dull brown, the sky full of menacing clouds. "We ended it. We killed everyone."

"They were already dead," Thurman said. "We all were. Everyone dies, son. The only thing that matters is—"

"No." Donald waved the words away as if they were buzzing things that could bite him. "There's no justifying this—" He felt spittle form on his lips, wiped it away with his sleeve. The tray on his lap slid dangerously, and Thurman moved swifter than his years to catch it. He placed what was left of the meal on the bedside table, and up close, Donald could see that he had gotten older. The wrinkles were deeper, the skin hanging from the bones. He wondered how much time Thurman had spent awake while Donald slept.

"I killed a lot of men in the war," Thurman said, looking down at the tray of half-eaten food.

Donald found himself focused on the old man's neck. He interlocked his hands to keep them still. This sudden admission about killing made it seem as if he could read Donald's mind, like this was some kind of a warning for Donald to stay his murderous plans.

Thurman turned to the dresser and picked up the folded report. He opened it, and Donald caught sight of the pale blue dollops, his ice-tinged tears from earlier.

"Some say killing gets easier the longer you're at it," Thurman said. He sounded sad, not threatening. Donald looked down at his own knees and saw that they were bouncing. He forced his heels against the carpet and tried to pin them there.

"For me, it only got worse. There was a man in Iran—"

"The entire goddamn planet," Donald whispered, stressing each word. This was what he said, but all he could think about was his wife. Bombs going off, the plans he'd drawn, Helen pulled down the wrong hill, marbles rolling apart, everything that had ever existed crumbling to ruin. "We killed everyone."

The senator took in a deep breath and held it a moment. "I told you," he said. "They were already dead."

Donald's knees began bouncing again. There was no controlling it. Thurman studied the report, seemed unsure of something. The paper faintly shook, but maybe it was the overhead vent blowing, which also stirred his hair.

"We were outside of Kashmar," Thurman said. "This was toward the end of the war, when we were getting our butts kicked and telling the world we were winning. I had a corporal in my squad, our team medic, a James Hannigan. Young. Always cracking jokes but serious when he needed to be. The kind of guy everyone likes. The hardest kind to lose."

Thurman shook his head. He stared off into the distance. The vent in the ceiling quieted, but the report continued to quiver.

"I killed a lot of men during the war, but only once to really *save* a life. The rest, you never knew what you were doing when you pulled the trigger. Maybe the guy you take out is never gonna find his own target, never hurt a soul. Maybe he's gonna be one of the thousands who drop their rifles and blend in with the civvies, go back to their families, open a kasava stand near the embassy and talk basketball with the troops stationed outside. A good man. You never knew. You're killing these men, and you never knew if you were doing it for a good reason or not."

"How many billions—?" Donald swallowed. He slid to the edge of the bed and reached toward the tray. Thurman knew what he was after and passed the glass of water, half empty. He continued to ignore Donald's complaints.

"Hannigan got hit with shrapnel outside of Kashmar. If we could get him to a medic, it was the kind of wound you survived, the kind you lift your shirt in a bar to show off the scars one day. But he couldn't walk, and it was too hot to send in an airlift. Our squad was hemmed in and would need to fight our way out. I didn't think we could get to a safe LZ in time to save him. But what I knew, because I'd seen it too many damn times before, is that two or three of my men would die trying to get him out. That's what happens when you're lugging a soldier instead of a rifle." Thurman pressed his sleeve to his forehead. "I'd seen it before."

"You left him behind," Donald said, seeing where this was going. He took a sip of water. The surface was agitated.

"No. I killed him." Thurman stared at the foot of the bed. He stared at nothing. "The enemy wouldn't have let him die. Not there, not like that. They would've patched him up so they could catch it on film. They would've stitched up his belly so they could open his throat." He turned to Donald. "I had to make a decision, and I had to make it fast. And the longer I've lived with it, the more I've come to agree with what I did. We lost one man that day. I saved two or three others."

Donald shook his head. "That's not the same as what we— what you—"

"It's precisely the same. Do you remember Safed? What the media called the outbreak?"

Donald remembered Safed. An Israeli town near Nazareth. Near Syria. The deadliest WMD strike of the war. He nodded.

"The rest of the world would've looked just like that. Just like Safed." Thurman snapped his fingers. "Ten billion lights go out all at once. We were already infected, son. It was just a matter of triggering it. Safed was . . . like a beta test."

Donald shook his head. "I don't believe you. Why would anyone do that?"

Thurman frowned. "Don't be naive, son. This life means nothing to some. You put a switch in front of ten billion people, a switch that kills every one of us the moment you hit it, and you'd have thousands of hands racing to be the one. Tens of thousands. It would only be a matter of time. And that switch *existed*."

"No." Donald flashed back to the first conversation he'd ever had with the senator as a member of Congress, after winning office the first time. It had felt like this, the lies and the truth intermingling and shielding one another. "You'll never convince me," he said. "You'll have to drug me or kill me. You'll never convince me."

Thurman nodded as if he agreed. "Drugging you doesn't work. I've read up on your first shift. There's a small percentage of people with some kind of resistance. I'd love to know why."

Donald laughed. He settled against the wall behind the cot and nestled into the darkness the top bunk provided. "Maybe I've seen too much to forget," he said.

"No, I don't think so." Thurman lowered his head so he could still make eye contact. Donald took a sip of water, both hands wrapped around the glass. "The more you see," Thurman said, "the worse the trauma is, the better it works. Except for some people. Which is why we took a sample."

Donald glanced down at his arm. A small square of gauze had been taped over the spot of blood left by the doctor's needle. He felt a caustic mix of helplessness and fear well up, the mix that moves caged animals to bite at curious hands. "You woke me to take my blood?"

"Not exactly." Thurman hesitated. "Your resistance is something I'm curious about. The reason you're awake is because I was asked to wake you. We're losing silos—"

"I thought that was the plan," Donald spat. "Losing silos. I thought that was what you wanted." He remembered crossing one out with red ink, all those many lives lost. They had accounted for this. Silos were expendable. That's what he'd been told.

Thurman shook his head. "Whatever's happening out there, we need to understand it. And there's someone here who . . . who thinks you may have stumbled onto the answer. A few questions, and then we can put you back under."

Back under. So he wasn't going to be out for long. They woke him to take his blood and to drill into his mind, and then back to sleep. Donald rubbed his arms, which felt thin and atrophied. He was dying in that pod. Only, more slowly than he would like.

"We need to know what you remember about this report." Thurman held it out. Donald waved the thing away.

"I already looked it over," he said. He didn't want to see it again. He could close his eyes and see people spilling out onto the dusty land, a cloud of killing mist, the people that he had ordered dead, more people being trampled inside.

"We have other medications that might ease the—"

"No. No more drugs." Donald crossed his wrists and spread his arms out, slicing the air with both hands. "Look, I don't have a resistance to your drugs." The truth. He was sick of the lies. "There's no mystery. I just stopped taking the pills."

It felt good to admit it. What were they going to do, anyway? Put him back to sleep? That was the answer no matter what. He took another sip of water while he let the confession sink in. He swallowed.

"I kept them in my gums and spat them out later. It's as simple as that. Probably the case with anyone else remembering. Like Hal, or Carlton, or whatever his name was."

Thurman regarded him coolly. He tapped the report against his open palm, seeming to digest this. "We know you stopped taking the pills," he finally said. "And when."

Donald waved his hand. "Mystery solved, then." He finished his water and put the empty glass back on his tray. It felt good to have that out in the open.

"The drugs you have a resistance to are not in the pills, Donny. The reason people stop taking the pills is because they begin to remember, not the other way around."

Donald studied Thurman, disbelieving.

"Your urine changes color when you get off them. You develop sores on your gums. These are the signs we look for."

"What?"

"There are no drugs in the pills, Donny."

"I don't believe you."

"We medicate everyone. There are those of us who are immune. But you shouldn't be."

"Bullshit. I remember. The pills made me woozy. As soon as I stopped taking them, I got better."

Thurman tilted his head to the side. "The reason you stopped taking them was because you were . . . I won't say getting better. It was because the fear had begun leaking through. Donny, the medication is in the water." He waved at the empty glass on the tray. Donald followed the gesture and immediately felt sick, even though he didn't believe him. The suspicion was enough.

"Don't worry," Thurman said. "We'll get to the bottom of it."

"I don't want to help you. I don't want to talk about this report. I don't want to see whoever it is you need me to see."

He wanted Helen. All he wanted was his wife.

"There's a chance that thousands will die if you don't help us. There's a chance that you stumbled onto something with this report of yours, even if I don't believe it."

Donald felt the weight of the soil piled on them both. He glanced at the door to the bathroom, thought about locking himself inside and forcing himself to throw up, to expunge the food and the water. But it was an insane thought. Maybe Thurman was lying to him. Maybe he was telling the truth. A lie would mean the water was just water. The truth would mean that he did have some sort of resistance. Either way, there was nothing—and everything—to fear.

"I barely remember writing the thing," he admitted. And who would want to see him? He assumed it would be another doctor, maybe a silo head, maybe whoever was running this shift.

He rubbed his temples, could feel the pressure building between them. Maybe he should just do this thing and go back to sleep, back to his skull-filled dreams. Now and then, he had dreamed of Helen. It was the only place left to see her. With this thought, his resistance crumbled like thousand-year-old bones.

"Okay," he said. "I'll go. But I still don't understand what I could possibly know." He rubbed his arm where they'd taken the blood. There was an itch there. An itch so deep it felt like a bruise.

Senator Thurman nodded. "I tend to agree with you. But that's not what she thinks."

Donald stiffened. "She?" He searched Thurman's eyes, wondering if he'd heard correctly. "She who?"

The old man frowned. "The one who had me wake you." He waved his hand at the bunk. "Get some rest. I'll take you to her in the morning."

· 32 ·

H e couldn't rest. How could he rest? The hours were cruel, slow, and unknowable. There was no clock to mark their passing, no answer to his frustrated slaps on the door. Donald was left to lie in his bunk and stare at the diamond patterns of interlocking wires holding the mattress above him, to listen to the gurgle of water in hidden pipes as it rushed to another room. He couldn't sleep. He had no idea if it was the middle of the night or the middle of the day. The weight of the silo pressed down. The world was his bunkmate. It lay still as death in the bed above him.

When the boredom grew intolerable, Donald eventually gave in and looked over the report a second time. He studied it more closely. It wasn't the original; the signature was flat, and he remembered using a blue pen. A red marker for the big X on the map and a blue pen for the reports. He was pretty sure.

He skimmed the account of the silo's collapse and his theory that IT heads shadowed too young. His recommendation was to raise the age. He wondered if they had. Maybe so, but the problems were persisting. There was also mention of a young man he had inducted, a young man with a question. His grandmother was one of those who remembered, much like Donald. Like Hal or Carter or whatever his name had been. Donald had suggested in the report that entertaining one question from inductees might be a good idea. They were given the Legacy, after all. Their cruel test was a severe application of the truth. Why not show them, in that final stage of indoctrination, that there were more truths to be had?

It had seemed like a good idea at the time, but Donald remembered being a mess when he wrote the report. Maybe it had been his own questions, his own need for answers, that had driven him to suggest this.

The tiny clicks of a key entering a lock. Thurman opened the door as Donald folded the report away.

"How're you feeling?" Thurman asked.

Donald didn't say.

"Can you walk?"

He nodded. A walk. When what he really wanted was to run screaming down the hallway, to kick things over and punch holes in walls. But a walk would do. A walk before his next long nap.

••••

They rode the elevator in silence. Donald noticed Thurman had scanned his badge before pressing one of the shiny buttons, level fifty-four. Its number stood bright and new while so many others had been worn away. There was nothing but supplies on that level if Donald remembered correctly, supplies they weren't supposed to ever need. The lift slowed as it approached a level it normally skipped. The doors opened on a cavernous expanse of shelves stocked with instruments of death.

Thurman led him down the middle of it all. There were wooden crates with "AMMO" stenciled on the side, longer crates beside them with military designations like "M22" and "M19" that Donald recognized as being guns. Not that he knew what those guns looked like or how to operate them, but he had been to movies, and like any other young boy he had known what to call his stick while he fired imaginary bullets at his friends.

More shelves with armor and helmets, with supplies, some boxes unlabeled. And beyond the shelves, tarps that covered bulbous and winged forms that he knew to be drones. UAVs. His sister had flown them in a war that now seemed pointless and distant, part of ancient history. But here these relics stood, oiled and covered, waiting, both proud and paranoid, confident and reeking of grease and fear.

Beyond the drones, Thurman led the way through a murky dimness that made the wide storehouse seem to go on forever. Donald padded quietly behind, fearful of waking these demon sentinels, this aviary that promised hell-rain from the skies.

At the far end of the wide room, a hallway leaked a glow of light. An arrangement of offices, a wall lined with filing cabinets spotted with dots of rust, not greased like the other things. And in one wide room, the sounds of paper stirring, a chair squeaking as someone turned. Thurman rapped his knuckles on the doorframe. Donald rounded the corner and saw, inexplicably, *her* sitting there.

"Anna?"

He remained frozen in the doorway. Anna sat behind a huge conference table ringed with identical chairs. She looked up from a wide spread of paperwork and a computer monitor. There was no shock on her part, just a smile of acknowledgment and a weariness that the smile could not conceal.

Her father crossed the room while Donald gaped. Thurman squeezed her arm and kissed her on the cheek, but Anna's eyes did not leave Donald's. The old man whispered something to his daughter, then announced that he had work of his own to see to. Donald did not budge until the Senator had left the room, the armory swallowing an old soldier's footsteps.

"Anna—"

She was already around the massive table, wrapping her arms around him. Donald sagged into her embrace, suddenly exhausted. She was whispering things, the sing-song tunes of placating mothers, the there-theres and shushes. It took this to inform Donald that he was shaking. He felt her hand come down the back of his head and rest on his neck, his own arms crossing her back like a spring-loaded habit. Here was why women didn't pull shifts. Here was a truth the shrinks knew. Donald could feel himself grow both weak and bold. He had dangerous thoughts of giving in and more dangerous thoughts of lashing out. Here was the love and violence in the hearts of men, all for their women.

"What're you doing here?" he whispered. Did she not know the danger? The disruptive power of her gender? And what weakness was this of a father to wake a child in the middle of a storm?

"I'm here for the same reason you are." She pulled back from the embrace. "I'm looking for answers." She stepped away and surveyed the mess on the table. "To different questions, perhaps."

Donald finally saw what the table was, what the *room* was. A familiar schematic—a grid of silos—covered the table. Each silo was like a small plate, all of them trapped under the glass. A dozen chairs were gathered around. It was a war room, where generals stood and pushed plastic models and grumbled over lives lost by the thousands. He glanced up at the maps and schematics plastered on the walls. There was an adjoining bathroom, a towel hanging from a hook on the door. A cot had been set up in the far corner and was neatly made. There was a lamp beside it sitting on one of the wooden crates from the storeroom. Extension cords snaked here and there, signs of a room long converted into an apartment of sorts.

Donald wanted desperately to fall into the cot. He looked to Anna, made sure she was still there, and in a disturbed corner of his mind he thought this meant Helen must also be somewhere that he could wake her. Life, death, sleeping, rising, the passage of time, the workings of his own mind—all of it was soft and without meaning.

He turned to the nearest wall and flipped through some of the drawings. They were three layers deep in places and covered in notes. It didn't look like a war was being planned. It looked like a scene from the crime shows that used to lull him to sleep in a former life.

"You've been up longer than me," he said.

Anna stood beside him. Her hand lighted on his shoulder like a bird, and Donald felt himself startle to be touched at all.

"Almost a year, now." Her hand slid down his back before falling away. "Can I get you a drink? Water? I also have a stash of scotch down here. Dad doesn't know half the stuff they hid away in these crates."

Donald shook his head. He turned and watched as she disap-peared into the bathroom and ran the sink. She emerged, sipping from a glass.

"What's going on here?" he asked. "Why am I up?"

She swallowed and waved her glass at the walls. "It's—" She laughed and shook her head. "I was about to say it's nothing, but this is the hell that keeps me out of one box and in another. It doesn't concern you, most of this."

Donald studied the room again. He could feel the dark halls of shelves and crates stretching back toward the elevator. A year, living like this. He turned his attention to Anna, the way her hair was balled up in a bun, a pen sticking out of it. Her skin was pale except for the dark rings beneath her eyes. He wondered how she was able to do this, live like this.

There was a printout on the far wall that matched the table, a grid of circles, the layout of the facilities. A familiar red X had been drawn across what he knew to be Silo 12 in the upper left corner. There was another X nearby, a new one. More lives lost while he slept. Thousands screaming while in his nightmares he could make no sound. And in the lower right-hand corner of the grid, a mess that made no sense. The room seemed to wobble a bit as he took a step closer.

"Donny?"

"What happened here?" he asked, his voice a whisper. Anna turned to see what he was looking at. She glanced at the table, and he realized that her paperwork was scattered around the same corner of the facility. The glass surface crawled with notes written in red and blue wax.

"Donny—" She stepped closer. "Things aren't well."

He turned and studied the scrawl of red marks on the wall schematic. There were Xs and question marks. There were notes in red ink with lines and arrows. Ten or a dozen of the silos were marked up to hell.

"How many?" he asked, trying to count, to multiply the thousands. "Are they gone?"

She took a deep breath. "We don't know." She finished her water, walked down the long line of chairs pushed up against the table, and reached down into the seat of one. She procured a bottle and poured a few fingers into her plastic cup. *Better than a blue pill*, Donald thought.

"It started with Silo 40," she said. "It went dark about a year ago—"

"Went dark?"

Anna took a sip of the scotch and nodded. She licked her lips. "The camera feeds went out first. Not at once, but eventually they got them all. We lost contact with the heads over there. Couldn't raise anyone. Erskine was running the shift at the time. He followed the Order and gave the okay to shut the silo down—"

"You mean kill everyone."

Anna shot him a look. "You know what had to be done."

Donald remembered Silo 12. He remembered making that same decision. As if there had been a decision to make. The system was automatic, wasn't it? Wasn't he just doing what came next, following a set of procedures written down by someone else? He remembered a debate from a history class in college, a group of students arguing that the first president to drop a bomb hadn't had any other choice. All that time and money invested, the military saying this was the only way. What was heroic or brave about carrying out the inevitable? What kind of man would it have taken to have bucked the expected? What if he hadn't aborted Silo 12? What if those people had scurried over the hills and had realized they weren't alone? Who would be the hero then? Who the villain?

He studied the poster with the red marks. "And the rest of them? The other silos?"

Anna finished the drink with one long pull and gasped for air afterward. Donald caught her eyeing the bottle. "They woke up Dad when 42 went. Two more silos had gone dark by the time he came for me—"

Two more silos. "Why you?" he asked.

She tucked a strand of loose hair behind her ear. "Because there was no one else. Because everyone who had a hand in designing this place was either gone or at their wits' end. Because Dad was desperate."

"He wanted to see you."

She laughed. "It wasn't that. Trust me." She waved her empty cup at the arrangement of circles on the table and the spread of papers. "They were using the radios at high frequencies. We think it started with 40, that maybe their IT Head went rogue. They hijacked their antenna and began communicating with the other silos around them, and we couldn't cut them off. They had taken care of that as well. As soon as Dad suspected this, he argued with the others that wireless networks were my specialty. They eventually relented."

"The others? Who all knows you're here?" Donald couldn't help but think how dangerous this could get, but maybe that was his own weakness screaming at him.

"My dad, Erskine, Dr. Henson, his assistants who brought me out. But those assistants won't work another shift—"

"Deep freeze?"

Anna frowned and splashed her cup, and it occurred to Donald how much could take place while a man slept. Entire shifts had gone by. Another silo had been lost, another red X drawn on the map. An entire corner of silos had run into some kind of trouble. Thurman, meanwhile, had been awake for a year, dealing with it. His daughter as well. So much had happened while Donald had dreamt of snarling dogs with bat-like wings and piles of bones. He waved his arm at the room. "You've been stuck in here for a year. Working on this."

She jerked her head at the door and laughed. "I've been cooped up in worse for a lot longer. But yeah, it sucks. I'm sick of this place." She took another sip, her cup hiding her expression, and Donald wondered if perhaps he was awake because of her weakness just as she might be awake because of her father's. What was next? Him searching the deep freeze for his sister Charlotte? How would it end?

"We've lost contact with eleven silos so far." Anna peered into her cup. "I think I've got it contained, but we're still trying to figure out how it happened or if anyone's still alive over there. I don't think so, but Dad wants to send scouts. Others say that's a bigger risk. And now it looks like 18 is going to burn itself to the ground."

"And I'm supposed to help? What does your dad think I know?" He stepped around the planning table and waved for the bottle. Anna splashed her cup and handed the drink to him; she reached for another cup by her monitor while Donald collapsed onto her cot. It was a lot to take in.

"It's not Dad who thinks you know anything. He didn't want you up at all. No one's supposed to come out of deep freeze." She screwed the cap back on the bottle. "It was his boss."

Donald nearly choked on his first sip of the scotch. He sputtered and wiped his chin with his sleeve while Anna looked on with concern.

"His *boss?*" he asked, gasping for air.

She narrowed her eyes. "Dad told you why you're here, right?"

He fumbled in his pocket for the report. "Something I wrote during my last . . . during my shift. Thurman has a boss? I thought he was in charge."

Anna laughed, but there was no humor there. "Nobody's in charge," she told him. "The system's in charge. It just runs. We built it to just *go.*" She got up from her desk and studied something on the wall for a moment, then walked over and joined him on the cot, the springs squeaking in complaint. Donald slid over to give her more room.

"Dad was in charge of digging the holes, that was his job. There were three of them who planned most of this. The other two had ideas for how to hide this place. Dad convinced them they should just build it in plain sight. The nuclear containment facility was his idea, and he was in a position to make it happen."

A flood of memories washed over Donald. He remembered being convinced to run for office. Was it Mick who had goaded him into it? Or was it Thurman?

"You said three. Who were the others?"

"Victor and Erskine." Anna adjusted a pillow and leaned back against the wall. "Not their real names, of course. But what does it matter? A name is a name. You can be anyone down here. Erskine was the one who discovered the original threat, who told Victor and Dad about the nanos. You'll meet him. He's been on a double shift with me, working on the loss of these silos, but it's out of his area of expertise. Do you need more?" She nodded at his cup.

"No. I'm already feeling dizzy." He didn't add that it wasn't from the alcohol. "I remember a Victor from my shift. He worked across the hall from me."

"The same." She looked away for a moment. "Dad refers to him as the boss, but I've been working with Victor for a while, and he never thought of himself that way. He thought of himself as a steward, joked once about feeling like Noah. He wanted to wake you months ago because of this Silo 18, but Dad vetoed the idea. I think Victor was fond of you. He talked about you a lot."

"Victor talked about *me?*" Donald remembered the man across the hall from him, the shrink. Anna reached up and wiped at the bottom of her eyes.

"Yes. He was a brilliant man, could tell what you were thinking, what anyone was thinking. He planned most of this. Wrote the Order, the original Pact. It was all his design."

"What do you mean *was?*"

Her lip trembled. She tipped her cup, but there was little solace left in it.

"Victor's dead," she said. "He shot himself at his desk two days ago."

• 33 •

"Victor? Shot himself?" Donald tried to imagine the composed man who had worked across the hall from him doing such a thing. "Why?"

Anna sniffed and slid closer to Donald. She twisted the empty cup in her hands. "We don't know. He was obsessed with that first silo we lost. Obsessed. It broke my heart to see how he blamed himself. He used to say that he could see certain things coming, that there were . . . probabilistic certainties." She said these two words in a mimic of his voice, which brought the old man's face even more vividly to Donald's mind.

"But it killed him not to know the precise when and where." She dabbed her eyes. "He would've been better off if it'd happened on someone else's shift. Not his. Not where he'd feel guilty."

"He blamed me," Donald said, staring at the floor. "It was on my shift. I was such a mess. I couldn't think straight."

"What? No. Donny, no." She rested a hand on his knee. "There's no one to blame."

"But my report—" He still had it in his hand, folded up and dotted here and there with pale blue.

Anna's eyes fell to the piece of paper. "Is that a copy?" She sniffed and reached for it, brushed the loose strands of hair off her face. "Dad had the courage to tell you about this but not about what Vic did." She shook her head. "Victor was strong in some ways, so weak in others." She turned to Donald. "He was found at his desk, surrounded by notes, everything he had on this silo, and your report was on top."

She unfolded the page and studied the words. "Just a copy," she whispered.

"Maybe it was—" Donald began.

"He wrote notes all over his copy." She slid her finger across the page. "Right about here, he wrote *'This is why.'*"

"This is why? As in why he did it?" Donald waved his hand at the room. "Shouldn't *this* be why? Maybe he realized he'd made a mistake." He held Anna's arm. "Think about what we've done. What if we followed a crazy man down here? Maybe Victor had a sudden bout of *sanity*. What if he woke up for a second and saw what we'd done?"

"No." Anna shook her head. "We had to do this."

He slapped the wall behind the cot. "That's what everyone keeps saying."

"Listen to me." She placed a hand on his knee, tried to soothe him. "You need to keep it together, okay?" She glanced toward the door, a fearful look in her eyes. "I asked him to wake you because I need your help. I can't do all of this alone. Vic was working on Silo 18. If it's up to Dad, he'll just terminate the place not to have to deal with it. Victor didn't want that. *I* don't want that."

Donald thought of Silo 12, which he'd terminated. But it was already falling, wasn't it? It was already too late. They had opened the airlock. He looked toward the schematic on the wall and wondered if it was too late for this silo as well. Maybe when they put him down again, maybe he would dream better dreams if this place could be saved. Maybe the pile of bones would have a summit this time.

"What did he see in my report?" he asked.

"I don't know. But he wanted to see you weeks ago. He thought you touched on something."

"Or maybe it was just because I was around at the time."

Donald looked at the room of clues. Anna had been digging, tearing into a different problem. So many questions and answers. His mind was clear, not like last time. He had questions of his own. He wanted to find his sister, find out what happened to Helen, dispel this crazy thought that she was still out there somewhere. He wanted to know more about this damnable place he'd helped build.

"You'll help us?" Anna asked. She rested her hand on his back. Her touch was comforting for a moment, and then he thought of Helen. He startled as if bit, some wild part of him thinking for a moment that he was still married, that she was alive out there, maybe frozen and waiting for him to wake her.

"I need—" He stood and glanced around the room. His eyes fell to the computer on the desk. "I need to look some things up."

Anna rose beside him. She fumbled for his hand. "Of course. I can fill you in with what we know so far. Victor left a series of notes. He wrote all over your report. I can show you. And maybe you can convince Dad that he was onto something, that this silo is worth saving—"

"Yes," Donald said. He would do it. But only so he could stay awake. That was his motivation. And he wondered for a moment if it was Anna's as well. To keep him around.

An hour ago, all he had wanted was to go back to sleep, to escape the world he had helped create. But now he wanted answers. He would look into this silo with its problems, but he would find Helen as well. Find out what'd happened to her, where she was. He thought of Mick, and Tennessee flashed in his mind. He turned toward the wall schematic with all the silos, tried to remember which state went with which number.

"What can we access from here?" he asked. His skin flushed with heat as he thought of the answers at his disposal. Maybe this computer wouldn't be locked down like his last one. No games of solitaire to subdue curious minds.

Anna turned toward the door. There were footsteps out there in the darkness.

"Dad. He's the only one with access to this level anymore."

"Anymore?" He turned back to Anna.

"Yeah. Where do you think Victor got the gun?" She lowered her voice. "I was in here when he came down and cracked open one of the crates. I never heard him. Look, my father blames himself for what happened, and he still doesn't believe this has anything to do with you or your report. But I know Vic. He wasn't crazy. If there's anything you can do, please. For me."

She squeezed his hand. Donald looked down, didn't realize she'd been holding it. The folded report was in her other hand. The footsteps approached. Donald nodded his assent.

"Thank you," she said. She dropped his hand, grabbed his empty cup from the cot, and nested hers with it. The cups and the bottle were tucked into one of the chairs, which slid against the table as Thurman arrived at the door and rapped the jamb with his knuckles.

"Come in," Anna said, brushing loose hair off her face.

Thurman studied the two of them a moment. "Erskine is planning a small ceremony," he said. "Just us. Those of us who know."

Anna nodded. "Of course."

Thurman narrowed his eyes and glanced from his daughter to Donald. Anna seemed to take it as a question.

"He thinks he can help," she said. "We both think it's best for him to work down here with me. At least until we make some progress."

Donald turned to her in shock. Thurman said nothing.

"We'll need another computer," she added. "If you bring one down, I can set it up."

That, Donald liked the sound of.

"And another cot, of course," Anna added with a smile.

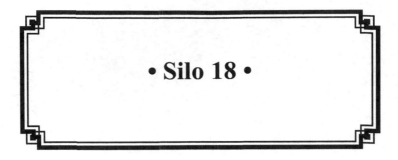

• Silo 18 •

Hush-a-bye baby
in the Up Top
When the wind blows,
the cradle will rock.
When the dust comes,
the cradle will fall.
And down will come baby,
Silo and All.

-Jennifer Plume, age 17

• 34 •

Mission slunk away after the fight with the farmers as the rest of the porters scattered. He stole a few hours of sleep at the upper waystation, his nose numb and lips throbbing from a blow he'd suffered. Tossing and turning, too restless to stay put, he rose in the dim-time and realized it was early yet to go to the Nest. The Crow would still be asleep. And so he headed to the cafeteria for a sunrise and a decent breakfast, the coroner's bonus burning in his pockets the way his knuckles burned from their scrapes.

He nursed his aches with a welcomed hot meal, eating with those coming off a midnight shift, and watched the clouds boil and come to life across the hills. The towering husks in the distance—the Crow called them buildings—were the first to catch the rising sun. It was a sign that the world would wake one more day. His birthday, Mission realized. And he regretted coming up there. He left his dishes on the table, a chit for whoever cleaned after him, and tried not to think of cleaning at all. Instead, he rushed down the eight flights of stairs before the silo fully woke. He headed toward the Nest, feeling not a day older at all.

Familiar words greeted him at the landing of the eighth. There, above the door, rather than a level number it read:

The Crow's Nest

The words were painted in bright and blocky letters. They followed the outlines from years and generations prior, color piled on color, letters crooked and bent from more than one young hand's involvement. Where the paint had gone outside the lines, silo gray had been slapped on top to try and cover it up.

Mission remembered helping with the latest coat. Another would be needed soon. Already, a prior color from another age could be seen through the blues and purples that he and his friends had chosen. And where the blue paint was thin and the color beneath had chipped away, a third layer could be seen beyond. It was like peering into the past. For all he knew, there could be five or six layers hidden beneath. The children of the silo came and went and left their marks with bristles, but the Old Crow remained.

Her nest comprised the nursery, day school, and classrooms that served the Up Top. She had been perched there for longer than any alive could remember. Some said she was as old as the silo itself, but Mission knew that was just a legend. He'd heard it said that the limits to the silo were the limits to life, that no one could ever reach a hundred and fifty in age. This, he believed. His uncle had been one third that when he died. Most people never reached half the levels in age. But the Crow wasn't most people.

He passed beneath the door and reached up to slap the paint as he went. A small hop where terrible leaps were once needed. He remembered employing a ladder before that, spilling a bucket of blue paint, hearing the complaints from Fourteen as it dribbled down. Maybe that's where the idea for the plasticwrap paintbombs had come from. It must've been. Kids playing at the wars their fathers had fought. Screams fading to laughter over time—warlike grunts into giggles—chasing each other with imaginary weapons and kitchen utensils, fighting over who got to be Security and who had to play the bad guys.

Mission remembered how exciting those adventures had felt. Such joyous times now seemed sad as they became truer and truer.

He entered the Nest to find the hallways empty and quiet, the hour early still. There was a soft screech from one classroom as desks were put back into order. Mission caught a glimpse of two teachers conferring in another classroom, their faces scrunched up with worry, probably wondering what to do with a younger version of himself. The scent of strong tea mixed with the odor of paste and chalk. There were rows of metal lockers in dire need of paint and stippled with dents from tiny fists; they transported Mission back to another age. Just yesterday, he was terrorizing that hall. He and all his friends whom he didn't see anymore—not as often as he'd like.

The Crow's room was at the far end adjoining the only apartment on the entire level. The apartment had been built especially for her, converted from a classroom, or so they said. And while she only taught the youngest children anymore, the entire school was hers. This was her nest, her aerie.

Mission remembered coming to her at various stages of his life. Early on, for comfort, feeling so very far from the farms. Later, for wisdom, when he was finally old enough to admit he had none. And more than once he had come for both, like the day he had learned the truth of his birth and his mother's death—that she had been sent to clean because of him. Mission remembered that day well. It was the only time he'd seen the Old Crow cry.

He knocked on her classroom door before entering and found her at the blackboard that'd been lowered so she could write on it from her chair. Mrs. Crowe stopped erasing yesterday's lessons, turned, and beamed at him.

"My boy," she croaked. She smiled and waved with the eraser to beckon him closer, a chalky haze filling the air. "My boy, my boy."

"Hello, Mrs. Crowe." Mission passed through the handful of desks to get to her. The power line for her electric chair drooped from the center of the ceiling to the pole that rose up from the chair's back. Mission ducked beneath it as he got closer and bent to give the Crow a hug. His hands wrapped around her and the chair both, and her smell was one of childhood and innocence. The yellow gown she wore, spotted with flowers, was her Wednesday fare, as good as any calendar. It had faded since Mission's time, as all things had.

"I do believe you've grown," she said, smiling up at him. Her voice was a bare whisper, and he recalled how it kept even the young ones quiet as death so they could hear what was being said. She brought her hand up and touched her own cheek. "What happened to your face?"

Mission laughed and shrugged off his porter's pack. "Just an accident," he said, lying to her like old times. He placed his pack at the foot of one of the tiny desks, could imagine squeezing into the thing and staying for the day's lesson. He noticed only a handful of the chairs were arranged for use. The rest were shoved against the back wall, waiting for the next boom, the next surge in population.

"How've you been?" he asked. He studied her face, the deep wrinkles and dark skin like a farmer's but from age rather than grow lights. Her eyes were rheumy, but there was a life behind them. They reminded Mission of the wallscreens on a bright day but in dire need of a cleaning.

"Not so good," Mrs. Crowe said. She twisted the lever on her armrest, and the chair built for her decades ago by some long-gone former student whirred around to better face him. Pulling back her sleeve, she showed Mission a gauze bandage taped to her thin and splotchy arm. "Those doctors came and took my blood away!" Her hand shook as she indicated the evidence. "Took half of it, by my reckoning."

Mission laughed. "I'm pretty sure they didn't take half your blood, Mrs. Crowe. The doctors are just looking out for you."

She twisted up her face, an explosion of wrinkles like a palm as it closed into a fist. She didn't seem so sure. "I don't trust them," she said.

Mission smiled. "You don't trust anyone. And hey, maybe they're just trying to figure out why you can't die like everyone else does. Maybe they'll come up with a way for everyone to live as long as you some day."

Mrs. Crowe rubbed the bandage on her withering arm. "Or they're sorting out how to *kill* me," she said.

"Oh, don't be so sinister." Mission reached forward and pulled her sleeve down to keep her from messing with the bandage. "Why would you think such a thing?"

She frowned and declined to answer. Her eyes fell to his sagging and mostly empty pack. "Day off?" she asked.

Mission turned and followed her gaze. "Hmm? Oh, no. I dropped off last night. I'll pick up another delivery in a little bit, take it wherever they tell me to."

"Oh, to be so young and free again." Mrs. Crowe spun her chair around and steered it behind her desk. Mission ducked beneath the pivoting wire out of habit; the pole at the back of the chair was made with younger heads in mind. She picked up a container of the vile vegetable pulp she preferred over water and took a sip. "Allie stopped by last week." She set the greenish-black fluid down. "She was asking about you. Wanted to know if you were still single."

"Oh?" Mission could feel his temperature shoot up. Mrs. Crowe had caught them kissing once, back before he knew what kissing was for. She had left them with a warning and a knowing smile. "I saw Jenine yesterday," Mission said, changing the subject, hoping she might take the hint. "Everyone's so spread out."

"As it should be." The Crow opened a drawer on her desk and rummaged around, came out with an envelope. Mission could see a half-dozen names scratched out across the thing. It'd been used a handful of times. "You're heading down from here? Maybe you could drop off something for Rodny?"

She held out the letter. Mission took it, saw his best friend's name written on the outside, all the other names crossed out.

"I can leave it for him, sure. The last two times I stopped by there, they said he was unavailable."

Mrs. Crowe nodded as if this was to be expected. "Ask for Jeffery, he's the head of security down there, one of my boys. You tell him that this is from me and that I said you should hand it to Rodny yourself. In person." She waved her hands in the air, little trembling blurs. "I'll write Jeffery a note."

Mission glanced up at the clock on the wall while she dug into her desk for a pen and ink. Soon, the hallways would begin filling with youthful chatter and the opening and slamming of lockers. He waited patiently while she scratched her note. In the while, he scanned the walls at the old motivators, as Mrs. Crowe like to call the posters and banners she made.

You can be anything, one of them said. It featured a crude drawing of a boy and a girl standing on a huge mound. The mound was green and the sky blue, just like in the picture books. Another one said: *Dream to your heart's delight*. It had bands of color in a graceful sweep. The Crow had a name for the shape, but he'd forgotten what it was called. Another familiar one: *Go new places*. It featured a drawing of a crow perched in an impossibly large tree, it's wings spread as if it were about to take flight.

"Jeffery is the bald one," Mrs. Crowe said. She waved a hand over her own white and thinning hair to demonstrate.

"I know the one," Mission said. It was a strange reminder that so many of the adults and elders throughout the silo had been her students as well. A locker was slammed in the hallway. Mission remembered when he was a kid how the rows and rows of tiny desks had filled the room. There were cubbies full of rolled mats for nap time, reminding him of the daily routine of clearing a space in the middle of the floor, finding his mat, and drifting off to sleep while the Crow sang to them. He missed those days. He missed the Old Time stories about a world full of impossible things. Leaning against that little desk, Mission suddenly felt as ancient as the Crow, just as impossibly distant from his youth.

"Give Jeffery this, and then see that Rodny gets my note. From you personally, okay?"

He grabbed his pack and slid both pieces of correspondence into his courier pouch. There was no mention of payment, just the twinge of guilt Mission felt for even thinking it. Digging into the pack reminded him of the items he had brought her, forgotten due to the previous night's brawl.

"Oh, I brought you these from the farm." He pulled out a few small cucumbers, two peppers, and a large tomato. He placed them on her desk. "For your veggie drinks," he said.

Mrs. Crowe clasped her hands together and smiled with delight.

"Is there anything else you need next time I'm passing by?"

"These visits," she said, her face a wrinkle of smiles. "All I care about are my little ones. Stop by whenever you can, okay?"

Mission squeezed her arm, which felt like a broomstick tucked into a sleeve. "I will," he said. "And that reminds me: Jenine, Frankie, and Steven all told me to tell you hello. And I'm probably forgetting someone."

"Those boys should come more often," she told him, her voice a quiver.

"Not everyone gets around like I do," he said. "I'm sure they'd like to see you more often as well."

"You tell them," she said. "Tell them I don't have much time left—"

Mission laughed and waved off the morbid thought. "You probably told my grandfather the same thing when he was young, and his father before him."

The Crow smiled as if this were true. "Predict the inevitable," she said, "and you're bound to be right one day."

Mission smiled. He liked that. "Still, I wish you wouldn't talk about dying. Nobody likes to hear it."

"They may not like it, but a reminder is good." She held out her arms, the sleeves of her flowered dress falling away and revealing the bandage once more. "Tell me, what do you see when you look at these hands?" She turned them over, back and forth. She studied them as if they belonged to another.

"I see time," Mission blurted out, not sure where the thought came from. He tore his eyes away, suddenly finding her skin to be grotesque. Like shriveled potatoes found deep in the soil long after harvest time. He hated himself for feeling it.

"Time, sure," Mrs. Crowe said. "There's time here aplenty. But there's remnants, too. I remember things being better, once. You think on the bad to remind yourself of the good."

She studied her hands a moment longer as if looking for something else. When she lifted her gaze and peered at Mission, her eyes were shining with sadness. Mission could feel his own eyes watering, partly from discomfort, partly due to the somber pall that had been cast like a cold and wet blanket over the conversation. It reminded him that today was his birthday, a thought that tightened his neck and emptied his chest. He was sure the Crow knew what day it was. She just loved him enough not to say.

"I was beautiful, once, you know." Mrs. Crowe withdrew her hands and folded them in her lap. "Once that's gone, once it leaves us for good, no one will ever see it again."

Mission felt a powerful urge to soothe her, to tell Mrs. Crowe that she was still beautiful in plenty of ways. She could still make music. Could paint. Few others remembered how. She could make children feel loved and safe, another bit of magic long forgotten.

"When I was your age," the Crow said, smiling, "I could have any boy I wanted."

She laughed, dispelling the tension and casting away the shadows that had fallen over their talk, but Mission believed her. He believed her even though he couldn't picture it, couldn't imagine away the wrinkles and the spots and the long strands of hair on her knuckles. Still, he believed her. He always did.

"The world is a lot like me, you know." She lifted her gaze toward the ceiling and perhaps beyond. "The world was beautiful once, too."

Mission sensed an Old Time story brewing like a storm of clouds. More lockers were slammed in the hallway, little voices gathering.

"Tell me," Mission said, remembering the hours that had passed like eyeblinks at her feet, the songs she sang while children slept. "Tell me about the old world."

The Old Crow's eyes narrowed and settled on a dark corner of the room. A deep breath rattled in her once-proud chest. Her lips, furrowed with the wrinkles of time, parted, and a story began, a story Mission had heard a thousand times before. But it never got old, visiting this land of the Crow's imagination. And as the little ones skipped into the room, they too fell silent and gathered around. They slipped into their tiny desks and followed along with the widest of eyes and the most open of unknowing minds these tales of a world, once beautiful, and now fairly forgotten.

· 35 ·

The stories Mrs. Crowe made up were straight from the children's books. There were blue skies and lands of green, white clouds and rainbows, animals like dogs and cats but bigger than people. Juvenile stuff. And yet, these fantastic tales of a better place somewhere impossibly distant left Mission feeling angry at the world he was stuck with. He thought this as he left the Up Top behind and wound his way past the farms and the levels of his youth. The promise of an *elsewhere* highlighted the flaws of the familiar. He had gone off to be a porter, to fly away and be all that he wished, and what he wished was to be further away than this world would allow.

These were dangerous thoughts. They reminded him of his mother and where she had been sent seventeen years ago to the day.

Past the farms, Mission noted something burning further down the silo. The air was hazy, and there was the bitter tinge of smoke on the back of his tongue. A trash pile, maybe. Someone who didn't want to pay the fee to have it ported to recycling. Or someone who didn't think the silo would be around long enough to *need* to recycle.

It could be an accident, of course. It could be a legitimate danger. But that's not where Mission's mind went. Nobody thought that way anymore. He could see it on the faces of those on the stairwell. He could see by the way belongings were clutched, children sheltered, that the future of everything was in doubt. There hadn't been nearly as much new graffiti lately. Even the delinquents had begun to wonder: *What's the point?*

Mission adjusted his light pack and hurried down to the IT levels. He remembered his father's talk of restoring the silo after the last outbreak of violence. There were physical things to patch, like the stairwell, but the population, too. Physical explosions led to population explosions. Record numbers of lottery winners followed the fighting. His father spoke of so many bodies to dispose of that the airlock had been employed, the great flames cremating the dead by the score, their ashes set loose to blur the view. It made clear the link between life and death, that each birth was owed to another's passing. The difference with Mission was that he *knew* who that other person was.

He reached IT and pushed his way through a crowd on landing thirty-four. It was mostly boys his age or a little older, many that he recognized, a lot from the mids. Several who didn't match this profile stood with computers tucked under their arms, wires dangling, jostling with the rest. Mission picked his way through the throng. A computer was dropped, which led to shouting and shoving. Inside, he found a barrier had been set up just beyond the door. Two men from Security manned the temporary gate and allowed only crumpled IT workers through.

"Delivery," Mission shouted. He worked his way to the front, carefully extracting the note Mrs. Crowe had written. "Delivery for Officer Jeffery."

One of the security men took the note. Mission was pressed against the barrier by those behind. A woman who belonged was waved through. She hurried toward the proper security gate leading into the main hall, smoothing her coveralls with obvious relief. There were crowds of young men being given instructions in one corner of the wide hall. They stood at attention in neat rank and file, but their eyes were wide as the stairwell.

"What the hell is going on?" Mission asked, as the barrier was parted for him.

"What the hell isn't?" one of the security guards rejoined. "Power spike last night took out a load of computers. Every one of our techs is pulling a double. There's a fire down in Mechanical or something, and some kinda violence up in the farms. Did you get the wire?"

Mechanical. That was a long way away to nose a fire. And word was out about last night's raid, making him self-conscious of the cut on his nose. "What wire?" he asked.

The security guard pointed to the groups of boys. "We're hiring. New techs."

All Mission saw were young men, and the guy talking to them was with Security, not IT. The security guard handed back the note to Mission and pointed toward the main security gate. The woman from earlier was already beeping her way through, a large and familiar bald head swiveling to watch her ass as she headed down the hall.

"Thanks," Mission said to the guard, hurrying away from the crush of people. "Sir?" he called out as he approached the gate.

Jeffery turned his head, the deep wrinkles and folds of flesh disappearing from his neck.

"Hmm? Oh—" he snapped his fingers, trying to place the name.

"Mission."

He wagged his finger. "That's right. You need to leave something with me, porter?" He held out a palm but seemed disinterested.

Mission handed him the note. "Actually, I have orders from Mrs. Crowe to deliver it in person." He pulled the sealed envelope with the crossed-out names from his courier pouch. "Just a letter, sir."

The old guard glanced at the envelope, then continued reading the note addressed to him. "Rodny isn't available." He shook his head. "I can't give you a timeframe, either. Could be weeks. You wanna leave it with me?"

Again, an outstretched palm; this time with more interest. Mission pulled the envelope back warily. "I can't. There's no way I can just hand it to him? This is the Crow, man. If it were the Mayor asking me, I'd say no problem."

Jeffery smiled. "You were one of her boys, too?"

Mission nodded. The head of Security looked past him at a man approaching the gate with his ID out. Mission stepped aside as the gentleman scanned his way through, nodding good morning to Jeffery.

"Tell you what. I'm taking Rodny his lunch in a little bit. When I do, you can come with me, hand him the letter with me standing there, and I won't have to worry about the Crow nipping my hide later. How's that sound?"

Mission smiled. "Sounds good, man. I appreciate it."

The officer pointed across the noisy entrance hall. "Why don't you go grab yourself some water and hang in the conference room. There's some boys in there filling out paperwork." Jeffery looked Mission up and down. "In fact, why don't you fill out an application? We could use you."

"I . . . uh, don't know much about computers," Mission said.

Jeffery shrugged as if that were irrelevant. "Suit yourself. One of the boys will be relieving me in a little bit. I'll come get you."

Mission thanked him again. He crossed the large entrance hall where neat columns and rows of young men listened to barked instructions. Another guard waved him inside the conference room while holding out a sheet of paper and a shard of charcoal. Mission saw that the back of the paper was blank and took it with no plan for filling it out. Half a chit right there in usable paper.

There were a few empty chairs around the wide table. He chose one. A number of boys scribbled with their charcoals on the pages, faces scrunched up in concentration. Mission sat with his back to the only window and placed his sack on the wide table, kept the letter in his hands. The application he slid inside his pack for future use. He studied for the first time the Crow's letter.

The envelope was old but addressed only a handful of times. One edge was worn tissue thin, a small tear revealing a folded piece of paper inside. Peering closer, Mission saw that it was pulp paper, probably made in the Crow's Nest by one of her kids, water and handfuls of torn paper blended up and pressed down on screens and left overnight to dry. Bits of thread and various colors could be seen in there, and just the hint of writing.

"Mission," someone at the table hissed.

He looked up to see Bradley sitting across from him. The fellow porter had his blue 'chief tied around his bicep. Mission had thought he was running a regular route in the Down Deep.

"You applying?" Bradley hissed.

One of the other boys coughed into his fist like he was asking for quiet. It looked like Bradley was already done with his application.

Mission shook his head. There was a knock on the window behind him, and he nearly dropped the letter as he whirled around. Jeffery stuck his head in the door. "Two minutes," he said to Mission, ignoring the other lads. He jabbed his thumb over his shoulder. "I'm just waiting on his tray."

Mission bobbed his head as the door was pulled shut. The other boys looked at him curiously.

"Delivery," Mission explained to Bradley loud enough for the others to hear. He pulled his pack closer and hid the envelope behind it. The boys went back to their scribbling. Bradley frowned and watched the others.

Mission studied the envelope again. Two minutes. How long would he have with Rodny? He tickled the corner of the sealed flap. The milk paste the Crow had used didn't stick very well to the months-old—maybe years-old—dried glue from before. He worked one corner loose without glancing down at the envelope. Instead, he watched Bradley as he disobeyed the third cardinal rule of porting, telling himself this was different, that this was two old friends talking and he was just in the room with them. Just friends talking as he peeled the flap away.

Even so, his hands trembled as he pulled the letter out. He glanced down, keeping the note hidden. Purple and red string lay strewn in with the dark gray of cheap paper. Kid paper. The writing was in chalk. It meant the words had to be big. White powder gathered in the folds as it shivered loose from the words like dust falling from old pipes:

> *Soon, soon, the momma bird sings.*
> *Take flight, take flight!*

Part of an old nursery rhyme. *Beat your wings,* Mission whispered, remembering the rest, a story about a young crow learning to be free. *Beat your wings and fly away to brighter things. Fly, fly with all your might!* He started to check the back for a real note, something beyond this fragment of a rhyme, when someone banged on the window again. Several of the other boys dropped their charcoals and visibly startled. One boy cursed under his breath. Mission whirled around to see Jeffery on the other side of the glass, a covered meal tray balanced on one palm, his bald head jerking impatiently.

Mission folded the letter up and stuffed it back in the envelope. He raised his hand over his head to let Jeffery know he'd be right there, licked one finger and ran it across the sticky paste, re-sealing the envelope as best he could. "Good luck," he told Bradley, even though he had no clue what the kid thought he was doing. He dragged his pack off the table, was careful to wipe away the chalk dust that had spilled, and hurried out of the conference room.

"Let's go," Jeffery said, clearly annoyed.

Mission hurried after him. He glanced back once at the window, then over at the noisy crowd jostling against the temporary barriers by the door. An IT tech approached the crowd with a computer, wires coiled neatly on top, and a woman reached out desperate arms from behind the barrier like a mother yearning for her baby.

"Since when did people start bringing their own computers up?" he asked, curious as a seasoned porter about how things got from there to here and back again. It felt as though he were witnessing yet another loop his kind was being sliced out of. Roker would have a fit.

"Yesterday. Mr. Wyck stopped sending our techs out. He says it's safer this way. People being robbed out there and not enough security to go around."

Jeffery was waved through the gates, Mission as well. They wound in silence through the hallways, every office full of clacking sounds or people arguing. Mission saw electrical parts and paper strewn everywhere. He wondered which office was Rodny's and why nobody else was having their food delivered. Maybe his friend was in trouble. That was it. Made sense of everything. Maybe he had pulled one of his stunts. Did they have a holding cell on thirty-four? He didn't think so. He was about to ask Jeffery if Rodny was in the pen when the old security guard stopped at an imposing steel door.

"Here." He held the tray out to Mission, who stuck the letter between his lips and accepted it. Jeffery glanced back, blocked Mission's view of a keypad with his body, and tapped in a code. A series of clunks sounded in the jamb of the heavy door. Fucking right, Rodny was in trouble. What kind of pen was this?

The door swung inward. Jeffery grabbed the tray and told Mission to wait there. Mission still had the taste of milk paste on his lips as he watched the security chief step inside a room that seemed to go back quite a ways. The lights inside pulsed as if something was wrong, red warning lights like a fire alarm. Jeffery called out for Rodny while Mission tried to peek around the guard for a better look.

Rodny arrived a moment later, almost as if expecting them. His eyes widened when he saw Mission standing there. Mission fought to close his own mouth, which he could feel hanging open at the sight of his friend.

"Hey." Rodny opened the heavy door a little further and glanced down the hallway. "What're you doing here?"

"Good to see you, too," Mission said. He held out the letter. "The Crow sent this."

"Ah, official business." Rodny smiled. "You're here as a porter, eh? Not a friend?"

Rodny smiled, but Mission could see that his friend was beat. He looked like he hadn't slept for days. His hair had been chopped short as if to keep it out of the way, but there was the shadow of a beard on his chin. Mission glanced into the room, wondering what they had him doing in there. Tall black metal cabinets were all he could see. They stretched out of sight, neatly spaced.

"You learning to fix refrigerators?" Mission asked.

Rodny glanced over his shoulder. He laughed. "Those are computers." He still had that tone like one who thought himself older or better. Mission nearly reminded his friend that today was his birthday, that they were the same age. Rodny was the only one he ever felt like reminding. Jeffery cleared his throat impatiently, seemed annoyed by the chatter.

Rodny turned to the security chief. "You mind if we have a few seconds?" he asked.

Jeffery shifted his weight, the stiff leather of his boots squeaking. "You know I can't," he said. "I'll probably get chewed out for allowing even this."

"You're right." Rodny shook his head like he shouldn't have asked. Mission studied the exchange. He sensed that his friend was the same one he'd ever known. He was in trouble for something, probably being forced to do the most reviled task in all of IT for a brash thing he'd said or done. He smiled at the thought.

Rodny tensed suddenly as though he'd heard something deep inside the room. He held up a finger to the others and asked them to wait there. "Just a second," he said, rushing off, bare feet slapping on the steel floors.

Jeffery crossed his arms and looked Mission up and down unhappily. "You two grow up down the hall from each other?"

"Went to school together," Mission said. "So what did Rod do? You know, Mrs. Crowe used to make us sweep the entire Nest and clean the blackboards if we cut up in class. We did our fair share of sweeping, the two of us."

Jeffery appraised him for a moment. And then his expressionless face shattered into tooth and grin. "You think your friend is in trouble," he said. He seemed on the verge of laughing. "Son, you have no idea."

Before Mission could inquire, Rodny returned, smiling and breathless.

"Sorry," he said to Jeffery. "I had to get that." He turned to Mission. "Thanks for coming by, man. Good to see you."

That was it?

"Good to see you, too," Mission sputtered, surprised that their visit would be so brief. "Hey, don't be a stranger." He went to give his old friend a hug, but Rodny stuck out a hand instead. Mission looked at it for a pause, confused, wondering if they'd grown apart so far so fast.

"Give my best to everyone," Rodny said, as if he might never see them again himself.

Jeffery cleared his throat, clearly annoyed and ready to go.

"I will," Mission said, fighting to keep the sadness out of his voice. He accepted his friend's hand. They shook like strangers, the smile on Rodny's face quivering, the folds of the note hidden in his palm digging sharply into Mission's hand.

· 36 ·

It was a miracle Mission didn't drop the note as it was passed to him, a miracle that he knew something was amiss, to keep his mouth closed, to not stand there a fool in front of Jeffery and say, "Hey, what's this?" Instead, he kept the wad of paper balled in his fist as he was escorted back toward the security station. They were nearly there when someone called "Porter!" from one of the offices they passed.

Jeffery placed a hand on Mission's chest, forcing him to a stop. They turned, and a familiar man strode down the hallway to meet them. It was Mr. Wyck, Head of IT, familiar to most porters. The endless shuffle of broken and repaired computers once kept the Upper Dispatch as busy as Supply kept the lower. Mission gathered that may have changed since yesterday.

"You on duty, son?" Mr. Wyck studied the porter's 'chief knotted around Mission's neck.

"Yessir." Mission hid the note from Rodny behind his back. He pressed it into his pocket with his thumb, like a seed going to soil. "You need something moved, sir?"

"I do." Mr. Wyck studied him for a moment. "You're the Jones boy, right? The zero."

Mission felt a flash of heat around his neck at the use of the term, a reference to the fact that no lottery number had been pulled for him. "Yessir. It's Mission." He offered his hand. Mr. Wyck accepted it.

"Yes, yes. I went to school with your father. And your mother, of course."

He paused to give Mission time to respond. Mission ground his teeth together and said nothing. He let go of the man's hand before his sweaty palms had a chance to speak for him.

"Say I wanted to move something without going through Dispatch." Mr. Wyck smiled. "And say I wanted to avoid the sort of nastiness that took place last night a few levels up from here."

Mission glanced over at Jeffery, who seemed disinterested in the conversation. It was strange to hear this sort of offer from a man of authority in front of a member of Security, but there was one thing Mission had discovered since he emerged from his shadowing days: things only got darker.

"I don't follow," Mission said. He fought the urge to turn and see how far they were from the security gate. A woman emerged from an office down the hall, behind Mr. Wyck. Jeffery made a gesture with his hand, and she stopped and kept her distance, out of earshot.

"I think you do, and I admire your discretion," Mr. Wyck said. "Two hundred chits to move a package a half dozen levels from Supply."

Mission tried to remain calm. Two hundred chits. A month's pay for half a day's work. But he feared this was some sort of test. Maybe Rodny had gotten in trouble for flunking a similar one.

"I don't know—" he said.

"It's an open invite," Wyck said. "The next porter that comes through will get the same offer. I don't care who does it, but the first will get the chits. You don't have to answer me. Just show up and ask for Joyce at the Supply counter. Tell her you're doing a job for Wyck. There'll be a delivery report detailing the rest."

"I'll think about it, sir."

"Good." Mr. Wyck smiled.

"Anything else?"

"No, no. You're free to go." He nodded to Jeffery, who snapped back from wherever he'd checked out to.

"Thank you, sir." Mission turned and followed the chief.

"Oh, and happy birthday, son," Mr. Wyck called out.

Mission glanced back, didn't say thanks, just hurried after Jeffery and through the security gate, past the crowds and out on the landing, down two turns of stairs, where he finally reached into his pocket for the note from Rodny. Paranoid he might drop it and watch it bounce off the stairs and through the rail, he gingerly and methodically unfolded the scrap of paper. It looked like the same rag blend Mrs. Crowe's note had been written on, the same threads of purple and red mixed in with the rough gray weave. For a moment, Mission feared the note would be addressed to the Crow rather than to him, maybe more lines in old nursery rhymes. He worked the piece of paper flat, one side blank, turned it over to read the other.

It wasn't addressed to anyone. Just two words, and Mission remembered the way his friend's smile had quivered while they shook hands.

Mission felt suddenly alone. There was the smell of something burning lingering in the stairwell, a tinge of smoke that mixed with the paint from drying graffiti. He took the small note and tore it into ever smaller pieces. He kept tearing until there was nothing left to pinch with his fingers, nothing left to shred. He waited until a passing man spiraled out of sight and then sprinkled the dull confetti over the rail to drift down and disappear into the void.

The evidence was gone, but the message lingered vividly in his mind. The hasty scrawl, the shadowy scratch the edge of a coin or a spoon made as it was dragged across paper, two words barely legible from his friend who never needed anybody or asked for anything:

Help me.

And that was all.

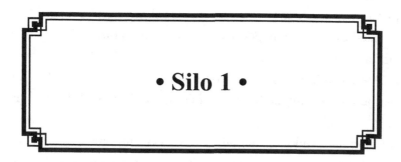

• Silo 1 •

Time is too slow for those who wait,
too swift for those who fear,
too long for those who grieve,
too short for those who rejoice,
but for those who love, time is eternity.

-Henry Van Dyke

•37•

Finding the right silo was easy enough. Donald could look at the old schematic and remember standing on those hills, peering down into the wide bowls that held each facility. The sound of grumbling four-wheelers came back, the plumes of dust kicked up as they bounced across the ridges where the grass had not yet filled in. He remembered that they had been growing grass over those hills, straw and seed spread everywhere, a bit of an illusion, a task hindsight made both pointless and sad.

Standing on that ridge in his memory, he was able to picture the Tennessee delegation. It would be Silo 2. Once he had this, he dug deeper. It took a bit of fumbling to remember how the computer program worked, how to sift through lives that lived in databases. There was an entire history there of each silo if you knew how to read it, all those souls trapped in little cells, but the history only went so far. It went back to made-up names, back to the orientation. It didn't stretch to the Legacy beyond. The old world was hidden behind bombs and a fog of mist and forgetting.

He had the right silo, but locating Helen might prove impossible. He worked frantically while Anna sang in the shower.

She had left the bathroom door open, steam and her melodic humming both billowing out. Donald ignored what he took to be an invitation. He ignored the throbbing, the yearning, the hormonal rush of being near an ex-lover after centuries of need. He searched instead for his wife.

There were four thousand names in that first generation of Silo 2. Four thousand, exactly. Roughly half were female. There were three Helens. Each had a grainy picture taken for her work ID stored on the servers. None of the Helens matched what he remembered his wife looking like, what he *thought* she looked like. Tears came unbidden. He wiped them away, furious at himself. From the shower, Anna sang a sad lament from long ago while Donald flipped through random photos. After a dozen, the faces of strangers began to meld together and threaten to erode the Helen in his memory. He went back to searching by name. Surely he could guess the name she would've chosen. He had picked Troy for himself those many years ago, a clue leading him back to her. He liked to think she would've done the same.

He tried Sandra, her mother's name, but neither of the two hits were right. He tried Danielle, her sister's name. One hit. Not her.

She wouldn't come up with something random, would she? They had talked once of what they might name their kids. It was gods and goddesses, a joke at first, but Helen had fallen in love with the name Athena. He did a search. Zero hits in that first generation.

The pipes squealed as Anna turned off the shower. Her singing subsided back into a hum, a song of sadness and grief, a hymn for the funeral they were about to attend. Donald tried a few more names, anxious to discover something, anything. He would search every night while the silo slept if he had to. He would search while he pretended to work on this problem with the silos. He wouldn't sleep until he knew, until he found her.

"Do you need to shower before the service?" Anna called out from the bathroom.

He didn't want to go to the service, he nearly said. He knew Victor as someone to fear, a boss sitting across the hallway, always watching, dispensing drugs, manipulating him. At least, that's how the paranoia of those days made it all seem.

"I'll go like this," he said. He still wore the beige coveralls they'd given him the day before. He flipped through random pictures again, starting at the top of the alphabet. What other name? The fear was that he'd forget what she looked like. Or that she'd look more and more like Anna in his mind. He couldn't let that happen.

"Find anything?"

She snuck up behind him and reached for something on the desk. A towel was wrapped around her breasts and reached the middle of her thighs. Her skin was wet. She grabbed a hairbrush and walked, humming, back to the bathroom. Donald forgot to answer. His body responded to Anna in a way that made him furious and full of guilt. The monitor fogged from the steam. He felt clammy from something else.

He was still married, he reminded himself. He would be until he knew what'd happened to Helen. He would be loyal to her forever.

Loyalty.

On a whim, he searched for the name Karma.

One hit. Donald sat up straight. His palms felt damp. He hadn't imagined a hit. It was their dog's name, the nearest thing he and Helen ever had to a child of their own. He brought up the picture.

"I guess we're all wearing these horrid outfits to the funeral, right?" Anna passed the desk as she snapped up the front of her white coveralls. Donald only noticed in the corner of his tear-filled vision. He covered his mouth and felt his body tremble with suppressed sobs. On the monitor, in a tiny square of black and white pixels in the middle of a work badge, was his wife.

"You'll be ready to go in a few minutes, won't you?"

Anna disappeared back into the bathroom, brushing her hair. Donald wiped his cheeks, salt on his lips while he read. Anna's humming made it nearly impossible.

Karma Brewer. There were several occupations listed, with a badge photo for each. Teacher, School Master, Judge—more wrinkles in each picture but always the same half-smile. He opened the full file, thinking suddenly what it would've been like to have been on the very first shift in Silo 1, to watch her life unfold next door, maybe even reach out and contact her somehow. A judge. It'd been a dream of hers to be a judge one day. Donald wept while Anna hummed. Through a lens of tears, he read about his wife.

Married, it said, which didn't throw up any flags at first. Married, of course. To him. Until he read about her death. Eighty-two years old. Survived by Rick Brewer and two children, Athena and Mars.

Rick Brewer.

The walls and ceiling bulged inward. Donald felt a chill, the cold of the pod and the deep sleep returning to his veins. There were more pictures. He followed the links to other files. To this husband's files.

"Mick," Anna whispered behind him.

Donald startled and turned to find her reading over his shoulder. Drying tears streaked his face, but he didn't care. His best friend and his wife. Two kids. He turned back to the screen and pulled up the daughter's file. Athena's. There were several pictures from different careers and phases of her life. She had Helen's mouth.

"Donny. Please don't."

A hand on his shoulder. Donald flinched from it and watched an animation wrought by furious clicks, this child growing into an approximation of his wife, until the girl's own children appeared in her file.

"Donny," Anna whispered. "We're gonna be late for the funeral."

Donald wept. Sobs tore through him as if he were made of tissue. "Late," he cried. "A hundred years too late." He sputtered this last, overcome with misery. There was a granddaughter on the screen that was not his, a great granddaughter one more click away. They stared out at him, all of them, none with eyes like his own.

D onald went to Victor's funeral numb. He rode the elevator in silence, watched his boots kick ahead of himself as he teetered forward, but what he found on the medical level wasn't a funeral at all—it was body disposal. It was them storing the remains back in a pod because they had no dirt in which to bury their dead. Their food came from cans. Their bodies returned to the same.

Donald was introduced to Erskine, who explained unprompted that the body would not rot. The same invisible machines that allowed them to survive the freezing process and turned their waking piss the color of charcoal would keep the dead as soft and fresh as the living. Donald heard all of this. He watched as the man he had known as Victor was prepped for deep freeze. As a reflex, he looked for something on a clipboard to sign, some nominal gesture that he was in charge, that anyone there was in charge.

They wheeled the body down a hall and through a sea of pods. The deep freeze was a cemetery, Donald saw. A grid of bodies laid flat, only a name to feebly encapsulate all that lay within. He wondered how many of the pods contained the dead. Some men must die on their shifts from natural causes. Some must break down as Victor had. They weren't immortal, he and these people, they were simply skipping through time. And some of those skipping undoubtedly stumbled and fell.

Donald helped with the physical task of moving the body into the pod. There were only four of them present, only four who could know how Victor had gone. The illusion that someone was in charge must be maintained. Donald thought of his last job, sitting at a desk, hands on a rudderless wheel, pretending. He watched Thurman as the old man kissed his palm and pressed his fingers to Victor's cheek. The lid was closed. The cold of the room made their exhalations visible, a funeral on a crisp fall day.

The others took turns speaking, but it was Helen's funeral that Donald attended. He did not cry. He had sobbed on the elevator, Anna holding him. Now, it was only the shock and the long years between. He did the math. Helen had died almost a century ago. It had been longer than that since he'd lost her over that hill, since missing her messages, since not being able to get through to her. He remembered the national anthem and the bombs filling the air. He remembered his sister being there.

His sister.

It was more than a century since those bombs had gone off, but that girl who had sung the national anthem would be stored in one of these cavernous rooms. Donald's sister would be there as well. Family. There was a fierce urge to find her and wake her, to bring someone he loved back to life. He wanted to hold a loved one while the last of the cold thawed from their veins.

Dr. Erskine paid his final respects. Only four of them present to mourn this man who had killed billions. Donald felt Anna's presence beside him and wondered if maybe the lack of a crowd was in fact due to her. Here were the four who knew not only that a man had taken his life, but that a woman had been woken. Her father knew, Dr. Henson, who had performed the procedure, Erskine, whom she spoke of as a friend, and himself.

The absurdity of Donald's existence, of the state of the world, swooped down on him in that gathering. He did not belong. He was only there because of a girl he had dated in college, a girl whose father was a senator, whose affections had likely gotten him elected, who had dragged him into a murderous scheme, and had now pulled him from a frozen death. All the great coincidences and marvelous achievements of his life disappeared in a flash. In their place were puppet strings. He was a pawn being shoved around a board while marveling at his great adventure. There was no coincidence at all, nothing to be amazed by, just dangerous affections.

"A tragic loss, this."

Donald emerged from his ruminations to discover that the ceremony was over. Anna and her father stood two rows of pods away discussing something. Dr. Henson was down by the base of the pod, the panel beeping as he made adjustments. That left Donald with Dr. Erskine, a thin man with glasses and a British accent. He surveyed Donald from the opposite side of the pod. Donald had been introduced to him earlier as he stepped off the elevator, but he'd been in a mournful haze.

"He was on my shift," Donald said inanely, trying to explain why he was present for the service. There was little else he could think to say of this man whom he had known as Victor. He stepped closer and peered through the little window at the calm face within.

"I know," Erskine said. This wiry man, probably in his early to mid sixties, adjusted the glasses on his narrow nose and joined Donald in peering through the small window. "He was quite fond of you, you know."

"I didn't," Donald blurted out, unable to censor himself. "I mean . . . he never said as much to me."

"He was peculiar that way." Erskine studied the deceased with a smile. "Brilliant perhaps for knowing the minds of others, just not so keen on communicating with them."

Donald studied this Dr. Erskine. He tried to remember what little Anna had told him about the man. "Did you know him from before?" he asked. He wasn't sure how else to broach the subject. The *before* seemed taboo with some, freely spoken of by others.

Erskine nodded. "We worked together. Well, in the same hospital. We orbited each other for quite a few years until my . . . discovery." He reached out and touched the glass, a final farewell to an old friend, it seemed.

"What discovery?" He vaguely remembered Anna mentioning something.

Erskine glanced up. Looking closer, Donald thought he may have been in his seventies. It was hard to tell. He had some of the agelessness of Thurman, like an antique that patinas and will grow no older.

"I'm the one who discovered the great threat," he said. It sounded more an admission of guilt than a proud claim. It was said with sadness. At the base of the pod, Dr. Henson finished his adjustments, stood, and excused himself. He steered the empty gurney toward the exit.

"The nanos." Donald remembered; Anna had said as much. He watched Thurman debate something with his daughter, his fist coming down over and over into his palm, and a question came to mind. He wanted to hear it from someone else. He wanted to see if the lies matched, if that meant they might be the truth.

"You were a medical doctor?" he asked.

Erskine considered the question. It seemed a simple enough one to answer.

"Not precisely," he said, his accent thick. "I *built* medical doctors. Wee ones." He pinched the air and squinted through his glasses at his own fingers. "We were working on ways to keep soldiers safe. Until I found someone else's handiwork in a sample of blood. It wasn't long before I was finding the little bastards everywhere."

Anna and Thurman headed their way, Anna with her cap donned once more, her hair in a bun that bulged noticeably through the top. It was little disguise for what she was, useful perhaps at a distance.

"I'd like to ask you about that sometime," Donald said hurriedly. "It might help my . . . help me with this problem the silos are having."

"Of course," Erskine said. His accent made him sound cheerier than he appeared.

"I need to get back," Anna told Donald. She set her lips in a thin grimace, like a scar on her face, a wound from the argument with her father, and Donald finally appreciated how powerless and trapped she truly was. He imagined a year spent in that warehouse of war, clues scattered across that planning table, sleeping on that small cot, not able even to ride up to the cafeteria to see the hills and the dark clouds or have a meal at the time of her own choosing, relying on others to bring her everything.

"I'll escort the young man up," Donald heard Erskine say, his hand resting on Donald's shoulder. "I'd like to chat with our boy for a bit."

Thurman narrowed his eyes but relented. Anna squeezed Donald's hand a final time, glanced at the humming pod, and headed toward the exit. Her father followed a few quiet paces behind.

"Come with me." Erskine's breath fogged the air. "I want to show you someone."

They left the cooling pod, and now it was just one of many. Identical. There were no flowers to mark what had happened, no mound of moist soil standing out like a brown scab on green grass. There was simply a lid closed on a life, no different from so many others. And a name. A made-up and pointless name.

• 39 •

Erskine picked his way through the grid of pods with purpose as though he'd walked the route dozens of times. Donald followed after, rubbing his arms for warmth. He had been too long in that crypt-like place. The cold was leeching back into his flesh.

"Thurman keeps saying we were already dead," he told Erskine, attacking the question head-on. "Is that true?"

Erskine looked back over his shoulder. He waited for Donald to catch up, seemed to consider this question.

"Well," Donald asked. "Were we?"

"I never saw a design with a hundred percent efficiency," Erskine said. "We weren't there with our own work, and theirs was much cruder. But what they had already would've taken out most. That part's true enough." He resumed his walk through the field of sleeping corpses. "Even the most severe epidemics burn themselves out," he said, "so it's difficult to say. I argued for countermeasures. Victor argued for this." He spread his arms over the quiet assembly.

"And Victor won."

"Indeed."

"Do you think he . . . had second thoughts? Is that why . . . ?"

Erskine stopped at one of the pods and placed both hands on its icy surface. "I'm sure we all have second thoughts," he said sadly. "But I don't think Vic ever doubted the rightness of this mission. I don't know why he did what he did in the end. It wasn't like him."

Donald peered inside the pod Erskine had led him to. There was a middle-aged woman inside, her eyelids covered in frost.

"My daughter," Erskine said. "My only child."

There was a moment of silence. It allowed the faint hum of a thousand pods to be heard. It could've been a choir of monks making that sound, a quiet hum on so many closed lips.

"When Thurman made the decision to wake his Anna, all I could dream about was doing the same. But why? There was no reason, no need for her expertise. Caroline was an accountant. And besides, it wouldn't be fair to drag her from her dreams."

Donald wanted to ask if it would ever be fair. What world did Erskine expect his daughter to ever see again? When would she wake to a normal life? A pleasant life?

"When I found nanos in her blood, I knew this was the right thing to do." He turned to Donald. "I know you're looking for answers, son. We all are. This is a cruel world. It's always been a cruel world. I spent my whole life looking for ways to make it better, to patch things up, dreaming of an ideal. But for every sot like me, there's ten more out there getting their jollies trying to tear things down. And it only takes one of them to get lucky."

Donald flashed back to the day Thurman had given him The Order. That thick book was the start of his plummet into madness. He remembered their talk in that massive lozenge of a medical unit, the feeling of being infected, the paranoia that something harmful and invisible was invading him. But if Erskine and Thurman were telling the truth, he'd been infected long before that.

"You weren't poisoning me that day." He looked from the pod to Erskine, piecing something together. "The interview with Thurman, the weeks and weeks he spent in that chamber having all of those meetings. You weren't infecting us."

Erskine nodded ever so slightly. "We were healing you," he said.

Donald felt a sudden flash of anger. "Then why not heal *everyone?*" he demanded.

"We discussed that. I had the same thought. To me, it was an engineering problem. I wanted to build countermeasures, machines to kill machines before they got to us. Thurman had similar ideas. He saw it as an invisible war, one we desperately needed to take to the enemy. We all saw the battles we were accustomed to fighting, you see. Me in the bloodstream, Thurman overseas. It was Victor who set the two of us straight."

Erskine pulled a cloth from his breast pocket and removed his glasses. He rubbed them while he talked, his voice echoing in whispers from the walls. "Victor said there would be no end to it. He pointed to computer viruses to make his case, how one might run rampant and cripple hundreds of millions of machines. Sooner or later, some nano attack would get through, get out of control, and there would be an epidemic built on bits of code rather than strands of DNA."

"So what?" Donald asked. "We've dealt with plagues before. Why would this be different?" He swept his arms at the pods. "Tell me how the solution isn't worse than the problem?"

As worked up as he felt, he also sensed how much angrier he would be if he heard this from Thurman. He wondered if he'd been set up to have a kindlier man, a stranger, take him aside and tell him what Thurman thought he needed to hear. It was hard not to be paranoid about being manipulated, to not feel the strings still knotted to his joints.

"Psychology," Erskine replied. He put his glasses back on. "This is where Victor set us straight, why our ideas would never work. I'll never forget the conversation. We were sitting in the cafeteria at Walter Reed. Thurman was there to hand out ribbons, but really to meet with the two of us." He shook his head. "It was crowded in there. If anyone knew the things we were discussing . . ."

"Psychology," Donald reminded him. "Tell me how this is better. *More* people die this way."

Erskine snapped back to the present. "That's where we were wrong, just like you. Imagine the first discovery that one of these epidemics was man-made—the panic, the violence that would ensue. That's where the end would come. A typhoon kills a few hundred people, does a few billion in damage, and what do we do?" Erskine interlocked his fingers. "We come together. We put the pieces back. But a terrorist's bomb." He frowned. "A terrorist's bomb does the same damage, and it throws the world into turmoil."

He spread his hands apart like an explosion going off.

"When there's only God to blame, we forgive him. When it's our fellow man, we must destroy him."

Donald shook his head. He didn't know what to believe. But then he thought about the fear and rage he'd felt when he thought he'd been infected by something in that chamber. Meanwhile, he never worried about the billions of creatures swimming in his gut and doing so since the day he was born.

"We can't tweak the genes of the food we eat without suspicion," Erskine added. "We can pick and choose the naturally mutated ones until a blade of grass is a great ear of corn, but we can't do it with *purpose*. Vic had dozens of examples like these. He rattled them off in the cafeteria that day." Erskine ticked his fingers as he counted. "Vaccines versus natural immunities, cloning versus twins, modified foods. Of course he was perfectly right. The bastard always was. It was the manmade part that would have caused the chaos. It would be knowing that people were out to get us, that there was danger in the air we breathed."

Erskine paused for a moment. Donald's mind was racing.

"You know, Vic once said that if these terrorists had an ounce of sense, they would've simply announced what they were working on and then sat back to watch things burn on their own. He said that's all it would take, us knowing that it was happening, that the end of any of us could come silent, invisible, and any damn time."

"And so the solution was to burn it all to the ground *ourselves?*" Donald ran his hands through his hair, trying to make sense of it all. His teeth began to clatter. He thought of a firefighting technique that always seemed just as confusing to him, the burning of wide swaths of forest to prevent a fire from spreading. And he knew in Iran, when oil wells were set ablaze during the first war, that sometimes the only cure was to set off a bomb, to fight the inferno with something greater.

"Believe me," Erskine said, "I came up with my own complaints. Endless complaints. But I knew the truth from the beginning, it just took me a while to accept it. Thurman was won over more easily. He saw at once that we needed to get off this ball of rock, to start over. But the cost of travel was too great."

"Why travel through space?" Donald said, "when you can travel through time?" He remembered a conversation in Thurman's office about making room on this planet rather than going off in search of another. The old man had told him what he was planning that very first day.

Erskine's eyes widened. "Yes. That was his argument. He'd seen enough war, I suppose. Me, I didn't have Thurman's experiences or the professional . . . *distance* Vic enjoyed. It was the analogy of the computer virus that wore me down, seeing these nanos like a new cyber war. I knew what they could do, how fast they could restructure themselves, evolve, if you will. We could've gone back and forth for ages, but there would've been no end to it. Once it started, it would only stop when we were no longer around. And maybe not even then. Every defense would become a blueprint for the next attack. The air would choke with our invisible armies. There would be great clouds of them, mutating and fighting without need of a host. And once the public saw this and *knew* . . ." he left the sentence unfinished.

"Hysteria," Donald muttered.

"Hysteria and homebrew. If you think affordable DNA sequencers were a scare, or those cloning kits that made the rounds, imagine kids programming nanos in their basements, sharing their designs on the web. It would be worse than when they started printing those plastic guns in those cheap extruder kits. Who knows what they might try and target just for fun? It starts with the neighbor's cat. The next weekend, someone wipes out an entire species by accident."

"You said it might not ever end, even if we were gone. Does that mean they're still out there? The nanos?"

Erskine glanced toward the ceiling. "The world outside isn't just being scrubbed of humans right now, if that's what you're asking. It's being reset. All of our experiments are being removed. By the grace of God, it'll be a very long time indeed before we think to perform them again."

Donald remembered from orientation that the combined shifts would last five hundred years. Half a millennia of living underground.

y

How much scrubbing was necessary? And what was to keep them from heading down that same path a second time? How would any of them unlearn the potential dangers? You don't get the fire back in the box once you've unleashed it.

"You asked me if Victor had regrets—" Erskine coughed into his fist and nodded. "I do think he felt something close to that once. It was something he said to me as he was coming off his eighth or ninth shift, I don't remember which. I think I was heading into my sixth. This was just after the two of you worked together, after that nasty business with Silo 12—"

"My first shift," Donald said, since Erskine seemed to be counting. He wanted to add that it was his only shift. It was his final shift.

"Yes, of course." Erskine adjusted his glasses. "I'm sure you knew him well enough to know that he didn't show his emotions often."

"He was difficult to read," Donald agreed. He knew almost nothing of the man he had just helped to bury.

"So you'll appreciate this, I think. We were riding the lift together, and Vic turns to me and says how hard it is to sit there at that desk of his and see what we were doing to the men across the hall. He meant you, of course. People in your position."

Donald tried to imagine the man he knew saying such a thing. He wanted to believe it.

"But that's not what really struck me. I've never seen him sadder than when he said the following. He said—" Erskine rested a hand on the pod. "He said that sitting there, watching you people work at your desks, getting to know you—he often thought that the world would be a better place with people like you in charge."

"People like me?" Donald shook his head. "What does that even mean?"

Erskine smiled. "I asked him precisely that. His response was that it was a burden doing what he knew to be correct, to be sound and logical." Erskine ran one hand across the pod as if he could touch his daughter within. "And how much simpler things would be, how much better for us all, if we had people brave enough to do what was *right*, instead."

· 40 ·

It was that night that Anna came to him. After a day of numbness and dwelling on death, of eating the meals brought down by Thurman and not tasting a bite, of watching her set up a computer for him and spread out folders of notes, she came to him in the darkness.

Donald complained. He tried to push her away. She sat on the edge of the cot and held his wrists while he sobbed and grew feeble. He thought of Erskine's story, on what it meant to do the right thing rather than the correct thing, what the difference was. He thought this as an old lover draped herself across him, her hand on the back of his neck, her cheek on his shoulder, lying there against him while he wept.

A century of sleep had weakened him, he thought. A century of sleep and the knowledge that Mick and Helen had lived a life together. He felt suddenly angry at her. Not at Anna, whose breath he could feel on his neck, but at Helen. Angry at her for not holding out, for not living alone, for not getting his messages and meeting him over the hill where he could store her beauty away forever.

Anna kissed his cheek and whispered that everything would be okay. Fresh tears flowed down Donald's face as he realized that he was everything Victor had assumed he wasn't. He was a miserable human being for wishing his wife to be lonely so that he could sleep at night a hundred years later. He was a miserable human being for denying her that solace when Anna's touch made him feel so much better.

"I can't," he whispered for the dozenth time.

"Shhh," Anna said. She brushed his hair back in the darkness. And the two of them were alone in that room where wars were waged. They were trapped together with those crates of arms, with guns and ammo, and far more dangerous things.

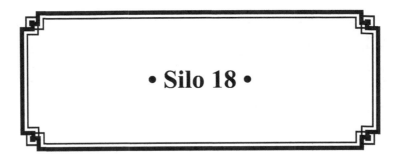

• Silo 18 •

Do not let me fear my death.
I beg you with my final breath.
Take and plant me 'neath the corn.
Take me, oh Lord, another born.
One for one, as per your plan.
One for one, come take my hand.
Bury me that I'll take root.
Plant me, oh Lord, and reap your fruit.

-Seth Hayden, age 5

· 41 ·

Mission wound his way toward Central Dispatch and agonized over what to do for his friend. He felt afraid for Rodny but powerless to help. The door they had him behind was unlike any he'd ever seen: thick and solid, gleaming and daunting. If the trouble his friend had caused could be read by where they were keeping him—

He shuddered to continue that line of thought. It'd only been a few months since the last cleaning. Mission had been there, had carried up part of the suit, a more haunting experience than porting a body for burial. Dead bodies at least were placed in those black bags the coroners used. There was something good and somber about them. The cleaning suit was a different sort of bag, tailored to a living soul that would crawl inside and be forced to die there.

Mission remembered where they had picked up the gear. It'd been a room right down the hall from where Rodny was being kept. Weren't cleanings run by the same department? He shivered. One slip of a tongue could land a body out there, rotting on the hills, and his friend Rodny was known to wag his dangerously.

First his mother, and now his best friend. Mission wondered what the Pact said about volunteering to clean in one's stead. If it said anything at all. Amazing that he could live under the rules of a document that he'd never read. He just assumed others had, all the people in charge, and that they were operating by its contents fairly.

On fifty-eight, a porter's 'chief tied to the downbound railing caught his attention. It was the same blue pattern as the 'chief worn around his neck, but with a bright red merchant's hem. Duty beckoned, dispelling thoughts that were spiraling nowhere. Mission unknotted the 'chief and searched the fabric for the merchant's stamp. It was Drexel's, the apothecary down the hall. Light loads and lighter pay, normally. But at least it was downbound, unless Drexel had been careless again with which rail he tied it to.

Mission was dying to get to Central where a shower and a change of clothes awaited, but if anyone spotted him with a flat pack marching past a signal 'chief, he'd hear it from Morgan and the others. He hurried inside to Drexel's, praying it wasn't a round of meds going to several dozen individual apartments. His legs turned to rubber just thinking about it.

Drexel was at the counter as Mission pushed open the apothecary's squeaky door. A large man with a full beard and a balding head, Drexel was something of a fixture in the mids. Many came to him rather than to the doctors, though Mission wasn't sure how sound a choice that was. Often, though, it was the man with the most promises who got the chits, not the one who made people better. And besides, the very worst cases rarely complained. If they did, only the roots heard.

The usual handful of sick people sat on Drexel's benches in the waiting room, sniffling and coughing. Mission felt the urge to cover his mouth with his 'chief. Instead, he innocuously held his breath and waited while Drexel filled a small square of paper with ground powder, folding it neatly like one might roll a cigarette, before handing it to the woman waiting. The woman slid a few chits across the counter. When she walked away, Mission tossed the signal 'chief on top of the money.

"Ah, Mish. Good to see you, boy. Looking fit as a fiddle." Drexel smoothed his beard and smiled, yellow teeth peering out from cornrows of drooping whiskers.

"Same," Mission said politely, braving a breath. "Got something for me?"

"I do. One sec."

Drexel disappeared behind a wall of shelves crammed full of tiny vials and jars. A baby in the waiting room wailed. The apothecary reappeared with a small sack. "Meds for down below," he said.

"I can take them as far as Central and have Dispatch send them from there," Mission told him. "I'm just finishing up a shift."

Drexel frowned and rubbed his beard. "I suppose that'll do. And Dispatch'll bill me?"

Mission held out a palm. "If you tip," he said.

"Aye, a tip. But only if you solve a riddle." Drexel leaned on the counter, which seemed to sag beneath his bulk. The snifflers and coughers waiting on their meds were ignored, and the last thing Mission wanted to hear was another of the old man's riddles and then not get paid. Always an excuse with Drexel to keep a chit on his side of the counter.

"Okay," the apothecary began, tugging on his whiskers. "Which one weighs more, a bag full of seventy-eight pounds of feathers, or a bag full of seventy-eight pounds of rocks?"

Mission didn't hesitate with his answer. "The bag of feathers," he declared. He'd heard this one before. It was a riddle made for a porter, and he had thought on it long enough between the levels to come up with his own answer, one different from the obvious.

"Incorrect!" Drexel roared, waving a finger. "It isn't the rocks—" His face dimmed. "Wait. Did you say the feathers?" He shook his head. "No, boy, they weigh the *same.*"

"The contents weigh the same," Mission told him. "The bag of feathers would have to be bigger. You said they were both full, which means a bigger bag with more material, and so it weighs more." He held out his palm. Drexel stood there, chewing his beard for a moment, thrown off his game. Begrudgingly, he took two coins from the lady's pay and placed them in Mission's hand. Mission accepted them and stuffed the sack of meds into his pack before cinching it up tight.

"The bigger bag—" Drexel muttered, as Mission hurried off, past the benches, holding his breath again as he went, the pills rattling in his sack.

The apothecary's annoyance was worth far more than the tip, but Mission appreciated both. The enjoyment faded, however, as he spiraled down through a tense silo. There was a fear invisible but still sensed like the rising smoke. He saw deputies on one landing, hands on their guns, trying to calm down fighting neighbors. The glass on the windows peeking into a shop on forty-two were broken and covered with a sheet of plastic. Mission was pretty sure that was recent. And down he went, the stairway trembling, the graffiti on the walls warning him with grammatical troubles of what was yet to come.

He arrived at Central Dispatch to find it eerily quiet. Marko passed him in the hall. The older porter had a black eye, and Mission had a good idea of where it came from. He nodded, and Marko nodded back, a bit of respect from a veteran porter who had warred with him in the dark the night before. Mission felt sad for the things he could imagine doing for a little respect. Braving violence was an ignoble way to earn it.

He made his way past the sorting rooms with their tall shelves of items needing delivery and went straight to the main counter. He would drop off his current package and pick out his next job before changing and showering. Katelyn was working the counter. There were no other porters queued up. Off licking their wounds, perhaps. Or maybe seeing to their families during this recent spate of violence.

"Hey, Katelyn."

"Mish." She smiled. "You look intact."

He laughed and touched his nose, which was still sore. "Thanks."

"Cam just passed through asking where you were."

"Yeah?" Mission was surprised. He figured his friend would be taking a day off with the bonus from the coroner. "Did he pick something up?"

"Yup. He requested anything heading toward Supply. Was in a better mood than usual, though he seemed miffed to have been left out of last night's adventures."

"He heard about that, huh?" Mission sorted through the delivery list. He was looking for something upbound. Mrs. Crowe would know what to do about Rodny. Maybe she could find out from the mayor what he was being punished for, perhaps put in a good word for him.

"Wait," he said, glancing up at Katelyn. "What do you mean he was in a good mood? And he was heading for *Supply?*" Mission thought of the job he'd been offered by Wyck. The head of IT had said Mission wouldn't be the last to hear of the offer. Maybe he hadn't been the *first*, either. "Where was Cam coming from?"

Katelyn touched her fingers to her tongue and flipped through the old log. "I think his last delivery was a broken computer heading to—"

"That little rat." Mission slapped the counter. "You got anything else heading down? Maybe to Supply or Chemical?"

She checked her computer, fingers clacking furiously, the rest of her perfectly serene. "We're so slow right now," she said apologetically. "I've got something from Mechanical back up to Supply. Forty five pounds. No rush. Standard freight." She peered across the counter at Mission, seeing if he was interested.

"I'll take it," he said. But he didn't plan on heading straight to Mechanical. If he raced, maybe he could beat Cam to Supply and do that other job for Wyck. That was the way in he was looking for. It wasn't the money he wanted, it was having an excuse to go back to thirty-four to collect his pay, another chance to see Rodny, see what kind of help his friend needed, what sort of trouble he was truly in.

• 42 •

Mission made record time downbound. It helped that traffic was light, but it wasn't a good sign that he didn't pass Cam on the way. The kid must've had a good head start. Either that, or Mission had gotten lucky and had overtaken the kid while he was off the stairway for a bathroom break.

Pausing for a moment on the landing outside of Supply, Mission caught his breath and dabbed the sweat from his neck. He still hadn't had his shower. Maybe after he found Cam and took care of this job in Mechanical, he could get cleaned up and get some proper rest. Lower Dispatch would have a change of clothes for him. And then he could figure out what to do about Rodny. So much to think about. A blessing that it took his mind off it being his birthday.

Inside Supply, he found a handful of people waiting at the counter. No sign of Cam. If the boy had come and gone already, he must've flown, and the delivery must've been heading further down. Mission tapped his foot and waited his turn. Once at the counter, he asked for Joyce, just like Wyck had said. The man helping him pointed to a heavyset woman with her hair up in a tight bun at the other end of the counter. Mission recognized her. She handled a lot of the flow of equipment marked special for IT. He waited until she was done with her customer, then asked for any deliveries under the name of Wyck.

She narrowed her eyes at him. "You got a glitch at Dispatch?" she asked. "Done handed that one off." She waved for the next person in line.

"Could you tell me where it was heading?" Mission asked. "I was sent to relieve the other guy. His . . . his mother is sick. They're not sure if she's gonna make it."

Mission winced at the lie. The lady behind the counter twisted her mouth in disbelief.

"Please," he begged. "It really is important."

She hesitated. "It was going six flights down to an apartment. I don't have the exact number. It was on the delivery report."

"Six down." Mission knew the level. Residential except for the handful of less-than-legal businesses being run out of a few apartments. "Thanks," he said. He slapped the counter and hurried toward the exit. It was on his way to Mechanical, anyway. He might be too late for Wyck's delivery, but he could ask Cam if he might pick up the pay for him, offer him a vacation chit in return. Or he could just flat out tell him an old friend was in trouble, and he needed to get through security. If not, he'd have to wait for an IT request to hit Dispatch and be the first to jump on it. And he'd have to hope that Rodny had that much time.

He was four levels down, formulating a dozen such plans, when the blast went off.

The great stairwell lurched as if thrown sideways. Mission slammed against the rail and nearly went over. He wrapped his arms around the trembling steel and held on.

There was a shriek, a chorus of groans. He watched, his head out in space beyond the railing, as the landing two levels below twisted away from the staircase. The metal sang and cried out as it was ripped free and went tumbling into the depths.

More than one body plummeted after. The receding figures performed cartwheels in space.

Mission tore himself away from the sight. A few steps down from him, a woman remained on her hands and knees, looking up at Mission with wild and frightened eyes. There was a distant crash, impossibly far below.

"I don't know," he wanted to say. There was that question in her eyes, the same one pounding in his skull, echoing with the sound of the blast. *What the hell just happened? Is this it? Has it begun?*

He considered running up, away from the calamity, but there were screams from below, and a porter had a duty to those on the stairwell in need. He helped the woman to her feet and bid her upward. Already, the smell of something acrid and the haze of smoke were upon them. "Go," he urged, and then he spiraled down against the sudden flow of traffic, responding on automatic to his shadowing days rather than to some deeply held sense of duty. And his friend. Cam was down there. Where the boy had gone and where the blast had occurred were still coincidence in Mission's rattled mind.

The landing below held a crush of people. Residents and shopkeeps crowded out of the doors and fought for a spot at the rail that they might gaze over at the wreckage one flight further down. Mission fought his way through, yelling Cam's name, keeping an eye out for his friend. A bedraggled couple staggered up to the crowded landing with hollow eyes, clutching the railing and each other. He didn't see Cam anywhere.

He raced down five turns of the central post, his normally deft feet stumbling on the slick treads, around and around. It'd been the level Cam was heading toward, right? Six down. Level one-sixteen. He would be okay. Mission convinced himself Cam would be okay. The sight of those people tumbling through the air flashed in Mission's mind. It was an image he knew he'd never forget. Surely, Cam wasn't among them. The boy was late or early to everything, never right on time.

He made the last turn, and where the next landing should've been was empty space. The stalwart rails of the great spiral staircase had been ripped outward before parting. A few of the steps sagged away from the central post, and gravity tugged at Mission's feet. He could feel a pull toward the edge, the void clawing at him. There was nothing there to stop him from going over. The steel felt slick beneath his boots.

Across a gap of torn and twisted steel, the doorway to one-sixteen was missing. In its place stood a pocket of crumbling cement and dark iron bars bent outward like hands reaching for the departed landing. White powder drifted down from the ceiling beyond the rubble. Unbelievably, there were sounds beyond the veil. Coughs and shouts. Screams for help.

People were yelling from the landing above as well. A fire hose slithered down, the nozzle clinking and banging against the wall of the stairwell. There was no one there to accept it, just an orange glow of fire deep inside that seemed to throb. It was as if the earth's chest had been torn open, exposing its bright red heartbeat, the bent rods of steel now like a shattered ribcage.

"Porter!" someone yelled from above.

Mission carefully slid to the edge of the sloping and bent steps. He held the railing where it had been torn free. It was warm to the touch. Leaning out, he studied the crowd fifty feet above him at the next landing. They were swinging the fire hose, trying to get it inside the busted door. But there was no landing rail to snag the nozzle on anymore, no one to grab it. Again, someone yelled something about a porter. Mission didn't know what was expected of him. He hadn't shadowed for this. The nozzle swung wildly a dozen feet away. Did they expect him to reach it? To swing over and douse that mad pulse in the heart of the burning earth?

Someone pointed when they spotted him leaning out, spotted the 'chief around his neck.

"There he is!" a woman shrieked, one of the mad-eyed women who had staggered past him as he hurried down, one of those who had survived. "The porter did it!" she yelled.

· 43 ·

Mission froze, uncomprehending, even as the stairway thundered and clanged with a descending mob. The loosened treads beneath his feet shook. He reached for the inner post and clung to it for a moment. Across the smoke-hazed void, a figure appeared at the hole in the earth. Someone was alive inside level one-sixteen. A man with his undershirt pulled up over his mouth stared across at Mission with wide, horror-filled eyes.

Mission turned and ran. He stumbled downward, a hand on the inner post, watching for the return of the railing. So much had been pulled away. The stairs were unstable from the damage. He didn't know why he was running beyond that he was being chased. It took a full turn of the staircase for the railing to reappear and for him to feel safe at such speeds. It took just as long to realize that Cam was dead. His friend had delivered a package, and now he was dead. He and others. One glance at his blue 'chief, and someone above thought it'd been Mission who'd made the delivery. It very nearly had been.

Another crowd at landing one-seventeen. Tear-streaked faces, a woman trembling, her arms wrapped around herself, a man covering his face, all looking up or down beyond the rails. They had seen the wreckage tumble past. Mission hurried on. Lower Dispatch was all that lay between him and Mechanical that he might call haven. He hurried there, his mind still grasping for a handhold that'd been wrenched away. A violent scream approached from above and came much too fast.

Mission startled and nearly fell as the wailing person flew toward him. He waited for someone to tackle him from behind, but the sound whizzed past beyond the rail. Another person. Falling, alive and screaming, plummeting toward the depths. The loose steps and empty space had claimed one of those chasing him.

He quickened his pace, leaving the inner post for the outer rail where the curve of the steps was broader and smoother, where the force of his descent tugged him against the steel bar. Here, he could move faster. He tried not to think of what would happen if he came across a gap in the steel. He ran, smoke stinging his eyes, the clang and clamor of his own feet and that of distant others, not realizing at first that the haze in the air wasn't from the ruin he had left behind. The smoke all around him was *rising*.

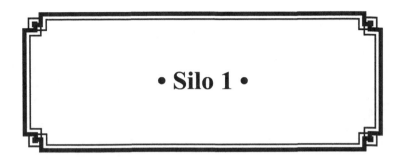

• Silo 1 •

If you do not change direction,
you may end up where you are heading.

-Lao Tzu

• 44 •

Donald's breakfast of powdered eggs and shredded potatoes had long grown cold. He rarely touched the food brought down by Thurman and Erskine, preferring instead the bland stuff in the unlabeled silver cans he had discovered among the storeroom's vacuum-sealed crates. It wasn't just the matter of trust—it was the rebelliousness of it all, the empowerment that came from foraging, from taking command of his own survival. He stabbed a yellowish-orange gelatinous blob that he assumed had once been part of a peach and put it in his mouth. He chewed, tasting nothing. He pretended it tasted like a peach.

Across the wide table, Anna fiddled with the dials on her radio and sipped loudly from a mug of cold coffee. A nest of wires ran from a black box to her computer, and a soft hiss of static filled the room. It was noise to Donald, but Anna squinted at a set of speakers and tilted her head like an animal with a higher sense. She seemed capable of listening to the indiscernible.

"It's too bad we can't get a better station," Donald said morosely. He speared another wedge of mystery fruit and popped it into his mouth. Mango, he told himself, just for variety.

"No station is the best station," she said, referring to her hope that the towers of Silo 40 and its neighbors would remain silent. She had tried to explain what she was doing to cut off unlikely survivors, but little of it made any sense to Donald. A year ago, supposedly, Silo 40 had hacked the system. It was assumed to have been a rogue Head of IT. No one else could be expected to possess the expertise and access required of such a feat. By the time the camera feeds were cut, every fail-safe had already been severed. Attempts to terminate the silo were made, but with no way to verify them. It was apparent these attempts had failed when the darkness began to spread to other silos.

Thurman, Erskine, and Victor had been woken according to protocol, one after the other. Further fail-safes proved ineffective, and Erskine worried the hacking had progressed to the level of the nanos, that everything was in jeopardy. After much cajoling, Thurman had convinced the other two that Anna could help. Her research at M.I.T. had been in wireless harmonics; remote charging technology; RFIDs; the ability to assume control of electronics via radio.

She'd eventually been able to commandeer the collapse mechanism of the afflicted silos. Donald still had nightmares thinking about it. While she described the process, he had studied the wall schematic of a standard silo. He had pictured the blasts that freed the layers of heavy concrete between the levels, sending them like dominoes down to the bottom, crushing everything and everyone in-between. Stacks of concrete fifty feet thick had been cut loose to turn entire societies into rubble. These underground buildings had been designed from the beginning so they could be brought down like any other—and remotely. The insight that such a fail-safe was even needed seemed as sick as the solution was cruel.

What now remained of those silos was all hiss and crackle, a chorus of ghosts. The silo Heads in the rest of the facilities hadn't even been told of the calamity. There would be no red Xs on their schematics to haunt their days. The various Heads had little contact with each other as it was. The greater worry was of panic spreading.

But everyone in Silo 1 knew. Victor had known. And Donald suspected it was this heavy burden that had led him to an unspeakable escape rather than any of the theories Thurman had offered. Thurman was so in awe of Victor's supposed brilliance that he searched for purpose behind his madness, some conspiratorial cause. Donald was verging on the sad realization that humanity had been thrown on the brink of extinction by insane men in positions of power following one another, each thinking the others knew where they were going.

He took a sip of tomato juice from a punctured can and reached for two pieces of paper amid the carpet of notes and reports surrounding his keyboard. The fate of a silo supposedly rested on something in these two pages. They were copies of the same report. One was a virgin printout of something he'd written long ago about the fall of another silo. Donald barely remembered writing it. And now he had stared at it so long, the meaning had been squeezed out of the ink. It had become like a word that, repeated, devolves into mere sound.

The other copy was of the notes Victor had scrawled across the face of this report. He had written his notes with a red pen, and someone upstairs had managed to pull just this color off in order to make both versions more legible. By copying the red, however, they had also transferred a fine mist and a few splatters. These marks were gruesome reminders that the report had been atop Victor's desk in the final moments of his life.

That could mean anything or nothing, Donald thought. In fact, after three days of study, he was beginning to suspect that the report was nothing more than a scrap of paper. Why else write across the top of it? And yet Victor had told Thurman several times that the key to quelling the violence in Silo 18 lay right there. He had argued strongly for Donald to be pulled from the deep freeze, but hadn't been able to get Erskine or Thurman to side with him. So this was all Donald had, a liar's account of what a dead man had said.

Liars and dead men—two parties unskilled at dispensing truth.

The scrap of paper with the red ink and rust-colored bloodstains offered little help. There were a few lines that resonated, however. They reminded Donald of how horoscopes were able to land vague and glancing blows, which gave credence to all their other feints.

"The One who remembers" had been written in bold and confident letters across the center of the report. Donald couldn't help but feel that this referred to him and his resistance to the medication. Hadn't Anna said that Victor spoke of him frequently, that he wanted him awake for testing or questioning? Other musings were vague and dire in equal measure. *"This is why,"* Victor had written. Also: *"An end to them all."*

Did he mean the why of his suicide or the why of Silo 18's violence? And an end to all of what?

In many ways, the cycle of violence in Silo 18 was no different than what took place elsewhere. Beyond being more severe, it was the same waxing and waning of the mobs, of each generation revolting against the last, a fifteen- to twenty-year cycle of bloody upheaval.

Victor had left reports behind about everything from primate behavior to the wars of the twentieth and twenty-first centuries. There was one report that Donald found especially disturbing: it detailed how primates came of age and attempted to overthrow their fathers, the alpha males. It told of chimps that committed infanticide, males snatching the young from their mothers and taking them into the trees where their arms and legs were ripped, limb by limb, from their small bodies. Victor had written that this put the females back into estrus. It made room for the next generation.

Donald had a hard time believing any of this was true. He had a harder time making sense of a report about frontal lobes and how long they took to develop in humans. Maybe this was important to unraveling some mystery. Or perhaps it was the ravings of a man losing his mind, or a man discovering his conscience and coming to grips with what he'd done to the world. Or maybe it was because of Silo 40, from watching impotently while his grand and twisted plans crumbled into ruin.

Donald studied his old report and Victor's notes and saw the same bit of nothing. Anna thought a people could be saved by what the report contained. Thurman was impatient to terminate the silo now before the violence spilled to some neighbor. Donald was reminded of his story, of having killed a man to save others. He thought about how bombs were used to douse fires, nukes used to end wars, fires to fight fires. He wanted no part of such a decision.

And so he searched. He fell into a routine that Anna had long ago perfected. They slept, ate, and worked. They emptied bottles of scotch at night one burning sip at a time and left them standing like factory smokestacks amid the diagram of silos. In the mornings, they took turns with the lone shower that adjoined what seemed an executive's office.

Or a general's office. Anna would be brazen with her nakedness, Donald wishing she wouldn't be. Her presence became an intoxicant from the past, and Donald began to confabulate a new reality in his mind: He and Anna were working on one more secret project together; Helen was back in Savannah; Mick wasn't making it to the meetings; Donald couldn't raise either of them because his cell phone wouldn't work.

It was always that his cell phone didn't work. Just one text getting through on the day of the convention, and Helen might be down in the deep freeze, asleep in her pod. He could visit her the way Erskine visited his daughter. They would be together again once all the shifts were over.

In another version of the same dream, Donald imagined that he was able to crest that hill and make it to the Tennessee side. Bombs exploded in the air, frightened people dove into their holes, a young girl sang with a voice so pure. In this fantasy, he and Helen disappeared into the same earth. They had children and grandchildren and were buried together.

Dreams such as these kept him sane as he slept and haunted him when he woke. They haunted him when he allowed Anna to touch him, to lay in his cot for an hour before bedtime, just the sound of her breathing, her head on his chest, the smell of alcohol on both their breaths, reminding him of college days. He would lay there and tolerate it, suffer how good it felt, her hand resting on his neck, and only fall asleep after she grew uncomfortable from the cramped quarters and moved back to her own cot.

In the morning, she would sing in the shower, steam billowing into the war room, while Donald returned to his studies. He would log onto her computer where he was able to dig through the files in Victor's personal directories. He could see when these files had been created, accessed, and how often. One of the oldest and most recently opened was a list with all the silos ranked. Number 18 was near the top, but it wasn't clear if this was a measure of trouble or worth. And why rank them to begin with? For what purpose?

He also used Anna's computer to search for his sister, Charlotte. She wasn't listed in the pods below, not under any name or picture that he could find. But she had been there during orientation. He remembered her being led off with so many others and being put to sleep. And now she seemed to have vanished. But where?

So many questions. He stared at the two reports, the awful sound of hissing ghosts leaking from the radio, and the weight of all the earth above him driving him mad. And he began to suspect that Silo 1 had certain fail-safes as well, that the lift took too long between levels, that a press of concrete hovered over all their heads that none of them could see. Such was his fear and his hope, two wildly different emotions that became difficult to distinguish as Donald followed Victor's messy trail. He began to wonder, if he followed this dead man too closely, if perhaps he would reach the same fateful conclusion in the end.

• 45 •

When he could no longer look at the notes and see anything but blood, Donald went for what had become his customary stroll among the guns and dozing drones. This was his escape from the hiss of Anna's work and the cramped confines of their makeshift home, and it was during these laps through the darkened storehouse that he came nearest to clearing his head from his dreams, from the prior night's bottle of scotch, and from the mix of emotions he was beginning to feel for Anna.

Most of all, he walked those laps and tried to make sense of this new world. He puzzled over what Thurman and Victor had planned for the silos. Five hundred years below ground, and then what? Donald desperately wanted to know. And here was when he felt truly alive: when he was taking action, when he was digging for answers. It was the same fleeting sense of power he had felt from refusing their pills, from staining his fingers purple and tonguing the ulcers that formed in his cheeks. It was the rattling of chains. Chains he could not hope to shake loose, but that he could shake nonetheless.

He passed the two lifts, feeling such courage, and tried both call buttons. He tried them several times a day, but neither would light without a badge. He was beginning to know the rules and secrets of that darkened place. In his explorations, he had discovered the plastic crate with the missing firearm, the one he assumed Victor had stolen. The airtight seal was broken, and the other guns inside reeked of grease.

It seemed strange at first that he was a prisoner locked away with instruments of war, but then he realized that he and Anna had simply been cloistered away with all the other forbidden things. They had been tucked away where they wouldn't be discovered.

It hadn't kept him from prying open other crates to see what was inside. Some contained folded uniforms and suits like astronauts wore, all vacuum sealed in thick plastic. Another held helmets with large domes and metal collars. There were flashlights with red lenses, food and medical kits, backpacks, rounds and rounds of ammo, and myriad other devices and gadgets he could only guess at. The day before, he had found a laminated map in one crate, a chart of the fifty silos. There were red lines that radiated from the silos, one from each, and met at a single point in the distance. Donald had traced the lines with his finger, holding the map up to catch the light spilling from the distant offices. These things were puzzled over and put back in their place, clues to a mystery he couldn't define.

He stopped during his lap to perform a set of jumping jacks in the wide aisles between the sleeping drones. The exercise had been a struggle just two days ago, but the chill seemed to be melting from his veins. And the more he pushed himself, the more awake and alert he seemed to become. He did seventy-five, which was ten more than yesterday. After catching his breath, he dropped down to see how many pushups he could do on his atrophied muscles. And it was here, on the third day of his captivity, that he discovered the launch lift, a garage door that barely came to his waist but was wide enough for the wings that lurked beneath the tarps.

Donald rose from his pushup and approached the low door. The entire storehouse was kept incredibly dim, this wall almost pitch black. He thought about going for one of the flashlights when he saw the red handle. A tug, and the door slid up into the wall. On his hands and knees, Donald explored the cavity beyond, which went back over a dozen feet. There were no buttons or levers that he could feel along the walls, no method of operating the lift.

Curious, he crawled out and decided to grab a flashlight. Before he turned, however, he saw another door along the darkened wall, a door he'd never noticed before, one he assumed led to a closet or a mechanical space. Donald tried the handle and found it unlocked, a dim hallway beyond. He glanced toward the spill of light in the direction of the offices, a barely audible hiss emanating from Anna's work. Reaching inside the hall, he fumbled for a light switch, and the overhead bulbs flickered hesitantly. Shielding his eyes—having grown used to the darkness in the warehouse—he crept inside. He pulled the door shut behind him so as not to disturb the sleeping drones.

The hallway beyond possessed the eerie calm of a place haunted. It ran fifty paces to a door at the far end, with a pair of doors on either side. More offices, he assumed, similar to the small home Anna had carved out in the back of the warehouse. He tried the first door, and the odor of mothballs or some cleaning chemical wafted out. Inside, he discovered where his cot had come from. There were rows of bunks, the shuffle of recent footsteps in a layer of dust, and a place where two small beds formerly lay. There were dressers built into the walls and a trunk at the foot of each bed. The absence of people could be felt. This was a place meant for the living, and Donald wondered briefly why the two cots had been removed at all, why not sleep here? His curiosity grew stronger as he peeked into the door across the hall and found bathroom stalls and a cluster of showers.

The next two doors were more of the same, except for a row of urinals in the bathroom. The sight of these made Donald need to go. He crept inside and tested one, was mildly surprised when it flushed and was startled by how loud it was. While he went, he had a fear that Anna was looking for him, that she might hear the water banging through the pipes and barge in.

He finished and flushed, then noted the layer of dust on the handle of the neighboring urinal. Perhaps this place had been taken off the maintenance rounds while Anna was awake. Maybe people had lived down here and kept up with the munitions once but had relocated to make room for her secret presence. But Donald didn't remember anyone coming to this level during his first shift. No, these were quarters kept for another time, much like the machines beneath the tarps. And rather than put Donald where it made the most sense, where there was plenty of room and a second shower, Anna had kept him in the suite she'd long ago made for herself. To keep him near, perhaps. And Donald wondered for the first time if he was awake not because he held the answer to any mystery, but simply because she wanted him to be.

He washed his hands and studied himself in the mirror. His eyes were red and puffy, his hair disheveled, his cheeks gaunt and bearing three days of growth. He was turning gray, he saw. The centuries spent asleep were aging him. He laughed at this, laughed at the idea that the man in the mirror was him at all, that he was still alive, his wife gone, that any of this were more than a dream. Flicking off the light, he left the bathroom to the ghosts and checked the door at the end of the hall.

Inside, he found furniture locked in ice, the light from the hallway shimmering as it caught what looked like massive cubes of frozen water. The illusion was dispelled as he fumbled for the switch. It was sheets of plastic thrown over tables and chairs, a fine mist of dust settled on top. Donald approached one of the tables and saw the computer display beneath the sheet. The chairs were attached to the desks, and there was something familiar about the knobs and levers. He knelt and fumbled for the edge of the plastic and peeled it up noisily. He turned and checked the empty hallway, unable to shake the feeling of others being present.

The flight controls he revealed took him back to another life. Here was the stick his sister had called a yoke, the pedals beneath the seat she had called something else, the throttle and all the other dials and indicators. Donald remembered touring her training facility after she graduated flight school. They had flown to Colorado for her ceremony. He remembered watching a screen just like this as her drone took to the air and joined a formation of others. He remembered the view of Colorado from the nose of her graceful machine in flight.

He glanced around the room at the dozen or so stations. The obvious need for the place slammed into what had felt like a secret discovery. He imagined voices in the hallway, men and women showering and chatting, towels being snapped at asses, someone looking to borrow a razor, a shift of pilots sitting at these desks where coffee could lie perfectly still in steaming mugs as death was rained down from above.

Donald returned the plastic sheet. Dust shivered off and ran down the gleaming material like an avalanche on a snowy hillside. He thought of his sister, asleep and hidden some levels below where he couldn't find her, and he wondered if she hadn't been brought there as a surprise for him at all. Maybe she had been brought as a surprise for some future *others*.

And suddenly, thinking of her, thinking of a time lost to dreams and lonely tears, Donald found himself patting his pockets in search of something. Pills. An old prescription with her name on it. Helen had forced him to see a doctor, hadn't she? And Donald suddenly knew why he couldn't forget, why their drugs didn't work on him. The realization came with a powerful longing to see his sister. Charlotte was the why. She was the answer to one of Thurman's riddles.

• 46 •

"**I** want to see her first," Donald demanded. "Let me see her, and then I'll tell you."

He waited for Thurman or Dr. Henson to reply. The three of them stood in Henson's office on the cryopod wing. Donald had bargained his way down the lift with Thurman, and now he bargained further. His sister was the answer to why he couldn't forget. He would exchange that answer for another. He wanted to know where she was, to see her.

Something unspoken passed between the two men. Thurman turned to Donald with a warning. "She will not be woken," he said. "Not even for this."

Donald nodded. He saw how only those who made the laws were allowed to break them.

Henson turned to the computer on his desk. "I'll look her up."

"No need," Thurman said. "I know where she is."

He led them out of the office and down the hall, past the main shift rooms where Donald had awoken as Troy all those years ago, past the deep freeze where he had spent nearly a century asleep, all the way to another door just like the others.

The code Thurman entered was different; Donald could tell by the discordant four-note song the buttons made. Above the keypad in small stenciled letters he made out the words: *Emergency Personnel*. Locks whirred and ground like old bones, and the door gradually opened.

Steam followed them inside, the warm air from the hallway hitting the mortuary cool. There were fewer than a dozen rows of pods, perhaps fifty or sixty units total, little more than a full shift. Donald peered into one of the coffin-like units, the ice a spiderweb of blue and white on the glass, and saw inside a thick and chiseled visage. A frozen soldier, or so his imagination informed him.

Thurman led them through the rows and columns before stopping at one of the pods. He rested his hands on its surface with something like affection. His exhalations billowed into the air. It made his white hair and stark beard appear as though they were frosted with ice.

"Charlotte," Donald breathed, peering in at his sister. She hadn't changed, hadn't aged a bit. Even the blue cast of her skin seemed normal and expected, as he was growing used to seeing people this way.

He rubbed the small window to clear the web of frost and marveled at his thin hands and seemingly fragile joints. He had atrophied. He had grown older while his sister remained the same.

"I locked her away like this once," he said, gazing in at her. "I locked her away in my memory like this when she went off to war. Our parents did the same. She was just little Charla. She was over there flying planes with her joystick like the video games she used to play."

He thought of Charlotte in front of her computer as a kid. He had thought she was overseas doing something innocent like that. Glancing away from her, he studied the two men on the other side of the pod. Henson started to say something, but Thurman placed a hand on the doctor's arm. Donald turned back to his sister.

"Of course, it wasn't a game. She was killing people. We talked about it years later, after I was in office and she'd figured I'd grown up enough." He laughed and shook his head. "My kid sister, waiting for *me* to grow up."

A tear plummeted to the frozen pane of glass. The salt cut through the ice and left a clear track behind. Donald wiped it away with a squeak, then felt frightened he might disturb her.

"They would get her up in the middle of the night," he said. "Whenever a target was deemed . . . what did she call it? *Actionable.* They would get her up. She said it was strange to go from dreaming to killing, how none of it made sense, how she would go back to sleep and see the video feeds in her mind—that last view from a missile's nose as she guided it into its target—"

He took a breath and gazed up at Thurman.

"I thought it was good that she couldn't be hurt, you know? She was safe in a trailer somewhere, not up there in the sky. But she complained about it. She told her doctor that it didn't feel right, being safe and doing what she did. The people on the front lines, they had fear as an excuse. They had self-preservation. A reason to kill. Charlotte used to kill people and then go to the mess hall and eat a piece of pie. That's what she told her doctor. She would eat something sweet and not be able to taste it."

"What doctor was this?" Henson asked.

"My doctor," Donald said. He wiped his cheek, but he wasn't ashamed of the tears. Being by his sister's side had him feeling brave and bold, less alone. He could face the past and the future, both. "Helen was worried about my reelection," he explained. "Charlotte already had a prescription, had been diagnosed with PTSD after her first tour, and so we kept filling it under her name, even under her insurance."

Henson waved his hand, stirring the air for more information. "What prescription?"

"Propra," Thurman said. "She'd been taking Propra, hadn't she? And you were worried about the press finding out."

Donald nodded. "Helen was worried. She thought it might come out that I was taking medication for my . . . wilder thoughts. The pills helped me forget them, kept me level. I could study the Order, and all I saw were the words, not the implications. There was no fear." He looked at his sister, understanding finally why she had refused to take the meds. She *wanted* the fear. It was necessary somehow. The medication they'd prescribed was the exact opposite of what she needed.

"I remember you telling me she was on them." Thurman said. "We were in the bookstore—"

"Do you remember your dosage?" Henson asked. "How long were you on it?"

"I started taking it after I was given the Order to read." He watched Thurman for any hint of expression and got nothing. "I guess that was two or three years before the convention. I took them nearly every day right up until then." He turned to Henson. "I would've had some on me during orientation if I hadn't lost them on the hill that day. I think I fell. I remember falling—"

Henson turned to Thurman. "There's no telling what the complications might be. Victor was careful to screen psychotropics from administrative personnel. Everyone was tested—"

"I wasn't," Donald said.

Henson faced him. "Everyone was tested."

"Not him." Thurman studied the surface of the pod, spoke to Henson. "There was a last minute change. A switch. I vouched for him. And if he was taking her meds, there wouldn't have been anything in his medical records."

"We need to tell Erskine," Henson said. "I could work with him. We might come up with a new formulation." He turned away from the pod like he needed to get back to his office.

Thurman looked to Donald. "Do you need more time down here?"

Donald studied his sister a moment. He wanted to wake her, to talk to her. Maybe he could come back another time just to visit.

"I might like to come back," he said.

"We'll see."

Thurman walked around the pod and placed a hand on Donald's shoulder, gave him a light, sympathetic squeeze. He led Donald away from the pod and toward the door, and Donald didn't glance back, didn't check the screen for his sister's new name. He didn't care. He knew where she was, and she would always be Charlotte to him. She would never change.

"You did good," Thurman said. "This is real good." They stepped into the hall and closed the thick doors with their massive locks. "You may have stumbled on why Victor was so obsessed with that report of yours."

"I did?" Donald didn't see the connection.

"I don't think he was interested in what you wrote at all," Thurman said. "I think he was interested in *you*."

· 47 ·

They rode the lift toward the cafeteria rather than drop Donald off on fifty-five. It was almost dinnertime, and he could help Thurman with the trays. While the lights behind the level numbers blinked on and off, following their progress up the shaft, the idea that Thurman might be right haunted him. What if Victor had been curious about his resistance to the medication? What if it wasn't anything in that report at all?

They rode past level 40, its button winking bright and then going dark, and Donald thought of the silo that had done the same. "What does this mean for 18?" he asked, watching the next number flash by.

Thurman stared at the stainless steel doors, a greasy palm print there from where someone had caught their balance.

"Vic wanted to try another reset on 18," he said. "I never saw the point. But after his death—" Thurman hesitated. "Maybe we give them one more chance."

"What's involved in a reset?"

"You know what's involved." Thurman faced him. "It's what we did to the world, just on a smaller scale. Reduce the population, wipe the computers, their memories, try it all over again. We've done that several times before with this silo. There are risks involved. You can't create trauma without making a mess. At some point, it's simpler and safer to pull the plug."

"End them," Donald said, and he saw what Victor had been up against, what he had worked to avert. He wished he could speak to the old man, now that he knew what he knew. Anna said Victor had spoken of him often. And Erskine had said he wished people like Donald were in charge. What did that mean, all that nonsense about names being all that mattered and doing what was right for a change?

The elevator opened on the top level. Donald stepped out, and it was strange to walk among those on their shift, to be present and at the same time invisible, a body moving among the chatter while not a part of it all.

He noticed that no one here looked to Thurman with deference. He was not that shift's head, and no one knew him as such. They were just two men, one in white and one in beige, grabbing food and glancing at the ruined wasteland on the wallscreen.

Donald took one of the trays and noticed again that most people sat facing the view. Only one or two ate with their backs to it, preferring not to see. He followed Thurman back to the elevator while longing to speak to these handful, to ask them what they remembered, what they were afraid of, to tell them that it was okay to be afraid.

"Why do the other silos have screens?" he asked Thurman, keeping his voice down. The parts of the facility he'd had no hand in designing made little sense to him. "Why show them what we did?"

"To keep them in," Thurman said. He balanced the tray with one hand and pressed the call button on the express. "It's not that we're showing them what we did. We're showing them what's out there. Those screens and a few taboos are all that contain these people. Humans have this disease, Donny, this compulsion to move until we bump into something. And then we tunnel through that something, or we sail over the edge of the oceans, or we stagger across mountains—"

The elevator arrived. A man in reactor red excused himself and stepped between the two. They boarded, and Thurman fumbled for his badge. "Fear," he said. "Even the fear of death is barely enough to counter this compulsion of ours. If we didn't show them what was there, they would go look for themselves. That's what we've always done."

Donald considered this. He thought about his own desire, his mad urge, to escape the confines of all that pressing concrete. Even if it meant death out there. The slow strangulation was worse, he decided. It was all about choosing the lesser of two evils.

"I'd rather see a reset than extinguish the entire silo," he said, watching the numbers race by. He didn't mention that he'd been reading up on the people who lived there. Bad things would happen to many of them, but there would be a chance at life afterward.

"I'm less and less eager to gas the place, myself," Thurman admitted. "When Vic was around, all I did was argue against wasting our time with any one silo like this. Now that he's gone, I find myself pulling for these people. It's like I have to honor his last wishes. And that's a dangerous trap to fall into."

The elevator stopped on twenty and picked up two workers, who ceased a conversation of their own and fell silent for the ride. Donald thought about this process of cleansing a silo only to watch the violence repeat itself. The great wars he remembered from the old days came like this, a new generation unremembering, so that sons marched into the wars their fathers had fought before them.

The two workers got off at the rec hall, resuming their conversation as the doors closed. Donald remembered how much he enjoyed punishing himself in the weight room. Now he was wasting away with little appetite, nothing to push against, no resistance.

"It makes me wonder sometimes if that was why he did what he did," Thurman said. The elevator slid toward fifty-five. "Vic calculated everything. Always with a purpose. Maybe his way of winning this argument of ours was to ensure he had the last word." Thurman glanced at Donald. "Hell, it's what finally got me to agree to wake you up."

Donald didn't say out loud how crazy that sounded. He thought Thurman just needed some way to make sense of the unthinkable. Of course, there was another way Victor's death had ended the argument. Not for the first time, Donald imagined that it hadn't been a suicide at all. But he didn't see where such doubts could get him except in trouble.

They got off on fifty-five and carried the trays through the aisles of munitions. As they passed the sleeping drones, Donald thought of his sister, similarly sleeping. It was good to know where she was, that she was safe. A small comfort.

They ate at the war table. Donald pushed his dinner around his plate while Thurman and Anna talked. The two reports sat before him, constant companions, a bevy of notes with a splatter of blood, a report that he'd been reading too much into, notes about him remembering, about this being the great *why* of it all.

Just a scrap of paper, he thought. No mystery. He had been looking at the wrong thing, assuming there was a clue in the words, but it was just Donald's *existence* that Victor had remarked upon. He had sat across the hall from Donald and watched him react to whatever was in their water or their pills. Victor had watched him go mad. And now when Donald looked at his notes, all he saw was a piece of paper with pain scrawled across it amid specks of blood. Blood that had been copied over with the handwritten notes, both now black as copier toner.

Ignore the blood, he told himself. The blood wasn't a clue. It had come after. There were several splatters in a wide space left in the notes. Donald had been studying the senseless. He had been looking for something that wasn't there. He may as well have been staring off into space.

Space. Donald set his fork down and grabbed the other report. Once you ignored the large spots of blood, there was a hole, a vacancy where nothing had been written. This was what he should've been focused on. Not what was there, but what wasn't.

He checked the other report—the corresponding location of that blank space—to see what was written there. He was grasping at air, he knew. Sure enough, when he found the right spot, his excitement vanished. It was the paragraph that didn't belong, the one about the young inductee whose great grandmother remembered the old times. It was nothing.

Unless—

Donald sat up straight. Thurman had said the report wasn't about its contents at all. But maybe they had been looking at the *wrong contents*. He took the two reports and placed them on top of each other. Anna was telling Thurman about her progress with the jamming of the radio towers, that she would be done soon. Thurman was saying that they could all get off shift in the next few days, get the schedule back in order. Donald held the overlapping reports up to the lights. Thurman looked on curiously.

"He wrote *around* something," Donald muttered. "Not *over* something."

He met Thurman's gaze and smiled. "You were wrong." The two pieces of paper trembled in his hands. "There is something here. He wasn't interested in me at all."

Anna set down her utensils and leaned over to have a look.

"If I had the original, I would've seen it straight away." He pointed to the space in the notes, then slid the top page away and tapped his finger on the one paragraph that didn't belong. The one that had nothing to do with Silo 12 at all.

"Here's why your resets don't work," he said. Anna grabbed the bottom report and read about the shadow Donald had inducted, the one whose great-grandmother remembered the old days, the one who had asked him a question about whether those stories were true.

"Someone in Silo 18 remembers," Donald said with confidence. "Maybe a bunch of people do, passing the knowledge down in secret from generation to generation. Or they're immune like me. They remember."

Thurman took a sip of his water. He set down the glass and glanced from his daughter to Donald. "More reason to pull the plug," he said.

"No," Donald told him. "No. That's not what Victor thought." He tapped the dead man's notes. "He wanted to find the one who remembers, but he didn't mean me." He turned to Anna. "I don't think he wanted me up at all. This isn't about me."

Anna looked up at her father, a puzzled expression on her face. She turned to Donald. "Are you saying there's another way?"

"Yes." He stood and paced behind the chairs, stepping over the wires that snaked across the tiles. "We need to call 18 and ask the head there if anyone fits this profile, someone or some group sowing discord, maybe talking about the world we—" He stopped himself from saying *destroyed*.

"Okay," Anna said, nodding her head. "Okay. Let's say they do know. Let's say we find these people over there like you. What then?"

He stopped his pacing. This was the part he hadn't considered. He found Thurman studying him, the old man's lips pursed.

"We find these people—" Donald said.

And he knew. He knew Thurman had been right. There was that story of a medic wounded, there was Donald's frustration with what had been done to the world. He imagined what it might take to save these people in this distant silo, these welders and shopkeeps and metalsmiths and their young shadows. He remembered being the one on a previous shift to press that button, to kill in order to save.

And he knew he would do it again.

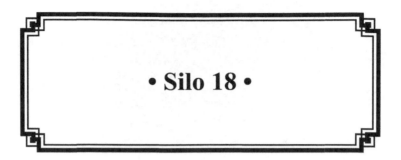

• Silo 18 •

Hush, my child, too late to cry
The skies are dark, the rivers dry
Our parents gave us lives to keep
Buried here beneath the deep

They sent us down below the dirt
They lied and said it wouldn't hurt
Their lies still shield us from our dread
Buried here beside our dead

We cannot leave, we must not cry
We'll show them that our cheeks are dry
Now sleep, my child, accept the dream
Buried here, unless you clean

-Mary Fonvielle, age 22

·48·

Mission's throat itched and his eyes stung, the smoke growing heavier and the stench stronger as he approached Lower Dispatch. At least the pursuit from above seemed to have faltered, perhaps from the gap in the rails that had claimed a life.

Cam was gone, of that he felt certain. How many others? A twinge of guilt accompanied the sick thought that the fallen would have to be carried up to the farms in plastic bags. Someone would have to do that job, and it wouldn't be a pretty one.

He shook this thought away as he got within a level of Dispatch. Tears streamed down his face and mixed with the sweat and grime of the long day's descent. He bore bad news. A shower and clean clothes would do little to alleviate the weariness he felt, but there would be protection here, help in clearing up the confusion about the blast. He hurried down the last half flight and remembered, perhaps due to the rising ash that reminded him of a note he'd torn to confetti, the reason he'd been chasing after Cam in the first place.

Rodny. His friend was locked away in IT, and his plea for help had been lost in the din and confusion of the explosion.

The explosion. Cam. The package. The *delivery*.

Mission wobbled and clutched the railing for balance. He thought of the ridiculous fee for the delivery, a fee that perhaps was never meant to be paid. He gathered himself and hurried on, wondering what in the depths was going on, what kind of trouble his friend might be in, and how to help him. How, even, to *get* to him.

The air grew thick and it burned to breathe as he arrived at Dispatch. A small crowd huddled on the stairway. They peered across the landing and into the open doors of one-twenty-two. Mission coughed into his fist as he pushed his way through the gawkers. Had the wreckage from above landed here? Everything seemed intact. Two buckets lay on their sides near the door, and a gray fire hose snaked over the railing and trailed inside. A blanket of smoke clung to the ceiling; it trailed out and up the wall of the stairwell shaft like water from a giant faucet defying gravity.

Mission pulled his 'chief up over his nose, confused. The smoke was coming from *inside*. He breathed in through his mouth, the fabric pressing against his lips and lessening the sting in his throat. Dark shapes moved inside the hallway. He unsnapped the strap that held his knife in place and crossed the threshold, keeping low to stay away from the smoke.

Eli, one of the senior dispatchers, met him in the hall. He had a basket of scorched paper in his hands, a mournful look on his face. The floors were everywhere wet and squished with the traffic from deeper inside. It was dark, but cones of light danced around like fretful things.

"Look what you've done," Eli cried to Mission. "Look what you've done."

Mission hurried past him and toward the flashlights. The smoke was thicker, the water on the floor deeper. Bits of pulp worth saving floated on the surface. He passed one of the dormitories, the sorting hall, the front offices.

Lily, an elder porter, ran by in slaps and spray, recognizable only at the last moment as the beam from her flashlight briefly lit her face. There was someone lying in the water, pressed up against the wall. As Mission approached and a passing light played over the form, he saw that they weren't lying there at all. It was Hackett, one of the few dispatchers who treated the young shadows with respect and never seemed to take delight in their burdens. The glimpse Mission got revealed half a face recognizable, the other half a red blister. Deathdays. Lottery numbers flashed in Mission's vision.

"Porter! Get over here."

It was Morgan's voice. The old man's cough joined a chorus of others. The hallway was full of ripples and waves, splashes and hacks, smoke and commands. Mission hurried toward the familiar silhouette, his eyes burning.

"Sir? It's Mission. The explosion—" He pointed toward the ceiling.

"I know my own shadows, boy." A light was trained on Mission's eyes, a physical lash of sorts. "Get in here and give these lads a hand."

The smell of cooked beans and burnt and wet paper was overpowering. There was a hint of fuel behind it all, a smell Mission knew from the Down Deep and its generators. He had lugged a massive filter once that reeked of this. And there was something else: the smell of the bazaar during a pig roast, a foul and unpleasant odor.

The water in the main hall was deep. It lapped up over Mission's halfboots and filled them with muck. Drawers of files were being emptied into buckets. An empty crate was shoved into his hands, cones of light swirling in the mist, shapes moving and kicking up splashes, his nose burning and running, tears on his cheeks unbidden.

"Here, here," someone said, urging him forward. They warned him not to touch the filing cabinet. Piles of paper went into the crate, heavier than they should be. Mission didn't understand the rush. The fire was out. The walls were black where the flames must've licked them with their orange tongues, and the grow plots along the far wall where rows of beans had run up tall trestles were all ash. The trestles stood like black fingers, those that stood at all.

The porter beside him, Mission couldn't see who, cursed the farmers before leaving with a load. Amanda was there at the filing cabinet, her 'chief wrapped around her hand, managing the drawers as they were emptied. The crate filled up fast. Mission spotted someone emptying the wall safe of its old books as he turned back toward the hallway. There was a body in the corner covered in a sheet. Nobody was in as much of a hurry to remove that.

He followed the others toward the landing, but they did not go all the way out. The emergency lights in the dorm room were on, mattresses stacked up in the corner. Carter, Lyn, and Jocelyn were spreading the files out on the springs. Mission unloaded his crate and went back for another load. He asked Amanda what had happened, if this was retribution of some sort.

"They came for the beans," she said. She used her 'chief to wrestle with another drawer. "They came for the beans, and they burned it all."

Mission took in the wide swath of damage. He recalled how the stairwell had trembled during the blast, still saw the bodies falling and screaming to their deaths. Something was going on. The months of small violences had ramped up like a switch had been flipped. He wasn't convinced that this was about the beans at all.

•••

"So what do we do now?" Carter asked. He was a powerful porter, in his early thirties where men find their strength and have yet to lose their joints, but he looked absolutely beat. His hair clung to his forehead in wet clumps. There were black smears on his face, and you could no longer tell what color his 'chief had been. All signs that he had been present for and had fought back the fire.

"Now we burn their crops," someone suggested.

"The crops we eat?"

"Just the upper farms. They're the ones that did this."

"We don't know who did this," Morgan said.

Mission caught his old caster's eye. "In the storehouse," he said. "I saw— Was that—?"

Morgan nodded. "Hendricks. Aye."

Carter slapped the wall and barked profanities. "I'll kill 'em!" he yelled.

"So you're . . ." Mission wanted to say *Lower Chief*, but it was too soon for that to make sense.

"Aye," Morgan said, and Mission could tell it made little sense to him as well.

"People will be carrying whatever they like for a few days," Joel said. He coughed into his palm while Lyn looked on with concern. "We'll appear weak if we don't strike back."

Mission had other concerns besides appearing weak. The people above thought a porter had attacked them. And now this with the farmers, so far from where they'd been hit the night before. Porters were the nearest thing to a roaming sentry, and they were being knocked out by someone, purposefully he thought. There were all those boys being recruited into IT. It wasn't computers they were being hired to fix. It was something else.

"I need to get home," Mission said. It was a slip. He meant to say Up Top. He worked to unknot his 'chief. The thing reeked of smoke, as did his hands and his coveralls. He would need to find another color to don. He needed to get in touch with his friends.

"What do you think you're doing?" Morgan asked. His former caster seemed ready to say something else as Mission tugged the 'chief away. Instead, the old man's eyes fell to the bright red whelp around Mission's neck, the stain of a rope's embrace.

"I don't think this is about us at all," he said. "I think this is bigger than that. A friend of mine's in trouble. He's at the heart of all that's going wrong. I think something bad is going to happen to him or that he might know something. They won't let him talk to anyone."

"Rodny?" Lyn asked. She and Joel had been two years ahead of him, but they both knew he and Rodny from the Nest.

He nodded. "And Cam is dead," he told the others. He explained what'd happened on his way down, the blast, the people chasing him, the gap in the rails. Hands covered gaping mouths. Someone whispered Cam's name in disbelief. "I don't think anyone cares that we know," Mission added. "I think that's the point. Everyone's supposed to be angry. As angry as possible."

"I need time to think," Morgan said. "To plan."

"I don't know that there is much time," Mission said. He told them about the new hires at IT. He told Morgan about seeing Bradley there, about the young porter applying for a different job.

"What do we do?" Lyn asked, looking to Joel and the others.

"We take it easy," Morgan said, but he didn't seem so sure. The confidence he displayed as a senior porter and caster seemed shaken now that he was a chief. It was how knees got wobbly when that last bit of weight went onto a heavy load.

"I can't stay down here," Mission said flatly. "You can have every vacation chit I own, but I've got to get up-top. I don't know how, but I have to."

Beffore he went anywhere, Mission needed to get in touch with friends he could trust, anyone who might be able to help, the old gang from the Nest. As Morgan urged everyone on the landing back to work, Mission slunk down the dark and smoky hallway toward the sorting room, which had a computer he might use. Lyn and Joel followed, more eager to help Rodny than to clean up after the fire.

They checked the monitor at the sorting counter and saw that the computer was down, possibly from the power outage the night before. Mission remembered all those people with their broken computers earlier that morning at IT and wondered if there would be a working machine anywhere on five levels. Since he couldn't send a wire, he picked up the hard line to the other Dispatch offices to see if they could get a message out for him.

He tried Central, first. Lyn stood with him at the counter, her flashlight illuminating the dials and highlighting the haze of smoke in the room. Joel splashed among the shelves, moving the reusable sorting crates on the bottom higher up to keep them from getting wet. There was no response from Central.

"Maybe the fire got the radio, too," she whispered.

Mission didn't think so. The power light was on and the thing was making that crackling sound when he squeezed the button. He heard Morgan splash past in the hallway, yelling and complaining that his workforce was disappearing. Lyn cupped her hand over her flashlight. "Something is going on at Central," he told Lyn. He had a bad feeling.

The second waystation he tried up-top finally won a response. "Who's this?" someone asked with none of the formality nor the jargon radio operators were known for.

"This is Mission. Who's this?"

"Mission? You're in big trouble, man."

Mission glanced at Lyn. "Who is this?" he asked.

"This is Robbie. They left me alone up here, man. I haven't heard from anybody. But everyone's looking for you. What's going on down there?"

Joel stopped with the crates and trained his flashlight on the counter.

"Everyone's looking for me?" Mission asked.

"You and Cam, a few of the others. There was some kind of fight at Central. Were you there for that? I can't get word from anyone!"

Mission told him to calm down, which seemed an unfair thing to expect when he could hardly think straight himself. "Robbie, I need you to get in touch with some friends of mine. Can you send out wires? Something's wrong with our computers down here."

"No, ours are all kind of sideways. We've been having to use the terminal up at the mayor's office."

"The mayor's office? Okay, I need you to send a couple of wires, then. You got something to write with?"

"Wait," Robbie said. "These are official wires, right? If not, I don't have the authority—"

"Damnit, Robbie, this is important! Grab something to write with. I'll pay you back. They can dock me for it if they want." Mission glanced up at Lyn, who was shaking her head in disbelief. He coughed into his fist, the smoke tickling his throat. They should be *moving*, not explaining this to someone else.

"All right, all right," Robbie said. "Who'm I sending this to? And you owe me for this piece of paper because it's all I have to write on."

Mission let go of the transmit button to curse the kid. Joel laughed from behind the sorting stacks. Composing himself a moment, Mission thought about who would be most likely to get a wire and send it along to the others. He ended up giving Robbie three names, then told him what to write. He would have his friends meet him at the Nest, or meet each other if he couldn't make it there himself. The Nest had to be safe.

Nobody would mess with the school or the Crow. Once the gang was together, they could figure out what to do. Maybe the Crow would know what to do. The hardest part for Mission would be figuring out how to join them.

"You got all that?" he asked Robbie, when the boy didn't reply.

"Yeah, yeah, man. I think you're gonna be over the character limit, though. This better come out of your pay."

"You've gotta be kidding me," Mission said, careful to release the mic first.

"Now what?" Lyn asked as he hung up the receiver. She played her flashlight around the sorting room, the beam catching in the smoke and dancing across the ripples in the water. Joel's boots had thrown the wet film into chaos. He had gotten most of the sorting crates moved up so they wouldn't get wet.

"I need coveralls," Mission said. He splashed around the counter and joined Joel by the shelves, began looking through the nearest crates. "They're looking for me, so I'm gonna need new colors if I'm getting up there."

"We," Lyn told him. "We need new colors. If you're going to the Nest, I'm coming with you."

"Me too," Joel said.

"I appreciate that," Mission said, "but company might make it more dangerous. We'd be more conspicuous."

"Yeah, but they're looking for you," Lyn said.

"Hey, we have a ton of these new whites." Joel pulled the lid off a sorting bin. "But they'll just make us stand out, won't they?"

"Whites?" Mission headed over to see what Joel was talking about.

"Yeah. For Security. We've been moving a ton of these lately. Came down from Garment a few days ago. No idea why they made up so many."

Mission checked the coveralls. The ones on top were covered in soot, more gray than white. There were dozens of them stacked in the reusable sorting crate. He remembered all the new hires. It was like they wanted half the silo to be dressed in white, the other half fighting one another. It made no sense. Unless the goal was simply to get everyone dead.

"Dead," Mission said out loud.

The others swung their flashlights at him. Mission was already splashing down the shelves to another crate. "I've got a better idea," he called out. A coughing fit seized him as he found the right bin. He and Cam had been given one of these just a few days ago. He reached in and pulled out a bag. "How would you two like to make some money?"

Joel and Lyn hurried over to see what he'd found, and Mission held up one of the heavy plastic bags with the bright silver zipper and the hauling straps.

"Three-hundred and eighty-four chits to divide between you," he promised. "Every chit I own. I just need you for one last tandem."

The two porters played their lights across the object in his hands. It was a black bag. A black bag made for hauls such as these.

· 50 ·

The ground was too wet to roll it out proper, so Mission used the main counter, instead. He promised Lyn and Joel that he would transfer every chit in his account as soon as they got to a working computer. Joel told him to save his breath. They were just as eager as he was to get to higher levels. The bag, with all of death's taboo, would afford protection to them all.

Lyn worked the bright zipper loose, and Joel peeled the flaps back. Mission sat on the counter and worked the laces on his boots free. They were soaked, his socks as well. He shucked them off to keep the water out of the bag and to save the weight. Always a porter, thinking about weight. Lyn handed him one of the Security coveralls, an extra precaution. He wiggled out of his porter blues and tugged the whites on while Lyn looked the other way. His knife, he strapped back to his waist.

Outside, flashlights danced in the main hall, the other porters still recovering from the damage wrought by fire and flood. Mission coughed into his palm and snapped up the coveralls, which were at least a size too big for him. "You guys sure you're up for this?" he asked.

Lyn helped him slide his feet into the bag and worked the inside straps around his ankles. Never before had a corpse made it so easy. "Are *you* sure?" she asked, cinching the straps tight.

Mission laughed, his stomach fluttering with nerves. He stretched out and let them work the top straps under his shoulders. It felt surreal to be placing himself inside one of the bags. He had never heard of anyone getting in one willingly.

"Have you both eaten?" he asked.

"We'll be fine," Joel said. "Stop worrying."

"If it gets late—"

"Lie your head back," Lyn told him. She began working the zipper from his feet. "And don't talk unless we tell you it's okay. You'll have people jumping the rails out there if they hear you or see you move."

"We'll take a break every twenty or so," Joel added. "We'll bring you into a restroom with us. You can stretch and get some water."

Mission lifted a hand out to stop the zipper from passing his stomach. "Don't mention water," he said. He listened to the sounds of lapping ripples against the counter, the squish of the other two porters moving about in their boots. He begged his bladder to ignore the cues.

"Get your hand inside," Lyn told him. She worked the zipper up over his chest to his chin, hesitated, then kissed the pads of her fingers and touched his forehead the same way he'd seen countless loved ones and priests bless the dead. "May your steps rise to the heavens," she whispered.

Her wan smile caught in the spill of Joel's flashlight before the bag was sealed up over Mission's face.

"Or at least until Upper Dispatch," Joel added.

••••

Getting out of the lower waystation proved simple. Their fellow porters made way for the dead, maybe thinking Roker was the one in the bag. Several hands reached out and touched Mission through the plastic, showing respect, and he fought not to flinch nor cough. It felt as though the smoke was trapped in the bag with him. It pervaded his hair and skin, despite the brand new coveralls.

Joel took the lead, which meant Mission's shoulders were pressed against his. He faced upward, his body swaying in time to their steps, the straps beneath his armpits pulling the opposite way he was used to. It grew more comfortable as they hit the stairs and began the long spiral up. His feet were lowered until the blood no longer pooled in his head. Lyn carried her half of his weight from several steps below.

The dark and quiet overtook him as they left the chaos of the waystation. The two porters didn't talk as some tandems might. They saved their lungs and kept their thoughts to themselves. Joel set an aggressive pace. Mission could almost hear Morgan's metronome ticking, that silver arm that rocked back and forth with the time. Mission was that arm, now. He could sense the pace in his own gentle swaying, his body suspended in space above the steel treads.

As the steps passed, the intolerableness grew. It wasn't the difficulty breathing, for he had been shadowed well to manage his lungs on a long climb. And he could handle the stuffiness with the plastic pressed against his face. Nor was it the dark; his favorite hour for porting had always been the dim-time, being alone with his thoughts, stirring while others slept. It wasn't the stench of plastic and smoke, the tickle in his throat, or the pain of the straps.

It took several spirals around the central post to put his finger on what discomforted him so, what caused a hollow pit to form in his stomach, a likewise gaping void in his chest, that mix of feelings he got when he had free time and nothing to fill it with. His entire body felt like his legs sometimes did when they needed to twitch but he forced them still. It was an anxiety, and one that went beyond fearing for his friends, beyond the death of Cam, beyond the terror of a silo crumbling down around him. He placed the sensation as he listened to Joel's heavy and steady breathing, as he felt in his motionless legs the work and agony of his friends', as he endured doing nothing while they hauled his burdens. This was what Mission felt knotting his gut above all else: It was the act of lying still. Of being carried.

He was a burden. A burden.

The straps pinched his shoulders until his arms fell numb, and he swayed in the darkness, the sounds of boots on steel, of breathing, as he was lifted toward the heavens. Too great a burden. This was his weakness, his inability to be carried.

Mission felt like sobbing—but the tears would not come. He thought of his mother carrying him for all those months, no one to tell and no one to support her. Not until his father found out, and by then it was too late.

He wondered how long his father had hated the bulge in her belly, how long he had wanted to cut Mission out like some cancer. Until it was too late and this was all his dad was left with, a tumor to raise, a reminder. Mission had never asked to be carried like that. And he had never wanted to be ported by anyone ever again.

Two years ago to the day. That was the last time he had felt this, this sense of being a burden to all. Two years since he had proved too much for even a rope to bear.

It was a poor knot he had tied. Morgan would've been disgusted by the effort. But his hands had been trembling and he had fought to see the knot through a film of tears. When it failed, the knot didn't come free so much as slide, and it left his neck afire and bleeding. His great regret was having jumped from the lower stairwell in Mechanical, the rope looped over the pipes above. If he had gone from a landing, the slipping knot wouldn't have mattered. The fall would've claimed him.

Now he was too scared to try again. He was as scared of trying again as he was of being a burden to another. Was that why he avoided seeing Allie, because she longed to care for him? To help support him? Was that why he ran away from home? Why he pined for a girl that he knew deep down cared more for another?

The intolerableness grew until Mission began to hate the boy stuffed in that bag with him. A boy too scared to live, too frightened to die.

The tears finally came. His arms were pinned, so he couldn't wipe them away. He thought of his mother, about whom he could only piece together a few details. But he knew this of her: She hadn't been afraid of life or death. She had embraced both in an act that he knew he would never make worthy.

More tears. And there weren't enough chits in the silo to pay back the debt of being carried by others. The silo spun slowly around him; the steps sank one at a time; and Mission endured the suffering of this self-discovery. He labored not to sob, seeing himself for the first time in that utter darkness, knowing his soul more fully in that deathly ritual of being ported to his grave, this sad awakening on his birthday.

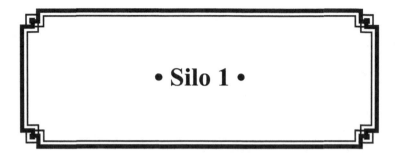

• Silo 1 •

Fear cannot be without hope nor hope without fear.

-Baruch Spinoza

•51•

Finding one among ten thousand should've been more difficult than this. It should've taken months of crawling through reports and databases, of querying the Head of 18 and asking for personality profiles, of looking at arrest histories, cleaning schedules, who was related to whom, where people spent their time, and all the gossip and chatter compiled from monthly reports.

But Donald found an easier way. He simply searched the database for *himself*.

One who remembers. One full of fear and paranoia. One who tries to blend in but is subversive. He looked for a fear of doctors, teasing out those residents who never went to see them. He looked for someone who shunned medication and found one who did not even trust the water. A part of him expected he might find several people to be causing so much havoc, a pack, and that locating one among them would lead to the rest. He expected to find them young and outraged with some way of handing down what they knew from generation to generation.

This was what he expected, and so he put it out of mind. He did not act on what was probable. He stayed up for most of the night searching simply for himself. He searched for himself the way he had searched for Helen and his sister. And what he found was both eerily similar and not like him at all.

The next morning, he showed his results to Thurman, who stood perfectly still for a long while.

"Of course," he finally said. He looked at Anna, his daughter, with tears in his eyes. "Of course."

A hand on Donald's shoulder was all the congratulations he got. Thurman explained that the reset was well underway. He admitted that it had been underway since Donald had been woken. Erskine and Dr. Henson were working through the night to make changes, to come up with a new formulation, but this component might take weeks. Looking over what Donald had found, he said he was going to make a call to 18.

"I want to come with you," Donald said. "It's my theory."

What he wanted to say was that he wouldn't take the coward's way. If someone was to be executed on his account—a life taken in order to save others—he didn't want to remove himself, to hide from it.

Thurman agreed.

They rode the lift almost as equals. Donald asked why Thurman had started the reset, but he thought he knew the answer.

"Vic won," was Thurman's reply.

Donald thought of the lives in a database that were now thrown into chaos. This is what generals and politicians felt, sitting in a room some comfortable distance away, gathered around a table where death was planned and hoped against. He made the mistake of asking how the reset was going, and Thurman told him about the bombs and the recruits, how these things typically went, that the recipe was as old as time.

"The combustibles are always there," he said. "You'd be surprised at how few sparks it takes."

They exited the lift and walked down a familiar hallway. This was Donald's old commute. Here, he had worked under a different name. He had worked without knowing what he was doing. They passed offices full of people clacking on keyboards and chatting with one another. Half a millennium of people coming on and off shifts, doing what they were told, following orders.

He couldn't help himself as they approached his old office: he paused at the door and peered in. A thin man with a halo of hair that wrapped from ear to ear, just a few wisps on top, looked up at him. He sat there, mouth agape, hand resting on his mouse, waiting for Donald to say or do something.

Donald nodded a sympathetic hello. He turned and looked through the door across the hall where a man in white sat behind a similar desk. The puppeteer. It was a wonder people didn't trip on the strings.

Thurman spoke to the man in white, who got up from his desk and joined them in the hall. Here was one who seemed to know that Thurman was in charge. Tiers of puppets.

Donald followed the two of them to the comm room, leaving the balding man at his old desk to his game of solitaire. He felt a mix of sympathy and envy for the man, this captain at a rudderless wheel. Sympathy and envy for those who don't remember. As they turned the corner, Donald thought back to those initial bouts of awareness on his first shift. He remembered speaking with a doctor who knew, and having this sense of wonder that anyone could cope with such knowledge. And now he saw that it wasn't that the pain grew tolerable or the confusion went away. Instead, it simply became familiar. It became a part of you. It was a nasty scar that still flared up now and then but that you lived with.

The comm room was quiet. Heads swiveled as the three of them entered. One of the operators hurriedly removed his feet from his desk. Another took a bite of his protein bar and turned back to his station.

"Get me Eighteen," Thurman said.

Eyes turned to the other man in white, who waved his consent. A call was patched through. Thurman held half a headset to one ear while he waited. He caught the expression on Donald's face and waved the operator for another set. Donald stepped forward and accepted it while the cable was slotted into the receiver. He could hear the familiar beeping of a call being placed, and his stomach fluttered as doubts began to surface. Finally, a voice answered. A shadow.

Thurman asked him to get Mr. Wyck, the silo Head.

"He's already coming," the shadow said.

When Wyck joined the conversation, Thurman told the Head what Donald had found, but it was the shadow who responded. The shadow knew the one they were after. He said that they were close. There was something in his voice, some shock or hesitation, and Thurman waved at the operator to get the sensors in his headset going. Suddenly, it was a

Rite of Initiation they were conducting. This shadow became Thurman's target, and Donald watched a master at work.

"Tell me what you know," he said. Thurman leaned over the operator and peered at a screen that monitored skin conductivity, heartbeat, and perspiration. Donald was no expert at reading the charts, but he knew something was up by the way the lines spiked up and down while the shadow spoke. He feared for the young man. He wondered if someone would die then and there.

But such was not Thurman's intent. Within moments, he had the boy speaking of his childhood, had him admitting to this rage he harbored, a sense of not belonging, the need to act up and lash out. He spoke of a childhood that seemed both ideal and frustrating, and Thurman was like a gentle but firm drill sergeant working with a troubled recruit: tearing him down, building him back up.

"You've been fed the truth," he told the young man. "And now you see why it must be divvied out carefully or not at all."

"I do."

The shadow sniffed as though he were crying. And yet: the jagged lines on the screen formed less precipitous peaks, less dangerous valleys.

Thurman spoke of sacrifice, of the greater good, of individual lives proving meaningless in the far stretch of time. He took that shadow's rage and redirected it until the work of being locked up for months with the Legacy was distilled down to its very essence. And through it all, it didn't sound as though the silo Head breathed once.

"Tell me what needs to be fixed," Thurman said, after their discussion. He laid the problem at the shadow's feet. Donald saw how this was better than simply handing him the solution.

The shadow spoke of a culture forming that overvalued individuality, of children that wanted to get away from their families, of generations living levels apart and independence stressed until no one relied on anyone and everyone was dispensable.

The sobs came. Donald watched as Thurman's face tightened, and he wondered again if he was about to see a death ordered, a young man put out of his misery. Instead, the white-haired general, this senator of another time, released the radio for a moment and said to those gathered around, simply, "He's ready."

And what started as an inquiry, a test of Donald's theory, concluded this boy's dose of the Legacy and his Rite of Initiation. A shadow became a man. Lines on a screen settled into steel cords of resolve as his anger was given a new focus, a new purpose. His childhood was seen differently. Dangerously.

Thurman gave this young man his first order. Mr. Wyck congratulated the boy and provided his freedom. And later, as Donald and Thurman rode the elevator back toward Anna, Thurman declared that this Rodny would make a fine silo Head. Even better than the last.

· 52 ·

That afternoon, Donald and Anna worked to restore order to the war room. They made it ready in case it was called upon during a future shift. All their notes were taken off the walls and filed away into airtight plastic crates, and Donald imagined these would sit on another level somewhere, another storeroom, to gather dust. The computers were unplugged, all the wiring coiled up, and these were hauled off by Erskine on a cart with squeaky wheels. All that was left were the cots, a change of clothes, and the standard issue toiletries. Enough to get them through the night and to their meeting with Dr. Henson the following day.

Several shifts were about to come to a close. For Anna and Thurman, it had been a long time coming. Two full shifts. Almost a year awake. Erskine and Henson would need a few weeks to finish their work, and by that time the next Head would come on, and the schedule would return to normal. For Donald, it had been less than a week awake after nearly a century of sleep. He was a dead man who had blinked his eyes open for but a moment. Just a peek, and now back again.

Something told him his dreams would be different this time. There might still be a mountain of skulls to climb, but some of those bleached skulls with their empty sockets would now have names. Names gleaned from a database. Families that may or may not survive the great reset of Silo 18. Some that would die so that others might live.

He thought of them as he took his last shower, as he brushed his teeth, took his first dose of the bitter drink so that no one would think anything was amiss. But Donald didn't plan on sleeping or dreaming. To him, this deep freeze was worse than death. Not only did it carry him farther and farther from Helen, whisking him through the years while she returned to dust, the deep freeze was a false sleep that could only be filled with nightmares and only be disturbed by tragedy.

If he went back to sleep, they would never get him up again. He knew that. Unless things were so bad that he wouldn't want to be woken anyway. Unless it were Anna once more, lonely, wishing for company, and willing to subject him to abuse in order to get it.

That wasn't sleep. That was a body and a mind stored away. There were other choices, more final ways out. Donald had discovered this resolve by following a trail of clues left behind by Victor, and he would soon arrive at the man's same fateful conclusion.

He walked a final lap amid the guns and drones. He touched the wings beneath the tarps, and finally retired to his cot. He thought of Helen as he lay there listening to Anna sing in the shower one last time. And he realized the anger he had felt for his wife having lived and loved without him was now gone. It had been wiped away by his guilt for coming to find solace in Anna's embrace. And when she came to him that night, straight from the shower with water beading on her flesh, he could not be strong. They had the same bitter drink on their breath, that concoction that prepped their veins for the deep sleep, and neither of them cared. Donald succumbed. And then he waited until she had returned to her cot and her breathing had softened before he cried himself to sleep. And in that sleep, he discovered no doubts about the voyage he had planned for the following day.

When he woke, Anna was already gone, her cot neatly made. Donald did the same, tucking the sheets beneath the mattress and leaving the corners crisp, even though he knew the sheets would be mussed as the cots were returned to their rightful place in the barracks. He checked the time. Anna had been put under during the early morning so as not to be spotted. He had less than an hour before Thurman would come for him. It was more than enough time.

He went out to the storeroom and approached the drone nearest the hangar door. Yanking the tarp off sent a cloud of dust into the air.

Donald coughed and covered his mouth. He waved his hand in the air, then dragged out the empty bin he had stuffed under one of the wings. He opened the low hangar door and arranged the tough plastic bin so that it was slightly inside the lift. He lowered the door onto the bin to keep the small hangar propped open.

Opening the adjacent door, he hurried down the hallway, past the empty barracks, and pulled the plastic sheet off the station at the very end. His explorations had recently turned from discovery into experimentation. Flipping the plastic cover off the lift switch, he threw it into the up position. The first time he'd done this, the door to the lift would no longer open, but he could hear the platform rumbling upward on the other side of the wall. It hadn't taken long to figure out a solution.

Replacing the plastic sheet, he hurried down the hall. He could still taste the bitter prepping agent in his mouth and wished he'd been able to avoid drinking that. It would be a horrible final taste.

He turned off the light in the hall and shut the door. The other bin was pulled out from under the drone's left wing. The contents had been assembled and arranged carefully. Donald stripped and tossed his clothes under the drone. He pulled out the thick plastic suit and sat down to work his feet into the legs. The boots went on next, Donald being careful to seal the cuffs around them. Standing up, he gripped the dangling shoelace stolen from an extra boot. The end had been tied to the zipper on the back of the suit. He pulled it over his shoulder and tugged upward, hand over hand, like he'd seen surfers and divers do. He made sure the zipper went to the top before pulling the gloves, flashlight, and helmet from the bin.

The helmet went on before the gloves, as the latches were difficult to operate. After tugging on the second glove, he did one final check of the suit to be sure everything was properly sealed. Satisfied, he closed the bin and slid the container back under the wing before covering the drone with the tarp. There would only be a single trunk out of place when Thurman arrived. Victor had left a mess to discover. Donald would hardly leave a trace.

He crawled inside the lift on his belly, pushing the flashlight ahead of him. He could hear the motor inside straining against the pinned bin to move upward, a whirring like an angry hive of bees. Turning on the flashlight, he took a last look at the storeroom, braced himself, then kicked the plastic tub with both boots.

It budged. There was a scraping sound. He kicked again, and the lift shook from the violence. Just a few more inches. A last kick, and he barely got his boots back inside in time. There was a thunderous racket as the door slammed shut, a bang like an explosion, and then he felt the shudder of movement. Cables rattled and sang above. The flashlight jittered and danced. Donald corralled the loose flashlight between his mitts and watched his exhalations fog the inside of his helmet. He had no idea what to expect, but he was causing it. For once, he was the agent of change. He was going somewhere by choice.

• 53 •

The ride up took much longer than he anticipated. There were moments when he wasn't sure whether or not he was still moving. His body told him several times that he was in fact heading back down, that he had changed direction. He grew worried that his plan had been discovered, that the misplaced bin had led them to his tracks in the dust, that he was being recalled. He urged the lift to hurry along.

His flashlight gave out. Donald tapped the cylinder in his mitt and worked the switch back and forth. It must've been on a weak charge from its long storage. He was left in the dark with all the sensation of a man beneath the sea on a moonless night, no way of knowing which way was up nor down, whether he was bobbing or sinking, rising or drowning. All he could do was wait. And again, he knew that this was the right decision. There was nothing worse than being trapped in the darkness, unable to do anything more than wait. This final time would mark the end of his suffering.

Arrival came with a jarring clank. The persistent hum of the motor disappeared, the ensuing quiet haunting. There was a second clank, and then the door opposite the one he'd entered slowly rose. A metal nub on the floor the size of a fist slid forward on a track that linked up with a groove outside. Donald scrambled after this nub, seeing how the drone might be guided forward.

He found himself in a sloping launch bay. He hadn't known what to expect, thought maybe he'd simply arrive above the soil on a barren landscape, but he was in a shaft. A dim light grew stronger. Above him, up the slope, a slit was opening. Beyond this slit, Donald spotted the roiling clouds he knew from the cafe. They were the bright gray that came with a sunrise. The doors at the top of the slope continued to slide apart like a maw opening wide.

Donald crawled up the steep slope as quickly as he could. The metal car in the track stopped and locked into place. Donald hurried, imagining he didn't have much time. He stayed off the track in case the launch sequence was automated, but the nub never moved, never raced by. He arrived at the open doors exhausted and perspiring and managed to haul himself out.

The world spread out before him. After a week of living in a windowless chamber and decades of sleeping in a virtual grave, the scale and openness were inspiring. Donald felt like tearing off his helmet and sucking in deep breaths of non-confinement. The oppressive weight of his silo imprisonment had been lifted. Above him were only the clouds.

He stood on a round concrete platform. Behind the opening for the launch ramp was a cluster of antennas. He went to these, held onto one of them, and lowered himself to the wide ledge below. From here it was a scramble on his belly, trying to hold onto the slick edge with bulky gloves, and then a graceless drop to the dirt.

He scanned the horizon for the city—had to work his way around the tower to find it. From there, he aimed forty-five degrees to the left. He had studied the maps to make sure, but now that he was there, he realized he could've done it by memory. Over there was where the tents had stood, and here the stage, and beyond them the dirt tracks through the struggling beginnings of grass as ATVs buzzed up the hillside. He could almost smell the food that'd been cooking, could hear the dogs barking and children playing, the anthems in the air.

Donald shook off thoughts of the past and made his time count. He knew there was a chance—a very good chance—that someone was sitting at breakfast in the cafe. They would be dropping their spoon into their reconstituted eggs right then and pointing at the wallscreen. But he had a head start. They would have to wrestle with suits and wonder if the risk was worth it. By the time they got to him, it would be too late. Hopefully, they would simply leave him.

He worked his way up the hillside. Movement was a struggle inside the bulky suit. He slipped and fell several times in the slick soil. When a gust of wind hammered the landscape, it peppered his helmet with grit and made a noise like the hiss of Anna's radio. There was no telling how long the suit would last. He knew enough of the cleaning to suspect it wouldn't be forever, but Anna had told him that the machines in the air were designed to attack only certain things. That was why they didn't destroy the sensors, or the concrete, or a proper suit. And he suspected his silo would only have proper suits.

All he hoped for as he labored up the hill was a view. He was so obsessed and determined to win this that he never thought to look behind him. Always ahead. Slipping and scrambling, crawling on his hands and knees the last fifty feet, until finally he was at the summit. He stood and staggered forward, exhausted, breathing heavily, remembering the bombs in the air and Anna pulling him back to safety, back to hell.

Not this time. He reached the edge and looked down into the adjacent bowl. There, a concrete tower stood like a gravestone, like a monument to Helen. She was buried below, and while he could never go to her, never be buried alongside her, he could lie down beneath the clouds and be close enough.

He wanted his helmet off. First, though, his gloves. He tugged one of them free—popping the seal—and dropped it to the soil. The heavy winds, heavy enough that he found himself leaning into them, sent the glove tumbling down the slope. The grit in the heavy breeze stung his hand. The peppering of fine particles burned like a day on a windy beach. Donald began tugging on his other glove, resigned to what would come next, when suddenly he felt a hand grip his shoulder, and he was yanked back from the edge of that gentle rise, that hard-fought and pleasant view.

• 54 •

Donald stumbled and fell. The shock of being touched sent his heart into his throat. He waved his arms to free himself, but someone had a grip on his suit. More than one person. They dragged him back until he could no longer see Helen's resting spot.

His screams of frustration filled his helmet. Couldn't they see that it was too late? Couldn't they leave him be? He flailed and tried to lunge out of their grip, but he was being pulled down the hill, back toward Silo 1.

When he fell the next time, he was able to roll over and face them, to get his arms up to fend for himself. And there was Thurman standing over him—wearing nothing more than his white coveralls. Dust from the dead earth gathered in the old man's gray brow.

"It's time to go!" Thurman yelled into the heavy wind. His voice seemed as distant as the clouds.

Donald kicked his feet and tried to move like a crab back up the hill, but there were three of them there. All in white, squinting against the ferocity of the driving wind and pelting soil. And they were, none of them, pleased.

"Nooo!" Donald yelled, as they seized him again. He tried to grab rocks and fistfuls of soil as they pulled him along by his boots. His helmet knocked against the lifeless pack of dirt. He watched the clouds boil overhead as his fingernails were bent back and broken in his struggle for some purchase.

By the time they got him to the flats, Donald was spent. They carried him down a ramp and through the airlock where more men were waiting. His helmet was tossed aside before the outer door fully shut. Thurman stood in a far corner and watched as they undressed him. The old man dabbed at the blood running from his nose. Donald had caught him with his boot.

Erskine was there, Dr. Henson as well, both of them breathing hard. As soon as they got his suit off, Henson plunged a needle into Donald's flesh. Erskine held his hand and seemed sad. A darkness like death spread through Donald's veins.

"A bloody waste," someone said, as the fog settled over him.

"Look at this mess."

Erskine placed a hand on Donald's cheek as Donald drifted deeper into the black. His lids grew heavy and his hearing distant.

"Be better if someone like you were in charge," he heard Erskine say.

But it was Victor's voice he heard. It was a dream. No, a memory. A thought from an earlier conversation. Donald couldn't be sure. The waking world of boots and angry voices was too busy being swallowed by the mist of sleep and the fog of dreams. And this time—rather than with a fear of death—Donald went into that darkness gladly. He embraced it hoping it would be eternal. He went with a final thought of his sister, of those drones beneath their tarps, and all that he hoped would never be woken.

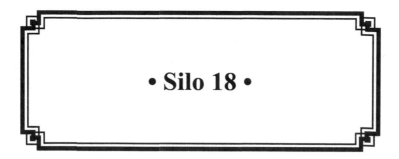

• Silo 18 •

Ring around the silo.
No one knows what I know.
Ashes! Ashes! We all fall down!

·55·

Mission felt buried alive. He fell into an uncomfortable trance, the bag growing hot and slick as it trapped his heat and exhalations. Part of him feared he would pass out in there and Joel and Lyn would discover him dead. Part of him hoped.

The two porters were stopped for questioning on one-seventeen, a landing below the blast that took Cam. Those working to repair the stairwell were on the lookout for a certain porter. Their description was part Cam, part Mission. Mission held deathly still while Joel complained of being stopped with so sensitive and heavy a load. It seemed that they might demand the bag be opened, but there were some things nearly as taboo as talk of the outside. And so they were let free with a warning that the rail was out above and that one person had already fallen to their death.

Mission fought off a coughing fit as the voices receded below. He wiggled his shoulders and struggled to cover his mouth to muffle the sound of his throat being cleared. Lyn hissed at him to be quiet. In the distance, Mission could hear a woman wailing. They passed through the wreckage from hours earlier, and Joel and Lyn gasped at the sight of an entire landing torn free from the stairwell.

Above Supply, they carried him into a restroom, opened the bag, and let him work the blood back into his arms. Mission peed and took a few sips of water. He assured the others that he was fine in there. Yes, it was hot, he told them. All three of them were damp with sweat, and there was a very long way to go. Joel especially seemed weary from the levels climbed thus far, or perhaps from seeing the damage wreaked by the blast. Lyn was holding up better but was anxious to get going again. She fretted aloud for Rodny and seemed as eager to get to the Nest as Mission.

Mission looked at himself in the mirror with his white coveralls and his porter's knife strapped to his waist. He was the one they were looking for. He drew his knife and held a handful of his hair. It made a crunching noise, like biting into celery, as he sawed through a clump close to his scalp. Lyn saw what he was doing and helped with her own knife. It hurt in a good way and made his head tingle. Joel grabbed the trashcan from the corner to collect the hair.

It was a rough job, but he looked less like the one they wanted. Before putting his knife away, he cut a few slits in the black bag, right by the zipper. He peeled off his undershirt and wiped the inside of the bag dry before throwing the shirt in the trashcan. It reeked of smoke and sweat, anyway. Crawling back inside, helping with the straps, they zipped him up and carried him back to the stairway to resume their ascent. Mission was powerless to do anything but worry.

He ran over the events of a very long day. Things had happened that morning that felt like they must've taken place yesterday. He remembered getting up early to watch the clouds brighten over breakfast. He had visited the Crow and delivered her note, had then lost a friend, and now was heading back to the Nest. The exhaustion of it all caught up to him. Or perhaps it was the lack of sleep from the fight the night before or the gentle swaying of the bag. Whatever the cause, he found himself sliding into unconsciousness.

He didn't sleep so much as cease to be for a while. Time marched along without him.

When he startled awake, it felt but a moment later. His coveralls were damp, the inside of the bag slick again with condensation. Joel must've felt him jerk to consciousness, as he quickly shushed Mission and told him they were coming up on Central.

Mission's heart pounded as he came to and remembered where he was, what they were doing. It felt difficult to breathe. The slits he had cut were lost in the folds of the plastic. He wanted the zipper cracked, just a slice of light, a whisper of fresh air. His arms were pinned and numb from the straps around his shoulders. His ankles were sore from where Lyn was hoisting him from below.

"Can't breathe," he gasped.

The others shushed him. But there was a pause, an end to the swaying. Someone fumbled with the bag over his head, a series of tiny clicks from a zipper lowering a dozen notches.

Mission sucked in cool gasps. The world resumed its swaying, boots striking the stairs in the distance—a commotion somewhere above or below, he couldn't tell. More fighting. More dying. He saw bodies spinning through the air. He saw Cam leaving the farm sublevels just the day before, a coroner's bonus in his pocket, no thought of how little time he had left for spending it. No thought from any of them how little time they had left to spend anything.

They rested at Central Dispatch. Mission was let out in the main hallway, which was frighteningly empty. "What the hell happened here?" Lyn asked. She dug her finger into a hole in the wall surrounded by a spiderweb of cracks. There were hundreds of holes like them. Boots rang on the landing and continued past.

"What time is it?" Mission asked, keeping his voice down.

"It's after dinner," Joel said. It meant they were making good time.

Down the hall, Lyn studied a dark patch of what looked to be rust. "Is this blood?" she hissed.

"Robbie said he couldn't reach anyone down here," Mission said. "Maybe they scattered."

Joel took a sip from his canteen. "Or were driven off." He wiped his mouth with his sleeve.

"Should we stay here for the night? You two look beat."

Joel frowned and shook his head. He offered Mission his canteen. "I think we need to get past the thirties. Security is everywhere. Hell, you could probably dash up with what you've got on the way they're running about. Might need to clean up your hair a bit."

Mission rubbed his scalp and thought about that. "Maybe I should," he said. "I could be up there before the dim-time." He watched as Lyn disappeared into one of the bunk rooms down the hall. She emerged almost immediately with her hand over her mouth, her eyes wide.

"What is it?" Mission asked, pushing up from a crouch and joining her.

She threw her arms around him and held him away from the door, buried her face into his shoulder. Joel risked a look.

"No," he whispered.

Mission pulled away from Lyn and joined his fellow porter by the door.

The bunks were full. Some lay sprawled on the floor, but it was obvious by the tangle of their limbs—the way arms hung useless from bunks or were twisted beneath them—that these porters weren't sleeping.

They discovered Katelyn among them. None of them could abide seeing her like that, which cemented Mission's plan to dash up on his own. Lyn shook with silent sobs as he and Joel retrieved Katelyn's body and loaded her into the bag. Mission felt a pang of guilt to think that it was nice how small Katelyn was. Awful porter thoughts.

They were securing the straps and zipping her up when the power in the hallway went out, leaving them in the pitch black. They groped for one another, even the light spilling through the doors leading out onto the landing suddenly gone.

"What the hell?" Joel hissed.

A moment later, the lights returned but flickered as though an unsteady flame burned in each bulb. Mission wiped the sweat from his forehead and wished he still had his 'chief.

"If you can't make it all the way tonight," he said to the others, "stop and stay at the waystation and check on Robbie."

"We'll be fine," Joel assured him.

Lyn squeezed his arm before he went. "Watch your steps," she said.

"And you," Mission told them.

He hurried toward the landing and the great stairway beyond. Overhead, the lights flickered like little flames. A sign that something, somewhere, perhaps was burning.

· 56 ·

He hurried upward amid a fog of smoke and rumor, and Mission's throat burned from the one, his mind from the other. An explosion in Mechanical was whispered to have been the reason for the blackout. Talk swirled of a bent or broken shaft and that the silo was on backup power. He heard such things from half a spiral away as he took the steps two and sometimes three at a time. It felt good to be out and moving, good to have his muscles aching rather than sitting still, to be his own burden.

And he noticed that when anyone saw him, they either fell silent or scattered beyond their landings, even those he knew. At first, he feared it was from recognition. But it was the Security white he wore. Young men just like him thundered up and down the stairwell terrorizing everyone. They were yesterday's farmers, welders, and pumpmen—and they brought order with their strange and dark weapons.

More than once, a group of them stopped Mission and asked where he was going, where his rifle was. He told them that he had been a part of the fighting below and was reporting back. It was something he'd heard another claim. Many of them seemed to know as little as he did, and so they would let him pass. As ever, the color you wore said everything. People could know you at a glance.

The activity grew thicker near IT. A group of new recruits passed, and Mission watched over the railing as they kicked in the doors to the level below and stormed inside. People screamed. There was a sharp bang like a heavy steel rod falling to the steel decking. A dozen of these bangs, and then less screaming. Fear was in everyone's eyes, no less those in white who seemed to know as little of what they were doing as Mission. Just chaos like a switch had been thrown. A steady pulse of light one day, and now the faltering of a dying flame.

He passed IT, the doors closed, and thought for a moment about barging in and trying to talk his way past the guards. But not alone. Tomorrow, with his friends.

His legs were sore, a stitch in his side, as he approached the farms. He caught sight of Winters and a few others out on the landing with shovels and rakes. Someone yelled something as he passed. Mission quickened his pace, thinking of his father and brother, seeing the wisdom for once in his old man's unwillingness to leave that patch of dirt.

A bag of berries on the stairwell looked at first like a blood stain. They had been stepped on and crushed, but Mission picked up the bag anyway. He scooped the mush out with his fingers as he hurried on, grateful for the find. He left the empty bag on the next landing, remembering days when such plastic was filled with paint and dropped on others. Those no longer seemed like the good times.

After a lifetime of racing up with the smoke as his company, of rising with the drifting ash, he reached the quiet of the Nest. The little chicks were gone. Most people were probably holed up in their apartments, families cowering together, hoping this madness would pass like others had. Inside, several lockers stood open. A child's backpack lay in the middle of the hall. Mission staggered forward on numb legs toward the sound of a familiar singing voice and the screech of something awful.

At the end of the hall, her door stood as welcome and open as always. The singing was from the Crow, whose voice seemed stronger than usual. Mission saw that he wasn't the first to arrive, that his wire had gone out. Frankie and Allie were there, both in the green and white of farm security. They were arranging desks while Mrs. Crowe sang. The sheets had been thrown off the stacks of desks kept in storage along one wall. Those desks now filled the classroom the way Mission remembered from his youth. It was as though the Crow was expecting them to be filled at any time.

Allie noticed him first. She rushed over, her coveralls bunched up around her boots, the straps knotted to make them shorter. They must've been Frankie's coveralls. As she threw herself into his arms, he wondered what the two of them had risked to meet him there.

"Mission, my boy." Mrs. Crowe stopped her singing, smiled, and waved him over. After a moment, Allie reluctantly loosened her grip.

Mission shook Frankie's hand and thanked him for coming. It took a moment to realize something was different, that his hair had been cut short as well. They both rubbed their scalps and laughed. Humor came easy in humorless times.

"What is this I hear about my Rodny?" the Crow asked him. Her chair twitched back and forth, her hand working the controls, her Thursday dress tucked under her narrow bones. Mission drew a deep breath, smoke lingering in his lungs, and he began to tell them all he had seen on the stairwell, about the bombs and the fires and what he had heard of Mechanical, the Security forces with their barking rifles like the dogs of Supply—but the Crow dispelled his frenzied chatter with a wave of her frail arms.

"Not the fighting," she said. "The fighting I've seen. I could paint a picture of the fighting and hang it from my walls. What of Rodny? What of our boy? Has he got them?" She made a small fist and held it aloft.

"No," Mission said. "He needs our help."

The Crow laughed, which took him aback. He tried to explain. "I gave him your note, and he passed me one in return. It begged for help. They have him locked up behind these great steel doors—"

"Not locked up," the Crow said.

"—like he'd done something wrong—"

"Something *right*," she said, correcting him.

Mission fell silent. He could see knowledge shining behind her old eyes, a sunrise on the day after a cleaning.

"Rodny is in no danger," she said.

Allie squeezed Mission's arm. "She's been trying to tell us," she whispered. "Everything's going to be okay. Come, help with the desks."

"But the note," Mission said, wishing he hadn't turned it to confetti.

"The note you gave him was to give him strength. To let him know it was time to begin." There was a wildness in the Crow's eyes, excitement and joy becoming something more combustible than either.

"No," Mission said. "Rodny was afraid. I know my friend, and he was afraid of something."

The Crow's face hardened. She relaxed her fist and smoothed the front of her faded dress. "If that be the case," she said, her voice trembling. "Then I judged him most wrongly."

• 57 •

The dim-time approached while they arranged desks and the Crow resumed her singing. Allie told him a curfew had been announced, and so Mission lost hope that the others would show up that night. They pulled out mats from the cubbies to rest, plan, and give the others until daybreak. There was much Mission wanted to ask the Crow, but she seemed distracted, her thoughts elsewhere, a joyousness that made her giddy.

Frankie felt certain he could get them through security and deeper into IT if only he could reach his father. Mission told them how well he'd been able to move about with the whites on. Maybe he could reach Frankie's dad in a pinch. Allie produced fresh fruits harvested from her plot and passed them around. The Crow drank one of her dark green concoctions. Mission grew restless.

He wandered out to the landing, torn between waiting for the others and his anxiety to get going. For all he knew, Rodny was being marched up to his death already. Cleanings tended to settle people down, to come after bouts of unrest, but this was unlike any of the spates of violence he had seen before. This was the burning his father spoke of, the embers of distrust and crumbling trade that jumped up all at once. He had seen this coming, but it had approached with the swiftness of a knife plummeting from the Up Top.

Out on the landing, he heard the sounds of a mob echoing from far below. Holding the landing rail, he could feel the hum of many marching boots. He returned to the others and said nothing of it. There was no reason to suspect those boots were marching for them.

Allie looked as though she'd been crying when he got back. Her eyes were moist, her cheeks flushed. The Crow was telling them an Old Time story, her hands painting a scene in the air. Mission asked Allie if everything was all right.

She shook her head like she'd rather not say.

"What is it?" he asked. He held her hand, heard the Crow speaking of Atlantis, another tale of the crumbling and lost city of magic beyond the hills, a bygone day when those ruins shone like a wet dime.

"Tell me," he said. He wondered if maybe those stories were affecting her the way they sometimes did him, making her sad and not knowing why.

"I didn't want to say anything until after," she cried, fresh tears welling up. She wiped them away, and the Crow fell silent, her hands falling to her lap. Frankie sat quietly. Whatever it was, the two of them knew as well.

"Father," Mission said. It had to do with his father. Allie was close to his father in a way that Mission had never been. And suddenly, he felt a powerful regret for ever having left home. While she wiped her eyes, the words unable to form on her trembling lips, Mission imagined himself on his hands and knees, in the dirt, digging for forgiveness. He thought of growing corn rather than hauling it. Of making something rather than being paid a chit for rumors that ought to be free.

Allie bawled, and the Crow hummed a tune of aboveground days. Mission thought of his father, gone, all he longed to say, and wanted nothing more than to hurl himself at the posters on the walls, to tear them down and rip to shreds their urgings to go and be free.

"It's Riley," Allie finally said. "Mish, I'm so sorry."

The Crow ceased her humming. All three of them watched him.

"No," Mission whispered.

"You shouldn't have told him—" Frankie began.

"He ought to know!" Allie demanded. "He's an only son, now. His father would want him to know."

Mission gazed at a poster of green hills and blue skies. That world blurred with tears as surely as it might with dust. "What happened?" he whispered.

She told him that there'd been an attack on the farms. Riley had begged to go and help fight, had been told no, and then disappeared. He'd been found with a knife from the kitchen still clutched in his hands.

Mission stood and paced the room, tears splashing from his cheeks. He shouldn't have gone. Ever. He should've been there. He wasn't there for Cam, either. Death preceded him in all the places he couldn't be. He had done the same to his mother. And now the end was coming for them all.

There was someone in the hallway. Mission wiped his cheeks. He had given up on any of the others coming and thought it might be Security with their guns, instead. They would ask him where his own gun was before realizing he was an impostor, before shooting them all. He thought about Jenine, had the sickening feeling that his call to arms had placed others in danger. More deathdays.

He pushed the door shut, saw that the Crow had no lock on the thing, and wedged a desk under the handle. Frankie grabbed another desk. Mission didn't see that they would do any good. He hurried toward Allie, told her to get behind the Crow's desk. He grabbed the back of the old teacher's wheelchair—the overhead wire swinging dangerously—but she insisted she could manage herself, that there was nothing to be afraid of.

Mission knew better. This was Security coming for them—Security or some other mob. He'd traveled the stairwell, knew what was out there. This was something bad coming, not his friends. There was no part of him that thought it might be *both*.

There was a knock on the door. The handle jiggled. The boots outside quieted as they gathered around. Frankie pressed his finger to his lips, his eyes wide. The wire overhead creaked as it swung back and forth.

The door budged. Mission hoped for a moment that they would go away, that they were just making their rounds. He thought about hiding under the sheets used to cover the unneeded desks, but the thought came too late. The door was shoved open, a desk crying as it skittered across the floor, and the first person through was Rodny.

His sudden appearance was as jarring as a bomb. He wore white coveralls, the creases still in them like a great letter H across his stomach and down his chest. His hair had been cut short, his face newly shaved, a nick on his chin.

Mission felt as though he were staring into a mirror, the two of them in costume, the same costume. More men in white crowded behind Rodny in the hallway, rifles in hand. Rodny ordered them back and stepped into the room where all those tiny desks lay neatly arranged and empty.

Allie was the first to respond. She gasped with surprise and hurried forward, arms wide as if for an embrace. Rodny held up a palm and told her to stop. His other hand held a small gun like the deputies wore. His eyes were not on his friends but on the Old Crow.

"Rodny—" Mission began. His brain attempted to grasp his friend's presence. They were there to go rescue him, but he looked in little need of it.

"The door," Rodny said over his shoulder.

A man twice Rodny's age hesitated before doing as he was asked and pulling the door shut. This was not the demeanor of a prisoner. It was one who held captive the attention of others. Frankie lurched forward before the door shut all the way, calling "Father," as he caught a glimpse of his old man in the hall with the others.

"We were coming for you," Mission said. He wanted to approach his friend, but there was something dangerous in Rodny's eyes. "Your note—"

Rodny finally looked away from the Crow.

"We were coming to help—" Mission said.

"Yesterday, I needed it," Rodny said. He circled around the desks, the gun at his side, his eyes flicking from face to face. Mission backed up and joined Allie in standing close to the Crow, whether to protect her or feel protected, he couldn't say.

"You shouldn't be here," Mrs. Crowe said with a lecturing tone. "This is not where your fight is."

The gun rose a little.

"What're you doing?" Allie asked of her old friend.

Rodny pointed at the Crow. "Tell them," he said. "Tell them what you've done. What you do."

"What've they done to you?" Mission asked. His friend was different beyond the garb.

"They showed me—" Rodny swept his gun at the posters on the wall. "That these stories are true." He laughed and turned to the Crow. "And I was angry, just like you said. Angry at what they did to the world."

"So hurt them," the Crow insisted, her voice creaking like a door about to slam.

"But now I know. They told me. We got a call. And now I know what you've been doing here—"

"What's this about?" Frankie asked, still in the middle of the room. He moved toward the door. "Why is my father—?"

"Stay," Rodny told him. He pushed one of the desks out of the way and moved down the aisle. "Don't you move." His gun swung from Frankie to the Crow, whose chair shivered in time with her palsied hand. "These sayings on the wall, the stories and songs, you made us what we are. You made us angry."

"You should be," she screeched. "You damn well should be!"

Mission moved closer to her. He kept his eye on the gun. Allie knelt and held the old woman's hand. Rodny stood ten paces away, the gun angled at their feet.

"They kill and they kill," the Crow said. "And this will go the way it always has. Wipe it all clean. Bury and burn the dead. And these desks—" Her arm shot up, her quivering finger aimed at the empty desks newly arranged. "These desks will be *full* again."

"No," Rodny said. He shook his head. "No more. It ends here. You won't terrify us anymore—"

"What're you saying?" Mission asked. He stepped close to the Crow, a hand on her chair. "You're the one with the gun, Rodny. You're the one scaring us."

Rodny turned toward Mission. "*She* makes us feel this way. Don't you see? The fear and hope go hand in hand. What she sells is no different than the priests, only she gets to us *first*. This talk of a better world. It just makes us hate *this* one."

"No—" Mission hated his friend for uttering such a thing.

"Yes," Rodny said. "Why do you think we hate our fathers? It's because her stories are true. But this won't make it better." He waved his hand. "Not that it matters. What I knew yesterday had me terrified for my life. For all of us. What I know now gives me hope." His gun came up. Mission couldn't believe it. His friend pointed the barrel at the Old Crow.

"Wait—" Mission raised a hand.

"Stand back," Rodny said. "I have to do this."

"No!"

His friend's arm stiffened. The barrel was leveled at a defenseless woman in a mechanical chair, the mother to them all, the one who sang them to sleep in their cribs and on their mats, whose voice followed them through their shadowing days and beyond.

Frankie shoved a desk aside and lurched toward Rodny. Allie screamed. Mission's legs coiled with the power of a thousand climbs. He threw himself sideways as the gun roared and flashed. There was a punch to his stomach, a fire in his gut. He crashed to the floor as the gun thundered a second time, the Crow's chair lurching to the side as her hand spasmed.

Mission clutched his stomach. His hands came away sticky and wet.

Lying on his back, he saw the Crow slump over in her chair, a chair that no longer moved. Again, the gun roared. Needlessly. Her body twitched as it was struck. Frankie flew into Rodny, and the two men went tumbling. Boots stormed into the room, summoned by the noise.

Allie was there, crying. She kept her hands on Mission's stomach, pressing so hard, and looked back at the Crow. She wailed for them both.

Mission tasted blood in his mouth. It reminded him of the time Rodny had punched him as a kid, only playing. They'd only ever been playing. Costumes and pretending to be their fathers.

There were boots everywhere. Shiny and black boots on some, scuffed with wear on others. Those who had fought before and those just learning.

Frankie screamed. Boots shuffled. And then Rodny appeared above Mission, his eyes wide with worry. He told him to hang in there. Mission wanted to say he'd try, but the pain in his belly was too great. He couldn't speak. They told him to stay awake, but all he'd ever wanted was to sleep. To not be. To not be a burden to anyone.

"Damn you!" Allie screamed, and it was at him, at Mission, not at Rodny. She blubbered that she loved him, and Mission tried to say he knew. He wanted to tell her that she was right all along. He imagined for a moment the kids they would have, the plot of soil if they combined their holdings, the long uninterrupted rows of corn like lives that stretched out for generations. Generations of people staying close to home, there for each other, doing what they knew best, enjoying being a burden to one another.

He wanted to say all these things and more. Much more. But as Allie bent close and he struggled to form the words, all that came out, a whisper amid the din of boots and shouts, was that today was his birthday.

Hush my Darling, don't you cry
I'm going to sing you a lullaby
Though I'm far away it seems
I'll be with you in your dreams.

Hush my Darling, go to sleep
All around you angels keep
In the morn and through the day
They will keep your fears at bay.

Sleep my Darling, don't you cry
I'm going to sing you a lullaby

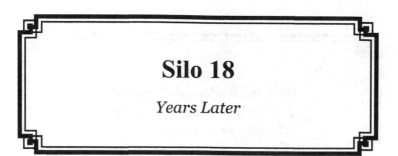

Silo 18

Years Later

•58•

Mission changed out of his work coveralls while Allie readied dinner. He washed his hands, scrubbing the dirt from beneath his fingernails, and watched the mud slide down the drain. The ring on his finger was getting more and more difficult to remove, his knuckles sore and stiff from the hoeing of a planting season.

He soaped his hands and finally managed to work the ring off. Remembering the time he'd lost it down the drain, he set it aside carefully. Allie whistled in the kitchen while she tended the stove. When she cracked the oven, he smelled the pork roast inside. He'd have to say something. They couldn't go buying roasts on no occasion.

His coveralls went into the wash. There were candles on the table when he got back to the kitchen. Lit candles. They were for emergencies, for the times when the fools below switched generators and worked on the busted main. Allie knew this. But before he could say anything about the roast or the candles, or tell her that the bean crop wouldn't be what he'd hoped come harvest, he saw the way she was beaming at him. There was only one thing to be that happy about—but it was impossible.

"No," he said. He couldn't allow himself to believe it.

Allie nodded. There were tears in her eyes. By the time he got to her, they were coursing down her cheeks.

"But our ticket is up," he whispered, holding her against him. She smelled like sweet peppers and sage. He could feel her trembling.

Allie sobbed. Her voice broke from being overfull of joy. "Doc says it happened last month. It was in our window, Mish. We're gonna have a baby."

A surge of relief filled Mission to the brim. Relief, not excitement. Relief that everything was legal, on the up-and-up. He wasn't sure why this is what he felt. He kissed his wife's cheek, salt to go with the pepper and sage. "I love you," he whispered.

"The roast." She pulled away and hurried to the stove. "I was gonna tell you after dinner."

Mission laughed. "You were gonna tell me now or have to explain the candles."

He poured two glasses of water, hands trembling, and set them out while she fixed the plates. The smell of cooked meat made his mouth water. He could anticipate the way the roast would taste like it was already in his mouth. A taste of the future, of what was to come. Like by the table, how he could already see two children, two more mouths to feed. He'd have to find a way to put in another row of corn. Or take that part time delivery job he'd been thinking about, just on weekends.

"Don't let it get cold," Allie said, setting the plates.

They sat and held hands. Mission cursed himself for not putting his ring back on.

"Bless this food and those who fed its roots," Allie said.

"Amen," said Mission. His wife squeezed his hands before letting go and grabbing her utensils.

"You know," she said, cutting into the roast, "if it's a girl, we'll have to name her Allison. Every woman in my family as far back as we can remember has been an Allison."

Mission wondered how far back her family could remember. Be unusual, if they could. The first piece of meat hit his tongue, an explosion of flavors. He chewed and thought on the name. "Allison it is," he said. And he thought that eventually they would call her Allie, too. "But if it's a boy, can we go with Cam?"

"Sure." Allie lifted her glass. "That wasn't your grandfather's name, was it?"

"Hmm? No. I don't know a Cam. I just like the way it sounds."

He picked up his glass of water, studied it a while. Or did he know a Cam? Where did he know that name from? There was something he was supposed to remember, something about the way water gets made, gets purified. But there were pockets of his past shrouded and hidden from him. There were things like the mark on his neck and the scar on his stomach that he couldn't remember coming to be. Everyone had their share of these things, parts of their bygone days they couldn't recall, but Mission more than most. Like his birthday. It drove him crazy that he couldn't remember when his birthday was. What was so hard about that?

All changes, even the most longed for, have their melancholy;
for what we leave behind us is a part of ourselves;
we must die to one life before we can enter another.

-Anatole France

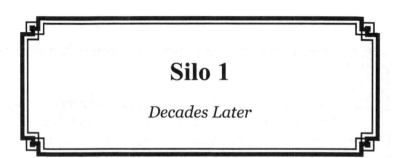

Silo 1

Decades Later

·59·

"**S**ir?"

There was a clatter of bones beneath his feet. Donald stumbled through the dark.

"Can you hear me?"

The haze parted, an eyelid cracking, just like the seal of his pod. A bean. Donald was curled inside that pod like a bean.

"Sir? Are you with me?"

Skin so cold. Donald was sitting up, steam rising from his bare legs. He didn't remember going to sleep. He remembered a doctor, remembered being in his office. Not his office, an airlock. They were talking. People were angry. Now he was being woken up.

"Drink this, sir."

Donald remembered this. He remembered waking over and over, but he didn't remember going to sleep. Just the waking. He took a sip, had to concentrate to make his throat work, had to fight to swallow. A pill. There was supposed to be a pill, but it wasn't offered.

"Sir, we had instructions to wake you."

Instructions. Rules. Protocol. Donald was in trouble again. Troy. Maybe it was that Troy fellow. Who was he? Donald drank as much as he could.

"Very good, sir. We're going to lift you out."

He was in trouble. They only woke him when there was trouble. A catheter was removed, a needle extracted from his arm.

"What did I—?"

He coughed into his fist. His voice was a sheet of tissue paper, thin and fragile. Invisible.

"What is it?" he asked, shouting to form a whisper.

Two men lifted him up and set him into a wheelchair. A third man held it still. There was a soft blanket instead of a paper gown. There was no rustling this time, no itching on his skin.

"We lost one," someone said.

A silo. A silo was gone. It would be Donald's fault again. "Eighteen," he whispered, remembering his last shift.

Two of the men glanced at each other, mouths open.

"Yes," one of them said, awe in his voice. "From Silo Eighteen, sir. We lost her over the hill. We lost contact."

Donald tried to focus on the man. He remembered losing someone over a hill. *Helen.* His wife. They were still looking for her. There was still hope.

"Tell me," he whispered.

"We're not sure how, but one of them made it out of sight."

"A cleaner, sir—"

A cleaner. Donald sank into the chair; his bones were as cold and heavy as stone. It wasn't Helen at all.

"Over the hill—" one said.

"We got a call from Eighteen—"

Donald raised his hand a little, his arm trembling and still half-numb from the sleep. "Wait," he croaked. "One at a time. Why did you wake me?" It hurt to talk. He remembered a hill. A view over a hill.

One of the men cleared his throat. The blanket was tucked up under Donald's chin to stop him from shivering. He hadn't known he was shivering. They were being so reverent with him, so gentle. What was this? He tried to clear his head.

"You told us to wake you—"

"It's protocol—"

Donald's eyes fell to the pod, still steaming as the chill escaped. There was a screen at the base, empty readouts without him in there, just a rising temp. A rising temp and a name. Not his name.

And Donald remembered a conversation. He didn't remember going to sleep, but he remembered a doctor, a man with glasses and an accent telling him how names meant nothing unless that was all we had to go by. Unless we didn't remember each other, didn't cross paths, and then a name was everything.

"Sir?"

"Who am I?" he asked, reading the little screen, not understanding. This wasn't him. "Why did you wake me?"

"You told us to, Mr. Thurman."

The blanket was wrapped snugly around his shoulders. The chair was turned. They were treating him with respect, like he had authority. The wheels on this chair did not squeak at all.

"It's okay, sir. Your head will clear soon."

He didn't know these people. They didn't know him.

"The doctor will clear you for duty."

Nobody knew anyone.

"Right this way."

And then anyone could be anybody.

"Through here."

Until it didn't matter who was in charge. One who might do what was needed, another who might do what was right.

"Very good."

One name as good as any other.

Third Shift
९ act

• Silo 17 •

Hour One

· 60 ·

The Loud came before the quiet. That was a Rule of the World, for the bangs and shouts need somewhere to echo, just as bodies need space in which to fall.

Jimmy Parker was in class when the last of the great Louds began. It was the day before a cleaning. Tomorrow, they would be off from school. For the death of a man, Jimmy and his friends would receive a few extra hours of sleep. His father would work overtime down in IT. And tomorrow afternoon, his mother would insist they go up with his aunt and cousins to watch the bright clouds drift over the clear view of the hills until the sky turned dark as sleep.

Cleaning days were for staying in bed and for seeing family. They were for silencing unrest and quieting the Louds. That's what Mrs. Pearson said anyway, as she wrote rules from the Pact up on the blackboard. Her chalk clacked and squeaked and left dusty trails of all the whys for which a man could be put to death. Civics lessons on a day before a banishment. Warnings on the eve of graver warnings. Jimmy and his friends fidgeted in their seats and learned rules. Rules that very soon would no longer apply.

Jimmy was sixteen. Many of his friends would move off and shadow soon, but he would need another year of study to follow in his father's footsteps. Mrs. Pearson marked the chalkboard and moved on to the seriousness of choosing a life partner, of registering relationships according to the Pact. Sarah Jenkins turned in her seat and smiled back at Jimmy. Civics lessons and biology lessons intermingled, hormones spoken of alongside the laws that governed their excesses. Sarah Jenkins was cute. Jimmy hadn't thought so at the beginning of the year, but now he was seeing it. Sarah Jenkins was cute and would be dead in just a few hours.

Mrs. Pearson asked for a volunteer to read from the Pact, and that's when Jimmy's mother came for him. She burst in unannounced. An embarrassment. The end of Jimmy's world began with an embarrassment, with hot cheeks and a burning collar and everyone watching. His mom didn't say anything to Mrs. Pearson, didn't excuse herself. She just stormed through the door and hurried among the desks the way she walked when she was angry. She pulled Jimmy from his desk and led him out with his arm in her fist, causing him to wonder what he'd done this time.

Mrs. Pearson didn't know what to say. Jimmy looked back at his best friend Paul, caught him smiling behind his palm, and wondered why Paul wasn't in trouble, too. They rarely got in or out of a fix alone, he or Paul. The only person to utter a word was Sarah Jenkins. "Your backpack!" she cried out, just before the classroom door slammed shut. Her voice was swallowed by the quiet.

There were no other mothers pulling their children down the hallway. If they came, it would be much later. Jimmy's father worked among the computers, and the computers were fast. Jimmy's father knew things before anyone else. This time, it was only moments before. There were others scrambling on the stairwell already. The noise was frightening. The landing outside the school level thrummed with the vibrations of distant and heavy traffic. A bolt in one of the railing's stanchions rattled as it worked its way loose. It felt like the silo would simply shake itself apart. Jimmy's mom took him by the sleeve and pulled him toward the spiral staircase like he was still twelve. She started down, even though home was up.

Jimmy pulled against her for a moment, confused. In the past year, he had grown bigger than his mom, as big as his father, and it was strange to be reminded that he had this power, that he was nearly a man. He had left his backpack and his friends behind. Where were they going? The banging from below seemed to be getting louder.

His mother turned as he gave resistance. Her eyes, he saw, were not full of anger. There was no glare, no furrowed brow, her eyes like tiny slits that tried to see less of him when he was bad. They were wide and wet, shiny like the times Grandma and Grandpa had passed. The noise below was frightful, but it was the look in his mother's eyes that put the start of a very long fear into Jimmy's bones.

"What is it?" he whispered. He hated to see his mother upset. Something dark and empty—like that stray and tailless cat that nobody could catch in the upper apartments—clawed at his insides.

His mother didn't say. She turned and pulled him down the stairs, toward the thundering approach of something awful, and Jimmy realized at once that he wasn't in trouble at all.

They all were.

·61·

Jimmy had never felt the stairs tremble so. The entire spiral staircase seemed to sway. It turned to rubber the way a length of charcoal appeared to bend between jiggled fingers, a parlor trick he'd learned in class. Though his feet rarely touched the steps—racing as he did to keep up with his mother—they tingled and felt numb from vibrations transmitted straight from steel to bone. He could barely feel the rail with his hand as it shook him to his elbow, and Jimmy tasted fear in his mouth like a dry spoon on his tongue.

There were angry screams from below. Jimmy's mother shouted her encouragement, told him to hurry, and down the staircase they spiraled. They raced toward whatever bad thing was marching upward. "Hurry," she cried again, and Jimmy was more scared of the tremor in her voice than the shuddering of a hundred levels of steel. He hurried.

They passed twenty-nine. Thirty. People ran by in the opposite direction. A lot of people in coveralls the color of his father's. On the landing of thirty-one, Jimmy saw his first dead body since his grandpa's funeral. It looked like a tomato had been smashed on the back of the man's head. Jimmy had to skip over the man's arms, sticking out into the stairwell. He hurried after his mother while some of the red dripped through the landing and splattered and slicked the steps below.

At thirty-two, the shake of the stairs was so great that he could feel it in his teeth. His mother grew frantic as the two of them bumped past more and more people hurrying upward. Nobody seemed to see anyone else, even though all eyes were surely wide enough.

The stampede could be heard. There were loud voices among the ringing footfalls. Jimmy stopped and peered over the railing. Below, as the staircase augured into the depths, he could see the elbows and hands of a jostling crowd jutting out. He turned as someone thundered by. His mother called for him to hurry, for the crowd was already upon them, the traffic growing. Jimmy felt the fear and anger in the people racing past, and it made him want to flee upward with them. But there was his mom yelling for him to come along, and her voice cut through his fear and to the center of his being.

Jimmy shuffled down and took her hand. The embarrassment of earlier was gone. Now, he wanted her clutching him. The people who ran past shouted for them to go the other way. Several held pipes and lengths of steel. There were some who were bruised and cut; blood covered the mouth and chin of one man. A fight somewhere. Jimmy thought that only happened in the Deep. Others seemed to be simply caught up in it all. They were without weapons and looked over their shoulders as if a sinister thing were coming. It was a mob scared of a mob. Jimmy wondered what caused it. What was there to be afraid of?

Loud bangs rang out among the footfalls. A large man knocked into Jimmy's mom and sent her roughly against the railing. Jimmy held her arm, and the two of them stuck to the inner post as they made their way down to thirty-three. "One more to go," she told him, which meant it was his father they were after.

The growing throngs became a crush a few turns above thirty-two. People pressed four wide where there was comfortable room for two. Jimmy's wrist banged against the inner rail. He wedged himself between the post and those forcing their way up. Moving a few inches at a time— those beside him shoving, jostling, and grunting with effort—he felt certain they would all become stuck like that. People crowded in and he lost his grip on her arm. She surged forward while he remained pinned in place. He could hear her yelling his name below.

A large man, dripping with sweat, jaw slack with fear, was trying to force his way up the downbound side. "Move!" he yelled at Jimmy, as if there were anywhere to go. There was nowhere to go but up. He flattened himself against the center post as the man brushed past. There was a scream by the outer rail, a jolt through the crowd, a series of gasps, someone yelling "Hold on!" another yelling to let them go, and then a shriek that plummeted away and grew faint.

The wedge of bodies loosened a little. Jimmy felt sick to his stomach at the thought of someone falling so near to him. He wiggled free and climbed up onto the inner rail. Jimmy hugged the central post and balanced there, careful not to let his feet slip into the six inches of space between the rail and the post, that gap that kids liked to spit into.

Someone in the crowd immediately took his place on the steps. Shoulders and elbows knocked into his ankles. He remained crouched there, the undersides of the steps above him transmitting the scrapes of shuffling boots from those overhead. He slid his feet along the narrow bar of steel made slick by the rubbing of thousands of palms and worked his way down the railing after his mom. His foot slipped into the gap by the center post. It seemed eager to swallow his leg. Jimmy righted himself, fearful as well of falling onto the lurching crowd, imagining how he could be tossed across their frenzied arms and shot out into space.

He was half a circuit around the inner post before he found his mom. She had been forced toward the outside by the crowds. "Mom!" he yelled. Jimmy held the edge of the steps above his head and reached out over the crowd for her. A woman in the middle of the steps screamed and disappeared, her head sinking below those who took her place. As they trampled her, the woman's screams disappeared. The crowd surged upward. They carried Jimmy's mom a few steps with them.

"Get to your father!" she screamed, cupping her hands around her mouth. "Jimmy!"

"Mom!"

Someone knocked into his shins, and he lost his grip on the stairs overhead. Jimmy waved his arms once, twice, in little circles, trying to keep his balance. He fell inward on the sea of heads and rolled. Someone punched him in the ribs as they protected themselves from his fall.

Another man threw Jimmy aside. He tumbled outward across an undulating platform of sharp elbows and hard skulls, and time slowed to a crawl. There was nothing but empty space beyond the crowd, now packed five wide. Jimmy tried to grab one of the hands pushing and shoving at him. His stomach lurched as the space grew nearer. The rail was below the screaming heads. The rail was invisible. He heard his mother's voice, a screech recognizable above all the others, as she watched, helpless. Someone screamed to help that boy as he slid down the spiral of heads, rolling and grasping, and that boy they were screaming after was him.

Jimmy went into open space. He was thrown aside by those trying to protect themselves. He slid between two people—a shoulder catching him in the chin—and he saw the railing at last. He clutched for it, got one hand wrapped around the bar. As his feet tumbled over his head, he was twisted around, his shoulder wrenched painfully, but he kept his grip. He hung there, clutching the railing with one hand and one of the vertical stanchions with the other, his feet dangling in the open air.

Someone's hip pinched his fingers against the rail, and Jimmy cried out. Hands scrambled at his arms to help, but these people and their concerns were pushed upward by the madness below.

Jimmy tried to pull himself up. He looked down past his kicking feet at the crowds jostling beyond the rail below him. Two turns below was the landing to thirty-four. Again he tried to hoist himself, but there was a fire in his wrenched shoulder. Someone scratched his forearm as they tried to help, and then they too were gone, surging upward.

Peering down his chest, between his feet, Jimmy saw that the landing to thirty-four was packed. The crowd spilled out of the crowded stairs and tried to shove their way back in again. Someone barged out of the doors to the IT level with a cleaning suit on, helmet and everything. They threw themselves into the crowd, silvery arms swimming amid the flesh, everyone trying to get up, more of the bangs and shouts from down below, a sudden pop like the balloons from the bazaar but much, much louder.

Jimmy lost his grip on the railing—his shoulder was too injured to bear the weight any longer. He clutched the stanchion with his other hand as he slid down, sweaty palm on steel adding one more squeal to the mob. He was left clutching the edge of the steps at the base of the stanchion. With his feet, he tried to feel for the railing one turn below, but all he felt were angry arms knocking his boots aside. His busted shoulder was alive with pain. He swung down on one hand, dangling for an instant.

Jimmy cried out in alarm. He cried out for his mother, remembering what she'd told him.

Get to your father.

There was no way he was getting back up on the stairwell. He didn't have the strength. There was no room. Nobody was going to help him. A surging crowd, and yet he hung there all alone.

Jimmy took a deep breath. He dangled for a moment longer, glanced down at the packed landing below him, and let go.

• 62 •

Two turns of the spiral staircase flew by. Two turns of wide eyes among the packed and crushing crowd. Jimmy felt the swoosh of wind on his neck grow and grow. His stomach flew up into his throat, and there was a glimpse of a face turning in alarm to watch him plummet past.

Slamming into the crowd on the landing below, he hit with a sickening thud. Grunts escaped him and those he landed on. The man in the silver suit, faceless behind his small visor, was pinned beneath him.

People yelled at him. Others crawled out from underneath him. Jimmy rolled away, an electric shock in his ribs where he'd hit someone, a throbbing pain in one knee, his shoulder burning. Limping, he hurried toward the double doors as another person barged out, a bundle in their arms. They pulled to a halt at the sight of the crowd on the stairs. Someone yelled about the forbidden Outside, and nobody seemed to care. Tomorrow, there was to be a cleaning. Maybe it was too late. Jimmy thought of the extra hours his dad had been putting in. He wondered how many more people would be sent out for all this violence.

He turned back to the stairs and searched for his mom. The screams and shouts for people to move, to get out of the way, made it impossible to hear. But her voice still rang in his ears. He remembered her last command, the plaintive look on her face, and hurried inside to find his father.

It was chaos beyond the doors, people running back and forth in the halls, loud voices arguing. Yani stood by the security gate, the large officer's hair matted with sweat. Jimmy ran toward him. He clutched his elbow to pin his arm to his chest and keep his shoulder from swinging. The sting in his ribs made it difficult to take in a full breath. His heart was still pounding from the rush of the long fall.

"Yani—" Jimmy leaned against the security gate and gasped for air. It seemed to take a moment for the guard to register his existence. Yani's eyes were wide; they darted back and forth. Jimmy noticed something in his hand, a pistol like the sheriff wore. "I need to get through," Jimmy said. "I need to find Dad."

The officer's wild eyes settled on Jimmy. Yani was a good man, a friend of his father's. His daughter was just two years younger than Jimmy. Their family came over for dinner around the holidays sometimes. But this was not that Yani. Some sort of terror seemed to have him by the throat.

"Yes," he said, bobbing his head. "Your father. Won't let me in. Won't let any of us in. But you—" It seemed impossible, but Yani's eyes grew wilder.

"Can you buzz me—?" Jimmy started to ask, nudging the turnstile.

Yani grabbed Jimmy by his collar. Jimmy was no small boy, was growing into his adult frame, but the massive guard practically lifted him over the turnstile like a sack of dirty laundry.

Jimmy struggled in the man's fierce grip. Yani pressed the end of the pistol against Jimmy's chest and dragged him down the hall. "I've got his boy!" he yelled. To whom, it wasn't clear. Jimmy tried to twist free. He was hauled past offices in disarray. The entire level looked cleared out. He thought of the prevailing color on the stairway early on, all the coveralls in silver and gray, and feared for a moment that his father had been among those he'd passed. The crowd had been littered with people from this level, as though they'd been leading the charge—or were the ones being chased.

"I can't breathe—" he tried to tell Yani. He got his feet beneath him, clutched the powerful man's forearm, anything to take the pinch off his collar.

"Where'd you assholes go?" Yani screamed, glancing up and down the halls. "I need a hand with this—"

There was a clap like a thousand balloons popping at once, a deafening roar. Jimmy felt Yani lurch sideways as if kicked. The guard's grip relaxed, allowing the blood to rush back to Jimmy's head. Jimmy danced sideways as the large man tumbled over like a lush with too much gin in him. He crashed to the floor, gurgling and wheezing, the black pistol skittering across the tile.

"Jimmy!"

His father was at the end of the hall, half around a corner, a long black object under his armpit, a crutch that didn't quite reach the floor. The end of this too-short crutch smoked as if it were on fire.

"Hurry, son!"

Jimmy cried out in relief. He stumbled away from Yani, who was writhing on the floor and making awful, inhuman sounds, and ran to his father, limping and clutching his arm.

"Where's your mother?" his dad asked, peering down the hall.

"The stairs—" Jimmy fought for a breath. His pulse had blurred into a steady thrum. "Dad, what's going on?"

"Inside. Inside." He pulled Jimmy down the hall toward a large door of stainless steel. There were shouts from around the corner. His father was on full alert; Jimmy could see the veins standing out in his dad's forehead, trickles of sweat beading beneath his thinning hair. His father keyed a code into the panel by the massive door. There was a whirring and a series of clunks before it opened a crack. His dad leaned into the door until there was room for the two of them to squeeze through. "C'mon, son. Move."

Down the hall, someone yelled at them to stop. Boots clomped their way. Jimmy squeezed through the crack, was worried his dad might close him up in there, all alone, but his old man worked his way through as well, then leaned on the inside of the door.

"Push!" he said.

Jimmy pushed. He didn't know why they were pushing, but he'd never seen his dad frightened before. It made his insides feel like jelly. The boots outside stomped closer. Someone yelled his father's name. Someone yelled for Yani.

As the steel door slammed shut, a slap of hands hit the other side. There was a whir and a clunk once more. His dad keyed something into the pad, then hesitated. "A number," he said, gasping for breath. "Four digits. Quick, son, a number you'll remember."

"One two one eight," Jimmy said. Level twelve and level eighteen. Where he lived and where he went to school. His father keyed in the digits. There were muffled yells from the other side, soft ringing sounds from palms slapping futilely against the thick steel.

"Come with me," his father said. "We've got to keep an eye on the cameras, find your mother." He slung the black machine over his back, which Jimmy saw was a bigger version of the pistol. The end was no longer smoking. His father hadn't kicked Yani from a distance; he had shot him.

Jimmy stood motionless while his father set off through the room of large black boxes. It dawned on him that he'd heard of the room. This was where his father had shadowed. The server room. The machines seemed to watch him as he stood there by the door. They were black sentries, quietly humming, standing guard.

Jimmy left the wall of stainless steel with its muffled slaps and muted shouts and hurried after his father. He had seen his dad's office before, back down the hall and around a bend, but never this place. The room was huge. He favored one leg as he ran the full length of it, trying to pick his way through the servers and keep track of where his dad had gone. At the far wall, he rounded the last black box and found his dad kneeling on the floor as if in prayer. Bringing his hands up around his neck, his dad dug inside his coveralls and came out with a thin black cord. Something silver danced on the end of it.

"What about Mom?" Jimmy asked. He wondered how they would let her in with the rest of those guys outside. He wondered why his father was kneeling on the floor like that.

"Listen carefully," his dad said. "This is the key to the silo. There are only two of these. Do not ever lose sight of it, okay?"

Jimmy watched as his father inserted the key into the back of one of the machines. "This is the comm hub," his dad said. Jimmy had no idea what a comm hub was, only that they were going to hide inside of one. That was the plan. Get inside one of the black boxes until the noise went away. His dad turned the key as if unlocking something, did this three more times in three more slots, then pulled the panel away. Jimmy peered inside and watched his dad pull a lever. There was a grinding noise in the floor nearby.

"Keep this safe," his father said. He squeezed Jimmy's shoulder and handed him the lanyard with the key. Jimmy accepted it and studied the jagged piece of silver amid the coil of black cord. One side of the key formed a circle with three wedges inside, the symbol of the silo. He teased the lanyard into a hoop and pulled it down over his head, then watched his dad dig his fingers into the grating by their feet. A rectangle of flooring was lifted out to reveal darkness underneath.

"Go on. You first," his father said. He waved at the hole in the ground and began unslinging the long pistol from his back. Jimmy shuffled forward a little and peered down. There were handholds on one wall. It was like a ladder, but much taller than any he'd ever seen.

"C'mon, son. We don't have much time."

Sitting on the edge of the grating, his feet hanging in the void, Jimmy reached for the steel rungs below and began the long descent.

The air beneath the floor was cool, the light dim. The horror and noise of the stairwell seemed to fade, and Jimmy was left with a sense of foreboding, of dread. Why was he being given this key? What was this place? He favored his injured arm and made slow but steady progress.

At the bottom of the ladder, he found a narrow passageway. There was a dim pulse of light at the far end. Looking up, he could see the outline of his father making his way down. The light above pulsed as well, a red throbbing, an unpleasant sight.

"Through there," his father said, indicating the slender hallway. He left the long pistol leaned up against the ladder.

"Shouldn't we cover the—?" Jimmy pointed up.

"I'll get it on my way out. Let's go, son."

Jimmy turned and worked his way through the passage. There were wires and pipes running in parallel across the ceiling. A light ahead beat crimson. After twenty paces or so, the passage opened on a space that reminded him of the school stockroom. There were shelves along two walls. Two desks as well—one with a computer, the other with an open book. His dad went straight for the computer. "You were with your mother?" he asked.

Jimmy nodded. "She pulled me out of class. We got separated on the stairs." He rubbed his sore shoulder while his father collapsed heavily into the chair in front of the desk. The computer screen was divided into four squares.

"Where did you lose her? How far up?"

"Two turns above thirty-four," he said, remembering the fall.

Rather than reach for the mouse or keyboard, his father grabbed a black box studded with knobs and switches. There was a wire attached to the box that trailed off toward the back of the monitor. In one corner of the screen, Jimmy saw a moving picture of three men standing over someone lying still on the floor. It was real. It was an image, a window, like the cafeteria wallscreen. He was seeing a view of the hallway they'd just left.

"Fucking Yani," his father muttered.

Jimmy's eyes fell from the screen to stare at the back of his dad's head. He'd heard his old man curse before, but never that word. His father's shoulders were rising and falling as he took deep breaths. Jimmy returned his attention to the screen.

The four windows had become twelve. No, sixteen. His father leaned forward, his nose just inches from the monitor, and peered from one square to the next. His old hands worked the black box, which clicked as the knobs and dials were adjusted. Jimmy saw in every square the turmoil he'd witnessed on the stairway. From rail to post, the treads were packed with people. They surged upward. His father traced the squares with a finger, searching.

"Dad—"

"Shhh."

"—what's going on?"

"We've had a breach," he said. "They're trying to shut us down. You said it was two turns above the landing?"

"Yeah. But she was being carried up. It was hard to move. I went over the rail—"

The chair squeaked as his father turned and sized him up. His eyes fell to Jimmy's arm, pinned against his chest. "You fell?"

"I'm okay. Dad, what's going on? Trying to shut what down?"

His father returned his focus to the screen. A few clicks from the black box, and the squares flickered and changed. They now seemed to be peering through slightly different windows.

"They're trying to shut down our silo," his father said. "The bastards opened our airlock, said our gas supply was tainted— Wait. There she is."

The many little windows became one. The view shifted slightly. Jimmy could see his mother pinned between a crush of people and the rail. Her mouth and chin were covered in blood. Gripping the rail and fighting for room, she lurched down one laborious step as the crowd coursed the other direction. It seemed as though everyone in the silo was trying to get topside. Jimmy's father slapped the table and stood abruptly. "Wait here," he said. He stepped toward the narrow passage, stopped, looked back at Jimmy, seemed to consider something. There was a strange shine in his eyes.

"Quick, now. Just in case." He hurried the other direction, past Jimmy, and through a door leading out of the room. Jimmy hurried after him, frightened, confused, and limping.

"This is a lot like our stove," his father said, patting an ancient thing in the corner of the next room. "Older model, but it works the same." There was a wild look in his father's eyes. He spun and indicated another door. "Storehouse, bunkroom, showers, all through there. Food enough to last four people for ten years. Be smart, son."

"Dad— I don't understand—"

"Tuck that key in," his father said, pointing at Jimmy's chest. Jimmy had left the lanyard outside of his coveralls. "Do not lose that key, okay? What's the number you said you'd never forget?"

"Twelve-eighteen," Jimmy said.

"Okay. Come in here. Let me show you how the radio works."

Jimmy took a last look around this second room. He didn't want to be left alone down there. That's what his father was doing, leaving him down between the levels, hidden in the concrete. The world felt heavy all around him.

"I'll come with you to get her," he said, thinking of those men slapping their hands against the great steel door. His father couldn't go alone, even with the big pistol.

"Don't open the door for anyone but me or your mother," his father said, ignoring his son's pleas. "Now watch closely. We don't have much time." He indicated a box on the wall. The box was locked behind a metal cage, but there were some switches and dials on the outside. "Power's here." His father tapped one of the knobs. "Keep turning this way for volume." His father did this, and the room was filled with an awful hiss. He pulled a device off the wall and handed it to Jimmy. It was attached to the noisy box by a wavy bit of stretchy cord. His dad grabbed another device from a rack on the wall. There were several of them there.

"Hear this? Hear this?" His father spoke into the portable device, and his voice replaced the loud hiss from the box on the wall. "Squeeze that button and talk into the mic." He pointed to the unit in Jimmy's hands. Jimmy did as he was told.

"I hear you," Jimmy said hesitantly, and it was strange to hear his voice emanate from the small unit in his father's hands.

"What's the number?" his dad asked.

"Twelve-eighteen," Jimmy said.

"Okay. Stay here, son." His father appraised him for a moment, then stepped forward and grabbed the back of Jimmy's neck. He kissed his son on the forehead, and Jimmy remembered the last time his father had kissed him like that. It was right before he had disappeared for three months, before his father had become a shadow, back when Jimmy was a little boy.

"When I put the grate back in place, it'll lock itself. There's a handle below to re-open it. Are you okay?"

Jimmy nodded. His father glanced up at the red, pulsing lights and frowned.

"Whatever you do," he said. "Do not open that door for anyone but me or your mother. Understand?"

"I understand." Jimmy clutched his arm and tried to be brave. There was another of the long pistols leaning up against the desk with the open book. He didn't understand why he couldn't come as well. He reached for the black gun. "Dad—"

"Stay here," his father said.

Jimmy nodded.

"Good man." He rubbed Jimmy's head and smiled, then turned and disappeared down that dark and narrow corridor. The lights overhead winked on and off, a red throbbing like a pulse. There was the distant clang of boots on metal rungs, swallowed by the darkness and soon silent. And then Jimmy Parker was alone.

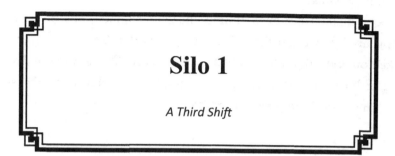

Silo 1

A Third Shift

· 63 ·

Donald couldn't feel his toes. His feet were bare and had yet to thaw. They were bare, but all around him were boots. Boots everywhere. Boots on the men pushing him through aisles of gleaming pods. Boots standing still while they took his blood and told him to pee. Stiff boots that squeaked in the lift as grown men shifted nervously in place. And up above, a frantic hall greeted them where men stomped by in boots, a hall laden with shouts and nervous, lowered brows. They pushed him to a small apartment and left him alone to clean up and thaw out. Outside his door, more boots clomped up and down, up and down. Hurrying, hurrying. A world of worry, confusion, and noise in which to wake.

Donald remained half asleep, sitting on a bed, his consciousness floating somewhere above the floor. Deep exhaustion gripped him. He was back to aboveground days, back when stirring and waking were two separate things. Mornings when he gained consciousness in the shower or behind the wheel on his way into work, long after he had begun to move. The mind lagged behind the body; it swam through the dust kicked up by numb and shuffling feet. Waking from decades of freezing cold felt like this. Dreams of which he was dimly aware slipped from his grasp, and Donald was eager to let them go.

The apartment they'd brought him to was down the hall from his old office. They had passed it along the way. That meant he was on the operations wing, a place he used to work. An empty pair of boots sat on the foot of the bed. Donald stared at them numbly. The name "Thurman" wrapped around the back of each ankle in faded black marker. Somehow, these boots were meant for him. They had been calling him Mr. Thurman since he woke up, but that was not who he was. A mistake had been made. A mistake or a cruel trick. Some kind of game.

Fifteen minutes to get ready. That's what they'd said. Ready for what? Donald sat on the double cot, wrapped in a blanket, occasionally shivering. The wheelchair had been left with him. Thoughts and memories reluctantly assembled like exhausted soldiers roused from their bunks in the middle of the night and told to form ranks in the freezing rain.

My name is Donald, he reminded himself. He must not let that go. This was the first and most primal thing. Who he was.

Sensation and awareness gathered. Donald could feel the dent in the mattress the size and shape of another's body. This depression left behind by another tugged at him. On the wall behind the door, a crater stood where the knob had struck, where the door had been flung open. An emergency, perhaps. A fight or an accident. Someone barging inside. A scene of violence. Hundreds of years of stories he wasn't privy to. Fifteen minutes to get his thoughts together.

There was an ID badge on the bedside table with a barcode and a name. No picture, fortunately. Donald touched the badge, remembered seeing it in use. He left it where it was and rose shakily on unsure legs, held the wheelchair for support, and moved toward the small bathroom.

There was a bandage on his arm where the doctor had drawn his blood. Doctor Wilson. He'd already given a urine sample, but he needed to pee again. Allowing his blanket to fall open, he stood over the toilet. The stream was pink. Donald thought he remembered it being the color of charcoal on his last shift. When he finished, he stepped into the shower to wash off the stink of flesh in a cast too long, that film of death on the surface of something that refuses to die.

The water was hot, his bones cold. Donald shivered in a fog of steam. He opened his mouth and allowed the spray to hit his tongue and fill his cheeks. He scrubbed at the memory of poison on his flesh, a memory that made it impossible to feel clean. For a moment, it wasn't the scalding water burning his skin—it was the air. The outside air. But then he turned off the flow of water and the burning lessened.

He toweled off and found the coveralls left out for him. They were too big. Donald shrugged them on anyway, the fabric rough against skin that had lain bare for a century. There was a knock at the door as he worked the zipper up to his neck. Someone called a name that was not his, a name scrawled around the backs of the boots lying perfectly still on the bed, a name that graced the badge sitting on the bedside table.

"Coming," Donald croaked, his voice thin and weak. He slid the badge into his pocket and sat heavily on the bed. He rolled up his cuffs, all that extra material, before pulling the boots on one at a time. He fumbled with the laces, stood, and found that he could wiggle his toes in the space left behind by another.

• • • •

Many years ago, Donald Keene had been elevated by a simple change in title. Power and importance had come in an instant. For all his life, he had been a man to whom few listened. A man with a degree, a string of jobs, a wife, a modest home. And then one night, a computer tallied stacks of ballots, and Donald Keene became Congressman Keene. He became one of hundreds with his hand on some great tiller—a struggle of hands pushing, pulling, and fitfully steering.

It had happened overnight, and it was happening again.

"How're you feeling, sir?"

The man outside his apartment studied Donald with concern. The badge around his neck read "Eren." He was the Ops Head, the one who manned the shrink's desk down the hall, one among the pairs of boots that had woken him.

"Still groggy," Donald said quietly. A gentleman in bright blue coveralls raced by and disappeared around the bend. A gentle breeze followed, a stir of air that smelled of coffee and perspiration, and then was gone.

"Are you good to walk? I'm sorry about the rush, but then I'm sure you're used to it." Eren pointed down the hall. "They're waiting in the comm room."

Donald nodded and followed. He remembered these halls being quieter, remembered them without the stomping and the raised voices. There were scuff marks on the walls that he thought were new. Reminders of how much time had passed.

In the comm room, all eyes turned to him. Someone was in trouble—Donald could feel it. Eren led him to a chair, and everyone watched and waited. He sat down and saw that there was a frozen image on the screen in front of him. A button was pressed, and the image lurched into motion.

Thick dust tumbled and swirled across the view, making it difficult to see. Clouds flew past in unruly sheets. But there, through the gaps, a figure in a bulky suit could be seen on a forbidding landscape, picking their ponderous way up a gentle swell, heading away from the camera. It was someone outside. Donald could sense that they shouldn't be. He wondered if this was *him* out there, if he was the one in trouble. He had lumbered up a hill like that once before. The suit looked familiar. Perhaps they'd caught his foolish act on camera, his attempt to die a free man. And now they'd woken him up to show him this damning bit of evidence. Donald braced for the accusation, for his punishment—

"This was earlier this morning," Eren said.

Donald nodded and tried to calm himself. This wasn't him on the screen. He had been asleep for longer than a day, which meant this was not him. They didn't know who he was. A surge of relief washed over him, a stark contrast to the nerves in the room and the shouts and hurrying boots in the hallway. Donald remembered being told that someone had disappeared over a hill when they'd pulled him from the pod. It was the first thing they'd told him. This was that person on the screen. This was why he'd been woken. He licked his lips and asked who it was.

"We're putting a file together for you now, sir. Should have it soon. What we do know is that there was a cleaning scheduled in eighteen this morning. Except . . ."

Eren hesitated. Donald turned from the screen and caught the Ops Head looking to the others for help. One of the operators—a large man in orange coveralls with wiry hair and headphones around his neck—was the first to oblige. "The cleaning didn't go through," the operator said flatly.

Several of the men in boots stiffened. Donald glanced around the room at the crowd that had packed into the small comm center, and he saw how they were watching him. Waiting on him. The Ops Head looked down at the floor in defeat. He appeared to be Donald's age, late thirties, and he was waiting to be chastised. These were the men in trouble, not him.

Donald tried to think. The people in charge were looking to *him* for guidance. Something was wrong with the shifts, something very wrong. He had worked with the man they thought he was, the man whose name graced his badge and his boots. A senator. Senator Thurman. It felt like yesterday that Donald had stood in that very same comm room and had felt that man's equal but for a moment. He had helped save a silo on his previous shift. And even though his head was in a mist and his legs were weak, he knew this charade was important to uphold. At least until he understood what was going on.

"What direction were they heading?" he asked, his voice a whisper. The others held perfectly still so that the rustle of their coveralls wouldn't compete with his words.

A man from the back of the room answered. "In the direction of seventeen, sir."

Donald composed himself. He remembered the Order, the danger of letting anyone out of sight. These people in their silos with a limited view of the world thought that they were the only ones alive. They lived in bubbles that must not be allowed to burst. "Any word from seventeen?" he asked.

"Seventeen is gone," the operator beside him said, dispensing more bad news with the same flat voice.

Donald cleared his throat. "Gone?" He searched the faces of the gathered. Foreheads creased with worry. Eren studied Donald, and the operator beside him adjusted his bulk in his seat. On the screen, the cleaner disappeared over the top of the hill and out of view. "What did this cleaner *do*?" he asked.

"It wasn't her," Eren said.

"Seventeen was shut down shifts ago," the operator said.

"Right, right." Donald ran his fingers through his hair. His hand was trembling.

"You feeling all right?" the operator asked. He glanced at the Ops Head, then back to Donald. He knew. Donald sensed that this man in orange with the headphones around his neck knew something was wrong.

"Still a bit woozy," Donald explained.

"He's only been up for half an hour," Eren told the operator.

There were murmurs from the back of the room.

"Yeah, okay." The operator settled back into his seat. "It's just . . . he's the Shepherd, you know? I pictured him waking up chewing nails and farting tacks."

Someone just behind Donald's chair chuckled.

"So what're we supposed to do about the cleaner?" a voice asked. "We need permission before we can send anyone out after her."

"She can't have gotten far," someone said.

The comm engineer on the other side of Donald spoke up. He had one side of his headphones still on, the other side pulled off so he could follow the conversation. A sheen of sweat stood out on his forehead. "Eighteen is reporting that her suit was modified," he said. "There's no telling how long it'll last. She could still be out there, Sirs."

This caused a chorus of whispers. It sounded like wind striking a visor, peppering it with sand. Donald stared at the screen, at a lifeless hill as seen from Silo 18. The dust came in dark waves. He remembered what it had felt like out there on that landscape, the difficulty moving in one of those suits, the hard slog up that gentle rise. Who was this cleaner, and where did she think she was going?

"Get me the file on this cleaner as soon as you can," he said. The others fell still and stopped their whispering arguments. Donald's voice was commanding because of its quietude, because of who they thought he was. "And I want whatever we have on seventeen." He glanced at the operator, whose brow was furrowed in either worry or suspicion. "To refresh my memory," he added.

Eren rested a hand on the back of Donald's chair. "What about the protocols?" he asked. "Shouldn't we scramble a drone or send someone after her? Or shut down eighteen? There's going to be violence over there. We've never had a cleaning not go through before."

Donald shook his head, which was beginning to clear. He looked down at his hand and remembered tearing off a glove once, there on the outside. He shouldn't be alive. How was he alive? He wondered what Thurman would do, what the old man would order. But he wasn't Thurman. Someone had told him once that people like Donald should be in charge. And now he was.

"We don't do anything just yet," he said, coughing and clearing his throat. "She won't get far."

The others stared at him with a mixture of shock and acceptance. There finally came a handful of nods. They assumed he knew best. He had been woken up, after all. It was all according to protocol. The system could be trusted—it was designed to just *go*. All anyone needed to do was their own job and let others handle the rest.

• 64 •

I t was a short walk from his apartment to the central offices, which Donald assumed was the point. It reminded him of a CEO's office he'd once seen with an adjoining bedroom. What had seemed impressive at first became sad after realizing why it was there.

He rapped his knuckles on the open door marked *Office of Psychological Services*. He used to think of these people as shrinks, that they were here to keep others sane. Now he knew that they were in charge of the insanity. All he saw on the door anymore was "OPS." Operations. The Head of the Head of the Heads. The office across the hall was where the busywork landed. Donald was reminded how each silo had a mayor for shaking hands and keeping up appearances, just as the world of yore had Presidents who came and went. Meanwhile, it was the men in shadows whose term limits were bounded by gravestones who wielded true power. That this silo operated by the same deceit should not be surprising; it was the only way such men knew to run anything.

He kept his back to his former office and knocked a little louder. Eren looked up from his computer and a hard mask of concentration melted into a wan smile. "Come in," he said as he rose from his seat. "You need the desk?"

"Yes, but stay." Donald crossed the room gingerly, his legs still half asleep, and noticed that while his own whites were crisp, Eren's were crumpled with the wear of a man well into his six-month shift. Even so, the Ops Head appeared vigorous and alert. His beard was neatly trimmed by his neck and only peppered with gray. He helped Donald into the plush chair behind the desk.

"We're still waiting for the full report on this cleaner," Eren said. "The Head of eighteen warned that it's a thick one."

"Priors?" Donald imagined anyone sent to clean would have priors.

"Oh, yeah. The word is that she was a sheriff, but I only heard that from Gable across the hall. Not sure if I'm buying it. Of course, it wouldn't be the first lawman to want out."

"But it would be the first time anyone's gotten out of sight," Donald said.

"From what I understand, yeah." Eren crossed his arms and leaned against the desk. "Nearest anyone got before now was that gentleman you stopped. I reckon that's why protocol says to wake you. I've heard some of the boys refer to you as the Shepherd." Eren laughed.

Donald cleared his throat into his fist. He was loath to admit that he had been more the loose sheep than the shepherd. "Tell me about seventeen," he said, changing the subject. "Who was on shift when that silo went down?"

"We can look it up." Eren waved a hand at the keyboard.

"My, uh, fingers are still a little tingly," Donald said. He slid the keyboard toward Eren, who hesitated before getting off the desk. The Ops Head bent over the keys and pulled up the shift list with a shortcut. Donald tried to follow along with what he was doing on the screen. These were files he didn't have access to, menus he was unfamiliar with.

"Looks like it was Cooper. I think I came off a shift once as he was coming on. Name sounds familiar. I sent someone down to get those files as well."

"Good, good."

Eren raised his eyebrows. "You went over the seventeen reports on your last shift, right?"

Donald had no clue if Thurman had been up since then. For all he knew, the old man had been awake when it happened. "It's hard to keep everything straight," he said, which was solid truth. "How many years has it been?"

"That's right. You were in the deep freeze, weren't you?"

Donald supposed he was. Eren tapped the desk with his finger, and Donald's gaze drifted to the man across the hall, sitting behind his computer. He remembered what it had been like to be that person over there, wondering what the doctors in white were discussing across the way. Now he was one of those in white.

"Yes, I was in the deep freeze," Donald said. They wouldn't have moved his body, would they? Erskine or someone could've simply changed entries in a database. Maybe it was that simple. Just a quick hack, two reference numbers transposed, and one man lives the life of another. "I like to be near my daughter," he explained.

"Yeah, I don't blame you." The wrinkles in Eren's brow smoothed. "I've got a wife down there. I still make the mistake of visiting her first thing every shift." He took a deep breath, then pointed at the screen. "Seventeen was lost over thirty years ago. I'd have to look it up to be exact. The cause is still unclear. There wasn't any sign of unrest leading up to it, so we didn't have much time to react. There was a cleaning scheduled, but the airlock opened a day early and out of sequence. Could've been a glitch or tampering. We just don't know. Sensors reported a gas purge in the lower levels and then a riot surging up. We pulled the plug as they were scrambling out of the airlock. Barely had time."

Donald recalled Silo 12. That facility had ended in similar fashion. He remembered people scattering on the hillside, a plume of white mist, some of them turning and fighting to get back inside. "No survivors?" he asked.

"There were a few stragglers. We lost the radio feed and the cameras but continued to put in a routine call over there, just in case anyone was in the safe room."

Donald nodded. By the book. He remembered the calls to 12 after it went down. He remembered nobody answering.

"Someone did pick up the day the silo fell," Eren said. "I think it was some young shadow or tech. I haven't read the transcripts in forever." He paged down on the shift report. "It looks like we sent the collapse codes soon after that call, just as a precaution. So even if the cleaner gets over there, she's gonna find a hole in the ground."

"Maybe she'll keep walking," Donald said. "What silo sits on the other side? Sixteen?"

Eren nodded.

"Why don't you go give them a call." Donald tried to remember the layout of the silos. These were the kinds of things he'd be expected to know. "And get in touch with the silos on either side of seventeen, just in case our cleaner takes a turn."

"Will do."

Eren stood, and Donald marveled again at being treated as if he were in charge. It was already beginning to make him feel as if he really were. Just like being elected to Congress, all that awesome responsibility foisted on him overnight—

Eren leaned across the desk and hit two of the function keys on the keyboard, logging himself out of the computer. The Ops Head hurried out into the hall while Donald stared at a login and password prompt.

Suddenly, he felt very much less in charge.

· 65 ·

Across the hall, a man sat behind a desk that once had belonged to Donald. Donald peered up at this man and found him peering right back. It was as though someone had installed a funhouse mirror in the hall, or some kind of tear in the cosmos had ripped open, allowing him to see into the past. That was him on the other side. He used to gaze across that hallway in the opposite direction. And while this man in his former office—who was heavier than Donald and had less hair—likely sat there playing a game of solitaire, Donald struggled with a puzzle of his own.

His old login of Troy with his passkey of 2156 wouldn't work. He tried old ATM codes, and they were just as useless. He sat, thinking, worried about performing too many incorrect attempts. It felt like just yesterday that this account had worked. But a lot had happened since then. A lot of shifts. And someone had tampered with them.

It pointed back to Erskine, the old Brit left behind to coordinate the shifts. Erskine had taken a liking to him. But what was the point? What was he expecting Donald to do?

For a brief moment, he thought about standing up and walking out into the hallway and saying, "I am not Thurman or Shepherd or Troy. My name is Donald, and I'm not supposed to be here."

He should tell the truth. He should rage with the truth, as senseless as it would seem to everyone else. "I am Donald!" he felt like screaming, just as old man Hal once had. They could pin his boots to a gurney and put him back to glorious sleep. They could send him out to the hills. They could bury him like they'd buried his wife. But he would scream and scream until he believed it himself, that he was who he thought he was.

Instead, he tried Erskine's name with his own passkey. Another red warning that the login was incorrect, and the desire to out himself passed as swiftly as it had come.

He studied the monitor. There didn't seem to be a trigger for the number of incorrect tries, but how long before Eren came back? How long before he had to explain that he couldn't log in? Maybe he could go across the hall, interrupt the Silo Head's game of solitaire, and ask him to retrieve his key. He could blame it on being groggy and newly awake. That excuse had been working thus far. He wondered how long he could cling to it.

On a lark, he tried the combination of Thurman and his own passkey of 2156.

The login screen disappeared, replaced by a main menu. The sense that he was the wrong person deepened. Donald wiggled his toes. The extra space in his loose boots gave him comfort. On the screen, a familiar envelope flashed. Thurman had messages.

Donald clicked the icon and scrolled down to the oldest unread message, something that might explain how he had arrived there, something from Thurman's prior shift. The dates went back centuries; it was jarring to watch them scroll by. Population reports. Automated messages. Replies and forwards. He saw a message from Erskine, but it was just a note about the overflow of deep freeze to one of the lower cryopod levels. The useless bodies were stacking up, it seemed. Another message farther down was starred as important. Victor's name was in the senders column, which caught Donald's attention. It had to be from before Donald's second shift. Victor was already dead the last time Donald had been woken. He opened the message.

••••

Old friend,

I'm sure you will question what I'm about to do, that you will see this as a violation of our pact, but I see it more as a restructuring of the timeline. New facts have emerged that push things up a bit. For me, at least. Your time will come.

I have in recent days discovered why one of our facilities has seen more than its share of turmoil. There is someone there who remembers, and she both disturbs and confirms what I know of humanity. Room is made that it might be filled. Fear is spread because the clean-up is addicting. Seeing this, much of what we do to one another becomes more obvious. It explains the great quandary of why the most depressed societies are those with the fewest wants. Arriving at the truth, I feel an urge from older times to synthesize a theory and present it to roomfuls of professionals. Instead, I have gone to a dusty room to procure a gun.

You and I have spent much of our adult lives scheming to save the world. Several adult lives, in fact. That deed now done, I ponder a question more dire, one that I fear I cannot answer and that we were never brave nor bold enough to pose. And so I ask you now, dear friend: Was this world worth saving to begin with? Were we worth saving?

This endeavor was launched with that great assumption taken for granted. Now I ask myself for the first time. And while I view the cleansing of the world as our defining achievement, this business of saving humanity may have been our gravest mistake. The world may be better off without us. I have not the will to decide. I leave that to you. The final shift, my friend, belongs to you, for I have worked my last. I do not envy you the choice you will have to make. The pact we formed so long ago haunts me as never before. And I feel that what I'm about to do . . . that this is the easy way.

-Vincent Wayne DiMarco

Donald read the last paragraph again. It was a suicide note. Thurman knew. All along, while Donald wrestled with Victor's fate on his last shift, Thurman knew. He had this note in his possession and didn't share it. And Donald had almost grown convinced that Victor had been murdered. Unless the note was a fake— But no, Donald shook that thought away. Paranoia like that could spiral out of control and know no end. He had to cling to something.

He backed out of the message with a heavy heart and scrolled up the list, looking for some other clue. Near the top of the screen was a message with the subject line: *Urgent - The Pact.* That word had appeared more than once in Victor's note. Donald clicked the message open. The body was short. It read, simply:

Wake me when you get this.
— Anna
(Locket 20391102)

Donald blinked rapidly at the sight of her name. He glanced across the hall at the silo Head and listened for footsteps heading his way. His arms were covered in gooseflesh. He rubbed them, wiped at the bottoms of his eyes, and read the note a second time.

It was signed Anna. It took him a moment to realize that it wasn't to him. It was a note between daughter and father. There was no send date listed, which was curious, but it was sorted near the very top. Perhaps it was from before their last shift together? Maybe the two of them had been awake recently. Donald studied the number at the bottom. *20391102.* It looked like a date. An old date. Inscribed on a locket, perhaps. Something meaningful between the two of them. And what of the mention of this Pact? That was the name the silos used for their constitutions. What was urgent about that?

Footsteps in the hallway broke his concentration. Eren rounded the corner and covered the office in a few steps. He circled the desk and placed two folders by the keyboard, then glanced at the screen as Donald fumbled with the mouse to minimize the message. "H-how'd it go?" Donald asked. "You got through to everyone?"

"Yeah." Eren sniffed and scratched his beard. "The Head of sixteen took it badly. He's been in that position a long time. Too long, I think. He suggested closing down his cafeteria or shutting off the wallscreen, just in case."

"But he's not going to."

"No, I told him as a last resort. No need to cause a panic. We just wanted them to have a heads-up."

"Good, good." Donald liked someone else thinking. It took the pressure off of him. "You need your desk back?" He made a show of logging off.

"No, actually, you're on if you don't mind." Eren checked the clock in the corner of the computer screen. "I can take the afternoon shift. How're you feeling, by the way? Any shakes?"

Donald shook his head. "No. I'm good. It gets easier every time."

Eren laughed. "Yeah. I've seen how many shifts you've taken. And a double a while back. Don't envy you at all, friend. But you seem to be holding up well."

Donald coughed. "Yeah," he said. He picked up the topmost of the two folders and read the tab. "This is what we have on Seventeen?"

"Yep. The thick one is your cleaner." He tapped the other folder. "You might want to check in with the Head of eighteen today. He's pretty shaken up, is shouldering all the blame. Name's Bernard. There are already grumblings from his lower levels about the cleaning not going through, so he's looking at a very probable uprising. I'm sure he'd like to hear from you."

"Yeah, sure."

"Oh, and he doesn't have an official second right now. His last shadow didn't work out, and he's been putting off a replacement. I hope you don't mind, but I told him to get on that. Just in case."

"No, no. That's fine." Donald waved his hand. "I'm not here to get in your way." He didn't add that he had absolutely no clue why he was there at all.

Eren smiled and nodded. "Great. Well, if you need anything, call me. And the guy across the hall goes by Gable. He used to hold down a post over here but couldn't cut it. Opted for a wipe instead of a deep freeze when given the choice. Good guy. Team player. He'll be on for a few more months and can get you anything you need."

Donald peered across the hall at the man in the funhouse mirror. He remembered the vacuous sensation of manning that desk, the hollow pit that had filled him. How Donald had ended up there had seemed unusual, a last-minute switch with his friend Mick. It never occurred to him how all the others were selected. To think that any might volunteer for such an empty post filled him with sadness.

Eren stuck out his hand. Donald studied it a moment, then accepted it.

"I'm really sorry we had to wake you like this," he said, pumping Donald's hand. "But I have to admit, I'm damn sure glad you're here."

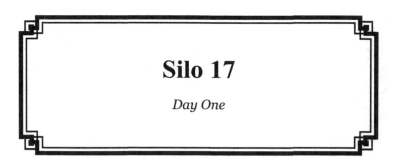

Silo 17

Day One

• 66 •

The box on the wall was unrelenting with its awful sounds. His father had called it a radio. The noise it made was like a person hissing and spitting. Even the steel cage surrounding it looked like a mouth with its lips peeled back and iron bars for teeth.

Jimmy wanted to silence the radio but was scared to touch it or adjust anything. He waited to hear from his father, who had left him in a strange room, a hidden warren between the silo's levels.

How many more of these secret places were there? He glanced through an open door at the other room his dad had shown him, the one like a small apartment with its stove, table, and chairs. When his parents got back, would they all stay here overnight? How long before the madness cleared from the stairs and he could see his friends again? He hoped it wouldn't be long.

He glared at the black box with its spitting sounds, patted his chest, felt for the key there. His ribs were sore from the fall, and he could feel a knot forming in his thigh from where he'd landed on someone. His shoulder hurt when he lifted his arm. He turned to the monitor to search for his mother again, but she was no longer on the screen. A jostling crowd moved in jerks and fits. A stairwell writhed with more traffic than it was meant to hold.

Jimmy reached for the box with the controls his father had used. He twisted one of the knobs, and the view changed. It was an empty hall. A faint number 33 stood in the lower left corner of the screen. Jimmy turned the dial once more and got a different hallway. There was a trail of clothes on the ground, like someone had walked by with a leaking laundry bag. Nothing moved.

He tried a different dial, and the number on the bottom changed to 32. He was going *up the levels*. Jimmy spun the first dial until he found the stairwell again. Something flashed down and off the bottom of the screen. There were people leaning over the railing with their arms outstretched, mouths open in silent horror. There was no sound from the little windows that allowed him to see the world, but Jimmy remembered the screams from the woman who fell earlier. This was too far up to be his mother, he consoled himself. His dad would find her and bring her back. His dad had a gun.

Jimmy spun the dials and tried to locate either of his parents, but it seemed that not every angle was covered. And he couldn't figure out how to make the windows multiply. He was decent on a computer—he was going to work for IT like his father someday—but the little box was unintuitive as the deeps. He dialed it back down to 34 and found the main hallway. He could see a shiny steel door at the far end of a long corridor. Sprawled in the foreground was Yani. Yani hadn't moved, was surely dead. The men standing over him were gone, and there was a new body at the end of the hall, near the door. The color of his coveralls assured Jimmy that it wasn't his father. His father probably put that man there on his way out. Jimmy wished he hadn't been left alone.

Overhead, the lights continued to blink angry and red, and nothing happened on the screen. Jimmy grew restless and paced in circles. He went to the small wooden desk on the opposite wall and flipped through the thick book. It was a fortune in paper, perfectly cut, and eerily smooth to the touch. The desk and chair were both made of real wood, not painted to look like that. He could tell by scratching it with his fingernail.

He closed the book and checked the cover. The word ORDER was embossed in shiny letters across the front. He reopened it, and realized he'd lost someone's place. The radio nearby continued to hiss noisily. Jimmy turned and checked the computer screen, but nothing was happening in the hallway. That noise was getting on his nerves. He thought about adjusting the volume, but was scared he might accidentally turn it off. His dad wouldn't be able to get through to him if he messed something up.

He paced some more. There was a shelf of metal containers in one corner that went from floor to ceiling. Pulling one out, Jimmy felt how heavy they were. He played with the latch until he figured out how to open it. There was a soft sigh as the lid came loose, and he found a book inside. Looking at all the containers filling the shelves, Jimmy saw what a pile of chits was there. He returned the book, assuming it was full of nothing but boring words like the one on the desk.

Back at the other desk, he examined the computer underneath and saw that it wasn't turned on. All the lights were dim. He traced the wire from the black box with all the switches and found a different wire led from the monitor to the computer. The machine that made the windows—that could see far distances and around corners—was controlled by something else. The power switch on the computer did nothing. There was a place for a key. Jimmy bent down to inspect the connections on the back, to make sure everything was plugged in, when the radio crackled.

"—need you to report in. Hello—?"

Jimmy knocked his head on the underside of the desk. He ran to the radio, which was back to hissing. Grabbing the device at the end of the stretchy cord—the thing his dad had named Mike—he squeezed the button.

"Dad? Dad, is that you?"

He let go and looked to the ceiling. He listened for footsteps and waited for the lights to stop flashing. The monitor showed a quiet hallway. Maybe he should go to the door and wait.

The radio crackled with a voice: "Sheriff? Who is this?"

Jimmy squeezed the button. "This is Jimmy. Jimmy Parker. Who—" The button slipped out of his hand, the static returning. His palms were sweaty. He wiped them on his coveralls and got the device under control. "Who is this?" he asked.

"Russ's boy?" There was a pause. "Son, where are you?"

He didn't want to say. So he didn't. The radio continued to hiss.

"Jimmy, this is Deputy Hines," the voice said. "Put your father on."

Jimmy started to squeeze the button and say that his father wasn't there, but another voice chimed in. He recognized it at once.

"Mitch, this is Russ."

Dad! There was a lot of noise in the background, people screaming. Jimmy held the device in both hands. "Dad! Come back, please!"

The radio popped with his father's voice. "James, be quiet. Mitch, I need you to—" Something was lost to the background noise. "—and stop the traffic. People are getting crushed up here."

"Copy."

That was his father talking to the deputy. The deputy was acting like his old man was in charge. Nothing made sense in the world.

"We've got a breach up-top," his father said, "so I don't know how long you've got, but you're probably the sheriff until the end."

"Copy," Mitch said again. The radio made his voice sound shaky.

"Son—" His father was yelling, now, fighting to be heard over some obnoxious din of screams and shouts. "I'm going to get your mother, okay? Just stay there, James. Don't move."

Jimmy turned to the monitor. "Okay," he said. He hung the Mike back on its hook, his hands trembling, and returned to the black box with all the controls. He felt helpless and alone. He should be out there, lending a hand. He thought about Nick and Seth and Sarah Jenkins. How long before he could see his friends again? He hoped it wouldn't be long.

· 67 ·

Hours passed, and Jimmy wanted to be anywhere but that place. He crept down the dark passage to the ladder and peered up at the grating, listening. There was a faint buzzing sound coming and going that he couldn't place. The hiss of the radio could barely be heard from the end of the corridor. He didn't want to be too far away from the radio, but he worried his dad might need him by the door as well. He wanted to be in two places at once.

He went back to the room with the desks. Another of the long guns like his father had used to kill Yani was propped against the wall. Jimmy was afraid to touch it. He wished his father hadn't left. It was all Jimmy's fault for being separated from his mom. They should've made it down together. But then he remembered the crush of people on the stairs. If only he'd been faster, they wouldn't have gotten caught up in the crowds. And it occurred to Jimmy that the only reason his mother was there at all was because she had come for him. If it weren't for that, his parents would be down in that room, safe and together.

He tried not to think of that. Jimmy glared at the throbbing red lights overhead. The hissing from the radio was getting on his nerves. He hissed back at the thing like Mrs. Pearson shushed the kids in the back row. The small room was strange and bewildering. On one desk, a book unlike any other. On another desk, windows into the whole of the silo. Drawings hung on the wall in the next room the size of blankets, and a gun rested idly, a big pistol that could kick men from a distance.

"James—"

Jimmy spun around. His father's voice was there in the room with him. It took a moment to realize the static from the radio was gone.

"—Son, are you there?"

He lunged for the radio, grabbed the Mike at the end of the cord. It had been hours without voices. Too long. As he squeezed the button, a flash of movement caught his eye. Someone was moving on the monitor.

"Dad?" He stretched the cord across the small room and looked closer. His father was outside the steel door, standing at the end of the hall. Yani was still in the foreground, unmoving. The other body was gone. His father had his back to the camera, the portable radio in his hand. "I'm coming!" Jimmy yelled into the radio. He dropped the Mike and dashed for the corridor and the ladder.

"Son! No—!"

His father's shouts were cut off by a grunt. Jimmy wheeled around, his boots squeaking. He clutched the desk for balance. On the screen, another man had emerged from around the corner. His father was doubled over in pain. This man held the long pistol, stooped to pick up something from the ground, held it to his mouth. It was the portable his father had taken from the room.

"Is this Russ's boy?"

Jimmy stared at the man on the screen. "Yes," he said out loud. "Don't hurt my dad."

The room was full of static. The lights overhead continued to throb red.

Jimmy cursed himself, pushed away from the desk, and grabbed the dangling Mike. "Please don't hurt him," he said, squeezing the button.

The man turned and looked directly at the camera. It was one of the security guards. There was a bit of movement peeking out from around the corner of the hall, more people out of sight.

"James, is it?"

Jimmy nodded. He watched his dad regain his composure and stand. His father made a gesture to someone out of sight. He patted the air with his palm as if to calm them.

"What's the new code?" the man with the radio asked.

Jimmy didn't want to tell him. But he wanted his father back inside. He wasn't sure what to do.

"The code," the man said. He aimed the gun at Jimmy's dad. Jimmy watched his father say something, then gesture for the portable. The security guard hesitated a moment before handing it over. His father lifted the unit to his mouth.

"They'll kill you," his father said, calm as if he were telling his son to tie his boots. The man with the gun waved an arm, and someone rushed into view to wrestle with his father. "They'll kill us all anyway," his father shouted, struggling to keep hold of the radio. "And they'll kill you the moment you open this door!"

Jimmy screamed as one of the men punched his father. His dad fought back, but they punched him again. And then the man with the gun waved the other guy away. And the room was full of static, so he couldn't hear the long pistol bark, but Jimmy could see the flashes of flame leap out, could see the way his father jerked as he was hit, watched him slump to the ground and become as still as Yani.

Jimmy dropped the Mike and grabbed the edges of the monitor. He yelled at this cruel window on the world while the guards in the silver coveralls surveyed the man who had been his father. And then more men appeared from around the corner. They dragged Jimmy's mom behind them, kicking and silently screaming.

68

"No, no, no, no—"

The room was static and pulse. The two men wrestled with Jimmy's mother, who lifted herself off the ground and writhed in their jerking grasps. Her feet kicked and whirled. Jimmy's father lay still as stone beneath her.

"Open this goddamn door!" the man with the portable yelled. The radio on the wall was deafening. Jimmy hated the radio. He ran to it, reached for the dangling cord, then thought better and grabbed the other portable from the rack. One of the knobs said "power." He twisted it until it made the hissing sound, turned to the screen, and held the radio to his mouth.

"Don't," he said, and Jimmy realized he was crying. Tears splashed his coveralls. "I'm coming."

It was hard to tear himself away from the view of his mother. Harder still to be far from her, to not be there for her or his father. As he rushed down the dark corridor, he continued to see her kicking and screaming, her boots in the air. He could hear her yelling in the background as the man radioed again: "Tell me the code!"

Jimmy held the portable's wrist strap between his teeth and attacked the ladder. His hands rang out like dull bells as he slapped his way up, ignoring the pain in his shoulder and knee. He found the release for the grating and threw it aside with a clang. Tossing the portable out, he scrambled after it on his knees. The lights above were on fire. His chest was on fire. His father was as dead as Yani.

"Coming, coming," he said into the radio.

The man yelled something back. All Jimmy could hear was his mother screaming and his pulse ringing in his ears. He ran beneath the angry lights and between the dark machines. The laces on one of his boots had come undone. They whipped about while he ran, and he thought of his mother's legs, up in the air like that, kicking and fighting.

Jimmy crashed into the door. He could hear muffled shouts on the other side. They came through the radio as well. His mother's screams could be heard both places at once, crackling and hissing in one ear and dull and distant in the other.

Jimmy slapped the door with his palm and shouted into his portable. "I'm here, I'm here!"

"The code!" the man screamed.

Jimmy went to the control pad. His hands were shaking, his vision blurred. He imagined his mother on the other side, the gun aimed at her. He could feel his father lying a few feet away, just on the other side of that wall of steel. Tears streamed down his cheeks. He put in the first two numbers, the level of his school, and hesitated. That wasn't right. It was twelve-eighteen, not eighteen-twelve. Or was it? He put in the other two numbers, and the keypad flashed red. The door didn't open.

"What did you do?" the man yelled through the radio. "Just tell me the code!"

Jimmy fumbled with the portable, brought it to his lips. "Please don't hurt her—" he said.

The radio squawked. "If you don't do as I say, she's dead. We'll all be dead. Do you understand?"

The man sounded terrified. Maybe he was just as scared as Jimmy. Jimmy nodded and reached for the keypad. He entered the first two numbers correctly, then thought about what his father had said. They would kill him. They would kill him and his mother both if he let these men inside. But it was his mom—

The keypad blinked impatiently. The man on the other side of the door yelled for him to hurry, yelled something about three wrong tries in a row and having to wait another day. Jimmy did nothing, paralyzed with fear. The keypad flashed red and fell silent.

There was a bang on the other side of the door, a muffled pop, a blast from a gun. Jimmy squeezed the radio and screamed. When he let go, he could hear his mom shrieking on the other side.

"The next one won't be a warning," the man said. "Now don't touch that pad. Don't touch it again. Just tell me the code. Hurry, boy."

The man was panicked, and Jimmy blubbered. He tried to form the sounds, to tell the numbers in the right order, but nothing came out. With his forehead pressed against the wall, he could hear his mother struggling and fighting on the other side.

"The code," the man said, calmer now.

Jimmy heard a distant grunt. He heard someone yell "Bitch," heard his mother scream for Jimmy not to do it, and then a slap on the other side of the wall, someone pressed up against it, his mother inches away. And then the muffled beeps of numbers being entered, four quick taps of the same number, and an angry buzz from the keypad as a third attempt failed.

More shouts. And then the roar of a gun, louder and angrier with his head pressed to the door. Jimmy screamed and beat his fists against the cold steel. The men were yelling at him through the radio. There were a lot of screams coming through the portable, screams leaking through the heavy steel door, but none of them came from his mother.

Jimmy slid to the floor. The angry yells bled through the wall. They bled and bled. They crackled from the radio in hissing bursts, and Jimmy buried the portable against his belly and curled into a ball. His body quivered with sobs and strange sounds, the floor grating rough against his cheek. And while the violence so very close raged impotently, the lights overhead continued to throb at him. They throbbed steady. They weren't like a pulse at all.

Silo 1

69

There was a plastic bag waiting on Donald's bunk when he got back to his room. He shut the door to block out the cacophony of traffic and office chatter, searched for a lock, and saw that there wasn't one. Here was a lone bedroom among workspaces, a place for men who were always on call, who were up for as long as they were needed.

Donald imagined this was where Thurman stayed when he was called forth in an emergency. He remembered the name on his boots and realized he didn't have to imagine; it was happening.

The wheelchair had been removed, he saw, and a glass of water stood on the nightstand. His caretakers had been upgraded from the sort who locked him away, who pinned him to gurneys, who dragged him kicking and screaming down dusty hills. He tossed the folders Eren had given him on the bed, sat down beside them, and picked up the curious plastic bag.

Shift, it read, in large stenciled letters. The clear plastic was heavily wrinkled, a few items appearing inside as inscrutable bulges. Donald slid the plastic seal to the side and peeled open the bag. Turning it over, there was a jingle of metal as a pair of dog tags rattled out, a fine chain slithering after them like a startled snake. Donald inspected the tags and saw that they were Thurman's. Dented and thin, and without the rubber edging he remembered from his sister's tags, they seemed like antiques. Which he supposed they were.

A small pocketknife was next. The handle looked like ivory but was probably a substitute. Donald opened the blade and tested it. Both sides were equally dull. The tip had been snapped off at some point, used to pry something open, perhaps. It had the look of a memento, no longer good for cutting. Like an old man who had seen war but would no longer be useful in one.

The only other item in the bag was a coin, a quarter. The shape and heft of something once so common made it difficult to breathe. Donald thought of an entire civilization, gone. It seemed impossible for so much to go away completely, but then he remembered Roman coins and Mayan coins and who knew what else pulled from the ocean floors and unearthed in deserts and jungles. He turned the coin over and over and contemplated the only thing unusual about him holding a trinket from a world fallen to ashes—and that was him being around to marvel at the loss. It was supposed to be people who died and cultures that lasted. Now, it was the other way around.

Something about the coin caught Donald's attention as he turned it over and over. It was heads on both sides. He laughed and inspected it more closely, wondering if it was a gag item, but the feel of the thing seemed genuine. On one of the sides, there was a faint arc where the stamp had missed its mark. A mistake coin. Perhaps a gift from a friend in the Treasury?

He placed the items on the bedside table and remembered Anna's note to her father. He was surprised there wasn't a locket in the bag. The note had been marked urgent and had mentioned a locket with a date. Donald folded the bag marked *Shift* and slid it beneath his glass of water. People hurried up and down the hall outside. The silo was in a panic. He supposed if the real Thurman were there, the old man would be storming up and down as well, barking orders, shutting down facilities, commanding lives to be taken.

Donald coughed into the crook of his arm, his throat tickling. Someone had put him in this position. Erskine, or Victor beyond the grave, or maybe a hacker with more nefarious designs. He had nothing to go on.

Lifting the two folders, he thought of the panic roused by a person meandering out of sight. He thought about the violence brewing in the depths of another silo. These were not his mysteries, he thought. What he wanted to know was why he was awake, why he was even *alive*. What exactly was out there beyond those walls? What was the plan for the world once these shifts were over? Was it getting better out there? Would there be a day when the people underground would be set free? What would be expected of them?

Something didn't sit right with him, imagining how that last shift would play out. There was a nagging suspicion that things wouldn't end so simply. Every layer he'd peeled back so far, every skin of this onion, possessed the sting of a lie. And he didn't think he'd reached the core just yet. Perhaps someone had placed him in Thurman's boots to keep digging.

He recalled what Erskine had said about people like himself being in charge. Or was it Victor who said it to Erskine? He couldn't remember. What he did know, patting his pocket for the badge there, a badge that would open doors previously locked to him, was that he was very much in charge now. There were questions he wanted answers to. And he was in a position to ask them.

Donald coughed into the crook of his elbow once more, an itch in his throat he couldn't quite soothe. He opened one of the folders and reached for his glass. Taking a few gulps of water and beginning to read, he failed to notice the faint stain left behind, the spot of blood in the crook of his elbow.

Silo 17

Week One

· 70 ·

Jimmy didn't want to move. He couldn't move. He remained curled on the steel grating, the lights flashing overhead, on and off, on and off, the color of crimson.

People on the other side of the door yelled at him and at each other. Jimmy slept in fits. There were dull pops from guns and zings that rang against the door. The keypad buzzed. Only a single digit entered, and it buzzed. The whole world was angry with him.

Jimmy dreamt of blood. It seeped under the door and filled the room. It rose up in the shape of his mother and father, and they stood there, great red puddles with arms and legs, and they lectured him, mouths yawning open in anger. But Jimmy couldn't hear.

He awoke to a great pressure in his skull. Clasping his hands over his eyes, he curled into a tighter and tighter ball, knees against his chin. Jimmy felt something crack within his skull, a pop like the sound a too-big yawn makes deep behind his ear. There was a great release of pressure that had built up and built up—and it sent him back to sleep.

There were no days, no time. The yelling on the other side of the door came and went. They were fighting, these men. Fighting to get inside where it was safe. Jimmy didn't feel safe. He felt hungry. He needed to pee.

Standing was the hardest thing he'd ever done. Jimmy's cheek made a tearing sound as he lifted it from the grating. He wiped the drool from the side of his face and felt the ridges there, the deep creases and the places his skin puffed out. His joints were stiff. His eyes were crusted together from crying. Jimmy staggered toward the far corner of the room and tugged at his coveralls, tried to get them free before he accidentally went with them on.

The great black machines hummed and whirred and watched him go. Urine splashed through the grating and trickled down on bright runs of wires in neat channels. His stomach rumbled and spun inside his belly, but he didn't want to eat. He wanted to not eat and to waste away completely. He glared up at the annoying lights overhead trying to drill into his skull. His stomach was angry with him. Everything was angry with him.

Back at the door, he waited for someone to call his name. He went to the keypad and pressed the number "1." The door buzzed at him immediately. It was angry, too.

Jimmy wanted to lie back down on the grating and curl back into a ball, but his stomach said to look for food. Below. There were beds and food below. Jimmy walked in a daze between the black machines. He touched their warm skin for balance, heard them clicking and whirring like everything was normal. The red lights flashed over and over. Jimmy weaved his way until he found the hole in the ground.

He lowered his feet to the rungs of the ladder and noticed the buzzing noise. It came and went in time with the throbbing lights. He pulled himself out of the shaft and crawled across the floor in pursuit of the sound. It was coming from the server with its back off. His father had called it a comm something. Where had his father gone? Off to find his mother. There was something else—

Jimmy couldn't remember. He patted his chest and felt the key against his breastbone. The buzzing came and went with the flashing lights in perfect synchrony. This machine was making that overhead throb drilling into his skull. He peered inside the machine. A comm hub, that's what his father had called it. There was a headset hanging on a hook. He wished his father were there, but that seemed an impossible wish. Jimmy fumbled with the headset. There was a wire dangling from it. The piece on the end looked like something from computer class. He searched for a place to plug it in and saw a bank of sockets. One of them was blinking. The number "40" was lit up above it.

Jimmy adjusted the headset around his ears. He lined up the jack with the socket and pressed in until he felt a click. The lights overhead fell silent immediately. A voice came through, like the radio, only clearer.

"Hello?" the voice asked.

Jimmy didn't say anything. He waited.

"Is anyone there?"

Jimmy cleared his throat. "Yes," he said, and it felt strange to talk to an empty room. Stranger even than the radio with its hissing. It felt like Jimmy was talking to himself.

"Is everyone okay?" the voice asked.

"No," Jimmy said. He remembered the stairs and falling and Yani and something awful on the other side of the door. "No," he said again, wiping tears from his cheeks. "Everyone is *not* okay!"

There was muttering on the other side of the line. Jimmy sniffled. "Hello?" he asked.

"What happened?" the voice demanded. Jimmy thought it was an angry voice. Just like the people outside the door. Scared and angry, both.

"Everyone was running—" Jimmy said. He wiped his nose. "They were all heading up. I fell. Mom and Dad—"

"There were casualties?" the man from level 40 asked.

Jimmy thought of the body he'd seen on the stairway with the awful wound on his head. He thought of the woman who had gone over the rails, her scream fading to a crisp silence. "Yes," he said.

The voice on the line spat an angry curse, angry but faint. And then: "We were too late." Again, it sounded distant, like the man was talking to someone else.

"Too late for what?" Jimmy asked.

There was a click, followed by a steady tone. The light above the socket marked "40" went out.

"Hello?"

Jimmy waited.

"Hello?"

He searched inside the box for some button to press, some way to make the voices come back. There were sockets with fifty numbers above them. Why only fifty levels? He glanced at the server behind him and wondered if there were other comm stations to handle the rest of the silo. This one must be for the Up Top. There would be one for the Mids and another for the Deep. He unplugged the jack, and the tone in the headset fell silent.

Jimmy wondered if he could call another level. Maybe the school. He ran his finger down the row looking for "18," and noticed that "17" was missing. There was no jack for "17." He puzzled over this as the overhead lights began to flash once more. Jimmy glanced at level 40's socket, but it remained dark. It was the top level calling. The light over the number "1" blinked on and off. The cabinet was back to buzzing, the lights to flashing. Jimmy glanced at the jack in his hand, lined it up with the socket, and pressed in until he heard a click.

"Hello?" he said.

"What the hell is going on over there?" a voice demanded.

Jimmy shrunk within himself. His father had yelled at him like this before, but not for a long time. He suddenly needed to pee again. He didn't answer because he didn't know what to say.

"Is this Jerry? Or Russ?"

Russ was his dad. Jerry was his dad's boss. Jimmy realized he shouldn't be playing with these things.

"This is Jimmy," he said.

"Who?"

"Jimmy. The guy on level forty said they were too late. I told him what happened."

"Too late?" There was some distant talking. Jimmy jiggled the cord in the socket. He was doing something wrong. "How did you get in there?" the man asked.

"My dad let me in," he said, the truth frightened out of him.

"We're shutting you down," the voice said. "Shut them down right now."

Jimmy didn't know what to do. There was a hiss somewhere. He thought it was from the headset until he noticed the white steam coming from the vents overhead. A fog descended toward him. Jimmy waved his hand in front of his face, expecting the sting of smoke like he'd smelled from a fire once as a kid, but the steam didn't smell like anything. It just tasted like a dry spoon in his mouth. Like metal.

"—on my goddamn shift—" the person in his headset said.

Jimmy coughed. He tried to say something back, but he had swallowed wrong. The steam stopped leaking from the vents.

"That did it," the man on the other line muttered.

Before Jimmy could say anything else, the various winking lights inside the box went dark. There was a click in the headset, and then it too fell silent. He pulled the headset off just as a louder "thunk" rang out in the ceiling and the lights in the room turned off. The whirring and clicking of the tall servers around him wound down. There was utter dark and complete silence. Jimmy couldn't see his own nose, couldn't see his hand as he waved it in front of his face. He thought he'd gone blind, wondered if this was what being dead was like, but then he heard his pulse, a thump-thump, thump-thump in his temples.

Jimmy felt a sob catch in his throat. He wanted his mother and father. He wanted his backpack, which he'd left behind like an idiot. For a long while, he sat there, waiting for someone to come to him, for an idea to form on what he should do next. He thought of the ladder nearby and the room below. As he began to crawl toward that hole, patting the grating ahead of him so he wouldn't fall down the long drop, the clunking in the ceiling came back. There was a blinding flash as the lights overhead wavered, shimmered, blinked on and off several times, then burned steady.

Jimmy froze. The red and angry lights went to flashing again. He went back to the box and looked inside. It was the light over "40" going on and off like mad. He thought about answering it, seeing what these people were so angry about, but maybe the power was a warning. Maybe he'd said something wrong.

The lights overhead were like bright heat. They reminded him of the farms, of the time years ago that his class had gone on a trip to the Mids and planted seeds beneath those harsh lights.

Jimmy turned to the server with the open back and fumbled for the jack inside. He hated the flashing lights, but he didn't want to get yelled at. So he jabbed the headphone jack into the socket marked "40" until he felt a click.

The lights stopped blinking immediately. There was a muffled voice from the headset, which lay in the bottom of the server. Jimmy ignored that. He took a step away from the machine, watching the overhead lights warily, waiting on the nice white ones to shut off again or the angry red ones to return. But everything stayed the same. The jack sat in its socket, the wire dangling, the voice in the headset distant now, unable to be heard.

Jimmy worked his way down the ladder, wondering how long it'd been since he last ate. He couldn't remember. Breakfast before school, but that was a day ago, maybe two. Halfway down the ladder, he thought of himself as a piece of food sliding through some great metal neck. This was what a swallowed bite felt like. At the bottom of the ladder, he stood in the bowels of the silo, a hollow thing lost in a hollow thing. There would be no end to the silo's hunger, chewing on something empty like him. They would both starve, he thought. His stomach grumbled; he needed to eat. Jimmy staggered down the dark corridor and through the silo's guts.

The radio on the wall continued to hiss. Jimmy turned the volume down until the spitting noise could barely be heard. His father wouldn't be calling him ever again. He wasn't sure how he knew this, but it was a Rule of the World.

He entered the small apartment. There was a table big enough for four with the pages of a book scattered across it, a needle and thread coiled on top like a snake guarding its nest. Jimmy thumbed the pages and saw that the place where the pages met was being repaired. His stomach hurt, it was so empty. His mind was beginning to ache as well.

Across the room, the ghost of his father stood and pointed out doors, told him what was behind each. Jimmy patted his chest for the key, remembered what he'd been told. "Don't open the door for anyone," he said out loud. He promised. His father smiled at him as Jimmy used the key to unlock the pantry. Food enough for two people for ten years, he'd said. Was that right?

The room made a sucking sound as he cracked the pantry door, and there was the tickle of a breeze against his neck. Jimmy found the lights on the outside of the door—plus a switch that ran a noisy fan. He turned the fan off, which only reminded him of the radio. Inside the room, he found shelves bulging with cans that receding so far he had to squint to see the back wall. These were cans like he'd never seen before. He squeezed between the tight shelves and searched up and down, his stomach begging him to choose and be quick about it. "Eat, eat," his belly growled. Jimmy said to give him a chance.

Tomatoes and beets and squash, stuff he hated. Recipe food. He wanted *food* food. There were entire shelves of corn with labels like colorful sleeves of paper, not the black ink scrawled on a tin like he was used to. Jimmy grabbed one of the cans and studied it. A large man with green flesh smiled at him from the label. Tiny words like those printed in books wrapped all around. The cans of corn were identical. They made Jimmy feel out of place, like he was asleep and dreaming every bit of this.

He kept one of the corn and found an aisle of labeled soups in red and white, grabbed one of these. Back in the apartment, he rummaged for an opener. There were drawers around the stove full of knives and forks and serving spoons. There was a cabinet with pots and lids. A bottom drawer held charcoal pencils, a spool of thread, batteries bulging with age and covered in gray powder, a child's whistle, a screwdriver, and myriad other things.

He found the can opener. It was rusty and appeared as if it hadn't been used in years. But the dull cutter still sank through the soft tin when he gave it a squeeze, and the handle turned if given enough force. Jimmy worked it all the way around and cursed when the lid sank down into the soup. He fished a knife out of the drawer to lever the lid out with the tip. Food. Finally. He plopped a pot onto the stove and turned the burner on, thinking of his apartment, of his mother and father. The soup heated. Jimmy waited, stomach growling, but some part of him was dimly aware that there was nothing he could put inside himself to touch the real ache, this mysterious urge he felt every moment to scream at the top of his lungs or to collapse to the floor and cry.

While he waited for the soup to bubble, he inspected the sheets of paper the size of small blankets hanging on one wall. It looked like they'd been hung out to dry, and he thought at first that the thick books must be made by folding up or cutting these. But the large sheets were already printed on, the drawings continuous. Jimmy ran his hands down the smooth paper and studied the details of a schematic, an arrangement of circles with fine lines inside each and labels everywhere. There were numbers over the circles. Three of them were crossed out with red ink. Each was labeled a "silo," but that didn't make any sense.

Behind him, a hissing like the radio, like someone calling for him, the whisperings of ghosts. Jimmy turned from the strange drawing to find his soup spitting bubbles, dripping down the edge and sizzling on the glowing-hot burner. He left the drawing alone for now.

· 72 ·

Days passed until they threatened to make a week, and Jimmy could glimpse how weeks might eventually become months. Outside the steel door in the upper room, the men outside were trying to get in. On the radio, they yelled and argued. Jimmy listened sometimes, but all they talked about were the dead and dying and forbidden things, like the great outside.

Jimmy cycled through camera angles of quietude and vast emptiness. Sometimes, these still views were interrupted with bursts of activity and violence. Jimmy saw a man held down on the ground and beaten by other men. He saw a woman dragged down a hall, feet kicking, and had to turn the cameras off. His heart raced the rest of the day and into the night, and he resolved to not look at the cameras anymore. That night, alone in the bunk room with all the empty beds, he hardly slept. But when he did, he dreamt of his mother.

The days would be like this, he thought the next morning. Each day would stretch out forever, but their counting would not take long. Their counting would run out for him. He felt it.

He moved one of the mattresses out into the room with the computer and the radio. There was a semblance of company in that room. Angry voices and scenes of violence were better than the emptiness of the other bunks. He forgot his promise to himself and ate warm soup in front of the cameras, looking for people. He listened to their soft voices bicker on the radio. When he dreamed that night, his dreams were filled with little square views of a distant past. A younger self stood in those windows, peering back at him.

In forays to the room above, Jimmy crept silently to the steel door and listened to men argue on the other side. They tried codes, three beeping entries at a time, followed by three angry buzzes. Jimmy rubbed the steel door and thanked it for staying shut.

Padding away quietly, he explored the grid of machines. They whirred and clicked and blinked their flashing eyes, but they didn't say anything. They didn't move. Their presence made Jimmy feel even more alone, like a classroom of large boys who all ignored him. Just a handful of days like this, and Jimmy felt a new Rule of the World: Man wasn't meant to live alone. This was what he discovered, day by day. He discovered it and just as soon forgot, for there was no one around to remind him. He spoke with the machines, instead. They clacked back at him and hissed deep in their metal throats that man wasn't supposed to live at all.

The voices on the radio seemed to believe this. They reported deaths and promised more of them to each other. Some of them had guns from the deputy stations. There was a man on the ninety-first who wanted to make sure everyone else knew he had a gun. Jimmy felt like telling this man about the storage facility his key had unlocked beyond the bunk room. There were racks and racks of guns like his father had used to kill Yani. And countless boxes of bullets. He felt like telling the entire silo that he had more guns than anyone, that he had the key to the silo, so please stay away, but something told him that these men would just try harder to reach him if he did. So Jimmy kept his secrets.

On the sixth night of being alone, unable to sleep, Jimmy tried to make himself drowsy by flipping through the book on the desk. It was a strange read. Each page referenced other pages. What dead ends he discovered were just that: they ended in death. Accounts of all the horrible things that could happen, how to prevent them, how to mitigate inevitable disaster. Jimmy looked for an entry on finding oneself completely and utterly alone. There was nothing in the index. And then Jimmy remembered what was in all the hundreds of metal cases lining the bookshelf beside the desk. Maybe there was something in one of those books that could help him.

He checked the small labels on the lower portion of each tin, went to the Li - Lo box for loneliness. There was a soft sigh as he cracked the tin, like a can of soup sucking at the air. Jimmy slid the book out and flipped toward the back where he thought he'd find the entry, the help on what to do.

He found a window on the world, instead. A view of a great machine with large wheels like the wooden toy dog he'd owned as a kid. Fearsome and black with a pointy nose, the machine loomed impossibly large over the man standing in front of it. Jimmy waited for the man to move, but rubbing the view, he found it to be a picture, just like on his dad's work ID. But a picture in bright color and such gloss that it looked to be real.

"Locomotive," Jimmy read. He knew these words. The first part meant "crazy." The second part was a person's reason for doing something. He studied this image, wondering what crazy reason someone would have of making this picture. It couldn't be real. Jimmy flipped a handful of pages, hoping to find more on this loco motive—

He screamed and dropped the book when he saw the next picture. Jimmy hopped around and brushed himself with both hands, waiting for the bug to disappear down his shirt or bite him. He stood on his mattress and waited for his heart to stop pounding. Turning to the books for sleep was having the opposite effect. Jimmy eyed the flopped-open tome on the ground, expecting a swarm to fly out like the pests in the farms, but nothing moved. The radio quietly hissed.

He approached the book and flipped it over with his foot. The damn bug was a picture, the page folded over and creased where he'd dropped it. Jimmy smoothed the page, read the word "locust" out loud, and wondered just what sort of book this was supposed to be. It was nothing like the children's books he'd grown up with, nothing like the pulp paper they taught with at school.

Flipping the cover over, Jimmy saw that this was different from the book on the desk, which had been embossed with the word "Order." This one was labeled "Legacy." He flipped through it a pinch at a time, bright pictures on every page, paragraphs of words and descriptions, a vast fiction of impossible deeds and impossible things, all in a single book.

Not in a single book, he told himself. Jimmy glanced up at the massive shelves bulging with metal tins, each one labeled and arranged in alphabetical order. He searched again for the locomotive, a machine on wheels that dwarfed a grown man. He found the entry and shuffled back to his mattress and his twisted tangle of sheets. A week of solitude was drawing to a close, but there was no chance that Jimmy would be getting any sleep. Not for a very long while.

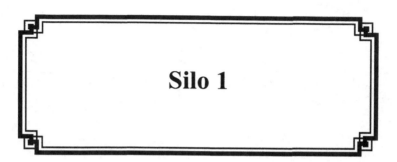

Silo 1

· 73 ·

Donald waited in the comm room for his first briefing with the Head of 18. To pass the time, he twisted the knobs and dials that allowed him to cycle through that silo's camera feeds. From a single seat—like a throne but with torn upholstery and squeaky wheels—he had a view of all a world's residents. He could nudge their fates from a distance if he liked. He could end them all with the press of a button. While he lived on and on, freezing and thawing, these mortals went through routines, lived and died, unaware that he even existed.

"It's like the afterlife," he muttered.

The operator at the next station turned and regarded him silently, and Donald realized he'd spoken aloud. He faced the man, whose bushy black hair looked like it'd last been combed a century ago. "It's just that . . . it's like a view from the heavens," he explained, indicating the monitor.

"It's a view of something," the operator agreed. He took another bite of his sandwich. On his screen, one woman seemed to be yelling at another, a finger jabbed in the other woman's face. It was a sitcom without the laugh track.

Donald worked on keeping his mouth shut. But it really did seem like an afterlife of sorts. He dialed in the cafeteria on 18 and watched its people huddle around a wallscreen. It was a small crowd. They gazed out at the lifeless hills, perhaps awaiting their departed cleaner's return, perhaps silently dreaming about what lay beyond those quiet crests. Donald wanted to tell them that she wouldn't be coming back, that there was nothing beyond that rise, even though he secretly shared their dreams. He longed to send up one of the drones to look, but Eren had told him the drones weren't for sightseeing—they were for dropping bombs. They had a limited range, he said. The air out there would tear them to shreds. Donald wanted to show Eren his hand, mottled and pink, and tell him that he'd been out on that hill and back. He wanted to ask if the air outside was really so bad.

Hope. That's what this was. Dangerous hope. He watched the people watch a wallscreen, feeling a kinship with them. This was how the gods of old got in trouble, how they ended up smitten with mortals and tangled in their affairs. Donald laughed to himself. He thought of this cleaner with her two-inch folder and how he might've intervened if he'd had the chance. He might've given her a gift of life if he were able. Apollo, doting on Daphne.

The comm officer glanced over at Donald's monitor, that view of the wallscreen, and Donald felt himself being studied. He switched to a different camera. It was the hallway of what looked like a school. Lockers lined either side. A child stood on her tiptoes and opened one of the upper ones, pulled out a small bag, turned and seemed to say something to someone off-camera. Life going on as usual.

"The call's coming through now," the operator behind them said. The man with the sandwich put it away and sat forward. He brushed the crumbs off his chest and switched the soap opera scene to a room full of black cabinets. Donald grabbed a pair of headphones and pulled the two folders off the desk. The one on the top was two inches thick. It was about his doomed mortal, the missing cleaner. Beneath that was a much thinner folder with a potential shadow's name on it. A man's voice came through his headphones.

"Hello?"

Donald glanced up at his monitor. A figure stood behind one of the black cabinets. He was pudgy and short, unless it was the distortion from the camera lens.

"Report," Donald said. He flipped open the folder marked *Lukas*. He knew from his last shift that the system would make his voice sound flat, make all their voices sound the same.

"I picked out a shadow as you requested, sir. A good kid. He's done work on the servers before, so his access has already been vetted."

How meek this man. Donald reckoned he would feel the same way, knowing his world could be smote at the press of a button. Fear like that puts a man at odds with his ego.

The operator beside Donald leaned over and peeled back the top page in the folder for him. He tapped his finger on something a few lines down. Donald scanned the report.

"You looked at Mr. Kyle as a possible replacement two years ago." Donald glanced up to watch the man behind the comm server wipe the back of his neck.

"That's right," the Head of 18 said. "We didn't think he was ready."

"Your office filed a report on Mr. Kyle as a possible gazer. Says here he's logged a few hundred hours in front of the wallscreen. What's changed your mind?"

"That was a preliminary report, sir. It came from another . . . potential shadow. A bit overeager, a gentleman we found more suited for the security team. I assure you that Mr. Kyle does not dream of the outside. He only goes up at night—" The man cleared his throat, seemed to hesitate. "To look at the stars, sir."

"The stars."

"That's right."

Donald glanced over at the operator beside him, who polished off his sandwich. The operator shrugged. The silo Head broke the silence.

"He's the best man for the job, sir. I knew his father. Stern sonofabitch. You know what they say about the treads and the rails, sir."

Donald had no idea what they said about the treads and the rails. It was nothing but stair analogies from these silos. He was reminded of how city people used to make him feel, growing up in Savannah. He wondered what this Bernard would say if the man ever saw an elevator. It would be like magic. The thought nearly elicited a chuckle.

"Your choice of shadow has been approved," Donald said. "Get him on the Legacy as soon as possible."

"He's studying right now, sir."

"Good. Now, what's the latest on this uprising?" Donald felt himself hurrying along, performing rote tasks so he could get back to his more interesting studies. This truly had become a job.

The silo Head glanced back toward the camera. This mortal knew damn well where the eyes of gods lay hidden. "Mechanical is holed up pretty tight," he said. "They put up a fight on their retreat down, but we routed them good. There's a . . . bit of a barricade, but we should be through it any time now."

The operator leaned forward and grabbed Donald's attention. He pointed two fingers at his eyes, then at one of the blank screens on the top row, indicating one of the cameras that had gone out during the uprising. Donald knew what he was getting at.

"Any idea how they knew about the cameras?" he asked. "You know we're blind over here from one-forty down, right?"

"Yessir. We . . . I can only assume they've known about them. They do their own wiring down there. I've been in person. It's a nest of pipes and cables. We don't think anyone tipped them off."

"You don't think."

"Nossir. But we're working on getting someone in there. I've got a priest we can send in to bless their dead. A good man. Shadowed with Security. I promise it won't be long."

"Fine. Make sure it isn't. We'll be over here cleaning up your mess, so get the rest of your house in order."

"Yessir. I will."

The three men in the comm room watched this Bernard gentleman remove his headset and return it to the cabinet. He wiped his forehead with a rag. While the others were distracted, Donald did the same, wiping the sweat off his brow with a handkerchief he'd requisitioned. He picked up the two folders and studied the operator, who had a fresh trail of breadcrumbs down his coveralls.

"Keep a close eye on him," Donald said.

"Oh, I will."

Donald returned his headset to the rack and got up to leave. Pausing at the door, he looked back and saw the screen in front of the operator had divided into four squares. In one, a roomful of black towers stood silent sentinel. Two women were having a row in another.

• 74 •

D onald took his notes and rode the lift to the cafeteria. He arrived to find it was too early for breakfast, but there was still coffee in the dispenser from the night before. He selected a chipped mug from the drying rack and filled it. A gentleman behind the serving line lifted the handle on an industrial washer, and the stainless steel box opened and let loose a cloud of steam. The man waved a dishrag at the cloud, then used the rag to pull out metal trays that would soon hold reconstituted eggs and slices of freeze-dried toast.

Donald tried the coffee. It was cold and weak, but he didn't mind. It suited him. He nodded to the man prepping for breakfast, who dipped his head in response.

Donald turned and took in the view splayed across the wallscreen. Here was the mystery. The documents in his folders were nothing compared to this. He approached the dusky vista where swirling clouds were just beginning to glow from a sun rising invisibly beyond the hills. He wondered what was out there. People died when they were sent to clean. They died on the hills when silos were shut down. But he hadn't. As far as he knew, the men who had dragged him back hadn't either.

He studied his hand in the dim light leaking from the wallscreen. His palm seemed a little pink to him, a little raw. But then, he had scrubbed it half a dozen times in the sink the last few nights and each morning. The feeling that it'd been tainted couldn't be shaken. But maybe it was his scrubbing that made it look red, that made it look like it needed even more scrubbing. He pulled his handkerchief out of his pocket and coughed into its folds.

"I'll have potatoes ready in a few minutes," the man behind the counter called out. Another worker in green coveralls emerged from the back, cinching an apron around his waist. Donald wanted to know who these people were, what their lives were like, what they thought about all this. For six months, they served three meals a day, and then hibernated for decades. Then they did it all over again. They must believe this is for some purpose, right? Or is this what any of them did for all their lives? Follow the tracks laid down yesterday. A boot in a hole, a boot in a hole, round and round. Did these men see themselves as deck hands on some great ark with a noble purpose? Or were they walking in circles simply because they knew the way?

Donald remembered running for Congress, thinking he was going to do real good for the future. And then he found himself in an office surrounded by a bewildering tempest of rules, memos, and messages, and he quickly learned to simply pray for the end of each day. He went from thinking he was going to save the world to passing the time until . . . until time ran out.

He sat down in one of the faded plastic chairs and studied the folder in his pink hand. It was two inches thick. *Nichols, Juliette* was written on the tab, followed by an ID number for internal purposes. He could still smell the toner from the printed pages. Seemed a waste, printing out so much nonsense. Somewhere, down in the vast storeroom, supplies were dwindling. And somewhere else, down the hall from his own office, a person was keeping track of it all, making sure there was just enough potatoes, just enough toner, just enough lightbulbs, to get them through to the end.

Donald glanced over the reports. He spread them out across the empty table and thought of Anna and his last shift as he did so, the way they had smothered that war room with clues. There was a pang of guilt and regret that Anna so often entered his thoughts before Helen. An affair hung but a long sleep ago, while his marriage had eroded to dust in a more distant past.

The reports were a welcome distraction while he awaited the sunrise and food. Here was a story about a cleaner who had been a sheriff, though not for long. One of the top reports in her folder was from the current Head of 18, a memo on this cleaner's lack of qualifications. Donald read a list of reasons this woman should not be given a mantle of power, and it was as though he were reading about himself. It seemed the mayor of 18—a politician like Thurman—had wrangled this woman into the job, had recruited her despite objections. It wasn't even clear that this woman, a mechanic from the lower levels, even *wanted* the job. In another report from the silo head, Donald read about her defiance, culminating in a walk out of sight and a refusal to clean. Again, it felt all too familiar to Donald. Or was he looking for these similarities? Isn't that what people did? Saw in others what they feared to see or hoped to see in themselves?

The hills outside brightened by degrees. Donald glanced up from the reports and studied the mounds of dirt. He remembered the video feed he'd been shown of this cleaner disappearing over a similarly gray dune. Now the panic among his colleagues was that the residents of 18 would be filled with a dangerous sort of hope—the kind of hope that leads to violence. The far graver threat was that this cleaner had made it to another facility, that those in another silo might discover they were not alone.

Donald did not think it likely. She couldn't have lasted long, and there was little to discover in the direction she had wandered. He pulled out the other folder, the one on Silo 17.

There had been no warning before its collapse, no uptick in violence. The population graphs appeared normal. He flipped through pages of typed documents from various division heads downstairs. Everyone had their theory, and of course each saw the collapse through the lens of their own expertise, or attributed it to the incompetence of another division. Population Control blamed a lax IT department. IT blamed a hardware failure. Engineering blamed programming. And the on-duty comm officer, who liaisons with IT and each individual silo head, thought it was sabotage, an attempt to prevent a cleaning.

Donald sensed something familiar about the breakdown of Silo 17, something he couldn't place. The camera feeds had gone out, but not before a brief view of people spilling out of the airlock. There had been an exodus, a panic, a mass hysteria. And then a blackout. Comm had placed several calls. The first had been answered by the IT shadow, 17's second in charge. There was a short exchange with this Russ fellow, questions fired from both ends, and then Russ had broken the connection.

The follow-up call went unanswered for hours. During this time, the silo went dark. And then someone else picked up the line.

Donald coughed into his handkerchief and read this strange exchange. The officer on duty claimed the respondent sounded young. It was a male, not a shadow nor the Head. A flurry of questions. One stood out to Donald. The person in 17, with only minutes left to live, had asked what was going on down on level forty.

Level forty. Donald didn't need to grab a schematic to check—he had designed the facilities. He knew every level like the back of his hand. Level forty was a mixed-use level with half to housing, a quarter to light agriculture, the rest to commercial. What could be going on down there? And why would this person, who must've been at the limits of survival, care?

He read the exchange again. It almost sounded as though the young man's last contact had been with level forty, as if he'd just spoken with them. Maybe he'd come from down there? It was only six levels away. Donald imagined a frightened boy storming up the stairwell with thousands of others. News of an opened airlock, of death below, people chasing upward. This young man gets to level thirty-four, and the crush of people is too much. IT has already emptied. He finds his way into the server room—

No. Donald shook his head. That wasn't right. None of that felt right. What was it about this that nagged him?

It was the blackout. Donald felt a chill run up his spine. It was the number 40. It was the *silo*, not the level. The report trembled in his hands. He wanted to jump up and pace the cafeteria, but all he had was the germ of a connection, the hint of an outline. He fought to connect the dots before the ideas shooed away, disturbed by a rush of adrenaline.

It was *Silo 40* he had spoken with. The boy had found himself at the back of 17's comm station. He didn't know it was a silo calling at all. That would be why he'd called it a level, had wondered what was happening down there. This blackout, this lack of contact, it was just like the silos Anna had been working on.

Anna—

Donald thought about the note she had left, asking Thurman to wake her. She was asleep below. She would know what to do. She should've been woken and put in charge, not him. He gathered the reports and papers and put them back into the proper folders. Workers were beginning to arrive from the lifts. The smells of eggs and biscuits floated out from the kitchen, the swinging doors pumping the aroma with the traffic of the bustling food staff, but Donald had forgotten his hunger.

He glanced up at the wallscreen. Would anyone on shift right now know of Silo 40? Maybe not. They wouldn't have made the same connection. Thurman and the others had kept the outbreak a secret, didn't want to cause a panic. But what if Silo 40 was still out there? What if they'd contacted 17? Anna said the master system had been hacked, that Silo 40 had hacked them. They had cut several facilities off from Silo 1 before Anna and Thurman had been awoken to terminate them all. But what if they hadn't? What if this Silo 17 wasn't destroyed? If it was still there, and this cleaner had stumbled into the bowl—

Donald had a sudden urge to go see for himself, to stroll outside and dash up to the top of the hill, suit be damned. He left the wallscreen and headed toward the airlock.

Perhaps he would need to wake Anna, just as Thurman had. He could set her up in the armory. There was a blueprint for doing this from his last shift, only he didn't have anyone he could trust to help. He didn't know the first thing about waking people up. But he was in charge, right? He could demand to know.

He left the cafeteria and approached the silo's airlock, that great yellow door to the open world beyond. The outside wasn't as bad as he had been led to believe. Unless he was simply immune. There were machines in his blood that kept him stitched up when he was frozen. Perhaps it was that. He approached the inner airlock door and peered through the small porthole. The memory of being in there struck him with sudden violence. He tucked the two folders under his elbow and rubbed his arm where the needle had bit into his flesh long ago, putting him to sleep. What was out there? The light spilling through the holding cell bars flickered as a dust cloud passed, and Donald realized how strange it was that they had a wallscreen in Silo 1. The people here knew what they'd done to the world. Why did they need to see the ruin they'd left behind?

Unless—

Unless the purpose was the same as for the other silos. Unless it was to keep them from going outside to see, a haunting reminder that the planet was not safe for them. But what did they really know beyond the silos? And how could a man hope to see for himself?

· 75 ·

It took a few days of planning and building up the nerve for Donald to make the request, and a few days more for Dr. Wilson to schedule an appointment. During that time he told Eren about his suspicions of Silo 40's involvement. The flurry of activity launched by this simple guess quickly consumed the silo. Donald signed off on a requisition for a bombing run, even though he didn't quite understand what he was signing. Little-used levels of the silo—levels familiar to Donald—were reawakened. Days later, he didn't feel the rumble or the ground shake, but others claimed to have. All he found was that a new layer of dust had settled over his things, shaken loose from the ceiling.

The day of his meeting with Dr. Wilson, he stole down to the main cryopod floor to test his code. He still didn't fully trust the fib offered by his loose coveralls and the badge with someone else's name on it. Just the day before, he had seen someone in the gym he thought he recognized from his first shift. It put him in the habit of slinking instead of strutting. And so he shuffled down the hall of frozen bodies and entered his code into the keypad warily. Red lights and warning buzzes were expected. Instead, the light above the "Emergency Personnel" label flashed green, and the door clanked open. Donald glanced down the hall to see if anyone was watching as he pulled the door far enough to slip inside.

The little-used cryochamber was a fraction of the size of the others and only one level deep. Standing inside the door, Donald could picture how the main deep freeze wrapped around this much smaller room. This was a mere bump along great walls that stretched nearly out of sight. And yet, it contained something far more precious. To him, anyway. There was danger in this room of square-jawed soldiers, but also glorious hope.

Donald picked his way through the pods and peeked in at the faces. It was difficult to remember being there with Thurman on his previous shift, hard to recall the exact spot, but he eventually found her. He checked the small screen and remembered thinking it didn't matter what her name was, saw that there wasn't one assigned. Just a number.

"Hey, Sis."

His fingertips sang against the glass as he rubbed the frost away. He recalled their parents with sadness. He wondered how much Charlotte knew of this place and Thurman's plans before she came here. He hoped nothing. He liked to think her less culpable than he.

Seeing her brought back memories of her visit to D.C. She had wasted a furlough on campaigning for Thurman and seeing her brother. Charlotte had given him a hard time when she found out he'd lived in D.C. for two years and hadn't been to any of the museums. It didn't matter how busy he was, she said. It was unforgivable. "They're free," she told him, as if that were reason enough.

So they had gone to the Air and Space Museum together. Donald remembered waiting to get in. He remembered a scale model of the solar system on the sidewalk outside the museum entrance. Although the inner planets were located just a few strides apart, Pluto was blocks away, down past the Hirshhorn, impossibly distant. Now, as he gazed at his sister's frozen form, that day in his memory felt the same way. Impossibly distant. A tiny dot.

Later that afternoon, she had dragged him to the Holocaust Museum. Donald had been avoiding going since moving to Washington. Maybe it was the reason he avoided the Mall altogether. Everyone told him it was something he had to see. "You must go," they said. "It's important." They used words like "powerful" and "haunting." They said it would change his life. From the day he arrived in Washington, Donald was urged to visit. Every mouth was in unison. But the eyes above those mouths—the eyes warned him.

His sister had pulled him up the steps, his heart heavy with dread. The building had been constructed as a reminder, but Donald didn't want to be reminded. He was on his meds by then to help him forget, to keep him from feeling as though the world might end at any moment. Such barbarisms as that building contained were buried in the past, he told himself, never to be unearthed nor repeated.

There were remnants of the Museum's sixtieth anniversary still hanging, somber signs and banners. A new wing had been installed, cords and stakes holding up fledgling trees and the air scented with mulch. Donald peered through the frosted glass at his sister and remembered what mulch smelled like. He remembered seeing a group of tourists file out, dabbing at their eyes and shielding themselves from the sun. He had wanted to turn and run, but his sister had held his hand, and the man at the ticket booth had already smiled at him. At least it'd been late in the day, so they couldn't stay long.

Donald rested his hands on the coffin-like pod and remembered the visit. There were scenes of torture and starvation. A room full of shoes beyond counting. Walls displayed naked bodies folded together, lifeless eyes wide open, ribs and genitals exposed, as mounds of people tumbled into a pit, into a hole scooped out of the earth. Donald couldn't bear to look at it. He tried to focus on the bulldozer instead, to look at the man driving the machine, that serene face, a cigarette between pursed lips, a look of steady concentration. A job. There was no solace to be found anywhere in that scene. The man driving the bulldozer became the most horrific part.

Donald had shrunk away from those grisly exhibits, losing his sister in the darkness. Here was a museum of horrors never to be repeated. Mass burials performed with whatever the opposite of ceremony was. Apathy. That was the absence of ceremony. People calmly marched into showers.

He sought refuge in a new exhibit called *Architects of Death,* drawn to the blueprints, to the promise of the familiar and the ordered. He found instead a claustrophobic space wallpapered with schematics of slaughter. That exhibit had been no easier to stomach. There was a wall explaining the movement to deny the Holocaust, even after it had happened. Here were those who willed themselves not to forget, but to not know in the first place.

The array of blueprints was shown as evidence. That was the purpose of the room. Blueprints that had survived the frantic burnings and purges as the Russians closed in, Himmler's signature on many of them. The layout of Auschwitz, the gas chambers, everything clearly labeled. Donald had hoped the plans would give him relief from what he saw elsewhere in the museum, but then he had learned that Jewish draftsmen had been forced to contribute. Their pens had inked in the very walls around them. They had been coerced into sketching the home of their future abuse.

Donald remembered fumbling for a bottle of pills as the small room spun around him. He remembered wondering how those people could've gone along with it, could have seen what they were drawing and not known. How could they not know? Not see what it was for?

Blinking tears away, he noticed where he was standing. The pods in their neat rows were alien to him, but the walls and floor and ceiling were familiar enough. Donald had helped design this place. It was here because of him. And when he'd tried to get out, to escape, they had brought him back screaming and kicking, a prisoner behind his own walls. And he still didn't know what it was all for.

The beeping of the keypad outside chased away disturbing thoughts. Donald turned as the great slab of steel hinged inward on pins the size of a man's arms. Dr. Wilson, the shift doctor, stepped inside. He spotted Donald and frowned. "Sir?" he called out.

Donald could feel a trickle of sweat working its way down his temple. His heart continued to race from the memory of that dark place in that dark past. He felt warm, despite being able to see his breath puff out before him.

"Did you forget about our appointment?" Dr. Wilson asked.

Donald wiped his forehead and rubbed his palm on the seat of his pants. "No, no," he said, fighting to keep the shakiness out of his voice. "I just lost track of time."

Dr. Wilson nodded. "I saw you on my monitor and figured that was it." He glanced at the pod nearest to Donald and frowned. "Someone you know?"

"Hm? No." Donald removed his hand, which had grown cold against the pod. "Someone I worked with."

"Well, are you ready?"

"Yes," Donald said. "I appreciate the refresher. It's been a while since I've gone over the protocols."

Dr. Wilson smiled. "Of course. I've got you lined up with the new reactor tech coming on his fourth shift. We're just waiting on you." He gestured toward the hall.

Donald patted his sister's pod and smiled. She had waited hundreds of years. Another day or two wouldn't hurt. And then they would see what exactly he had helped to build. The two of them would find out together.

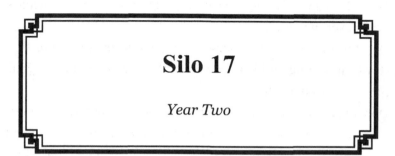

Silo 17

Year Two

J immy couldn't bring himself to write on the paper. He was drowning in paper, was surrounded by paper, but he didn't dare use even the margins for notes. Those pages were sacrosanct. Those books were too valuable. And so he counted the days using the key around his neck and the black panels of the server labeled "17."

This was his silo, he had learned. It was the number stamped on the inside of his copy of The Order. It was the label on the wall chart of all the silos. He knew what this meant. He might be all alone in his world, *but this was not the only world.*

Every evening before he went to bed, he scratched another bright silver mark in the black paint of the massive server. Jimmy only marked the days off at night. It seemed premature to do it in the morning.

The Project started sloppy. He had little confidence that the marks would amount to much, and so he made them in the middle of the machine and much too large. Two months into his ordeal, he began to run out of room and realized he would need to start adding marks up above, so he had scratched through the ones he'd already made and went around to the other side of the server to start anew. Now he made them tiny and neat. Four ticks and then a slash through them, just like his mom used to mark the days in a row that he was good. Six of these in a line to mark what he now thought of as a month. Twelve of these rows with five left over, and he had a year.

He made the final mark in the last set and stepped back. A year took up half the side of a server. It was hard to believe a whole year had gone by. A year of living in the half-level below the servers. He knew this couldn't last. Imagining the other servers covered in scratches was too much to bear. His dad had said there was enough food for ten years for some number of people. Maybe that meant twenty with him all alone. Twenty years. He stepped around the edge of the server and looked down the aisle between the rows. The massive silver door sat at the very end. At some point, he knew he would have to go out. He would go crazy if he didn't. He was already going crazy. The days were much too full of the same.

He went to the door and listened for some sound on the other side. It was quiet, as it sometimes was. Quiet, but he could still hear faint bangs echo from some memory. Jimmy thought about entering the four numbers and peeking outside. It was the worst sensation imaginable, not being able to see what was on the other side. When the camera screens had stopped working, Jimmy felt a primal sense stripped away. He was partially blind, could now see only a small slice of his world, and that made him feel broken. The desire was strong to open the door, like cracking an eyelid held shut for too long. A year of counting days. Of counting minutes within those days. A boy could only count so long.

He left the keypad alone. Not yet. There were bad people out there, people who wanted in, who wanted to know what was in there, why the power on the level still worked, and who he was.

"I'm nobody," Jimmy told them when he had the courage to talk. "Nobody."

He didn't have the courage often. He felt brave enough just listening to the men with the other radios fight. Brave to allow their arguments to fill his world and his head, to hear them argue and report about who had killed whom. One group was working on the farms, another was trying to stop the floods from creeping out of the mines and drowning Mechanical. One had guns and took whatever little bit the others were able to squeeze together. A lone woman called once and screamed for help, but what help was Jimmy? By his figuring, there were a hundred or more people out there in little pockets, fighting and killing. But they would stop soon. They had to. Another day. A year. They couldn't go on like this forever, could they?

Maybe they could.

Time had become strange. It was a thing *believed* rather than seen. There was no dimming of the stairwell and lights-out to signify a night. No trips to the Top and the glow of sunshine to say that it was day. There were simply numbers on a computer screen counting so slowly one could scream. Numbers that looked the same day and night. It took careful counting to know a day had passed. The counting let him know he was alive. Every day like a school day, numbing with its foreverness, a feeling like he didn't want to live any more, but he got hungry and ate. He got sleepy and slept. And so a life was lived accidental. It was lived because he wasn't brave enough to do anything else.

Jimmy thought about playing chase between the servers before he went to bed, but he had done that yesterday. He thought about arranging cans in the order he would eat them, but he already had three months lined up. There was target practice, books to read, a computer to fiddle with, chores to do, but none of that sounded like fun. He knew he would probably just crawl into bed and stare at the ceiling until the numbers told him it was tomorrow. He would think about what to do then.

• 77 •

Weeks passed, scratches accumulated, and the tip of the key around Jimmy's neck wore down. He woke to another morning with crust in his eyes like he'd been crying in his sleep and took his breakfast—one can of peaches and one of pineapple—up to the great steel door to eat. Unshouldering his gun, Jimmy sat down with his back against server number eight, enjoying the warmth of the busy machine against his spine.

The gun had taken some figuring out. His father had disappeared with the loaded one, and when Jimmy discovered the crates of arms and ammo, the method of inserting the latter into the former had posed a puzzle. He made the task a Project, like his father used to make their chores and tinkering. Ever since he was little, Jimmy had watched his dad disassemble computers and other electronics, laying out all the pieces—each screw, every bolt, the nuts spun back onto the bolts—all arranged in a neat pattern so he knew where they went again. Jimmy had done the same with one of the rifles. And then with a second rifle after he'd accidentally knocked the pieces from the first with his boot.

With the second, he saw where the ammo ended up and how it got there. The spring in the ammo holder was stiff, which made it difficult to load. Later, he learned that this was called a "clip," after reading the entry for "gun" under "G" in the tins full of books. That had come weeks after he'd figured out how the thing worked on his own, with a hole in the ceiling to show for it.

He kept the gun in his lap, across his thighs, and balanced the cans of fruit on the wide part of the stock. The pineapple was his favorite. He had some every day and watched with sadness as the supply on the shelves dwindled. He'd never heard of such a fruit, had to look the thing up in another of the books. The pineapples had led him on a dizzying tour through the tins. "Be" for "Beach" had led to "Oa" for "Ocean." This one confused him with its sense of scale. And then the "Fish" under "F." He had forgotten to eat that day as he explored, and the room with the radio and his little mattress had become a hazard of open books and empty tins. It had taken him a week to get things back in order. Countless times since then, he had lost himself in such excursions.

Pulling his rusty can opener and favorite fork from his breast pocket, Jimmy worked the peaches open. There was the whispering pop of air as he made the first cut. Jimmy had learned not to eat the contents if it didn't make that pop. Luckily, the toilets were still in operation back when he'd learned that lesson. Jimmy missed the toilets something fierce.

He worked his way through the peaches, savoring each bite before drinking down the juice. He wasn't sure if you were supposed to drink that part—the label didn't say—but it was his favorite. He grabbed the pineapples and his opener, was listening for the pop of air, when he heard the keypad on the great steel door beep.

"Little early," he whispered to his visitors. He set the can aside, licked his fork, and put it back in his breast pocket. Cradling the gun against his armpit, he sat and watched for the door to move. One crack, and he would open fire.

Instead, it was four beeps from the keypad as a set of numbers was entered, followed by a buzz to signal that it was the wrong code. Jimmy tightened his grip on the gun while they tried again. The screen on the keypad only had room for four digits. That meant ten thousand combinations if you included all zeros. The door allowed three incorrect attempts before it wouldn't take any more until the following day. Jimmy had learned these things a long time ago. He felt like his mom had taught him this rule, but that was impossible. Unless she'd done it in a dream.

He listened to the keypad beep with another guess and then buzz with the good news. Good news for him, anyway. Still, that was another number down, which meant time was running out. Twelve-eighteen was the number. Jimmy cursed himself for even thinking the code; his finger went to the trigger, waiting. But thoughts couldn't be heard. You had to speak to be heard. He tended to forget this, because he heard himself thinking all the time.

The third and final attempt for the day began, and Jimmy couldn't wait to eat his pineapples. He and these people had this routine, these three tries every morning. It was a bit of human contact, if scary. On the server behind him, he had done the math. He assumed they'd started at 0000 and were working their way up. That's how he would do it. Three a day meant they would stumble on the right code on day 406 on the second try. That was less than a month away.

But Jimmy's counting didn't figure for everything. There was the lingering fear that they might skip some numbers, that they had started somewhere else, or that they might get lucky if they were going random. For all Jimmy knew, more than one code could open the door. And since he didn't pay attention to how his father had changed the code, he couldn't move it higher. And what if that only got them closer? Maybe they started at 9999. He could move it lower, of course, hoping to pass one they'd already tried, but what if they hadn't tried it yet? To take action and let them in by accident would be worse than doing nothing and then dying. And Jimmy didn't want to die. He didn't want to die, and he didn't want to kill anyone.

This is how his brain whirled as the next four digits were entered. When the keypad chirped angrily at the good news, he was slow to relax his grip on the gun. Jimmy wiped his sweaty palms off on his thighs, and picked up his pineapples.

"Hello, pineapples," he whispered. He bent his head toward his lap and punctured the can, listening closely.

The pineapples whispered back. They told him they were safe to eat.

· 78 ·

Life at its essence, Jimmy learned, was a series of meals and bowel movements. There was some sleep mixed in as well, but little effort was required for that. He didn't learn this great Rule of the World until the water stopped flushing. Nobody thinks about their bowel movements until the water stops flushing. And then it's all one thinks about.

Jimmy started going in the corner of the server room, as far from the door as possible. He peed in the sink until the tap ran out of water and the smell got bad. Once that happened, he tapped into the cistern. The Order told him which page to look on and what to do. It was a boring book, but handy at times. Jimmy figured that was the point. The water in the cistern wouldn't last forever, though, so he took to drinking as much of the juice in the bottom of the cans as he could. He hated tomato soup, but he drank a can every day. His pee turned bright orange.

Jimmy was draining the last drops out of a can of apples one morning when the keypad beeped. It didn't buzz. It didn't bark or scream or sound angry. It beeped. And a light long red—red for as long as Jimmy could remember—flashed brilliant and scary green.

Jimmy startled. The open can of peaches on his knee leaped away and tumbled to the ground, juice splashing everywhere. It was two days early for this. It was two days early.

The time had gone by so fast, and now it decided to go slowly. The great steel door made noises. Jimmy dropped his fork and fumbled with the gun. Safety off. A *click* with his thumb, a *thunk* from the door. Voices, voices. Excitement on one side, dread on the other. Jimmy felt the need to pee. He pulled the gun against his shoulder and wished he'd practiced yesterday. Tomorrow. Tomorrow was when he was gonna get ready. They were two days too early.

The door made noises, and Jimmy wondered if he'd missed a day or two. There was the time he'd gotten sick and had a fever. There was the day he fell asleep reading and couldn't remember what day it was when he woke. Maybe he'd missed a day. Maybe the people in the hall had skipped a number. The door opened a crack. The slow time gave him all sorts of space to fill with dread.

Jimmy wasn't ready. His palms were slick on the gun, his heart racing. This was one of those things expected and expected. Expected so hard, with so much fervor and concentration, like blowing up a plastic bag over and over, watching it stretch out big and thin in front of your eyes, knowing it was about to burst, knowing, knowing, and when it comes, it scares you like it'd never been expected at all.

This was one of those things. The door opened further. There was a person on the other side. A person. And for a moment, for the briefest of pauses, Jimmy reconsidered a year of planning, a calendar of fear. Here was someone to talk to and listen to. Someone to take a turn with the screwdriver and hammer now that the can opener was broke. Someone with a *new* can opener, perhaps. Here was a Project Partner like his dad used to—

A face. A man with an angry sneer. And a year of planning, of shooting empty tomato cans, of ringing ears and reloading, of oiling barrels and reading, reading—and now a human face in a crack in the door.

Jimmy pulled the trigger. The barrel leaped upward like barrels do. And the angry sneer turned to something else: startlement mixed with sorrow. Jimmy had done a sad, sad thing. The man fell down, but another was pushing past him, bursting into the room, something black in his hand.

Again, the barrel leaped and leaped, and Jimmy's eyes blinked with the bangs. Three shots. Three bullets. The running man kept coming, but he had the same sad look on his face, a look fading as he fell, crumbling just a few paces away.

Jimmy waited for the next man. He heard him out there, cursing and cursing. And the first man he'd shot was still moving around, like an empty can that danced and danced long after it was hit. The door was open. The outside and the inside were connected. The man who had opened the door lifted his head, something worse than sorrow on his face, and suddenly it was his father out there. His father lying just beyond the door, dying in the hallway. And Jimmy didn't know why that would be.

The cursing grew faint. The unseen man out in the hallway was moving away. Jimmy took his first full breath since the door beeped and the light turned green. He didn't have a pulse; his heart was just one long beat that wouldn't stop. A thrumming like the insides of a whirring server.

He listened to the last man slink away, slink away, and now Jimmy could close the door. He got up and ran around the dead man who had fallen inside the server room, a black pistol near his lifeless hand. Lowering his gun, Jimmy prepared to shoulder the door shut, when the thought of tomorrow, or that night, or the next hour occurred to him.

The retreating man now knew the number. He was taking it with him.

"*Twelve-eighteen*," Jimmy whispered.

He poked his head out the door for a quick look. There was a brief glimpse of a man disappearing into an office. Just a flash of green coveralls, and then an empty hall, impossibly long and bright.

The dying man outside the door groaned and writhed. Jimmy ignored him. He pulled the gun against his arm and braced it like he'd practiced how. The little notches lined up with each other and pointed toward the edge of the office door. Jimmy imagined a can of soup out there, hovering in the hall. He breathed and waited. The groaning man on the other side of the threshold crawled closer, bloody palms slapping a spot of floor that made Jimmy feel funny to look at. There was that ache in the center of his skull, an ancient scar across his memories. Jimmy aimed at the nothingness in the hallway and thought of his mother and father.

Some part of him knew they were gone, that they had left somewhere and would never return, and the notches became unaligned as his barrel trembled.

The man by his feet drew closer. Groans had turned to a hissing. Jimmy glanced down and saw red bubbles frothing on the man's lips. His beard was fuller than Jimmy's and soaked in blood. Jimmy looked away before his father's face appeared on the man again. He watched the spot in the hall and counted.

He was at thirty-two when he felt fingers pawing weakly at his boots.

It was on fifty-one that a head peeked out like a sneaky soup can.

Jimmy's finger squeezed. There was a kick to his shoulder and a blossom of bright red down the hall.

He waited a moment, took a deep breath, then pulled his boot away from the hand reaching up his ankle. He placed his shoulder against a door hanging dangerously open and pushed. Locks whirred and made *thunking* sounds deep within the walls. He only heard them dimly. He dropped his gun and covered his face with his palms while nearby, a man lay dying in the server room. Inside the server room. Jimmy wept, and the keypad chirped happily before falling silent, patiently waiting for yet another day.

Silo 1

79

A row of familiar clipboards hung on the wall in Dr. Wilson's office. Donald remembered scratching his name on them with mock ceremony. He remembered signing off on himself once, authorizing his own deep freeze. There was a twinge of unease at the thought of signing those forms right then. What would he write? His hand would shake as he scribbled someone else's name, and it would strike midnight at the masquerade ball.

In the middle of the office, an empty gurney brought back bad memories. A fresh sheet had been tucked military crisp on top of it, ready for the next body. Dr. Wilson checked his computer to find that next body while his two assistants prepped. One of them stirred two scoops of green powder into a container of warm water. Donald could smell the concoction across the room. It made his cheeks pucker, but he took careful note of which cabinet the powder came from, how much was spooned in, and asked any question that came to mind.

The other assistant folded a clean blanket and draped it over the back of a wheelchair. There was a paper gown. An emergency medical kit was unpacked and repacked. Gloves, meds, gauze, bandages, tape. It was all done with a quiet efficiency. Donald was reminded of the men behind the serving counter who laid out breakfast with the same habitual care.

A number was read aloud to confirm who they were waking. This reactor tech, like Donald's sister, had been reduced to a number, a place within a grid, a cell in a spreadsheet. As if made-up names were any better. Suddenly, Donald saw how easily his switch could've taken place. He watched as paperwork was filled out—his signature not needed—and dropped into a box. This was a part of the process he could ignore. There would be no trace of what he had planned.

Dr. Wilson led them out the door. The wheelchair full of supplies followed, with Donald trailing behind.

The tech they were waking was two levels down, which meant taking the lift. One of the assistants idly remarked that he had only three days left on his shift.

"Lucky you," the other assistant said.

"Yeah, so be easy with my catheter," he joked, and even Dr. Wilson laughed.

Donald didn't. He was busy wondering what the *final* shift would be like. Nobody seemed to think much past the next shift. They looked forward to one ending and dreaded seeing another. It reminded him of Washington, where everyone he worked alongside hoped to make it to the next term even as they loathed running for another. Donald had fallen into that same trap.

The lift doors opened on another chilled hall. Here were rooms full of shift workers, the majority of the silo's population-in-waiting spread out across two identical levels. Dr. Wilson led them down the hall and coded them through the third door on the right. A hall of sleeping bodies angled off into the distance until it met the concrete skin of the silo. "Twenty down and four over," he said, pointing.

They made their way to the pod. It was the first time Donald had seen this part of the procedure. He had helped put others under, but had never helped wake anyone up. Storing Victor's body away was something altogether different. That had been a funeral.

The assistants busied themselves around the pod. Dr. Wilson knelt by the control panel, paused, glanced up at Donald, waiting.

"Right," Donald said. He knelt and watched over the doctor's shoulder.

"Most of the process is automated," the doctor admitted sheepishly. "Frankly, they could replace me with a trained monkey and nobody would know the difference." He glanced back at Donald as he keyed in his code and pressed a red button. "I'm like you, Shepherd. Only here in case something goes wrong."

The doctor smiled. Donald didn't.

"It'll be a few minutes before the hatch pops." He tapped the display. "The temperature here will get up to thirty-one Celsius. The bloodstream is getting an injection when this light is flashing."

The light was flashing.

"An injection of what?" Donald asked.

"The good little doctors. This procedure would kill a normal human being, which I suppose is why it was outlawed."

A normal human being. Donald wondered what the hell that made him. He lifted his palm and studied the red splotchiness. He remembered a glove tumbling down a hill.

"Twenty-eight," Dr. Wilson said. "When it hits thirty, the lid will release. Now's when I like to go ahead and dial the pod back down, rather than wait until the end. Just so I don't forget." He twisted the dial below the temp readout. "It doesn't stop the process. It only runs one direction once it starts."

"What if something goes wrong?" Donald asked.

Dr. Wilson frowned. "I told you. That's why I'm here."

"But what if something happened to you? Or you got called away?"

Dr. Wilson tugged his earlobe, thinking. "I would advise putting them back under until I could get to them." He laughed. "Of course, the little doctors might just fix what's wrong before I could. As long as you dial it back down, all you have to do is close the lid. But I don't see how that could come up."

Donald did. He watched the temperature tick up to twenty-nine. The two assistants prepped while they waited for the pod to open. One had a towel set aside along with the blanket and the paper gown. The medical kit sat in the wheelchair, the top open. Both men wore blue rubber gloves. One of them peeled off strips of tape and hung them from the handle of the wheelchair. A packet of gauze was preemptively torn open, the bitter drink given a vigorous shake.

"And my code will start the procedure?" Donald asked, thinking of anything he might be missing.

Dr. Wilson chuckled. He placed his hands on his knees and was slow to stand. "I imagine your code would open the airlock. Is there anything you don't have access to?"

A glove was snapped. The hatch hissed as the lock disengaged.

The truth, Donald wanted to say. That was what he didn't have access to. But he was planning on getting it soon.

The lid opened a crack on its own, and one of the assistants lifted it the rest of the way. A handsome young man lay inside, his cheeks twitching as he came to. The assistants went to work, and Donald tried to make note of every little part of the procedure. He thought of his sister in a hall above him, lying asleep, waiting.

"Once we get him up to the office, we'll check his vitals and take our samples for analysis. If they have any items in their locker, I send one of the boys to retrieve them."

"Locker?" Donald asked. He watched as a catheter was removed, a needle extracted from an arm. The tape and gauze were applied while the man in the pod sucked from a straw, wincing from the bitterness as he did so.

"Personal effects. Anything set aside from their previous shift. We retrieve those for them."

The assistants helped the man into a paper gown, then grunted as they lifted him from the steaming pod. Donald moved the medical kit and steadied the wheelchair for them. The blanket was already laid out across the seat. While they settled the man into place, Donald thought of the bag marked *Shift* left on his bed, the one with Thurman's things in them. There had been a small number marked on the bag similar to the one in Anna's note. That number in the note wasn't a date at all.

And then it hit him. It hit with such surety that he didn't trust the conclusion at all. *Locket* was a typo. He tried to picture where the R and T were on a keyboard, if this was a likely mistake. Had she meant to say *locker*, instead?

The confluence of clues cut through the chill in the room, and for a moment, the idea of waking his sister was forgotten. Other sleeping ghosts were whispering to him, clouding his mind.

80

D onald helped escort the groggy man up to the medical offices while one of the assistants stayed behind to scrub the pod. Not caring to see Dr. Wilson take his samples, he volunteered to go grab the tech's personal items. The assistant gave him directions to one of the storage levels in the heart of the silo.

There were sixteen levels of stores in all, not counting the armory. Donald entered the lift and pressed the worn out button for the storeroom on fifty-seven. The reactor tech's ID number had been scribbled on a piece of paper. The number from Anna's note to Thurman was vivid in his mind. He had assumed it was a date: November 2nd, 2039. It made the number easy to recall.

The lift slowed to a stop, and Donald stepped through the doors and into darkness. He ran his hand down the bank of light switches along the wall. The bulbs overhead sparked to life with the distant and muted *thunks* of ancient transformers and relays jolting into action. A maze of tall shelves revealed itself in stages as the lights popped on first in the distance, then close, then off to the right, like some mosaic unmasked one random piece at a time. The lockers were in the very back, past the shelves. Donald began the long walk while the last of the tremulous bulbs flickered on.

Cliffs of steel shelves laden with sealed plastic tubs swallowed him. The containers seemed to lean in over his head. If he glanced up, he almost expected the shelves to touch high above, to meet like train tracks. Huge swaths of tubs were empty and unlabeled, he saw, waiting for future shifts to fill them. All the notes he and Anna had generated on his last shift would be in tubs like these. They would preserve the tale of Silo 40 and all those unfortunate facilities around them. They would tell of the people of Silo 18 and Donald's efforts to save them. And maybe he shouldn't have. What if this current debacle, this vagabond cleaner, was his fault in some way?

He passed crates sorted by date, by silo, by name. There were cross-cuts between the shelves, narrow aisles wide enough for the carts used to haul blank paper and notebooks out and then bring them back in weighing just a little more from the ink. With relief from his claustrophobia, Donald left the shelves and found the far wall of the facility. He glanced back over his shoulder at how far he'd come, could imagine all the lights going out at once and him not being able to pick his way back to the elevator. Maybe he would stagger in circles until he thirsted to death. He glanced up at the lights and realized how fragile he was, how reliant on power and light. A familiar wave of fear washed over him, the panic of being buried in the dark. Donald leaned against one of the lockers for a moment and caught his breath. He coughed into his handkerchief and reminded himself that dying wouldn't be the worst of things.

Once the panic faded and he'd fought off the urge to sprint back to the lift, Donald entered the rows of lockers. There must've been thousands of them. Many were small, like post office boxes, six or so inches to a side and probably as deep as his arm judging by the width of the units. He mumbled the number from Anna's note to himself. Erskine's would be down here as well, and Victor's. He wondered if those men had any secrets squirreled away and reminded himself to come back and check.

The numbers on the lockers ascended as he walked down one of the rows. The first two digits were far away from Anna's number. He turned down one of the connecting aisles to search for the correct row and saw a group that started with 43. His ID number started with 44. Perhaps his locker was near here.

Donald imagined it would be empty, even as he found himself honing in on his ID number. He had never carried anything from shift to shift. The numbers marched in a predictable series until he found himself standing before a small metal door with his ID number on it, Troy's ID number. There was no latch, only a button. He pressed it with his knuckle, worried it might have a fingerprint scanner or something equally deserving of his paranoia. What would someone think if they saw Thurman looking in this man's locker? It was easy to forget the ruse. It was similar to the delay between hearing the senator's name and realizing Donald was the one being spoken to.

There was a soft sigh as the locker cracked open, and then the squeak of old and unused hinges. The sigh reminded Donald that everything down there—the bins and tubs and lockers—was protected from the air. The good, normal air. Even the air they breathed was caustic and full of invisible things, like corrosive oxygen and other hungry molecules. The only difference between the good air and the bad air was the speed at which they worked. People lived and died too quickly to see the difference.

At least they used to, Donald thought as he reached inside his locker.

Surprisingly, it wasn't empty. There was a plastic bag inside, crinkled and vacuum-packed like Thurman's. Only, this bag read *Legacy* across the top rather than *Shift.* Inside, he could see a familiar pair of tan slacks and a red shirt. The clothes hammered him with memories. They reminded him of a man he used to be, a world he used to live in. Donald squeezed the bag, which was dense from the absence of air, and glanced up and down the empty aisle.

Why would they keep these things? Was it so he could emerge from deep underground dressed just as he had been when he arrived? Like an inmate staggering out, blinking and shielding his eyes, having served his penance and now dressed in outdated fashion. Or was it because storage was the same thing as disposal? There were two entire levels above this one where unrecyclable trash was compacted into cubes as dense as iron and stacked to the ceiling. Where else were they supposed to put their garbage? In a hole in the ground? They lived in a hole in the ground.

Donald puzzled over this as he fumbled with the plastic zipper at the top and slid the bag open. A faint odor of mud and grass escaped, a whiff of bygone days. Donald vividly remembered a slick hill, falling down, and then his nostalgia was pierced by the dropping of bombs, by screams, by the image of a dog staked out to a tent pole, barking and left behind. He opened the bag further, and his clothes blossomed to life as air seeped inside. There was an impulse to change into this costume of normalcy, to pretend, to fake like his world wasn't dead. Instead, he began to shove the bag back into the locker—and then a glimmer caught his eye, a flash of yellow.

Donald dug down past his clothes and reached for the wedding ring. As he was pulling it out, he felt a hard object inside the slacks. He palmed the ring and reached inside again, felt around, squeezed the folds of his clothes. What had he been carrying that day? Not his pills. He'd lost those in a fall. Not the keys to the quad, Anna had taken those from him. His own keys and wallet had been in his jacket, had never even made it beneath the earth to orientation—

His cell phone. Donald found it in the pocket of his slacks. The heft of the thing, the curve of the plastic shell, felt right at home in his hand. He returned the bag to the locker, tucked the wedding ring into the pocket of his coveralls, and pressed the power button on the old phone. But of course it was dead. Long-dead. It hadn't even been working the day he'd lost Helen.

Donald placed the phone in his pocket out of habit, the sort of habit that time could not touch. He felt the ring in his pocket and pulled it out, made sure it still fit, and thought of his wife. Thoughts of her led to thoughts of she and Mick having children together. Sadness and sickness intermingled. He stuffed his clothes deep into the locker and shut the door, took the ring off and slipped it into his pocket with the old phone. Donald turned and headed off in search of Anna's locker. He still had to get the tech's personal items as well—

As he tracked down their lockers, something nagged at him, some connection, but he couldn't sort out what.

Off to one side, there was a patch of the storeroom still in darkness, a lightbulb out, and Donald thought of Silo 40 and the spread of darkness on a previous shift. Eren had brought an end to whatever was going on over there. A bomb had caused dust to shiver from overhead pipes. And now his deep mind whirred and made deeper connections. He could feel some thought attempting to notify his consciousness. Something about Anna. Some reason he'd been drawn to his locker. He wrapped his hand around the phone in his pocket and remembered why she'd been woken the last time. He remembered her expertise with wireless systems, with hacking.

In the distance, a light went out with a pop, and Donald felt the darkness closing in on him. There was nothing down here for him, nothing but awful memories and horrible realizations. His heart pounded as it began to come together, something he dearly wanted to disbelieve. His cell phone hadn't worked the day the bombs fell; he hadn't been able to contact Helen. And then there were all the times before when he couldn't reach Mick, the nights he and Anna had found themselves alone.

And now they'd been left alone again, in this silo. Mick had changed places with him at the last moment. Donald remembered a conversation in a small apartment. Mick had given him a tour, had taken him down into a room and said to remember him down there, that this was what he wanted.

Donald slapped one of the lockers with his palm; the loud bang drowned out his curse. This should've been Mick over here, freezing and thawing, going mad. Instead, Mick had stolen the domestic life he often teased Donald for living. And he'd had help doing it.

Donald sagged against the lockers. He reached for his handkerchief, coughed into it. He imagined his friend consoling Helen. He thought of the kids and grandkids they'd had together. A murderous rage boiled up. All this time, blaming himself for not getting to Helen. All this time, blaming Helen and Mick for the life he'd missed out on. And it was Anna, the engineer. Anna who had hacked his life. She did this to him. She brought him here.

·81·

The haze of new awareness was similar to the haze of more literal awakenings. Donald retrieved the items from the other two lockers as if in a dream. Numb, he rode the lift back down to Dr. Wilson's office, dropped off the reactor tech's personal effects. He asked Dr. Wilson for something to help him sleep that night, remembered where the pill came from. When Wilson left with his samples to go to the lab, Donald helped himself to more of the pills. Crushing them up, he added two scoops of the powder and made a most bitter drink. He had no plan. The actions followed one after the other. There was a cruelness in his life that he wished to end.

Down to the deep freeze. He found her pod effortlessly. Donald traced a finger down the skin of the machine. He touched its smooth surface warily, as if it might cut him. He remembered touching her body like this, always afraid, never quite able to give in or let go. The better it felt, the more it hurt. Each caress was a blow to himself and an affront to Helen.

He pulled his finger back and held it in his other hand to stop some imaginary bleeding. There was danger in being near her. Anna's nakedness was on the other side of that armored shell, and he was about to open it. He glanced around the vast halls of the deep freeze. Crowded, and yet all alone. Dr. Wilson would be in his lab for some while.

Donald knelt by the end of the pod and entered his keycode. Some small part of him hoped it wouldn't work. This was too great a power, the ability to give a life or take it. But the panel beeped. Donald steadied his hand and turned the dial just as he'd been shown.

The rest was waiting. Temperatures rose; doubts simmered; anger faded. Donald retrieved the drink and gave it a stir. He made sure everything else was in place.

When the lid sighed open, Donald slid his fingers into the crack and lifted it the rest of the way. Sleep looked so much like death, he saw. Every night people perished, if but for a moment. The cryopods and this hopping through the centuries suddenly seemed less strange. It was no more crazy than dying each evening, a head filled with nightmares and dreams, and trying to remember who he was in the morning.

He reached inside and carefully removed the tubing from the needle in Anna's arm. A thick fluid leaked out of the needle. He saw how the plastic valve on the end worked and turned it until the dripping stopped. Unfolding the blanket from the back of the wheelchair, he tucked it around her. Her body was already warm. Frost dripped down the inner surface of the pod and collected in little channels that served as gutters. The blanket, he realized, was mostly for him.

Anna stirred. Donald brushed the hair off her forehead as her eyes fluttered. Her lips parted and a groan decades old leaked out. Donald knew what that stiffness felt like, that deep cold frozen in one's joints. He hated doing this to her. He hated what had been done to him.

"Easy," he said, as she began to grope the air with shivering limbs. Her head lolled feebly from side to side, murmuring something. Donald helped her into a sitting position and rearranged the blanket to keep her covered. The wheelchair sat quietly beside him with a medical bag and a thermos. Donald made no move to lift her out and help her into the chair.

Blinking and darting eyes finally settled on Donald. They narrowed in recognition.

"Donny—"

He read his name on her lips as much as heard her.

"You came for me," she whispered.

Donald watched as she trembled; he fought the urge to rub her back or wrap her in his arms. He longed to put an end to all this torture in everyone.

"What year?" she asked, licking her lips. "Is it time?" Her eyes were now wide and wet with fear. Melting frost slid down her cheeks in pretend tears.

Donald remembered waking like this with his most recent dreams still clouding his thoughts. "It's time for the truth," he said. "You're the reason I'm here, aren't you?"

Anna stared at him blankly, her mind in a fog. He could see it in the twitch of her eyes, the way her dry lips remained parted, the processing delay he well knew from the times they did this to him, from the times they had woken him.

"Yes." She nodded ever so slightly. "Father was never going to wake us. The deep freeze—" Her voice was a whisper. "I'm glad you came. I knew you would."

A hand escaped from the blanket and gripped the edge of the pod as if to pull herself out. Donald placed a hand on her shoulder. She was in a weakened state. He turned and grabbed the thermos from the wheelchair. Peeling her hand from the lip of the pod, he pressed the drink into her palm. She wiggled her other arm free and held the thermos against her knees.

"I want to know why," he said. "Why did you bring me *here*. To this place." He looked around at the pods, these unnatural graves that kept death at bay.

Anna gazed at him. She studied the thermos and the straw. Donald let go of her arm and reached into his pocket. He pulled out the cell phone. Anna shifted her attention to that.

"What did you do that day?" he asked. "You kept me from her, didn't you? And the night we met to finalize the plans—all the times Mick missed a meeting—that was you as well."

A shadow slid across Anna's face. Something deep and dark registered. Donald had expected a harsh defiance, a steel resolve, denials. Anna looked sad, instead. It was as though the conversation had taken a turn she didn't expect.

"So long ago," she said, shaking her head. "I'm sorry, Donny, but it was so long ago." Her eyes flitted beyond him toward the door as if she were expecting danger. Donald glanced back over his shoulder and saw nothing. "We have to get out of here," she croaked, her voice feeble and distant. "Donny, my father, they made a pact—"

"I want to know what you did," he said. "Tell me."

She shook her head. "I need to tell you something else." Her voice was small and quiet. She licked her lips and glanced at the straw, but Donald kept a hand on her arm. "Dad woke me for another shift." She lifted her head and fixed her eyes on him. Her teeth chattered together while she collected her thoughts. "And I found something—"

"Stop," Donald said. "No more stories. No lies. Just the truth."

Anna looked away. A spasm surged through her body, a great shiver. Steam rose from her hair, and condensation raced down the skin of the pod in sudden bursts of speed.

"It was meant to be this way," she said. The admission was in the way she said it, her refusal to look at him. "It was meant to be. You and me together. We built this."

Donald seethed with renewed rage. Confirmation was like a second discovery of an awful truth. His hands trembled more than hers.

Anna leaned forward. "I couldn't stand the thought of you dying over there, alone."

"I wouldn't have been alone," he hissed through clenched teeth. "And you don't get to decide such things." He gripped the edge of the pod with both hands and squeezed until his knuckles turned white.

Anna nodded. It was hard to tell if she agreed with him or if she meant to say, "It's always up to people like me."

"You need to hear what I have to say," she said.

Donald waited. What explanation or apology was there? She had taken from him what little Thurman had left behind. Her father had destroyed the world. Anna had destroyed Donald's. He waited to hear what she had to say.

"My father made a pact," she said, her voice gaining strength. "We were never to be woken. We need to get out of here—"

This again. She didn't care that she had destroyed him. Donald felt his rage subside. It dissipated throughout his body, a part of him, a powerful surge that came and went like an ocean wave, not strong enough to hold itself up, crashing down with a hiss and a sigh.

"Drink," he told her, lifting her arm gently. "Then you can tell me. You can tell me whatever you like."

Anna blinked. Donald reached for the straw and steered it toward her lips. Such dangerous lips. They would tell him anything, keep him confused, use him so that she might feel less hollow, less alone. He had heard enough of her lies, her brand of poison. To give her an ear was to give her a vein.

Anna's lips closed around the straw, and her cheeks dented as she sucked. A column of foul green surged up the straw.

"So bitter," she whispered after her first swallow.

"Shhh," Donald told her. "Drink. You need this."

She did, and Donald held the thermos for her. Anna paused between sips to tell him they needed to get out of there, that it wasn't safe. He agreed and guided the straw back to her lips. The danger was her.

There was still some of the drink left when she gazed up at him, confused. "Why am I . . . feeling sleepy?" she asked. Anna blinked slowly, fighting to keep her eyes open.

"You shouldn't have brought me here," Donald said. "We weren't meant to live like this."

Anna lifted an arm, reached out, and seized Donald's shoulder. Awareness seemed to grip her. Donald sat on the edge of the pod and put an arm around her. As she slumped against him, he flashed back to the night of their first kiss. Back in college, her with too much to drink, falling asleep on his frat house sofa, her head on his shoulder. And Donald had stayed like that for the rest of the night, his arm trapped and growing numb while a party thrummed and finally faded. They had woken the next morning, Anna stirring before he did. She had smiled and thanked him, called him her guardian angel, and gave him a kiss.

That seemed several ages ago. Eons. Lives weren't supposed to drag on so long. But Donald remembered like it was yesterday the sound of Anna breathing that night. He remembered from their last shift, sharing a cot, her head on his chest as she slept. And then he heard her, right then in that moment as she took in one last sudden, trembling lungful. A gasp. Her body stiffened for a moment, and then cold and trembling fingernails sank into his shoulder. And Donald held her as that grip slowly relaxed, as Anna Thurman breathed her very last.

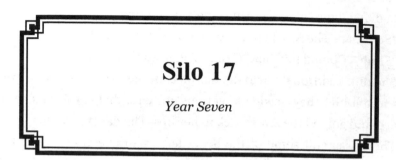

Silo 17

Year Seven

• 82 •

Something bad was happening with the cans. Jimmy couldn't be sure at first. He had noticed little brown spots on a can of beets months ago and hadn't thought anything of it. Now, there were more and more cans getting like that. And some of the contents tasted a little different, too. That part may've been his imagination, but he was for sure getting sick to his stomach more often, which was making the server room smell awful. He didn't like getting anywhere near the poop corner—the flies were getting bad over there—which meant going number two farther and farther out. Eventually he would be going everywhere, and the flies didn't carry his poop as fast as he made it. Especially not once he discovered that hidden cache of beef stew in the back of the soup shelves.

And so it was decided that he needed to go out. He hadn't heard any activity in the halls of late, no one trying the door. But what had once felt like a prison now felt like the only safe place to be. And the idea of leaving, once desirable, now turned his insides to water. The sameness, the routines, were all he knew. Doing something different seemed insane.

He put it off for two days by making a Project out of preparing. He took his favorite rifle apart and oiled all the pieces before putting it back together. There was a box of lucky ammo where very few had failed or jammed during games of Kick the Can, so he emptied two clips and filled them with only these magic bullets. A spare set of coveralls was turned into a backpack by knotting the arms to the legs for loops and cinching up the neck. The zipper down the front made for a nice enclosure. He filled this with two cans of sausage, two of pineapple, and two of tomato juice. He didn't think he'd be gone that long, but one never knew.

Patting his chest, he made sure he had his key around his neck. It never came off, but he habitually patted his chest anyway to make sure it was there. A purple bruise on his sternum hinted that he did this too often. A fork and a rusty screwdriver went in his breast pocket, the latter for jabbing open the cans. Jimmy really needed to find a can opener. That and batteries for his flashlight were the highest of priorities. The power had only gone out twice over the years, but both times had left him terrified of the dark. And checking to make sure his flashlight worked all the time tended to wear down the batteries.

Scratching his beard, he thought of what else. He didn't have much water left in the cistern, but maybe he'd find some out there, so he threw in two empty bottles from years prior. These took some digging. He had to rummage behind the hill of empty cans in one corner of the storeroom, the flies pestering him and yelling at him to leave them alone.

"I see you, I see you," he told them. "Buzz off."

Jimmy laughed at his own joke.

In the kitchen, he grabbed the large knife, the one he hadn't broken the tip off of. He put that in his pack as well. By the time he worked up his nerve to leave on the second day, he decided it was too late to get started. So he took his gun apart and oiled it up one more time and promised himself that he would leave in the morning.

Jimmy didn't sleep well that night. He left the radio on in case there was any chatter, and the hissing made him dream of the air from the outside leaking in through the great steel door. The air hissed and hissed and filled his home with poison. He woke up more than once gasping for a breath and found it difficult to get back to sleep.

In the morning, he checked the cameras, but they were still broken. He wished he had the one of the hallway. All it showed was black. He told himself there was no one there. But soon, he would be. He was about to go outside. *Outside.* Was it okay to think that?

"It's okay," he told himself. He grabbed his rifle, which reeked of oil, and lifted his homemade pack, which he thought suddenly he could wear as clothes in a pinch, if he had to. He laughed some more and headed for the ladder.

"C'mon, c'mon," he said, urging himself as he climbed up. He tried to whistle, was normally a very good whistler, but his mouth was too dry. He hummed, instead.

The pack and the gun were heavy. Dangling from the crook of his elbow, they made it difficult to unlock the hatch at the top of the ladder. But he finally managed. He stuck his head out and he paused to admire the gentle hum of the machines. Some of them made little clicking sounds as if their innards were busy. He'd taken most of the backs off over the years to peer inside and see if any contained secrets, but they all looked like the guts of the computers his dad used to build.

The stench of his own waste greeted him as he moved between the tall towers. That wasn't how you were supposed to greet someone, he thought. His poop was rude. And the black boxes radiated an awful heat, which only made the smell worse.

He stood in front of the great steel door and hesitated. Jimmy's world had been shrinking every day. It had been these two levels, the room with the black machines and the labyrinth beneath. And then he'd only been comfortable below. And then even the dark passageway and the tall ladder had frightened him. And soon it was the back room with all the beds and the storerooms with their funny smells, until the only place he felt safe was on his makeshift cot by the computer desk, the sound of the empty radio crackling in the background.

And now he stood before that door his father had dragged him through, the place where he'd killed a man, and he thought about his world expanding.

His palms were damp as he reached for the keypad. A part of him feared the air outside would be toxic, but he was probably breathing the same air, and people had lived for years out there, talking now and then on the radio. He keyed in the first two digits, level 12, his home. Jimmy thought about going home to get some different clothes, to go to the bathroom in a toilet. He pictured his mother sitting on his parents' bed, waiting for him. He saw her lying on her back, arms crossed, nothing but bones.

He messed up the next two digits, hitting the 4 instead of the 1, and wiped his hands on his thighs. "There's no one on the other side," he told himself. "No one. I'm alone. I'm alone."

Somehow, this comforted him.

He entered the two digits again, and then the digits of his school.

The keypad beeped. The door began to make noises. And Jimmy Parker took a step back. He thought of school and his friends, wondered if any of them were still alive. If *anyone* was still alive. He hooked his finger under the strap of his rifle and pulled it over his head, tucked it against his shoulder. The door clanked free. All he had to do was pull.

There were signs of life and death waiting for him in the hall. A charred ring on the tile and a scatter of ash marked the corpse of an old fire. The outside of the steel door was lined with scratches and marked with dings. The latter reminded him of his misses during Kick the Can, the ineffectual kiss of bullet against solid steel. Right by his feet, Jimmy noticed a stain on the floor—a patch of dappled brown—that touched some small broken bone deep within his brain. He remembered a man dying there with his father's face. Jimmy looked away from these signs of the living and the dying and stepped into the hall.

As he began to pull the door shut, something made him hesitate, some worry in the fiber of his muscles, some constriction of blood vessels. Jimmy wondered if perhaps his code wouldn't work from the outside. What if the door locked and he could never get back in? He checked the keypad and saw the gouges around its steel plate where someone had tried to pry it off the wall. He was reminded how desperately so many others had wanted in over the years. Remembering this made him feel crazy for wanting out. He was wanting in the wrong direction.

Before he could worry further, he shut the steel door, and his heart sank a little as the gears whirred and the locks slid into the wall. There was a hollow *thunk*, like a period on the end of a dreadful thought, the sound of awful finality.

Jimmy rushed to the keypad, his chest pounding in his throat, the feeling of men running down all three hallways to get him, blood-curdling screams and bludgeoning weapons held high over their heads—

He entered the code, and the door whirred open. Pushing on the handle, he took a few deep breaths of home, and nearly gagged on the smell of his own waste warmed by hot and buzzing servers.

There was no one running down the halls. He needed a new can opener. He needed to find a toilet that worked. He needed coveralls that weren't worn to tatters. He needed to breathe and find another stash of canned food and water.

Jimmy reluctantly closed the door again. And even though he had just tested the keypad, the fear that he would never get back inside returned. The gears would be worn out. The code would only work from the outside once per day, once per year. A part of him knew—the obsessive part of him knew—that he could check the code a hundred times and still worry it wouldn't work the very next. He could check forever and never be satisfied. His pulse pounded in his ears as he tore himself from the door.

The hallway was brightly lit. Jimmy kept his rifle against his arm and slid silently past ransacked offices. Everything was quiet except for the buzzing of one light fixture on its last leg and the flutter of a piece of paper on a desk beneath a gushing vent. The security station was unmanned. Jimmy crawled over the gate, remembering Yani, imagining the stairwell outside crowded with people, a man in a cleaning suit barging out and wading into the masses, but when he opened the door and peered outside, the landing was empty.

It was also dim. Only the green emergency lights were on. Jimmy shut the door slowly so that rusty hinges would groan rather than squeal. There was a roll of paper on the grating by his feet. Not a roll of paper. Jimmy nudged the object with his boot, a white cylinder the length of his forearm with knobby ends. A bone. He recognized it from the jumble of a man who had wasted away by the servers, dragged close to his piles of shit.

Jimmy felt with keen surety that his bones would be exposed someday. Perhaps this day. He would never make it back inside his sturdy little home beneath the servers. And this frightened him less than it should have. The heady rush of being out in the open, the cool air and the green glow of the stairwell, even the remnants of another human being, were a sudden and welcome relief from the insanity of being closed in. What had once been his pen—the floors and levels of the silo—was now the great outside. Here was a land of death and of hopeful opportunity.

· 84 ·

He had no great plan, no real direction, but the tug was upward. His flashlight was on its dimward way to death, so he explored the levels cautiously. Groping in an apartment, he fumbled for a toilet, took a crap the way God intended, and was disheartened by the lack of a flush. The sink didn't run, either. Neither did the wash nozzle beside the toilet, which left him using a bedsheet in perfect darkness.

He continued up. There was a general store on nineteen, just below his home. He would check there for batteries, though he feared most useful things would be quite consumed by now. The garment district would have coveralls, though. He felt sure of that. A plan was forming.

Until a vibration in the steps altered them.

Jimmy stopped and listened to the clang of footsteps. They were coming from above. He could see the next landing jutting off overhead, one turn around the central post. It was nearer than the landing below. So he ran, rifle clattering against the jugs tied to his makeshift backpack, boots clomping awkwardly on the treads, his heart both fearful and relieved to not be alone.

He tugged the doors open on the next landing and pulled them shut all but a crack. Pressing his cheek against the door, he peered through the slit, listening. The clanging grew louder and louder. Jimmy held his breath. A figure flew by, hand squeaking along the railing, and then another figure close behind, shouting threats. Both were little more than blurs. Once the noise faded, Jimmy decided they might've been ghosts. He remained in the darkness at the end of a strange and silent hall until he could feel things creeping across the tile toward him, hands with claws reaching through the inky black to tangle up in his wild and long hair, and Jimmy found himself back on the landing in the dull green glow of emergency lights, panting and not knowing what to believe.

He was alone, one way or the other. Even if people survived around him, the only company one found was the kind that chased you or killed you. He would rather remain alone.

Upward again, listening more closely for footfalls, keeping a hand on the rail for a vibration, he spiraled his way past the dirt farm and water plant, past sanitation, keeping to the green light and aiming for the general store. The muscles in his legs grew warm from the use, but in a good way. He passed familiar landmarks that seemed out of time, levels from another life with an accumulation of wear and a tangle of wires and pipes. The world had grown as rusty as his memory of it.

He arrived at the general store to find it mostly bare, except for the remains of someone trapped under a spilled stand of shelves. The boots sticking out were small, a woman's or a child's. White ankle bones spanned the gap between boot and cuff. There were goods trapped underneath the shelf with the person, but Jimmy wasn't about to investigate. He searched the scattering of items for batteries or a can opener. There were toys and trinkets and useless things. Jimmy sensed that many a shadow had fallen over those goods. He saved his flashlight by sneaking out in the darkness.

Searching his old apartment wasn't worth the juice, either. It no longer felt like home. There was a sadness inside that he couldn't name, a sense that he had failed his parents, an old ache in the center of his mind like he used to get from sucking on ice. Jimmy left the apartment and continued up. Something called to him from above. And it wasn't until he got within half a spiral from the schoolhouse that he knew what it was. The distant past was reaching out to him. The day it all began. His classroom, where he could last remember seeing his mother, where his friends still sat in his disordered mind, where if he remained, if he could just go back and sit at his desk and unwind events once more, they would have to come out differently. The world would go to right if he could get back to the day when last the world had been right at all.

Jimmy kept his flashlight powered up as he made his way to the classroom. There was no going back, he quickly saw. There, in the middle of the room, his old backpack lay lifeless like a small animal abandoned and starved. Several of the desks were askew, the neat rows snapped like broken bones, and Jimmy could see in his mind his friends rushing out, could see the paths they took, could watch them spill toward the door like transparent ghosts. They had taken their bags with them. Jimmy's remained and lay still as a corpse.

He could hear Sarah's voice somehow, clear as glass. She called out as his mother pulled him away, called out that he was leaving his backpack. Jimmy stood frozen in the doorway. He thought maybe Sarah had been calling out not to leave her behind.

A step inside, the room aglow from his torch, Mrs. Pearson looked up from a book, smiled and said nothing. Barbara sat at her desk, right by the door. Jimmy remembered her hand in his during a class trip to the livestock pens. It was on the way back, after the strange smells of so many animals, hands reaching through bars to stroke fur and feather and fat, hairless pigs. Jimmy had been fourteen, and something about the animals had excited or changed him. So that when Barbara hung back at the end of the corkscrew of classmates making their way up the staircase and had reached for his hand, he hadn't pulled back.

Jimmy didn't think of Barbara the same way he dreamed about Sarah, but that prolonged touch was a taste of what-might-have-been with another. He brushed the surface of her desk with his fingertips and left tracks through the dust. Paul's desk—his best friend's—was one of those disturbed. He stepped through the gap it left, seeing everyone leaving at once, his mother giving him a head start, until he stood in the center of the room, by his bag, completely alone.

"I am all alone," he said. "I am solitude."

His lips were dry and stuck together. They tore apart when he spoke as if opened for the very first time.

Approaching his bag, he noticed that it'd been gutted. He knelt down and tossed open the flap. There was a scrap of plastic like his mom used and reused to wrap his lunch, but his lunch was gone. Two cornbars and an oatmeal brownie. Amazing how he remembered some things and not others. Someone in the early days had taken his meal, and Jimmy was somewhat glad.

He dug deeper, wondering if they'd taken much else. The calculator his father had built from scratch was still in there, as were the glass figurine soldiers his uncle gave him on his thirteenth. He took the time to transfer everything from his makeshift bag to his old backpack. The zipper was stiff, but it still worked. He studied the knotted coveralls and decided they were in worse shape than the ones he had on, so he left them.

Jimmy stood and surveyed the room, sweeping his flashlight across the chaos. A part of him didn't want to go. When he left, it would be as another ghost, and the room would be empty once more. On the blackboard, he saw someone had left their mark. He played the light across the scene and saw the word Fuck written over and over. It looked like a string of letters like that, fuckfuckfuckfuck. Someone having a bad day.

Jimmy found the erasing rag behind Mrs. Pearson's desk. It was stiff and crusty, but the words still came off. Left behind was a smear, and Jimmy remembered the good days of writing on the board in front of the class. He remembered writing assignments. Mrs. Pearson complimented him on his poetry once, probably just to be nice. Licking his lips, he fished a nub of old chalk from the tray and thought of something to write. There were no nerves from standing before the class. No one was watching. He was well and truly all alone.

I am Jimmy, he wrote on the board, the flashlight casting a strange halo, a ring of dim light, as he wrote. The nub of chalk clicked and clacked as he made each stroke. It squeaked and groaned between the clicks. The noise was like company, and yet he wrote a poem of being alone, an assignment in front of an empty class, a mechanical act from bygone days.

The ghosts are watching, he wrote. The ghosts are watching. They watch me stroll alone. The corpses are laughing. The corpses are laughing. They go quiet when I step over them. My parents are missing. My parents are missing. They are waiting for me to come home.

He wasn't sure about that last line. Jimmy ran the light across what he'd written, which he didn't think was very good. More wouldn't make it better, but he wrote more, anyway.

The silo is empty. The silo is empty. It's full of death from pit to rim. My name was Jimmy, my name was Jimmy. But nobody calls me any longer. I am alone, the ghosts are watching, and solitude makes me stronger.

The last part was a lie, but it was poetry, so it didn't count. Jimmy stepped away from the board and studied the words with a flickering flashlight. The words were like a voice. His voice. They trailed off to the side and dipped down, each line sagging more than the last, the letters getting smaller toward the end of each sentence. It was a problem he always had with the blackboard. He started big and seemed to shrink as he went. Scratching the stubble on his chin, he wondered what this said of him, what it portended.

There was a lot wrong with what he'd written, he thought. The fifth line was untrue, the one about nobody calling him Jimmy. Above the poem, he had called himself this. I am Jimmy, he had written. He still thought of himself as Jimmy.

He grabbed the stiff rag he'd left in the chalk tray, stood before his poem, and went to erase the line that wasn't right. But something stopped him. It was the fear of making the poem worse by attempting to fix it. The fear of taking a line away and having nothing good to put in its place. This was his voice, and it was too rare a thing to quash.

Jimmy felt Mrs. Pearson's eyes upon him. He felt the eyes of his classmates. The ghosts were watching, the corpses laughing, while he studied the problem on the board.

When the solution came, it brought a familiar thrill of arriving at the right place, of connecting the dots. Jimmy reached up and slapped the dusty rag against the board and erased the first thing he'd written. The words I am Jimmy disappeared into a white smear and a tumbling haze of powder. He set the rag aside and began to write a truth in its place.

I am Solitude, he started to write. He liked the sound of that. It was poetic and full of meaning. But like all great poetry, the words had a mind of their own, his deep thoughts intervened, and so he wrote something different. He shortened it to two little neat circles, a swerve, and a slash. Grabbing his bag, he left the room and his old friends behind. All that remained was a poem and the call to be remembered, a mark to prove he'd been there.

I am Solo.

And a haze of chalk fell through the air like the ghost of unwritten words.

Silo 1

· 86 ·

Donald steered the empty wheelchair back to Dr. Wilson's office. A damp blanket was draped over the armrests and dragged across the tile. He felt numb. His dream that morning had been to give life, not take it. The permanence of what he'd done began to set in, and Donald found it difficult to swallow, to breathe. He stopped in the hallway and took stock of what he'd become. Unknowing architect. Prisoner. Puppet. Hangman. He wore a different man's clothes. The transformation horrified him. Tears welled up in his eyes, and he wiped them away angrily. All it took was thinking of Helen and Mick, of the life taken from him, to renew the justification. Everything leading up to that point in time, to him awakening in that silo, had been someone else's doing. He could feel parted strings dangling from his elbows and knees. He was a loose puppet steering an empty wheelchair back to where it belonged.

Donald parked the chair and set the brakes. He took the plastic vial out of his pocket and considered stealing another dose or two. Sleep would be hard to come by, he feared.

The vial went back into the cabinet full of empties. Donald turned to go when he saw the note left in the middle of the gurney.

You forgot this.

-Wilson

The note was stuck to a slender folder. Donald remembered handing it to Dr. Wilson along with the reactor tech's belongings. The trip to the other two lockers had been a blur. All he could remember was clutching his cell phone, facts coming together, realizing that Anna had played Mick and Thurman to engineer a last-minute switch that made no sense, that could only happen with a daughter bending her father's ear, and thus his life had been stolen away.

The folder had been in the locker Anna had mentioned to her father in the message. It seemed inconsequential, now. Donald balled up the note from Dr. Wilson and tossed it in the recycling bin. He grabbed the folder with the intention of staggering back to his cot and searching for sleep. But he found himself opening it up, instead.

There was a single sheet of paper inside. An old sheet of paper. It had yellowed, and the edges were rough where bits had flaked off over the years. Small pieces were still in the folder, caught in its spine. Below the single-spaced typing there were five signatures, a mix of florid and subdued penmanship. At the top of the document, boldly typed, it read: RE: THE PACT.

Donald glanced up at the door. He turned and went to the small desk with the computer, placed the folder by the keyboard, and sat down. Anna's note to her father had the same words in the subject line, along with *Urgent*. He had read the note a dozen times to try and divine its meaning. And the number in the note had led him to this folder.

He was familiar enough with the Pact of the silos, the governing document that kept each facility's inhabitants in line, that managed their populations with lotteries, that dictated their punishments from fines to cleanings. But this was too brief to be that Pact. It looked like a memo from his days on Capitol Hill.

Donald read:

All—

It has been previously discussed that ten facilities would suffice for our purposes, and that a time frame of one century would perform an adequate cleanse. With members of this pact both familiar with budget under-runs and how battle plans prove fruitless upon first firing, it should surprise no one that facts have changed our forecast. We are now calling for thirty facilities and a two century time frame. The tech team assures me their progress makes the latter feasible. These figures may be revisited once again.

There was also discussion in the last meeting of allowing two facilities to reach E-Day for redundancy (or the possibility of holding one facility back in reserve). That has been deemed inadvisable. Having all baskets in one egg is better than the danger of allowing two or more eggs to hatch. As it is a source of growing contention, this amendment to the original Pact shall be hereby undersigned by all founding persons and considered law. I will take it upon myself to work E-shift and pull the lever. Longterm survivability prospects are at 42% in the latest models. Marvelous progress, everyone.

V—

Donald scanned the signatures a second time. There was Thurman's simple scrawl, recognizable from countless memos and bills on the Hill. Another signature that might be Erskine's. One that looked like Charles Rhodes. Illegible others. There was no date on the memo.

He read over it again. Understanding dawned slowly, full of doubts at first, but solidifying. There was a list he remembered from his previous shift, a ranking of silos. Number 18 had been near the top. It was why Victor had fought so hard to save the facility. This decision he mentions in the memo, pulling the lever. Had he said something about this in his note to Thurman? In his admission before he killed himself? Victor had grown unsure of whether or not he could make some decision.

Baskets in one egg. That wasn't how the saying went. Donald leaned back in the chair, and one of the lightbulbs in Dr. Wilson's desk lamp flickered. Bulbs were not meant to last so long. They went dark, but there were redundancies.

One egg. Because what would they do to each other if more than one were allowed to hatch?

The list.

And the reason it all fell together for Donald so easily was because he always knew. He had to know. How could it be otherwise? They had no plan, these bastards, of allowing the men and women of the silos to go free. No. There could be only one. For what would they do to each other if they met on the landscape? What would they do if they met hundreds of years hence? Donald had drawn this place. He should've always known. He was an architect of death.

He thought about the list, the rankings of the silos. The one at the top was the only one that mattered. But what was their metric? How arbitrary would that decision be? All those eggs slaughtered except for one. With what hope? What plan? That the differences and struggles among a silo's people can be overcome? And yet the differences between the silos themselves was too much?

Donald coughed into his trembling hand. He understood what Anna was trying to tell him. And now it was too late. Too late for answers. This was the way of life and death, and in a place that ignored both, he'd forgotten. There was no waking anyone. Just confusion and grief. His only ally, gone.

But there was another he could wake, the one he'd hoped to from the beginning. This was a grave power, this ability to bestir the dead. And weren't they all? Donald shivered as he realized what the Pact truly meant, this pact between the madmen who had conspired to destroy the word.

"It's a suicide pact," he whispered, and the concrete walls of the silo closed in around him; they wrapped him like the shell of an egg. An egg never meant to be hatched. For they were the most dangerous of them all, this pit of vipers, and no world would ever be safe with them in it. The women and children were in lifeboats only to urge the men of Silo 1 to keep working their shifts. But they were all meant to drown. Every last one of them.

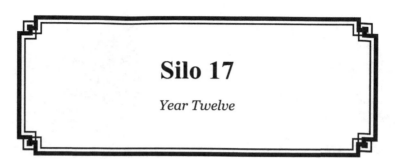

Silo 17

Year Twelve

• 87 •

Solo didn't set out one day to plumb the silo's depths—it simply happened. He had explored enough in both directions over the years, had hidden from the sound of others fighting, had found the messes they left behind, but such encounters grew rarer, and so his explorations grew bolder. It was curiosity as much as gravity and despair that drove him down. It was these things that ended his days alone.

He scavenged as he went. On one-twenty he discovered the lower farms and the signs of those who had lived there. This was farther than he'd ever been before. Those who had survived the early days had rigged the farms with wires and makeshift pipes. Solo took some carrots and beets from the overgrowth and left with the feeling of ghosts watching him. Outside, realizing how close he was to fabled Supply—the subject of so much radio chatter—he spiraled deeper. Supply was the land of plenty, or so they used to say. The promise of batteries and a can opener tugged him along.

The door to Supply was locked. Solo felt eyes on him as he crouched by the entrance and pressed his ear against the cool steel. There was a thrumming he felt as much as heard. It seemed far away, like the lungs of the silo somewhere distant rattling and wheezing. He tried the door again. It wouldn't budge. There were no locks visible on the outside, just the standard vertical handles big enough for one hand to grab and pull.

Solo retreated to the staircase. He lightly gripped the railing with both hands and listened. He listened hard. Eventually, he heard his own pulse in his ears. That's when he knew he was listening best.

No ghosts. No tremble to the rail. He checked his rifle, made sure the safety was off, then pulled it tight against his shoulder. He aimed for the place between the double doors where the handles met. He pictured a can sitting there, imagined kicking it, tried not to see the chest of a man. He squeezed the trigger so lightly and gradually that when the bullet exploded out the barrel, it startled him. The boom of the shot reverberated up and down the silo. A loud crack, and then a dozen echoes. Solo took aim again and fired a second round. A third. BOOM. BOOM. The ghosts would be everywhere cowering, he figured. He was Solo, but his rifle gave him noisy company.

He slipped the rifle strap over his head and tried the doors. One of them moved a little. Solo stepped back and kicked the door, even though they opened outward, just to put some violence into whatever bits continued to hold. When he pulled it the next time, the door came free with a grinding noise. Debris rained out of the insides and clattered onto the landing. The holes on the inside of the door were much larger than the holes on the outside, and the metal was bright and shiny where it had peeled away. Sharp to the touch, too, Solo discovered, sucking on his finger.

The silence within Supply seemed powerful after the boom of his rifle. Solo approached the counter that stretched from wall to wall. There were places he could crawl under where the counter wasn't solid. Then he saw the metal hinges and how the surface lifted up and folded away so he could step through.

Behind the counter were tall shelves and aisles littered with odds and ends. Solo thought he heard a scratching noise, but it was just one of the doors pulling itself shut on its spring-loaded hinges. He tiptoed through the debris and removed his rifle from his back. Just in case.

The bins on the shelves had been rummaged through. Many were missing altogether. Some were upside down, their contents scattered across the floor. To Solo's eye, Supply looked like little more than a bolt and screw store. Bins full of machined metal—rivets, nuts, bolts, washers, hooks and hinges. He dipped his hand into a tub of tiny washers and scooped up a fistful, allowed them to spill out between his fingers. They made a clumsy song as they landed.

Farther down the aisle, the parts became larger. There were pumps and lengths of pipe, bins full of attachments to split the pipe, make it turn corners, and cap it. Solo made mental note of where things were. He thought of all the incredible Projects he could start.

Beyond the aisles, a corridor stretched in both directions with doors on either side. It was dark down the halls. He fished his flashlight from his breast pocket and trained the feeble beam on the pitch black. He should be searching the shelves for another battery, but something tugged him down the corridor. There was something wrong. Trash on the ground. It was the smell of tomatoes. The canned kind, the kind that smelled sweet like the sauce it was preserved in, not sweet like the vine.

He bent and picked up a discarded can. Red tomato paste clung to the lid. Dabbing it with his finger, he found it wet, not hardened like he knew it got within days. Solo touched his finger to his tongue, the taste a jolt to his senses, awareness a shock to his nerves. He clutched his rifle and pulled the strap over his head, wedged the stock against his shoulder. Holding the flashlight and the grip of the gun in the same hand, he balanced the barrel on top of the light. The barrel split the beam in two where it hit the ceiling, leaving a dark shadow above him.

Solo trained the sights down the hall and listened. His flashlight wavered. He crept down a corridor that seemed to be holding its breath.

The doorknobs he tried were all unlocked. He pushed the doors inward, his finger resting on the trigger, finding rooms full of shadows. There were machines on stands with no power. Cutting and welding machines, shaping and joining machines, all splashed with orange rust. They revealed themselves only as his flashlight danced across them. For a split second, each machine loomed in the darkness as a man with his arms up and ready to pounce. There were more doors off the backs of these rooms. A labyrinth of storerooms. Debris scattered everywhere. Evidence of the original exodus was lost amid the struggle to survive ever since.

One of the rooms smelled funny, like hot electrics, like the smell of his rifle after a shell was ejected. The walls in that room were charred black. The darkness swallowed his flashlight's beam. He moved to the next door, leaving far behind the wan green emergency light trickling from the stairwell and through the tall shelves of bolts and screws.

An ominous glow emanated from down the hall. An open door. Solo thought he heard something. He stilled his breathing and waited. Not a whisper, just his heartbeat, probably nothing. He thought of the thousands who had lived in the silo before. How many like him had survived? How many tended the remnants of the farms, scraped the insides of cans with the flat of a knife, digging for those calories at the bottom, watching for spots of rust? Maybe it was just him anymore. Just Solo.

The next door leaked a faint spill of light. Solo approached warily, annoyed at his boots for squeaking, and nudged the door open with the end of his barrel. He remembered what it felt like to kick a man from a distance, to watch the blood spurt from his chest. His flashlight blinked on and off, the battery acting up again. Solo let go of his rifle and knocked the light against his thigh until the beam woke up. He aimed photons and bullets into the room, searching for the source of the glow.

A wedge of light sliced up from the floor inside the room. A wedge of light from a glowing circle. It was the lens of another flashlight.

Solo sucked in a shallow breath at the fortuitous discovery. He hurried forward, scattering cans and wads of trash, and crouched by the lit torch. He flicked his own flashlight off and tucked it into his pocket, picked up this other one. It shone brightly. He aimed it around the room, excited. This was what he had come for. Better than just batteries, a new flashlight as well. The batteries inside would last him years if he was careful, if he conserved. But they wouldn't last him more than a few days if he accidentally left it on.

A few days.

A bucket of cold water spilled down Solo's spine. The darkness all around him crowded closer. He heard imagined whispers from the shadows, and the flashlight was warm in his grip. Had it been warm when he picked it up?

He stood. An empty can clattered noisily from his boot. Solo realized how much of a racket he was making, how much light and life he had brought into this dark and deathly place. He backed toward the door, pulled his gun against his shoulder, the feeling of hands coming at him from every direction, long fingernails of the unkempt about to sink into his flesh.

He nearly dropped the flashlight as he turned to run. The rifle knocked against the doorjamb and pressed into his finger. There was a blinding flash in the coal-dark corridor, a bang like the end of the world, a kick from the rifle. And then Solo was running. Running back toward the shelves with their trickle of stairlight. Running away while imaginary things chased him, no room in his startled mind for the truth that he had brought terror to those who lived there, that his swinging new flashlight, bright and harmonious, had left someone else in the echoing bang and the pitch black that he left behind.

• 88 •

He fled from Supply and headed deeper, a second flashlight his reward for the scare. On one-twenty-eight, he stopped in an apartment to empty his bladder, which seemed to fill whenever he was afraid. There was a thought of getting some rest on the apartment's bare mattress, but he suspected it wasn't yet nighttime. It was just the fading adrenaline that made him feel sleepy.

Back on the landing, he considered his options. He had seen almost all that was left of the silo. It was just him and the ghosts. He had plenty of notes in his head on where things were, had discovered a second farm full of food, had found the water stock on one-twelve, had used his gun to bust open a door. Still no can opener, but he could make do with his screwdriver and hammer. Things were looking up the more he explored down, so that's the way he went.

A dozen levels deeper, the temperature really began to dip. The air grew cool and moist and blossomed in clouds when he blew his breath. An emergency fire hose had been left out on one-thirty-six, unspooled from its little rusted closet. The hose lay tangled on the landing. Water dripped from the nozzle, and Solo could hear the plummeting impacts ring out like tiny bells somewhere farther below. He was almost at the end. The Deep. He had never been to the Deep before.

He filled his water jug from the nozzle. Normally, even a slight crack from those valves would let loose a powerful torrent. Solo was able to open this one all the way, and even then he had to lift the tangle of hose from the landing and coax out half a jugful. He took a few sips, wincing at the bitter taste of the hose's fabric, then screwed the lid back on the jug. It hung from his pack, which jangled with the odds and ends he'd picked up since he'd left home the day before. Along with the rifle, it was a lot to carry.

Solo peered over the railing and spotted the bottom of the silo below: the floor of the Deep, slick and shiny. All he knew of Mechanical—the levels beneath the last twist of the stairway—was that power and air came from there. Since there was still some of both, maybe that meant people. Solo clutched his rifle warily. He wasn't sure if he ever wanted to see people again, ever.

He twisted his way down another few flights, his boots clomp-clomping. Anyone with an ear pressed to the railing would hear his progress. The thought sent chills down his arms. Solo imagined ten thousand people lining the rail, noses touching the crowns of those before them, all listening to him as he descended, an uninterrupted spiral of disembodied noggins attuned to his every move.

"Go away, ghosts," he whispered. He hugged the inner rail, just in case. The steps made less noise near the post. He flashed back to years ago when there'd been no space on the steps, when it'd been hard to breathe as people packed in around him, and his mother had yelled for him to go on without her. Solo felt sixteen again, except his tears disappeared into his beard where before he could wipe them away. He was sixteen again. Would always be sixteen.

His boots splashed into cold water. Solo startled and lost his grip on the rail. He slid, fought for balance, and fell to one knee, water soaking him up to his crotch, his rifle slipping off his shoulder, his bag getting wet.

Cursing, he struggled to his feet. Water dripped from the barrel of his rifle, a stream of liquid bullets. His coveralls were freezing cold and clung to his skin where they'd gotten soaked. Solo wiped at his eyes, which were full of tears, and wondered briefly if all that water at his feet had come from his years of crying.

"Stupid," he said. It was a stupid thought. The water had probably drained from all the toilets that didn't work. Or maybe this is where they flushed to, and now the mechanics weren't around to filter it and pump it back to the Top.

He retreated up a step and watched the agitated surface slowly settle. This was the shiny floor he'd seen from above. Peering through its murky surface—a colorful film across the top with all the colors that existed—he saw that the stairs spiraled out of sight and into the dark depths of the water. The silo was flooded.

Solo watched where the water met the railing and waited to see if the flood was rising. If so, it was far slower than he could tell. It was slower than he was patient enough to sit and stare.

One of the open doors on level one-thirty-seven moved back and forth with the waves his splashing had caused. He watched this gentle undulation, which made him sleepy. The water was two feet or more above the level of the landing. It was that high inside the door as well. The entire silo was filling up with water, he thought. It had taken years for it to get this high. Would it go on forever? How long before it filled his home up on thirty-four? How long before it reached the Top?

Thinking of slowly drowning elicited a strange sound from Solo's mouth, a noise like a sad whimper. His clothes dripped water back to where it had come from, and then Solo heard the whimpering sound again. It wasn't coming from him at all.

He crouched down and peered into the flooded level, listening. There. The sound of someone crying. It was coming from inside the flooded levels, and Solo knew he was not alone.

·89·

It sounded like an infant. Solo peered down at the water. He would have to wade through it to get inside the level. The dim green lights overhead lent the world a ghostly pallor. The air was cold, and the water colder.

He retreated up the steps and left his heavy pack on one of the dry treads—toward the outside, where the steps were wider. He lowered himself, his gun clattering on the stairs. The cuffs of his coveralls were soaked. He rolled them up over his calves, then began unknotting the laces of his boots.

He listened for the cry again. It did not come. He wondered if he would be braving the wet and cold for something he'd imagined, for another ghost who would disappear as soon as he paid it any mind. He dumped the water out of his boots before setting them aside. He pulled off his socks—his big toe poking through a hole in one of them. He squeezed and twisted these, then draped them across the railing to dry.

He left his bag four steps above the waterline. Surely it wasn't coming up fast enough to worry. It didn't appear to have moved since he'd arrived. He glanced at the doorway again, noted the height of the waterline, and imagined the flood surging up while he was trapped inside. Solo shivered, and not from the cold. He thought he heard the baby cry again.

He was enough years old to have a baby, he thought. He did the math. He rarely did this math. Was he twenty-six? Twenty-seven? Another birthday had come and gone with no one to remind him. No sweetbread, no candle lit and just as quickly blown out. "Blow it quick," his mother used to say. His father would barely get the thing lit before Jimmy leaned forward to puff it out. Just an instant of fire, barely a warming of the wax, and the family candle would be put away for his father, whose birthday came next.

A silly tradition, he thought. But supposedly each family had as many birthdays among them as there was wax. The Parker candle was many generations old and not yet half gone. Jimmy used to think he'd live forever if he blew swiftly enough. He and his parents would all live forever. But none of that was true. It would only be him until he died, and so the candle had been a lie.

He stepped into the water and waded toward the door, his feet shocked half-numb from the cold. The colorful film on the surface of the water swirled and mixed and flowed around the stanchions that held up the landing rail. Solo paused and peered beyond the landing. It seemed strange to be so high off the bottom of the silo and see this fluid stretching out to the concrete walls. If he were to fall over, would the water slow his plummet to the bottom? Or would he bob on the surface like that bit of trash over there? He thought he would sink. The most water he'd ever been in before was a tubful, and he'd sat right on the bottom. He was sinking up to his shins right then. The fear of slipping through some unseen crack and dropping to his death caused him to shuffle his feet cautiously. He fought to feel the metal grating beneath his soles, even as his feet grew colder and colder. Something silver seemed to flash beneath the grating, but he thought it was just his reflection or the dance of the metallic sheen on the surface.

"You better be worth this," he told the ghost of some baby down the hall.

He listened for the ghost to call back, but it was no longer crying. The light beyond the doors fell away to blackness, so he pulled his flashlight out of his chest pocket and turned it on. The layer of rippling water caught the beam and magnified it. Waves of light danced across the ceiling in a display so mesmerizing and beautiful that Solo forgot the freezing water. Or perhaps it was that his feet no longer had any feeling at all.

"Hello?" he called out.

His voice echoed softly back to him. He played the light down the hall, which branched off in three directions. Two of the paths curved around as if to meet on the other side of the stairwell. It was one of the hub-and-spoke levels. Solo laughed. *Bi* for *Bicycles*. He thought of that entry and realized where the words *hub and spoke* came from. These were magical discoveries, how old words came to be—

A cry.

For certain, this time, or he truly was losing his senses. Solo spun around and aimed his flashlight down the curving corridor. He waited. Silence. The whisper of ripples as they crashed into the hallway wall. He picked his way the direction he'd heard the noise, throwing up new waves with the push of his shins. He floated like a ghost. He couldn't feel his feet.

It was an apartment level. But why would anyone live down here with the waters seeping in? He paused outside a community rec room and dispelled pockets of darkness with his flashlight. There was a tennis table in the middle of the room. Rust reached up the steel legs as if the water had chased it there. The paddles were still on the warped surface of the rotting green table. *Green for grass*, Solo thought. The Legacy books made his own world look different to him.

Something bumped into his shin, and Solo startled. He aimed his light down and saw a foam cushion floating by his feet. He pushed it away and waded toward the next door.

A community kitchen. He recognized the layout of wide tables and all the chairs. Most of the chairs lay on their sides, partly submerged. A few legs stuck up where chairs had been overturned. There were two stoves in the corner and a wall of cabinets. The room was dark; almost none of the light from the stairwell trickled back this far. Solo imagined that if his batteries died, he would have to grope to find his way out. He should've brought the new flashlight, not his old one.

A cry. Louder this time. Near. Somewhere in the room.

Solo waved his flashlight about but couldn't see every corner at once. Cabinets and countertops. A spot of movement, he thought. He trained his light back a little, and something moved on one of the counters. It leapt straight up, the sound of claws scratching as it caught itself on an open cabinet above the counter, then the whisking of a bushy tail before a black shadow disappeared into the darkness.

· 90 ·

A cat! A living thing. A living thing he need not fear, that could do him no harm. Jimmy trudged into the room, calling "kitty, kitty, kitty." He recalled neighbors trying to corral that tailless animal that lived down the hall from his old apartment.

Something rummaged around in the cabinets. One of the closed doors rattled open and banged shut again. He could only see a spot at a time, wherever he aimed the flashlight. His shins brushed against something. He aimed the beam down to see trash and debris floating in the water. There was a squeak and a splash. Searching with the flashlight, he saw a V of ripples behind what he took for a swimming rat. Jimmy no longer wanted to be in that room. He shivered and rubbed his arm with his free hand. The cat made a racket inside the cabinet.

"Here, kitty, kitty," he said with less gusto. Reaching into his breast pocket, he pulled out one of his ration bars and tore the packaging off with his teeth. Taking a stale bite for himself, he chewed and held the rest out in front of him. The silo had been dead for twelve years. He wondered how long cats lived, how this one had made it so long. And eating what? Or were old cats having new cats? Was this a new cat? They didn't have a lottery, did they?

His bare feet brushed through something beneath the water. The reflection of the light made it difficult to see, and then a white bone broke the surface before sinking again. There was a loose jumble of someone's remains around his ankles.

Jimmy pretended it was just trash. He reached the cabinet making all the noise, grabbed a handle, and pulled it open. There was a hiss from the shadows. Cans and rotting boxes shifted about as the cat retreated further. Jimmy broke off a piece of stale bar and set it on the shelf. He waited. There was another squeak from the corner of the room, the sound of water lapping at furniture, a stillness inside the cabinet. He kept the flashlight down so as not to spook the animal.

Two eyes approached like bobbing lights. They fixed themselves on Jimmy for a small eternity. He began to seriously wonder if his feet might fall off from the cold, if that's what feet did when you subjected them to such abuse. The eyes drew closer and diverted downward. It was a black cat, the color of wet shadow, slick as oil. The piece of ration bar crunched as the cat chewed.

"Good kitty," he whispered, ignoring the scattered bones beneath his feet. He broke off another small piece of the bar and held it out. The cat withdrew a pace. Jimmy set the food on the edge and watched as the animal came forward more quickly this time to snatch it up. The next piece, the cat took from his palm. He offered the last piece, and as the cat came to accept it, Jimmy tried to pick it up with both hands. And this thing, this company he hoped would do him no harm, latched onto one of his arms and sank its claws into his flesh.

Jimmy screamed and threw up his hands. The flashlight tumbled end over end in the air. There was a splash as the cat disappeared. A shriek and a hiss, a violent noise, Jimmy fumbling beneath the water for the dull glow of the light, which flickered once, twice, then left him in darkness.

He groped blindly, seized a solid cylinder, and felt the knobby ends where the leg sockets into the hip. He dropped the bone in disgust. Two more bones before he found the flashlight, which was toast. He retrieved it anyway as the sound of frantic splashing approached. His arms were on fire; he had seen blood on them in the last of the spinning light. And then something was against his leg, up his shin, claws stinging his thighs, the damn cat climbing him like the leg of a table.

Jimmy reached for the poor animal to get its claws out of his flesh. The cat was soaked and hardly felt bigger around than his flashlight. It trembled in his arms and rubbed itself against a dry patch of his coveralls, mewing in complaint. It began to sniff at his breast pocket.

Jimmy held the animal with one forearm across his chest, making a perch, and reached inside his pocket for the other ration bar. It was perfectly dark in the room, so dark it made his ears ache. He ripped the package free and held the bar steady. Tiny paws wrapped around his hand, and there was a crunching sound.

Jimmy smiled. He worked his way toward where he thought the door might be, bumping through furniture and old bones as he went, Solo no more.

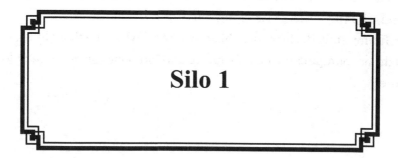

Silo 1

Donald's apartment had transformed into a cave, a cave where notes lay strewn like bleached bones, where the carcasses of folders decorated his walls, and where boxes of more notes were ordered up from archives like fresh kill. Weeks had passed. The stomping in the halls had dwindled. Donald lived alone with ghosts and slowly pieced together the purpose of what he'd helped to build. He was beginning to see it, the entire picture, zooming out of the schematic until the whole was laid bare.

He coughed into a pink rag and resumed examination of his latest find. It was a map he'd come across once before in the armory, a map of all the silos with a line coming out of each and converging at a single point. Here was one of many mysteries left. The document was labeled Seed, but he could find nothing else about it.

He shuffled through his piles—he had a system, the stacks had meaning—and found what he was looking for. A list similar to the one he'd uncovered on his last shift. A ranking of all the silos. Victor had spent a lot of time looking at this list before he killed himself. The ordering was different than Donald remembered. Different silos were near the top of this one. It was a version of the list that'd been updated weeks ago by Eren. Or generated by a computer and signed off by him. Donald had printed it from the Ops directory, which his Thurman account had access to. He scratched his beard. Silo 18 was near the bottom, down near the silos that no longer harbored life. Silos 12, 17, 40, and a dozen others were labeled N/A. He could tell the list was gravely important by who had access to it and who didn't. Silo 6 was at the very top. The one hopeful egg in the basket.

Donald could hear Anna approaching while he worked; he could hear her whispers getting louder. She had been trying to tell him something. The note in Thurman's account, she was trying to say, it had been left for him. So obvious, now. She could never be woken, not a woman. She needed him, needed his help. Donald imagined her piecing all of this together on some recent shift, alone and terrified, scared of her own father, no one left to turn to. So she had taken her father out of power, had entrusted Donald, had left him a note. And what did Donald do?

He heard her whispers and did not startle as she burst up through the film of white pages, a swimmer emerging from a frothy sea. Her arms flailed and splashed as she gasped for air, as she came back to life. Donald watched her struggle for a while. He imagined a hand on her head, pushing her back under. He willed the guilt to subside until the splashes and ripples settled and were pages once more.

Scratching his beard, he looked elsewhere. He nearly told himself that he wasn't mad, but that would be a small consolation. Sane people never said that to themselves.

The reports. Anna had spent a year like this once, down in the armory, surrounded by notes. Living alone, meals delivered, lonely and wishing for company. He was only a few weeks into what she had suffered and already cracking. Anna had been so much stronger than he, but now she was dead. She'd been dead for over two weeks, and nobody knew. Maybe they never would.

Donald groaned and picked up a piece of paper, a distraction.

It was from his Silo 18 stack, an old mystery he no longer cared about. They had sent drones up to look for a wayward cleaner. They had sent drones up to bomb Silo 40 because of a connection he'd made. There was no cleaner out there on the hills. The hills were littered with cleaners.

Donald remembered the video feed he'd been shown of a woman disappearing over a gray dune. Because of this, the residents of 18 had been filled with a dangerous hope—the sort of hope that leads to violence. And in the halls outside of Donald's door, scraps of conversation passed with squeaking boots, rumors and stories about this cleaner surviving, making it somewhere, joining another silo.

It was nothing but legends made up and circulated to entertain bored minds. Poison. It was stupid to hope. Crazy to dream. The less he did it—the more the nightmares guided him—the more clearly he saw the danger in others. He was becoming the man whose boots he wore. Even as he sorted out what they'd done and what they had planned, he was becoming him. Donald sometimes embraced this, sometimes raged against it.

He picked up the folder on Silo 17. As he did, he noticed the splotches on the back of his hand. Purplish and red, it looked like a rash. He held his hand up and studied the patterns, remembered tugging a glove off and watching it tumble down a windswept hill. Donald wanted to die up there with that view, anywhere but buried. Flexing his hand into a fist, squeezing the air and relaxing over and over, he waited for the blood to return to his hand, to normalize. He should see the doctor, but tell him what? When Donald coughed up blood, his greatest fear was that he would be discovered. Death was no longer a thing.

There was a knock on his door.

"Who is it?" Donald asked, his voice not sounding like his own.

The door opened a crack. "It's Eren, sir. We've got a call from eighteen. The shadow is ready."

"Just a second," he said.

Donald coughed into his handkerchief. He rose slowly and moved to the bathroom, stepping over two trays of old dishes. He emptied his bladder, flushed, and studied himself in the mirror. Gripping the edge of the counter, he grimaced at his reflection, this man with scraggly hair and the start of a beard. He looked insane, and yet people trusted him. That made them crazier than he was. But he was in charge, and the small duties that came from being in charge disturbed his private digging. Donald smiled a yellowing smile and thought of the long history of madmen who remained in charge simply because they already were.

Hinges squealed as Eren poked his head in the door.

"I'm coming," Donald said. He pushed away from a stranger, who pushed away from him in equal measure. Stomping across the reports, leaving a trail of footprints behind, he also left a bloody palm print on the edge of the counter, the mark of a man getting worse.

· 92 ·

Donald joined Eren in the hall. The state of his being was acutely felt in the presence of another. He wasn't cycling his coveralls through the wash the way he should be. He smelled himself with another man's nose—another man's cleanliness—in his presence.

"They're calling the shadow now, sir."

Donald cringed at the "sir." The deferential treatment felt more and more vacuous as the days wore on. Donald had been awoken for answers, but he had found nothing but questions. He sat alone in a room full of notes and pages, growing mad. He felt conspicuously mad.

"You want to freshen up?" Eren asked.

"No," Donald said. "I'm good." He stood in the doorway, struggling to remember what this meeting was about. A Rite of Initiation. He remembered those, thought it was something Raymond would handle. "Why am I needed, again?" he asked. "Shouldn't our Head be conducting this?" Donald remembered being the one to conduct such a Rite on his first shift.

Eren popped something into his mouth and chewed. He shook his head. "You know, with all that reading you're doing in there, you could bone up on the Order a bit. It sounds like it's changed since the last time you read it. The ranking officer on shift completes the Rite. That would normally be me—"

"But since I'm up, it's me." Donald pulled his door shut. The two of them started down the hall.

"That's right. The Heads here do less and less every shift. There have been . . . problems. I'll sit in with you though, help you get through the script. Oh, and you wanted to know when the pilots were heading off-shift. The last one is going under right now. They're just straightening up down there."

Donald perked up at this. Finally. What he'd been waiting for. "So the armory's empty?" he asked, unable to hide his delight.

"Yessir. No more flight requisitions. I know you didn't like chancing them to begin with."

"Right, right." Donald waved his hand as they turned the corner. "Restrict access to the armory once they're done. Nobody should be able to get in there but me."

Eren slowed his pace. "Just you, sir?"

"For as long as I'm on shift," Donald said.

They passed Raymond in the hall, who had three cups of coffee nestled in a web of fingers. Raymond smiled and nodded. Donald remembered fetching coffee for people when he was Head of the silo. Now, that was about all the Head did. Donald couldn't help but think his first shift was partly to blame.

Eren lowered his voice. "You know the story behind him, right?" He took another bite of something and chewed.

Donald glanced over his shoulder. "Who, Raymond?"

"Yeah. He was in Ops until a few shifts back. Broke down. Tried to get himself into deep freeze. The duty doc at the time talked him into a demotion. We were losing too many people, and the shifts were starting to get some overlap." Eren paused and took another bite. There was a familiar scent. Eren caught him watching and held out something. "Bagel?" he asked. "They're fresh baked."

Donald could smell it. Eren tore off a piece. The feeling of having become a stray animal or a homeless man was complete as he accepted the offering. It was still warm. "I didn't know they could make these," he said, popping the morsel into his mouth.

"New chef just came on shift. He's been experimenting with all kinds of stuff. He—"

Donald didn't hear the rest. He chewed on memories. A cool day in D.C., Helen up to visit, had the dog with her, drove all the way from Savannah. They walked around the Lincoln Memorial a week too early for the cherry blossoms, but still a spot of color here and there. Stopped for fresh bagels, still warm, the smell of coffee—

"Put an end to this," Donald said, indicating the rest of Eren's bagel.

"Sir?"

They were nearly to the bend in the hall that led to the comm room. "I don't want this chef experimenting anymore. Have him stick to the usual."

Eren seemed confused. After some hesitation, he nodded. "Yes sir."

"Nothing good can come of this," Donald explained. And while Eren agreed more strenuously this time, Donald realized he had begun to think like the people he loathed. A veil of disappointment fell over his face, this Ops Head, who in truth outranked him, who should by all rights be in charge, and Donald felt a sudden urge to take it back, to grab the man by the shoulders and ask him what the hell they thought they were doing, all this misery and heartache. They should eat memory foods, of course, and talk about the days they'd left behind.

Instead, he said nothing, and they continued down the hall in quiet and discomfort.

"Quite a few of our silo Heads came from Ops," Eren said after a while, steering the conversation back to Raymond. "I was a comms officer for my first two shifts, you know. The guy I took over for, the Ops Head from the last shift, was from medical."

"So you're not a shrink?" Donald asked.

Eren laughed, and Donald thought of Victor, blowing his brains out. This wasn't going to last, this place. There were cracked tiles in the center of the hall. Tiles that had no replacement. The ones at the edge were in much better shape, and Donald had an epiphany. He stopped outside the comm room and surveyed the wear on this centuries-old place. There were scuff marks low on the walls, hand-high, shoulder-high, fewer anywhere else. The traffic patterns on the floors throughout the facility showed where people walked. It wasn't evenly distributed.

"Are you okay, sir?" Eren asked.

Donald held up his hand. He could sense those in the comm room were waiting on him. But he was thinking on how an architect designs a structure to last. A certain calculus was used, an averaging of forces and wear across an entire structure, letting every beam and rivet shoulder its share of the load. All together, the resulting building could take the force of a hurricane, an earthquake, with plenty of redundancies to boot. But real stress and strain weren't as kind as the hurricanes computers simulated. Hidden in those calculus winds were hurtling rods of steel and two by fours. And where they slammed it was like bombs going off. Just as the center of a hall bore an unfortunate share of strain, some people would be on shift for the worst of it.

"I believe they're waiting on us, sir."

Donald looked away from the scuff marks to Eren, this young man with bright eyes and bagel on his breath. He was like a corner of the hall lightly touched, his hair full of color, an uptick at the corners of his mouth, a wan smile like a scar of hope.

"Right," Donald said. He waved Eren inside the comm room before following behind, stepping dead center like everyone else.

Donald familiarized himself with the script while Eren plopped into the chair beside him and pulled a headset on. The software would mask their voices, make them featureless and the same. The silo Heads need not know when one man went off shift and another replaced him. It was always the same voice, the same person, as far as they were concerned.

The shift operator lifted a mug and took a sip. Donald could see something written on the mug with a marker. It said: We're #1. Donald wondered if whoever wrote it meant the silo. The operator set the mug down and twirled his finger for Donald to begin.

Donald covered his mic and cleared his throat. He could hear someone talking on the other line as a distant headset was pulled on. There was a script to follow for the first half. Donald remembered most of it. Eren turned to the side and polished off the bagel guiltily. When the operator gave them the thumbs up, Eren gestured to Donald to do the honors, and all Donald could think about was getting this over with and getting down to that empty armory.

"Name," he said into his mic.

"Lukas Kyle," came the reply.

Donald watched the graphs jump with readings taken from the headset. He felt sorry for this person, signing on to head a silo rated near the bottom. It all seemed hopeless, and here Donald was going through the motions. "You shadowed in IT," he said.

There was a pause. "Yessir."

The boy's temperature was up. Donald could read it on the display. The operator and Eren were comparing notes and pointing to something. Donald checked the script. It listed easy questions everyone knew the answers to.

"What is your primary duty to the silo?" he asked, reading the line.

"To maintain the Order."

Eren raised a hand as the readouts spiked. When they settled, he gave Donald the sign to continue.

"What do you protect above all?" Even with the software helping, Donald tried to keep his voice flat. There was a jump on one of the graphs. Donald's thoughts drifted to the news of the pilots gone from his space, a space that he felt belonged to him. He would get through this and set his alarm clock. Tonight. Tonight.

"Life and Legacy," the shadow recited.

Donald lost his place. It took a moment to find the next line. "What does it take to protect these things we hold so dear?"

"It takes sacrifice," the shadow said after a brief pause.

The comm head gave Donald and Eren an OK signal. The formal readings were over. Now to the baseline, to get off-script. Donald wasn't sure what to say. He nodded to Eren, hoping he'd take over.

Eren covered his mic for a second as if he was about to argue, but shrugged. "How much time have you had in the Suit Labs?" he asked the shadow, studying the monitor in front of him.

"Not much, sir. Bernar— Uh, my boss, he's wanting me to schedule time in the labs after, you know . . ."

"Yes. I do know." Eren nodded. "How's that problem in your lower levels going?"

"Um, well, I'm only kept apprised of the overall progress, and it sounds good." Donald heard the shadow clear his throat. "That is, it sounds like progress is being made, that it won't be much longer."

A long pause. A deep breath. Waveforms relaxed. Eren glanced at Donald. The operator waved his finger for them to keep going.

Donald had a question, one that touched on his own regrets. "Would you have done anything differently, Lukas?" he asked. "From the beginning?"

There were red spikes on the monitors, and Donald felt his own temperature go up. Maybe he was asking something too close to home. He realized suddenly that these people they watched over were aliens, a different race, hundreds of years removed from his own kind. His pity for them grew. Such was how gods began doting on mortals, with pity.

"Nossir," the young shadow said. "It was all by the Order, sir. Everything's under control."

The comm head reached to his controls and muted all of their headsets. "We're getting borderline readings," he told them. "His nerves are spiking. Can you push him a little more?"

Eren nodded. The operator on the other side of him shrugged and took a sip from his #1 mug.

"Settle him down first, though," the comm head said.

Eren turned to Donald. "Congratulate him and then see if you can get him emotional," he suggested. "Level him out and tweak him."

Donald hesitated. It was all so artificial and manipulative. He forced himself to swallow. The mics were unmuted.

"You are next in line for the control and operation of Silo eighteen," he said stiffly, sad for what he was dooming this poor soul to.

"Thank you, sir." The shadow sounded relieved. Waveforms collapsed as if they'd struck a pier.

Now Donald fought for some way to push the young man. The comm head waving at him didn't help. Donald glanced up at the map of the silos on the wall. He stood, the headphone cord stretching, and studied the several silos marked out, the one there with the number '12.' Donald considered the seriousness of what this young man had just taken on, what his job entailed, how many had died elsewhere because their leaders had let them down.

"Do you know the worst part of my job?" Donald asked. He could feel those in the comm room watching him. Donald was back on his first shift, initiating that other young man. He was back on his first shift, shutting a silo down. There was silence, and he worried that the shadow on the other end had removed his headset.

"What's that, sir?" the voice asked.

"Standing here, looking at a silo on this map, and drawing a red cross through it. Can you imagine what that feels like?"

"I can't, sir."

Donald nodded. He appreciated the honest answer. He remembered what it felt like to watch those people spill out of 12 and perish on the landscape. He blinked his vision clear. "It feels like a parent losing thousands of children all at once," he said.

The world stood still for a heartbeat or two. The operator and the comm head were both fixated on their monitors, looking for a crack. Eren watched Donald.

"You will have to be cruel to your children so as not to lose them," Donald said.

"Yessir."

Waveforms began to pulse like gentle surf. The comm head gave Donald the thumbs-up. He had seen enough. The boy had passed, and now the Rite was truly over.

"Welcome to Operation Fifty of the World Order, Lukas Kyle," Eren said, reading from the script and taking over for Donald. "Now, if you have a question or two, I have the time to answer, but briefly."

Donald remembered this part. He had a hand in this. He settled back into his chair, suddenly exhausted.

"Just one, sir. And I've been told it isn't important, and I understand why that's true, but I believe it will make my job here easier if I know." The young man paused. "Is there . . . ?" A new red spike on his graph. "How did this all begin?"

Donald held his breath. He glanced around the room, but everyone else was watching their monitors as if any question was as good as another.

Donald responded before Eren could. "How badly do you wish to know?" he asked.

The shadow took in a breath. "It isn't crucial," he said, "but I would appreciate a sense of what we're accomplishing, what we survived. It feels like it gives me—gives us a purpose, you know?"

"The reason is the purpose," Donald told him. This was what he was beginning to learn from his studies. "Before I tell you, I'd like to hear what you think."

He thought he could hear the shadow gulp. "What I think?" Lukas asked.

"Everyone has ideas," Donald said. "Are you suggesting you don't?"

"I think it was something we saw coming."

Donald was impressed. He had a feeling this young man knew the answer and simply wanted confirmation. "That's one possibility," he agreed. "Consider this—" He thought how best to phrase it. "What if I told you that there were only fifty silos in all the world, and that we are in this infinitely small corner of that world?"

On the monitor, Donald could practically watch the young man think, his readings oscillating up and down like the brain's version of a heartbeat.

"I would say that we were the only ones . . ." A wild spike on the monitor. "I'd say we were the only ones who knew."

"Very good. And why might that be?"

Donald wished he had the jostling lines on the screen recorded. It was serene, watching another human being clutch after his vanishing sanity, his disappearing doubts.

"It's because . . . It's not because we knew." There was a soft gasp on the other end of the line. "It's because we did it."

"Yes," Donald said. "And now you know."

Eren turned to Donald and placed his hand over his mic. "We've got more than enough. The kid checks out."

Donald nodded. "Our time is up, Lukas Kyle. Congratulations on your assignment."

"Thank you." There was a final flutter on the monitors.

"Oh, and Lukas?" Donald said, remembering the young man's predilection for staring at the stars, for dreaming, for filling himself with dangerous hope.

"Yessir?"

"Going forward, I suggest you concentrate on what's beneath your feet. No more of this business with the stars, okay, son? We know where most of them are."

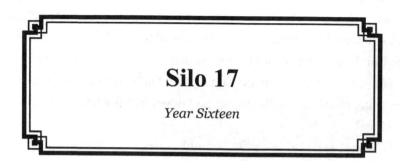

Silo 17

Year Sixteen

·94·

Jimmy wasn't sure how the math worked, but feeding two mouths was more than just twice the work. And yet—it felt like less than half the chore. The addition didn't add up, but he suspected it had to do with how nice it felt to provide for something besides himself. It was the satisfaction of seeing the cat eat and of it growing used to his presence that made him relish meals more and travel outside more often.

It had been a rough start, though. The cat had been skittish after its rescue. Jimmy had dried himself off with a towel scavenged two levels up, and the cat had acted insane as he dried it off after. It seemed to both love and hate the process, rolling around one minute and batting at Jimmy's hands the next. Once dry, the animal had blossomed to twice its wet size. And yet, he was still pathetic and hungry.

Jimmy found a can of beans beneath a mattress (always the first place he looked, though it was often useless chits he found there). The can wasn't too rusty. He opened it with his screwdriver and fed the slick pods to the cat one at a time while his own feet went from blue to normal, tingling like electricity the entire time.

After the beans, the cat had taken to following him wherever he went to see what he might find next. It made the hunt for food fun, rather than a never ending war against his own growling stomach. Fun, but lots of work. Up the staircase they went, him back in his boots, the cat silently pawing behind and sometimes ahead.

Jimmy had learned early on to trust the thing's balance. The first few times it rubbed itself against the outer stanchions, even twisting itself beyond them and back through as it ascended the steps, Jimmy nearly had a heart attack. The cat seemed to have a death wish, or just an ignorance of what it meant to fall. But he soon learned to trust the cat even as the cat began to trust him.

And that first night, as he lay huddled under his tarp in the lower farms, listening to pumps and lights click on and off and noises he mistook for hiding others, the cat tucked itself under his arm and curled against the crook his belly made when his legs were bent and began to rattle like a pump on loose mounts.

"You were lonely, huh?" Jimmy had whispered. He had grown uncomfortable but was unwilling to move. A cramp had formed in his neck while a different tightness disappeared from deep in his gut, a tightness he didn't know was there until it was gone.

"I was lonely, too," he had told the cat softly, fascinated by how much more he talked with the animal around. It was better than talking to his shadow and pretending it was a person.

"That's a good name," Jimmy had whispered. He didn't know what people named cats, but Shadow would work. Like the shadows in which he'd found the thing, another spot of blackness to follow Jimmy around. And that night, years back, the two of them had fallen asleep amid the clicking pumps, the dripping water, the buzzing insects, and all the stranger sounds deep within the farms that Jimmy preferred not to name.

••••

That was years ago. Now, cat hair and beard hair gathered together in the spines of the Legacy books. Jimmy trimmed his beard while he read about snakes. The scissors made crunching noises as he pinched a load of hair, held it away from his chin, and hacked it off with the dull shears. He sprinkled most of the hair in an empty can. The rest drifted down among the words, large swoops of meddling punctuation to mingle with the cat's hair, who kept walking back and forth under his arms, arching his back, and stepping across his sentences.

"I'm trying to read," Jimmy complained. But he put down the scissors and dutifully stroked the animal from neck to tail, Shadow pressing his spine up into Jimmy's palm as he got to the end of each pet. The animal lost its mind when Jimmy did this. He meowed and made that grumbling sound like his heart was going to burst and begged for more.

Tiny claws clenched into little fists and punctured a photo of a corn snake, and Jimmy guided the animal toward the floor. Shadow lay on his back with his feet in the air, watching Jimmy carefully. It was a trap. Jimmy could rub his belly for only a moment before the cat would suddenly decide it hated this and attack his wrist. Jimmy didn't understand cats that well, but he'd read the entry on them a dozen times. One thing he hated to learn was that they didn't live as long as humans. He tried not to think of that day. On that day he would go back to being Solo, and he much preferred being Jimmy. Jimmy talked more. Solo was the one with the wild thoughts, the one who gazed over the rails, who spat toward the Deep and watched as his spit trembled and tore itself apart from the wild speeds of its racing fall.

"Are you bored?" Jimmy asked Shadow.

Shadow looked at him like he was bored. It was similar to the look that said he was hungry.

"Wanna go explore?"

The cat's ear twitched, which was enough of a sign.

Jimmy decided to check the Top again. He had only been once since the days went dark, and just for a peek. If there was a working can opener in the silo, it would be there. An end to crusty screwdrivers and slicing his hands on roughly opened lids.

They set out after lunch with a short break at the farms. When they got to the cafeteria, they found it perfectly silent and glowing in the green cast from the stairwell. Shadow scampered up the last steps alone, intrepid as usual. Jimmy headed straight for the kitchen and found it a looted wreck.

"Who took all the openers?" he called out to Shadow.

But Shadow wasn't there. Shadow was off to the far wall, acting agitated.

Jimmy ranged behind the serving line and sorted through the forks, eager to replace his usual one, when he noticed the mewing. He peered across the wide cafeteria hall and saw Shadow rubbing back and forth against a closed door.

"Keep it down," Jimmy yelled to Shadow. Didn't the cat know he'd only bring trouble making such a racket? But Shadow wasn't in a listening mood. He mewed and mewed and scratched his claws at the door and stretched until Jimmy relented. He hurried through the maze of upturned chairs and crooked tables to see what the fuss was about.

"Is it food?" he asked. With Shadow, it was almost always food. His companion was drawn to meals like a magnet, which Jimmy had come to find quite handy. Approaching the door, he saw the remnants of a rope looped around the handle, the years reducing it to tatters. Jimmy tried the handle and found it unlocked. He eased it open.

The room beyond was dark, none of the emergency lights like at the top of the stairwell. Jimmy fumbled for his flashlight while Shadow disappeared through the cracked door, his tail swishing into the void.

There was a startled hiss just as the flashlight came on. Jimmy paused, a boot nearly through the door, as the cone of his flashlight fell upon a face staring up at him with open and lifeless eyes. Bodies shifted against the door, and an arm flopped out against his foot.

Jimmy screamed and fell backward. He kicked at the pale and fleshy hand and called for Shadow, who came screeching out the door, fur standing on end. There was the taste of metal on Jimmy's tongue, a rush of adrenaline as he scrambled to get the door shut. He lifted the limp arm and shoved it back inside, the clothes disintegrating at his touch, the flesh beneath whole and spongy.

Open mouths and curled fingers were the last things he saw. Piles of bodies, as fresh as the morning dead, frozen where they'd crawled over one another, hands reaching for the door.

Once it clicked shut, Jimmy began sliding tables and chairs against the door. He created a huge tangle of them, tossing more chairs on top of the pile, shivering and cursing beneath his beard while Shadow spun in circles.

"Gross, gross, gross," he told Shadow, whose hair had not yet settled. He studied his barricade against the piles of dead and hoped it would be adequate, that he hadn't let out too many ghosts. The remnants of old rope swayed on the door's handle, and Jimmy thanked whomever had kept these people at bay.

"Let's go," he said, and Shadow swished against his leg for comfort. There was no view on the wallscreen to see, no food or tools of any use. He'd had quite enough of the Top, which suddenly felt crowded to the walls with the dead.

95

Besides food, Shadow had a nose for trouble. A nose for causing it. Jimmy woke one morning to an awful screeching sound, a pathetic and plaintive hiss spilling down the corridor. Jimmy had climbed the ladder half-asleep to find Shadow stuck near the top rung. He didn't know how the cat had got there, and the cat didn't know how to get down. Jimmy released the hatch over their heads and threw it aside. He watched as Shadow clawed up the metal mesh behind the ladder, his back pressed against the rungs, and scampered over the top.

Two mornings later, the same thing happened, and that's when Jimmy decided to leave the hatch open all the time. He was sick of opening and closing as he came and went, and Shadow liked being able to explore the server room whenever he liked. There hadn't been any fighting in a long time, and the great steel door still winked red.

Shadow loved the servers. Most times, Jimmy would find him up on server number 40, where the metal was so hot Jimmy could hardly touch. But Shadow didn't mind. He slept up there or peered over the edge at the ground far below, watching for bugs and mice on which to pounce.

Other times, Jimmy found him standing in the corner where that man he'd shot forever ago had wasted away. Shadow liked to sniff the rust stains and touch his tongue to the grating, divining what had happened there. It was for these freedoms that the hatch remained off. And this was how, when the power went out big-time, the bad men got inside. This was how Jimmy woke up one morning with a stranger standing over his bed.

••••

The outage had woken him in the middle of the night. Jimmy slept with the lights full-on, keeping the ghosts at bay. He even liked a little of the radio static to fill the room, so he couldn't hear any whisperings. When the silence and darkness hit at once with a loud thump, Jimmy had startled awake and scrambled for his flashlight, stepping on Shadow's tail in the process. He waited for the lights to come on, but they never did. Too tired to think what to do, he went back to sleep, both hands wrapped around his torch, Shadow curling up warily against his neck.

The noise of someone coming down the ladder was likely what stirred him later. Jimmy was dimly aware of a presence in the room. It was a sensation often felt, but this presence seemed to change the way the silence bounced around, the way even the noise of his breathing echoed. He opened his eyes to find a flashlight shining down on him, a man standing at the foot of his bed.

Jimmy screamed, and the man pounced with half a mind to silence him. A bearded snarl of yellowed teeth caught the beam of light, and then the arc of a steel rod—

There was a flash of pain in Jimmy's shoulder. The man hauled back to hit him again with his length of pipe. Jimmy got his arms up to protect his head. The pipe cracked him on the wrist. There was a screech and a hiss by his head, and then a darting piece of black amid the shadows.

The man with the pipe screamed and dropped his flashlight, which doused itself in the bedsheets. Jimmy scrambled away, his mind unable to come to grips with a person in his home. A person in his home. The fear of years and years came true in an instant. All his precautions had loosened. All the venturing out. Slack, slack, he told himself, crawling on his hands and knees.

Shadow screeched an awful sound, the noise he made when his tail got stepped on. A howl of pain followed. Jimmy felt anger rise up and mix with fear, a potent brew. He crawled toward the corner, banged into the desk, reached for where it should be propped—

His hands settled around the gun. It'd been years since he'd fired it. Couldn't remember if it was even loaded. But he could still swing it like a club if he had to. He cradled it against his shoulder and waved the barrel through the pitch black. Shadow screeched again. There was a thump of a small body hitting something hard. Jimmy couldn't breathe or swallow. He couldn't see anything but the dim glow of light rising up from the folds of his bed.

He pointed the barrel at a patch of blackness that seemed to move, and squeezed the trigger. There was a blinding flash of light from the muzzle, a roar that filled the small space to the seams. In that brief strobe flashed the searing image of a man whirling toward him. Another wild shot. Another glimpse of this stranger in Jimmy's space, a thin man with a long beard and white eyes. And now Jimmy knew where he was, and the third shot did not zing. Its impact was lost in screams. The screams filled the darkness, and then a final shot put an end to even these.

•••

Shadow's eyes glowed beneath the desk. He peered our warily at Jimmy and his new flashlight.

"You okay?" Jimmy asked.

The cat blinked.

"Stay here," Jimmy whispered.

He cradled the flashlight between his cheek and shoulder and checked the clip. Before he left, he nudged the man who was bleeding on his sheets. Jimmy felt a strange numbness at seeing someone down there, even dead. He listened for more intruders as he stole his way toward the ladder.

The power outage and this attack were no coincidence, he told himself. Someone had gotten the door open. They had figured the keypad or pulled a breaker. Jimmy hoped this man had done it alone. He didn't recognize the face, but a lot of years had passed. Beards got long and turned gray. The silver coveralls hinted at someone who might know how to break in. The pain in his shoulder and wrist hinted at no friend of his.

There was no one on the ladder. Jimmy slipped the rifle over his shoulder and doused the flashlight so no one would see him coming. His palms made the softest of rings on the metal rungs. He was halfway up when he felt Shadow slithering and clacking his way up between the ladder and the wall.

Jimmy hissed at the cat to stay put, but it disappeared ahead of him. At the top of the ladder, Jimmy unslung his rifle and held it in one hand. With the other, he pressed the flashlight against his stomach and turned it on. Peeling the lens away from his coveralls a little at a time, he cast just enough glow to pick his way through the servers.

There was a noise ahead of him, Shadow or another person, he couldn't tell. Jimmy hesitated before continuing on. It took forever to cross the wide room with the dark machines like this. He could hear them still clacking, still whirring, still putting off heat. But when he got close to the door, the keypad was no longer blinking its sentinel light at him. And there was a void beyond the gleaming door—a door that stood halfway open.

More noise outside. The rustle of fabric, of a person moving. Jimmy killed the flashlight and steadied his rifle. He could taste the fear in his mouth. He wanted to call out for these people to leave him alone. He wanted to say what he had done to all those who came inside. He wanted to drop his gun and cry and beg to never have to do it again.

He poked his head out into the hall and strained to see in the darkness, hoped this other person couldn't see him back. The hall contained nothing but the sound of two people breathing. There was this growing awareness that a dark space was shared with another.

"Hank?" someone whispered.

Jimmy turned and squeezed the trigger. There was a flash of light. The rifle kicked him in the shoulder and kicked someone else worse. He retreated into the server room and waited for screams and stomping boots. He waited what felt like forever. Something touched his boot, and Jimmy screamed. It was Shadow purring and rubbing against him.

Chancing his torch, he peered around the corner and allowed some light to dribble out. There was a form there, a person on their back. He checked the deep and dark hallways and saw nothing. "Leave me alone!" he yelled out to all the ghosts and more solid things.

Not even his echo called back.

Jimmy looked over this second man only to discover it wasn't a man at all. It was a woman. Her eyes had thankfully fallen shut. A man and a woman coming for his food, coming to steal from him. It made Jimmy angry. And then he saw the woman's swollen and distended belly, and got doubly angry. It wasn't like they were hurting for food, he thought.

96

A fter the incident with the bad people, it was good to get away for a while. Locating the missing breaker hadn't fixed the doors, and two days of playing with the wires hanging from the keypad had gotten him nowhere. It made a night of sound sleep impossible, even with the grate back in place. Shadow climbed to the top of the ladder at night and mewed and mewed. Jimmy thought they needed to get away and go do their favorite thing.

Sitting on the lowest of the dry landings, Jimmy watched flashes of silver dart below, watched them twist beneath and through the flooded stairs. They looked like flashlights aimed from the drowned deep, like beams pointed skyward toward him and Shadow as the two of them peered over the edge of the landing.

Shadow's black tail swished back and forth in the air. His paws hugged the edge of the rusted steel grating, whiskers twitching. For all his consternation, however, Jimmy's bobber remained unmoved.

"Not hungry today," Jimmy said. He whistled a tune for the fish, a catching-fish tune, and Shadow peered up at him, a critic with an unreadable face. Jimmy's stomach growled. "I don't mean us," he told Shadow. "We're plenty hungry. I mean the fish."

Jimmy was hungry from digging for worms all morning. They were hard to find among the overgrowth of the farms. It was hot work when the lights were on, but it kept his mind off the people he'd hurt. He'd been so consumed by that and the promise of a day fishing that he hadn't eaten the veggies that were right there as he dug with his shovel. It was a lot of damn work, catching these fish. First, you had to catch the worms! Jimmy wondered, if the fish liked them so much, why he and Shadow didn't save themselves the trouble and just eat worms. But when he'd held one out, the cat had looked at him like he was crazy.

"I'm not crazy," he had assured Shadow.

He found himself insisting this more and more.

While Jimmy explained that it was the fish that weren't hungry that day, Shadow went back to studying the darting swimmers below. Jimmy did the same. They reminded him of spilled mercury, of a thermometer he broke years back. They changed directions and moved so fast.

He grabbed his pole, lifted his bobber out of the water, and checked the hook. The worm was still on there. Good thing. He only had a few left, and the nearest dirt was a dozen flights up. He lowered the line back into the water, the ping-pong ball resting on the surface. He had learned about fishing from the Legacy. Learned how to tie knots and fix a bobber and sinker, what kind of bait to use, all these instructions that came in perfect handy. It was as if the people who wrote those books somehow knew these things would be important some day.

He watched the fish swim and wondered how they'd gotten in the water. The tanks were a bunch of levels up above the farms, and now they were empty of fish. Jimmy had checked. All he found was algae that looked awful but that made the water in the vats taste pretty good. There were cups and jugs and even the beginnings of a hose to carry the water off to other levels, a Project someone had abandoned years back. Jimmy wondered if they'd dumped the fish over the railing, and now here they were. However it'd happened, he was glad.

There were only a dozen or so of them left. They didn't breed as fast as he could catch them. And the ones that remained were the hardest to catch. They'd watched what happens. They'd seen. They were like Jimmy in those early days, watching the people spiral up to their deaths. They knew like his mother had known that they didn't want to go that way. So they nibbled and nibbled until the worms were gone. But sometimes they couldn't help themselves. They'd get a taste and take a bite instead of a nibble, and then Jimmy would have them up in the air, dripping and dancing, flopping on the rusted grate until he could wrangle their slippery flesh in his fist and work the hook loose.

First, though, the waiting. Jimmy's bobber sat motionless on the rainbow-hued water. Shadow mewed impatiently.

"Listen to you," Jimmy said. "Two years ago, you didn't know what a fish tasted like."

Shadow crouched down on his belly and pawed at the air between the landing and the water as if to say, "I used to catch these all the time."

"I'm sure you did," Jimmy said, rolling his eyes. He watched the water, which had come up quite a ways since his first time down. The level he had rescued Shadow from was now completely gone. Fish likely lived in the room he'd found Shadow in. He peered down at his feline friend, a new thought coming to him.

"Is that what you were doing in there all that time ago?" he asked.

Shadow looked up at him with a face full of innocence.

"You devil."

The cat licked his paw, turned a circle, and watched for the bobber to move.

It moved.

Jimmy gave the pole a yank and felt resistance, the weight of a fish on his hook. He squealed and lifted the pole and reached out over the rail to grab the line. Shadow mewed and danced and tried to help by swiping at the air and swishing his tail.

"Here, here," Jimmy told the fish. He hauled the line up and rested the pole against the railing, reached over and grabbed more line, the flopping of the fish causing it to dig into his fingers. "Easy, now." He pursed his lips, could never feel like he'd truly caught one of the buggers until he got them over the rail and above the grate of the landing. Sometimes they spit the hook and got the worm for free and laughed at him as they splashed back home.

"Here we go," he told Shadow. He lowered the fish to the metal and got a boot on its tail. He hated this part. The fish looked so upset. This was when he would change his mind and wish he could throw the thing back, but Shadow was already swirling around his legs and swishing his tail. Jimmy held the fish still with his boot and dug the homemade hook out of its lip. The little barb he'd made by bending the needle back before pounding a new point made it hard to get free, but Jimmy had learned that this was the point.

"The point," he said, laughing at his own joke.

Shadow told him to hurry up.

Jimmy tossed the hook and line over the top of the rail to get it out of the way. The fish threw itself against the grating a few times. It peered up at him with its wide eye, its mouth panting frantically. Jimmy reached for his knife.

"I'm sorry," he said. "So, so sorry."

He stuck the knife in the fish's head to stop its pain. He looked away while he did this. So much death. Lifetimes of death. But Shadow was already acting so happy. The life dribbled out of the fish and into the water below. The handful of fish that remained darted up to gobble at the places the blood hit the water, and Jimmy wondered why they did that. There was none of this that he enjoyed, not the digging for worms, or the long hike, or the setting of hooks, or the killing, or the cleaning—but he did it anyway.

He cleaned the fish the way the Legacy showed, a slice behind the gills, and then a swipe along the bone toward the tail. Two runs of the knife like this, and he had two pieces of meat. He left the scales on, since Shadow never touched that part. Both fillets went onto a chipped plate near the stairwell.

Shadow spun in circles a few times, his belly making that thrumming noise, then began tearing at the flesh with his teeth.

Jimmy retired to the other end of the railing. He had a towel there. He wiped his hands of the foul slickness and sat down, his back against the closed doors of level one-thirty-one, and watched the cat eat. Silvery shapes darted below. The landing and all else seemed calm in the pale green glow of the emergency stairwell lights.

Before long, there wouldn't be any fish left. Another year at this rate, and Jimmy figured he'd catch them all.

"But not the last one," he told himself as he watched Shadow eat. Jimmy hadn't tasted a fish yet and didn't think he ever would. The catching of them was too much work, little of it fun, much of it disgusting. But he thought, when he came down one day with his rod and his jar of dirt and worms and saw only one fish remained, that he would leave it alone. Just the one, he thought, as he watched Shadow eat. It would be scared enough down there. No need to go yanking it out into the frightful air. Just let the poor thing be.

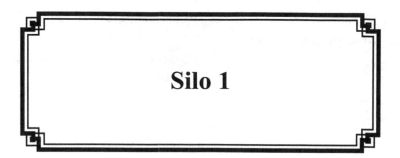

Silo 1

•97•

onald set his alarm for three in the morning, but there was little chance of him falling asleep. He'd waited weeks for this. A chance to give a life rather than take one. A chance at redemption and a chance for the truth, a chance to satisfy his growing suspicions.

He stared at the ceiling and considered what he was about to do. It wasn't what Erskine or Victor had hoped he would do if someone like him was ever in charge, but those men had gotten a lot wrong, least of all who he was. This wasn't the end of the end of the world. This was the beginning of something else. An end to the not knowing what was out there.

He studied his hand in the dim light spilling from the bathroom and thought of the outside. At two-thirty, he decided he'd waited long enough. He got up, showered and shaved, put on a fresh pair of coveralls, tugged on his boots. He grabbed his badge and clipped it to his collar. He had a mind to sneak out, to slink down the hallway, but that was the wrong way. He left his apartment with his head up and shoulders back, instead. Long strides took him down a hall with a few lights still on and the distant clatter of a keyboard, someone working late. The door to Eren's office was closed. Donald called for the elevator and waited.

Before heading all the way down, he checked to see if it would be all for naught by scanning his badge and pressing the shiny button marked fifty-four. The light flashed, and the lift lurched into motion. So far, so good. The elevator didn't stop until it reached the armory. The doors opened on a familiar darkness studded with tall shadows—black cliffs of shelves and bins. Donald held his hand on the edge of the door to keep it from shutting and stepped out into the room. The vastness of the space could somehow be felt, like the echoes of his racing pulse were being swallowed by the distance. He waited for a light to flick on at the far end, for Anna to walk out brushing her hair or with a bottle of scotch in her hand. But nothing in that room moved. Everything was quiet and still. The pilots and the temporary activity were gone.

He returned to the lift and pressed another button. The elevator sank. It drifted past more storage levels, past the reactor. The doors cracked on the medical wing. Donald could feel the tens of thousands of bodies arranged all around him, all facing the ceiling, eyelids closed. Some of them were well and truly dead, he thought. One was about to be woken.

He went straight to the doctor's office and knocked on the jamb. The assistant on duty lifted his head from behind the monitor. He wiped his eyes behind his glasses, adjusted them on his nose, and blinked at Donald.

"How's it going?" Donald asked.

"Hmm? Good. Good." The young man shook his wrist and checked his watch, an ancient thing. "We got someone going into deep freeze? I didn't get a call. Is Wilson up?"

"No, no. I just couldn't sleep." Donald pointed at the ceiling. "I went to see if anyone was up at the cafeteria, then figured since I was restless, I might as well come down here and see if you wanted me to finish out your shift. I can sit and watch a film as well as anyone."

The assistant glanced at his monitor and laughed guiltily. "Yeah." He checked his watch again, had somehow already forgotten what it just told him. "Two hours left. I wouldn't mind slagging off. You'll wake me if anything pops up?" He stood and stretched, covered his yawn with his hand.

"Of course."

The medical assistant staggered out from behind the desk. Donald stepped around and pulled the seat away, sat down and propped up his feet as though he wouldn't be going anywhere for hours.

"I owe you one," the young man said, collecting his coat from the back of the door.

"Oh, we're even," Donald said under his breath as soon as the man was gone.

He waited for the elevator to chime before launching into action. There was a plastic drink container on the drying rack by the sink. He grabbed this and filled it with water, the musical pitch of the vessel filling like a rising anxiety.

The lid came off the powder. Two scoops. He stirred with one of the long plastic tongue depressors and twisted the lid on, put the powder back in the fridge. The wheelchair wouldn't budge at first. He saw that the brakes were on, the little metal arms pressing into the soft rubber. He freed these, grabbed one of the blankets from the tall cabinet and a paper gown, tossed them onto the seat. Just like before. But he'd do it right this time. He collected the medical kit, made sure there was a fresh set of gloves.

The wheelchair rattled out the door and down the hall, and Donald's palms felt sweaty against the handles. To keep the front wheels silent, he rocked the chair back on its large rubber tires. The small wheels spun lazily in the air as he hurried.

He entered his code into the keypad and waited for a red light, for some impediment, some blockade. The light winked green. Donald pulled the door open and swerved between the pods toward the one that held his sister.

There was a mix of anticipation and guilt. This was as bold a step as his run up that hill in a suit. The stakes were higher for involving family, for waking someone into this harsh world, for subjecting her to the same brutality Anna had foisted upon him, that Thurman had foisted upon her, on and on, a never ending misery of shifts.

He left the wheelchair in place and knelt by the control pad. Hesitant, he lurched to his feet and peered through the glass porthole, just to make sure.

She looked so serene in there, probably wasn't plagued by nightmares like he was. Donald's doubts grew. And then he imagined her waking up on her own; he imagined her conscious and beating on the glass, demanding to be let out. He saw her feisty spirit, heard her demand not to be lied to, and he knew that if she were standing there with him, she would ask him to do it. She would rather know and suffer than be left asleep in ignorance.

This is what Donald told himself, anyway. He crouched by the keypad and entered his code. The keypad beeped cheerfully as he pressed the red button. There was a click from within the pod, like a valve opening. He turned the dial and watched the temperature gauge, waited for it to start climbing.

Donald rose and stood by the pod, and time slowed to a crawl. He expected someone to come find him before the process was complete. But there was another clack and a hiss from the lid. He laid out the gauze and the tape. He separated the two rubber gloves and began pulling them on, a cloud of chalk misting the air as he snapped the elastic.

He opened the lid the rest of the way.

His sister lay on her back, her arms by her side. She had not yet moved. Donald seemed to remember having moved by the time the lid opened, but he couldn't remember. A panic seized him as he went over the procedure again. Had he forgotten something? Dear god, had he killed her?

Charlotte coughed. Water trailed down her cheeks as the frost on her lids melted. And then her eyes fluttered open weakly before returning to thin slits against the light.

"Hold still," Donald told her. He pressed a square of gauze to her arm and removed the needle. He could feel the steel slide beneath the pad and his fingers as he extracted it from her arm. Holding the gauze in place, he took a length of tape hanging from the wheelchair and applied it across the gauze. The last was the catheter. He covered her with the towel, applied pressure, and slowly removed the tube. And then she was free of the machine, crossing her arms and shivering. He helped her into the paper gown, left the back open.

"I'm lifting you out," he said.

Her teeth clattered in response.

Donald shifted her feet toward her butt to tent her knees. Reaching down beneath her armpits—her flesh cool to the touch—and another arm under her legs, he lifted her easily. It felt like she weighed so little. He could smell the cast-stink on her flesh.

Charlotte mumbled something as he placed her in the wheelchair. The blanket was draped across so that she sat on the fabric rather than the cold seat. As soon as she was settled, he wrapped the blanket around her. She chose to remain in a ball with her arms wrapped around her shins rather than place her feet on the stirrups.

"Where am I?" she asked, her voice a sheet of crackling ice.

"Take it easy," Donald told her. He closed the lid on the pod, tried to remember if there was anything else, looked for anything he'd left behind. "You're with me," he said as he pushed her toward the exit. That was where both of them were: with each other. There was no home, no place on the Earth to welcome one to anymore, just a hellish nightmare in which to drag another for sad company.

•98•

The hardest part was making her wait to eat. Donald knew what it felt like to be that hungry. He put her through the same routine he'd endured a number of times: made her drink the bitter concoction, made her use the bathroom to flush her system, had her sit on the edge of the tub and take a warm but not hot shower, then put her in a fresh set of clothes and a new blanket.

He watched as she finished the last of the drink. Her lips gradually faded to pink from pale blue. Her skin was so white. Donald couldn't remember if it'd been white like that before orientation. Maybe it'd happened overseas, sitting in those dark trailers with only the light of a monitor to bathe in.

"I need to go make an appearance," he told her. "Everyone else will be getting up. I'll bring you breakfast on my way back down."

Charlotte sat quietly in one of the leather chairs around the old war planning table, her feet tucked up under her. She tugged at the collar of the coveralls as if they itched her skin. "Mom and Dad are gone," she said, repeating what he'd told her earlier. Donald wasn't sure what she would and wouldn't remember. She hadn't been on her stress medications as long or as recently as him. But it didn't matter. He could tell her the truth. Tell her and hate himself for doing it.

"I'll be back in a little bit. Just stay here and try to get some rest. Don't leave this room, okay?"

The words echoed hollow as he hurried through the warehouse and toward the elevator. He remembered hearing from others as soon as they woke him that he should get some rest. He was usually on the other side of that advice, thinking those dispensing it were out of their minds. Charlotte had been asleep for three centuries. As he scanned his badge and waited for the elevator, Donald thought on how much time had passed and how little had changed. The world was still the ruin they'd left it. Or if it wasn't, they were about to find out.

He rode up to the operations level. The express was anything but. It stopped twice to pick up four others with sleep in their eyes and a shuffle in their step. They rode in silence, all in coveralls of various hues, like men in a factory from the olden days heading to another Monday morning. Always Mondays in that place. Six months of Mondays. No weekends to look forward to.

The lift spilled them into the hall. Donald felt a chill from the thought that his sister was down below, awake and alone. He felt an impatience like bugs beneath his skin, urging him forward faster than he could go.

He checked with Eren, knocked on his doorframe. The Ops Head was already at his desk, surrounded by files, one hand tangled in his hair, his elbow on piles of paperwork. There was no steam from his mug of coffee. He'd been at his desk a while.

"Thurman," he said, glancing up.

Donald startled and glanced down the hall, looking for someone else.

"Any progress with 18?"

"I, uh . . ." Donald tried to remember. "Last I heard, they'd breached the barrier in the lowest levels. The Head over there thinks the fighting will be over in a day or two."

"Good. Glad the shadow is working out. Scary time not to have one. There was this one time on my third shift I think it was when we lost a Head while he was between shadows. Helluva time finding a recruit." Eren leaned back in his chair. "The mayor wasn't an option; the head of Security was as bright as a lump of coal; so we had to—"

"I'm sorry to interrupt," Donald said, pointing down the hall. "I need to get back to—"

"Oh, of course." Eren waved his hand, seemed embarrassed. "Right. Me too."

"—just a lot to do this morning. Grabbing breakfast and then I'll be in my room." He jerked his head toward the empty office across the hall. "Tell Gable I took care of myself, okay? I don't want to be disturbed."

"Sure, sure." Eren shooed him with his hand.

Donald spun back to the elevator. Up to the cafeteria. His stomach rumbled its agreement. He'd been up all night without eating. He'd been up and empty for far too long.

• 99 •

He was pushing the time limit by letting her eat an hour early, but it was hard to say no. Donald encouraged her to take small bites, to slow down. And while Charlotte chewed, he caught her up. She knew about the silos from orientation. He told her about the wallscreens, about the cleaners, that he was woken because someone had disappeared. Charlotte had a hard time grasping these things. It took saying them several times until they became strange even to his ears.

"They let them see outside, these people in the other silos?" She chewed on a small bite of biscuit.

"Yeah. I asked Thurman once why we put them there. You know what he told me?"

Charlotte shrugged and took a sip of water.

"They're there to keep them from wanting to leave. We have to show them death to keep them in. Otherwise, they'll always want to see what's over the rise. Thurman said it's human nature."

"But some of them go anyway." She wiped her mouth with her napkin, picked up her fork, her hand trembling, and pulled Donald's half-eaten breakfast toward her.

"Yeah, some of them go anyway," Donald said. "And you need to take it easy." He watched her dig into his eggs and thought about his own trip up the drone lift. He was one of those people who had gone anyway. It wasn't something she needed to know.

"We have one of those screens," Charlotte said. "I remember watching the clouds boil." She looked up at Donald. "Why do we have one?"

Donald reached quickly for his handkerchief and coughed into its folds. "Because we're human," he answered, tucking the cloth away. "If we think there's no way to see what's out there—that we'll die if we go—we'll stay here and do what we're told. But I know of another way to see what's out there."

"Yeah—?" Charlotte scraped the last of his eggs onto her fork and lifted them to her mouth. She waited.

"And I'm going to need your help to get there."

• • • •

They pulled the tarp off one of the drones. Charlotte ran her hand down its wing and walked around the machine like a jockey circling a horse before a race. Grabbing the flap on the back of a wing, she worked it up and down. Did the same for the tail. The drone had a black dome and nose that gave it something like a face. It sat silently, unmoving, while Charlotte inspected it. Donald noticed that three of the other drones were missing—the floor was glossy where their tarps used to drape. And the neat pyramid of bombs in the munitions rack was missing its top cheerleader. Signs of the armory's use these past weeks. Donald went to the hangar door and worked it open.

"No hardware?" Charlotte asked. She peered under one of the wings where bad things could be attached.

"No," Donald said. "Not for this." He ran back and helped her push. They steered the drone toward the open maw of the lift. The wings just barely fit.

"There should be a strap or a linkage," she said. She crawled behind the drone and wiggled in beneath the wing.

"There's something in the floor," Donald said, remembering the nub that moved along the track. "I'll get a light."

He retrieved a flashlight from one of the bins, made sure it had a charge, and brought it back to her. Charlotte hooked the drone into the launch mechanism and squirmed her way out. She seemed slow to stand. He gave his sister a hand, remembering when they were young.

"And you're sure this lift'll work?" She brushed hair, still wet from the shower, off her face.

"Very sure," Donald said. He led her down the hall, past the barracks and bathrooms.

Charlotte stiffened when he led her into the piloting room and pulled back the plastic sheets. He flipped the switch on the lift controls. She stared blankly at one of the stations with its joysticks, readouts, and screens.

"You can operate this, right?" he asked.

She broke from her trance and stared at him a moment, then nodded her head. "If they'll power up."

"They will." He watched the light above the lift controls flash while Charlotte settled behind one of the stations. The room felt overly quiet and empty with all those other stations sitting under sheets of plastic. The dust was gone from them, Donald saw. The place was recently lived in. He thought of the requisitions he'd signed for flights, each one at considerable cost. Eren had stressed the one-use nature of the drones. The air outside was bad for them, he'd said. Their range was limited. Donald had thought about why this might be as he dug through Thurman's files.

Charlotte flicked several switches, the neat clicks breaking the silence, and the control station whirred to life.

"The lift takes a while," he told her. He didn't say how he knew, but he thought back to that ride up all those years ago. He remembered his breath fogging the dome of his helmet as he rose to what he had hoped might be his death. Now he had a different hope. He thought of what Erskine had told him about wiping the Earth clean. He thought about Victor's suicide note to Thurman. This project of theirs was about resetting life. And Donald, whether by madness or reason, had grown convinced that the effort was more precise than anyone had rights to imagine.

Charlotte adjusted her screen. She flicked a switch, and a light bloomed on the monitor. It was the glare of the steel door of the lift, lit up by the drone's headlamp and viewed by its cameras.

"It's been so long," she said. Donald looked down and saw that her hands were trembling. She rubbed them together before returning them to the controls. Wiggling in her seat, she located the pedals with her feet, and then adjusted the brightness of the monitor so it wasn't so blinding.

"Is there anything I can do?" Donald asked.

Charlotte laughed and shook her head. "No. Feels strange not to be filing a flight plan or anything. I usually have a target, you know?" She looked back at Donald and flashed a smile.

He squeezed her shoulder. It felt good to have her around. He thought of their parents and Helen and everyone else he'd let down. She was all he had left. "Your flight plan is to fly as far and as fast as you can," he told her. His hope was that without a bomb, the drone would go farther. His hope was that the limited range wasn't programmed somehow. There was a flashing light from the lift controls. Donald hurried over to check them.

"The door's coming up," Charlotte said. "I think we've got daylight."

Donald hurried back over. He glanced out the door and down the hall, thinking he'd heard something.

"Engine check," Charlotte said. "We've got ignition."

She wiggled in her seat. The coveralls he'd stolen for her were too big, were bunched around her arms. Donald stood behind her and watched the monitor, which showed a view of swirling skies up a sloped ramp. He remembered that view. It became difficult to breathe, seeing that. The drone was pulled from the lift and arranged on the ramp. Charlotte hit another switch.

"Brakes on," she said, her leg straightening. "Applying thrust."

Her hand slid forward. The camera view dipped as the drone strained against its brakes.

"Been a long time since I've done this without a launcher," she said nervously.

Donald was about to ask if that was a problem when she shifted her feet and the view on the screen lifted. The metal shaft he remembered climbing up vibrated and began to race by. The swirling clouds filled the viewscreen until that was all that existed. Charlotte said, "Liftoff," and worked the yoke with her right hand. Donald found himself leaning to the side as the view banked and the ground came into view.

"Which way?" she asked.

"I don't think it matters," he said. "Just straight." He leaned closer to watch the strange but familiar landscape slide by. There were the great divots he had helped create. There was another tower down in the middle of a depression. The remnants of the convention—the tents and fairgrounds and stages—were long gone, eaten by the tiny machines in the air. "Just a straight line," he said, pointing. It was a theory, a crazy idea, but he needed to see before he dared say anything. There was the danger of making it not true by voicing his most cherished hope. The world seemed to sense these things from him. He had learned to guard his wishes, just to be safe. Thinking them was like shining a light out to sea, and Donald lived among reef and rock. Drawing good things toward him was unwise.

The pattern of depressions ended in the distance. Donald strained to see beyond when Charlotte let go of the throttle and reached for a bank of dials and indicators. "Uh . . . I think we have a problem." She flipped a switch back and forth. "I'm losing oil pressure."

"No." Donald watched the screen as the clouds swirled and the land seemed to heave upward. It was too early. Unless he'd missed some step, some precaution, some way of turning off other, smaller, flying things. "Keep going," he breathed, as much to the machine as to its pilot.

"She's handling screwy," Charlotte said. "Everything feels loose."

Donald thought of all the drones in the hangar. They could launch another. But he suspected the results would be the same. He might be resistant to whatever was out there, but the machines weren't. He thought of the cleaning suits, the way things were meant to break down at a certain time, a certain place. Invisible destroyers so precise that they could let loose their vengeance as soon as a cleaner hit a hill, reached a particular altitude, as soon as they dared to rise up. He reached for his cloth and coughed into it, and had a vague memory of them scrubbing the airlock after pulling him back inside.

"You're at the edge," he said, pointing to the last of the silos as its bowl disappeared beneath the drone's camera. "Just a little further."

But in truth, he had no idea how much further it might take. Maybe you could fly straight around the world and right back where you started, and that still wouldn't be far enough. But he didn't think so.

"I'm losing lift," Charlotte said. Her hands were twin blurs. They went from the controls to switches and back again. Donald thought of the seals and gaskets. Maybe they could be replaced. Beefed up.

"Engine two is out," she said. "Altitude oh-two-hundred."

It looked like far less on the screen. They were beyond the last of the hills, now. There was a scar in the earth, a trench that may have been a river, black sticks like charred bones that stuck up in sharp points like pencil lead, all that remained of ancient trees, perhaps. Or the steel girders of a large security fence, eaten away by time.

"Go, go," he whispered. Every second aloft was a new sight, a new vista. Here was a breath of freedom, a giant's step, a leap of leagues. Here was escape from hell.

"Camera's going. Altitude oh-one-fifty."

There was a bright flash on the screen like the shock of dying electrics. A purplish cast followed from the frying sensors, then a wash of blue where once there was nothing but browns and grays.

"Altitude fifty feet. Gonna touch down hard."

Donald blinked away tears as the drone plummeted and the earth rushed up to meet the machine. He blinked away tears at the sight on the monitor, nothing wrong with the camera at all.

"Blue—" he said.

It was an utterance of confirmation just before a vivid green landscape swallowed the dying drone, just as the monitor faded from color to black. Charlotte released the controls and cursed. She slapped the console with her palm. But as she turned and apologized to Donald, he was already wrapping his arms around her, squeezing her, kissing her cheek.

"Did you see it?" he asked, his voice a breathless whisper. "Did you see?"

"See what?" Charlotte pulled away, her face a hardened mask of disappointment. "Every gauge was toast there at the end. Blasted drone. Probably been sitting too long—"

"No, no," Donald said. He pointed to the screen, which was now dark and lifeless. "You did it," he said. "I saw it. There were blue skies and green grass out there, Charla! I saw it!"

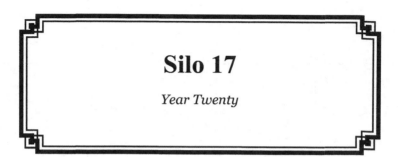

Silo 17

Year Twenty

· 100 ·

Without wanting to, Solo became an expert in how things broke down. Day by day, he watched steel and iron crumble to rust, watched paint peel and orange flecks curl up, saw the black dust gather as metal eroded to powder. He learned what rubber hoses felt like as they hardened, dried up, and cracked. He learned how adhesives failed, things appearing on the floor that once were affixed to walls and ceilings, objects moved suddenly and violently by the twin gods of gravity and dilapidation. Most of all, he learned how bodies rot. They didn't always go in a flash—like a mother pushed upward by a jostling crowd or a father sliding into the shadows of a darkened corridor. Instead, they were often chewed up and carried off in invisible pieces. Time and maggots alike grew wings; they flew and flew and took all things with them.

Solo tore a page from one of the boring articles in the Ri - Ro book and folded it into a tent. The silo, he thought, belonged to the insects in many ways. Wherever the bodies were gathered, the insects swarmed in dark clouds. He had read up on them in the books. Somehow, maggots turned into flies. White and writhing became black and buzzing. Things broke down and changed.

He threaded lengths of string into the folded piece of paper to give something to hang the weight on. This was when Shadow would normally get in the way, would come and arch his back against Solo's arm, step on whatever he was doing, make him annoyed and make him laugh at the same time. But Shadow didn't interrupt.

Solo made small knots in the string to keep them from pulling through. The paper was doubled over across the holes so it wouldn't tear. He well knew how things broke down. He was an expert in things he wished he could unlearn. Solo could tell at a glance how long it'd been since someone had died.

The people he'd killed years back had been stiff when he moved them, but this only lasted a while. People soon swelled up and stank. Their bodies let off gasses, and the flies swarmed. The flies swarmed and the maggots feasted.

The stench would make his eyes water and throat burn. And the bodies would soon grow soft. Solo had to move some on the stairs once, tangled where they lay and difficult to step over, and the flesh came right apart. It became like cottage cheese he'd had back when there was still milk and goats to get them from. Flesh came apart once the person was no longer inside, holding themselves together. Solo concentrated on holding himself together. He tied the other ends of the strings to one of the small metal washers from Supply. Chewing his tongue, he made the finest of knots.

String and fabric didn't last either, but clothes stayed around longer than people. Within a year, it was clothes and bones that were left. And hair. The hair seemed to go last. It clung to bones and sometimes hung over empty and gazing sockets. The hair made it worse. It lent bones an identity. Beards on most, but not on the young or the women.

Within five years, even the clothes would break down. After ten, it was mostly bones. These days, so very long after the silo had gone dark and quiet—over twenty years since he'd been shown the secret lair beneath the servers—it was only the bones. Except for up in the cafe. The rot everywhere else made those bodies behind that door curiouser and curiouser.

Solo held up his parachute, a paper tent with little strings fastened to a tiny washer. He had dozens and dozens of bits of string laying in tangles across the open book. A handful of washers remained. He gave one of the strings on his parachute a tug and thought of the bodies up in the cafeteria. Behind that door, there were dead people who wouldn't break down like the others. When he and Shadow had first discovered them, he'd assumed they'd recently passed. Dozens of them, dying together and piled on one another like they'd been tossed in there or had been crawling atop the others. The door to the forbidden outside was just beyond them, Solo knew. But he hadn't gone that far. He had closed the door and left in a hurry, spooked by the lifeless eyeballs and the strange feeling of seeing a face other than his own peering back at him like that. He had left the bodies and not come back for a long time. He had waited for them to become bones. But they refused.

He went to the rail and peered over, made sure the piece of paper was tented, ready to grab the air. There was a cool updraft from the flooded deep. Solo leaned out beyond the third level railing, the fine paper pinched in one hand, the washer resting in his other palm. He wondered why some people rotted and others kept going. What made them break down?

"Break down," he said aloud. He liked the way his voice sounded sometimes. He was an expert in how things broke down. Shadow should've been there, rubbing against his ankles, but he wasn't.

"I'm an expert," Solo told himself. "Breaking down, breaking down." He stretched out his arms and released the parachute, watched it plummet for a moment before the strings went taut. And then it bobbed and twisted in the air as it sank into the dwindling depths. "Down down down," he called after the parachute. All the way to the bottom. Sinking until it splashed invisible or got caught up along the way.

Solo knew well how bodies rot. He scratched his beard and squinted after the disappearing chute, then sat back down and crossed his legs, the knee torn completely out of his old coveralls. He mumbled to himself, delaying what needed to be done, his Project for the day, and instead tore another page from the shrinking book, trying not to think about yet another carcass that would soon dwindle with time.

· 101 ·

There had been items Solo spent days and weeks searching for. There had been some things he'd needed that had consumed his hunts for years. Often, he found useful things much later, when he needed them no longer. Like the time he had come across a stash of razors. A great big bin of them in a doctor's office. All the important stuff—the bandages, medicine, the tape—had long ago been snagged by those fighting over the scraps. But a bin of new razors, many of the blades still shiny, taunted him. He had long before resigned himself to his beard, but there had been times before that when he would've killed for a razor.

Other times, he found a thing before he even knew he needed it. The machete was like that. A great blade found beneath the body of a man not long dead. Solo had taken it simply so nobody else would have the murderous thing. He had locked himself below the server room for three days, terrified of the sight of another still-warm body. That had been many years ago. It took a while longer for the farms to thicken up where the machete became necessary. By then, he had taken to leaving his gun behind—no longer any use for it—and the machete became a constant companion. Something found before he knew he needed it.

Solo set the last of the parachutes free and watched as it narrowly missed the landing on level nine. The folded paper vanished out of sight. He thought of the things Shadow had helped him find over the years, mostly food, but then the one bonanza. He laughed and recalled the prick of claws from the cat climbing up and riding on his shoulders, or curling up in his arms, purring happily at the luxury of being ported.

Most days, Shadow followed him. Some days, the cat slunk off on his own. And then there were the days when no Projects loomed and Solo was the one who followed along behind. Some days *he* was the shadow.

Like the day after fishing when Shadow had run off with a mind of his own. It was on the way back up to Supply, with his belly full of fish and Solo stuffed on corn and beans, that Shadow had raced ahead and had disappeared across a landing. Solo had followed with his flashlight to what he later would suspect to have been the cat's home. Otherwise, how would he know what was there?

Mewing and mewing by a door—Solo wary of another pile of bodies— but the apartment had been empty. Up on the kitchen counter, twirling, pawing at a cabinet full of little cans. Ancient and spotted with rust, but with pictures of cats on them. A madness in Shadow, and there, with a short cord plugged into the wall, a battered contraption, a mechanized can opener.

Solo smiled and gazed over the rail, thinking on the things found and lost over the years. He remembered pressing the button on the top of that gadget the first time, and how Shadow had whipped into a frenzy, how neatly the tops had come off. He remembered not being impressed at all with how the stuff in the cans tasted, but Shadow had a mind of his own.

Solo turned and studied the book with the torn pages. He was out of washers, so he left the book behind and reluctantly headed down to the farms. He headed off to do what needed to be done.

••••

Hacking at the greenery with his machete, Solo marveled that the farms hadn't long ago rotted to ruin without people around to tend them. But the lights were rigged to come on and off, and more than half of them still could. Water continued to dribble from pipes. Pumps kicked on and off with angry buzzes and loud grumbles. Electricity stolen from his realm down below was brought up on wires that snaked the stairwell walls. Nothing worked perfectly, but Solo saw that man's relationship to the crops mostly consisted of eating them. Now it was only him eating. Him and the rats and the birds and the worms and the other loose and lonely things.

The crops, with less tending and much less eating, were doing quite well. Life seemed to have some things figured out. But the machete knew the way through, and for years and years Solo whistled while he worked, tomatoes and corn falling at his feet with the great green stalks and vines until time and critter carried it all away.

He did not whistle this day. Even the machete sang a dull lament as it listlessly beat on stalk and vine. *Clang clang* where once it was *shing shing*. A sad sound from sad steel swung by a sad arm.

He continued through the thickest plots, needing to reach the far corners of the farm where the lights no longer burned, where the soil was cool and damp, where nothing grew anymore. A special place. Away from his weekly trips to gather food. A place he would come to as a destination rather than simply pass because it was along the way. Nothing lazy like that. He had passed enough death during his days, enough rusted patches and remnants of old bones. Every spot of the silo seemed to bear a stain, a spot the color of rust, where he could remember finding a body or a tangle of bones. Reminders. Reminders with no good memories.

A stalk of corn rebounded and swung at Solo's face with its leafy fingers. He batted it away and said nothing. He was in no mood to curse the corn. On happier days, maybe.

Leaving the heat of the lights, he entered a dark place. He liked it back here. It reminded him of the room beneath the servers, a private and safe place where one could hide and not be disturbed. And there, scattered among other abandoned and forgotten tools, a shovel. A thing he needed right when he needed it. This was the other way of finding things. It was when the silo was in a gifting mood. It wasn't a mood the silo got in often.

Solo knelt and placed his burden by the edge of the three-railing fence. The body in the bag had gone into that stiff phase. Soon, it would soften. After that . . .

Solo didn't want to think after that. He was an expert in some things he'd rather not know.

He collected the shovel and scampered over the top rail, too dark to hunt for the gate. The shovel growled and crunched through the dirt. He lifted each scoop into the air. Soft sighs and little piles slid out. Some things, you found just when you needed them, and Solo thought of the years that had passed so swiftly with his friend. He already missed the way Shadow rubbed on his shin while he worked, always in the way but clever enough not to be stepped on, coming in a flash whenever Solo broke out in a whistle, there at just the right time. A thing, found, before he even knew he needed it.

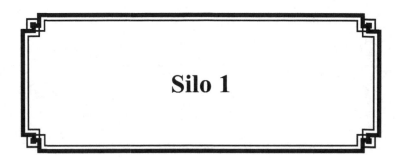

Silo 1

· 102 ·

Donald's boots echoed in the lower level shift storage, where thousands of pods lay packed together like gleaming stones. He stooped to check another nameplate. He had lost count of his position down the aisle and was worried he'd have to start over again. Bringing a rag to his mouth, he coughed. He wiped his lip and carried on. Something heavy and cold weighed down one pocket and pressed against his thigh. Something heavy and cold lay within his chest.

He finally found the pod marked "Troy," a jarring discovery, a self-discovery. Donald rubbed the glass and peered inside. There was a man in there, older than he seemed. Older than Donald remembered him. A blue cast overwhelmed pale flesh. White hair and white brows possessed an azure tint.

Donald studied the man, hesitated, reconsidered. He had come there with no wheelchair, no medical kit. Just a cold heaviness. A slice of truth and a desire to know more. Sometimes a thing needed opening before closure was found.

He bent by the control pad and repeated the procedure that had freed his sister, that had killed another. He thought of Charlotte up in the barracks as he entered his code. She couldn't know what he was doing down there. She couldn't know. Thurman had been like a second father to them both.

The dial was turned to the right. Numbers blinked, then ticked up a degree. Donald stood and paced. He circled that pod with a name on it, the name of a man they'd turned him into, this sarcophagus that now held his creator. The cold in Donald's heart spread into his limbs while Thurman warmed. Donald coughed into a rag stained pink. He tucked it back into his pocket and drew out the length of cord.

A report from Victor's files came to him as he stood there, roles reversed, thawing the Thaw Man. Victor had written of old experiments where guards and prisoners switched places, and the abused soon became the abuser. Donald found the idea detestable, that people could change so swiftly. Unbelievable. But he had seen good men and women arrive on the Hill with noble intentions, had seen them change. He had been given a dose of power on this shift and could feel its allure. His discovery was that evil men were made from evil systems, and that any man had the potential to be perverted. Which was why some systems needed to end.

A brief forever passed before temperatures rose and the lid was triggered. It opened with a sigh. Donald reached in and lifted it the rest of the way. He half expected a hand to shoot out and snatch his wrist. He half expected someone to clutch him by the neck, a fist to pummel him senseless. But there was just a man lying inside, still and steaming. Just a man pathetic and naked, a tube running into his arm, another between his legs. Muscles sagged. Pale flesh gathered in folds of wrinkles. Hair clung in wisps. Donald took Thurman's hands and placed them together on his chest. He looped the cord around his wrists, threaded it between Thurman's hands and around the loops of cord, then cinched a knot to draw the loops tight. Donald stood back and watched wrinkled lids for any sign of life. A sea of wet cobblestones stretched out in all directions, waiting patiently.

Thurman's lips moved. They parted and seemed to take a first, experimental gasp. It was like watching the dead become reanimated, and Donald appreciated for the first time the miracle of these machines. He coughed into his fist as Thurman stirred. The old man's eyes fluttered open, melted frost tracking from their corners, lending him a degree of false humanity. Wrinkled hands came up to wipe away the crust, and Donald knew what that felt like, lids that wouldn't fully part, that felt as though they'd grown together. A grunt spilled out as Thurman struggled with the cord. He came to more fully and saw that all was not right.

"Be still," Donald told him. He placed a hand on the old man's forehead, could feel the chill still in his flesh. "Easy."

"Anna—" Thurman whispered. He licked his lips, and Donald realized he hadn't even brought water, hadn't brought the bitter drink. There was no doubting what he was there to do.

"Can you hear me?" he asked.

Thurman's eyelids fluttered open again; his pupils dilated. He seemed to focus on Donald's face, eyes flicking back and forth in stunted recognition.

"Son—?" His voice was hoarse.

"Lie still," Donald told him, even as Thurman turned to the side and coughed into his bound hands. He peered confusedly at the cord knotted around his wrists. Donald turned and checked the door in the distance. "I need you to listen to me."

"What's going on here?" Thurman gripped the edge of the pod and tried to pull himself upright. Donald fished into his pocket for the pistol. Thurman gaped at the black steel as the barrel was leveled on him. His awareness thawed in an instant. He remained perfectly still, only his eyes moving as he met Donald's gaze. "What year is it?" he asked.

"Another two hundred years before you kill us all," Donald said. The barrel trembled with hate. He wrapped his other hand around the grip and took half a step back. Thurman was weak and bound, but Donald took no chances. The old man was like a coiled snake on a cold morning. He couldn't help but think of what he would be capable of as the day warmed.

Thurman licked his lips and studied Donald. Curls of steam rose from the old man's shoulders. "Anna told you," he finally said.

Donald felt a sadistic urge to tell him that Anna was dead. He felt a prideful twinge and wanted to insist that he'd figured it out for himself. He simply nodded, instead.

"You have to know this is the only way," Thurman whispered.

"There are a thousand ways," Donald said. He moved the gun to his other hand and dried his sweaty palm on his coveralls.

Thurman glanced at the gun, then searched the room beyond Donald for help. After a pause, he settled back against the pod. Steam rose from within the unit, but Donald could see him begin to shiver against the cold. He felt bad for not bringing a blanket. He held a gun, and felt bad for not bringing a blanket.

"I used to think you were trying to live forever," Donald said.

Thurman laughed. He inspected the knotted cord once more, looked at the needle and tube hanging from his arm. "Just long enough."

"Long enough for what? To whittle humanity down to nothing? To let one of these silos go free and kill the rest?"

Thurman nodded. He pulled his feet closer and hugged his shins. He looked so thin and fragile without his coveralls on, without his proud shoulders thrown back.

"You saved all these people just to kill most of them. And us as well."

Thurman whispered a reply.

"Louder," Donald said.

The old man mimed taking a drink. Donald showed him the gun. It was all he had. Thurman tapped his chest and tried to speak again, and Donald took a wary step closer. "Tell me why," Donald said. "I'm the one in charge here. Me. Tell me or I swear I'll let everyone out of their silos right now."

Thurman's eyes became slits. "Fool," he hissed. "They'll kill each other."

His voice was barely audible. Donald could hear all the cryopods around them humming. He stepped closer, more confident with each passing moment that this was the right thing to do.

"I know what you think they'll do to one another," Donald said. "I know about this great cleanse, this reset." He jabbed the gun at Thurman's chest. "I know you see these silos as starships taking people to a better world. I've read every note and memo and file you have access to. But this is what I want to hear from you before you die—"

Donald felt his legs wobble. A coughing fit seized him. He fumbled for his cloth, but pink spittle struck the silver pod before he could cover his mouth. Thurman watched. Donald steadied himself, tried to remember what he was saying.

"I want to know why all the heartache," Donald said, his voice scratchy, his throat on fire. "All the miserable lives coming and going, the people down here you plan on killing, on never waking. Your own daughter . . ." He searched Thurman for some reaction. "Why not freeze us for a thousand years and wake us when it's done? I know now what I helped you build. I want to know why we couldn't sleep through it all. If you wanted a better place for us, why not take us there? Why the suffering?"

Thurman remained perfectly still.

"Tell me why," Donald said. His voice cracked, but he pretended to be okay. He lifted the barrel, which had drooped.

"Because no one can know," Thurman finally said. "It has to die with us."

"What has to die?"

Thurman licked his lips. "Knowledge. The things we left out of the Legacy. The ability to end it all with the flip of a switch."

Donald laughed. "You think we won't discover them again? The means to destroy ourselves?"

Thurman shrugged his naked shoulders. The steam rising from them had dissipated. "Eventually. Which is a longer time than right now."

Donald waved his gun at the pods all around him. "And so all this goes as well. We're supposed to choose one tribe, one of your starships to land, and everything else is shut down. That's the pact you made."

Thurman nodded.

"Well someone broke your pact," Donald said. "Someone put me here in your place. I'm the shepherd, now."

Thurman's eyes widened. His gaze traveled from the gun to the badge clipped on Donald's collar. Clattering teeth were silenced by the clenching and unclenching of his jaw. "No," he said.

"I never asked for this job," Donald said, more to himself than to Thurman. He steadied the barrel. "For any of these jobs."

"Me neither," Thurman replied, and Donald was again reminded of those prisoners and those guards. This could be him in that pod. It could be anyone standing there with that gun. It was the system.

There were a hundred other things he wanted to ask or say. He wanted to tell this man how much like a father he'd been to him, but what did that mean when fathers could be as abusive as they were loving? He wanted to scream at Thurman for the damage he'd done to the world, but some part of Donald knew the damage had long ago been done and that it was irreversible. And finally, there was a part of him that wanted to beg for help, to free this man from his pod, a part that wanted to take his place, to curl up inside, and go back to sleep—a part that found being the prisoner was so much easier than remaining on guard. But his sister was up above, recovering. They both had more questions that needed answering. And in a silo not far away, a transformation was taking place, the end of an uprising, and Donald intended to see how that played out.

All this and more flitted through a brain on fire while another looked on and thawed. It wouldn't be long before Dr. Wilson returned to his desk and possibly glanced at a screen just as the right camera cycled through. It wouldn't be long. And even as Thurman's mouth parted to say something, Donald realized that waking the old man for these excuses had been a mistake. There was little to learn here.

Thurman leaned forward. He seemed to sense the accumulation of second thoughts. "Donny," he said. He reached out with bound wrists for the pistol in Donald's hand. His arms moved slowly and feebly, not with the hope—Donald didn't think—of snatching the gun away, but possibly with the desire to pull it close, to press it against his chest or his mouth the way Victor had, such was the sadness in the old man's eyes.

Thurman reached past the lip of the pod and groped for the gun, and Donald very nearly handed it to him, just to see what he would do with it.

He pulled the trigger instead. He pulled the trigger before he could regret it.

The bang was unconscionably loud. There was a bright flash, a horrid noise echoing out across a thousand sleeping souls, and then a man slumping down into a coffin.

Donald's hand trembled. He remembered his first days in office, all this man had done for him, that meeting very early on. He had been hired for a job for which he was barely qualified. He had been hired for a job he could not at first discern. That first morning, waking up a congressman, realizing he and only a handful of others stood at the helm of a powerful nation, had filled him with as much fear as accomplishment. And all along, he had been an inmate asked to erect the walls of his own cell. All along.

This time would be different. This time, he would accept responsibility and lead without fear. He and his sister in secret. They would find out what was wrong with the world and fix it. Restore order to all that had been lost. An experiment had begun in another silo, a changing of the guard, and Donald intended to watch it play out.

He reached up and closed the lid on the pod. There was pink spittle on its shiny surface. Donald coughed once, not a bad fit, and wiped his mouth. He stuffed the pistol away and left the pod behind, his heart racing from what he'd done, and the pod with a dead man inside—it quietly hummed.

Silo 17

Year Thirty-Four

· 103 ·

Solo worked the rope through the handles of the empty plastic jugs. They rattled together and made a kind of sonorous music. Holding them up, he thought they looked like the silver fish that hung on a string in the book marked "Me" for Mediterranean. He laughed at this and jiggled the jugs. "Here, fishy," he said. And then he grew sad. He remembered catching the fish and leaving the last of them all alone. All by himself.

Solo collected his canvas bag and stood there a moment, scratching his beard, forgetting something. What had he forgotten? Patting his chest, he made sure he had the key. It was an old habit from years ago that he couldn't shake. The key, of course, was no longer there. He had tucked it in a drawer when things no longer needed locking, when there was no one left to be afraid of.

He took two bags of empty soup and veggie cans with him—hardly a dent in the massive pile of garbage. With his hands full and every step causing a clang and a clatter, he carried his things down the dark passage to the shaft of light at the far end.

It took two trips up the ladder to unload everything. He passed between the black machines, many of which had gone silent over the years, succumbing to the heat, perhaps. The filing cabinet had to be moved before the door would open. The silo had no locks and no people— but no dummies, either. He pulled the heavy door, could feel his father's presence as always, and stepped out into the wide world crowded with nothing but ghosts and things so bad he couldn't remember them.

The hallways were bright and empty. Solo waved to where he knew the cameras were as he passed. He often thought that he'd see himself on the monitors one day, but the cameras had quit working forever ago. And besides, there'd have to be two of him for that to happen. One to stand there and wave, another down by the monitors. He laughed at how silly he was. He was Solo.

Stepping out on the landing brought fresh air and a troubling sense of height. Solo thought of the rising water. How long before it reached him? Too long, he thought. He would be gone by then. But it was sad to think of his little home under the servers full of water one day. All the empty cans in the great pile by the shelves would float to the top. The computer and the radio would gurgle little bubbles of air. That made him laugh, thinking of them gurgling and the cans bobbing around on the surface, and he no longer cared if it happened or not. He tossed both bags of empty cans over the railing and listened for them to crunch down on the landing at fifty-two. They dutifully did. He turned to the stairs.

Up or down? Up meant tomatoes, cucumbers, and squash. Down meant berries, corn, and digging for potatoes. Down required more cooking. Solo marched up.

He counted the steps as he went. "Eight, nine, ten," he whispered. Each of the stairs was different. There were a lot of stairs. They had all kinds of company, all kinds of fellow stairs like friends to either side. More things just like them. "Hello, step," he said, forgetting to count. The step said nothing. He didn't speak whatever they spoke, the ringing singing of lonely boots clanging up and down.

A noise. Solo heard a noise. He stopped and listened, but usually the noises knew when he was doing that and they got shy. This was another of those noises. He heard things that weren't there all the time. And there were pumps and lights wired all over the place that turned on and off at their whim and choosing. One of these pumps had sprung a leak years ago, and Solo had fixed it himself. He needed a new Project. He was doing a lot of the same ones over and over, like chopping his beard when it got to his chest, and all of them were boring.

Only one break to drink and pee before he reached the farms. His legs were good. Stronger, even, than when he was younger and never got out.

The hard things got easier the more you did them. It didn't make it any more fun to do the hard things, though. Solo wished they would just be easy the first time.

He rounded the last bend before the landing on twelve, was just about to start whistling a harvest tune, when he saw that he'd left the door open. He wasn't sure how. Solo never left the door open. Any doors.

There was something propped up in the corner against the rail. It looked like scrap from one of his Projects. A broken piece of plastic pipe. He picked it up. There was water in it. Solo sniffed the tube. It smelled funny, and he started to dump the water over the rail when the pipe slipped from his fingers. He froze and waited for the distant clatter. It never came.

Clumsy. He cursed himself for being forgetful and clumsy. Left a door open. He was headed inside when he saw what was holding it open. A black handle. He reached for it, saw that it was a knife plunged down through the grating.

There was a noise inside, deep within the farms. Solo stood very still for a moment. This was not his knife. He was not this forgetful. He pulled the blade out and allowed the door to close as a thousand thoughts flitted through his waking mind. A rat couldn't do something like this. Only a person could. Or a powerful ghost.

He should do something. He should tie the handles together or wedge something under the doors, but he was too afraid. He turned and ran, instead. He ran down the stairs, jugs clattering together, his empty pack flopping on his back, someone else's knife clutched in his hand. When the jugs caught on the railing, the rope snagged, and he tugged twice before giving up and letting them go. His hole. He had to get to his hole. Breathing heavily, he hurried on, the clangs and vibrations of some *other* disrupting his solitude. He didn't have to stop to listen for them. This was a loud ghost. Loud and solid. Solo thought of his machete, which had snapped in half years ago. But he had this knife. This knife. Around and around the stairs he went, sorely afraid. Down to the landing. Wrong landing! Thirty-three. One more to go. Stopped counting, stopped counting. He nearly stumbled, he ran so fast. Sweating. Home.

Solo pushed through the busted gate and hurried down the halls. One of the lights overhead was out. A Project. But no time. He reached the metal door and heaved. Ran inside. Stopped and ran back. He leaned on the door and pushed it closed. He got low and put his shoulder into the filing cabinet, slid that against the door, an awful screech. He thought he heard footsteps outside. Someone fast. Sweat dripped off his nose. He clutched the knife and ran, ran through the servers. There was a squeal behind him, metal on metal. Solo was not alone. They had come for him. They were coming, coming. He could taste the fear in his mouth like metal. He raced to the grate, wished he'd left it open. At least the locks were busted. Rusted. No, that wasn't good. He needed the locks. Solo lowered himself down the ladder and grabbed the grating, began to pull it over his head. He would hide. Hide. Like the early years. And then someone was tugging the grate from his hand. He was swiping at them with the knife. There was a startled scream, a woman, breathing heavy and looking down at him, telling him to take it easy.

Solo trembled. His boot slipped a little on the ladder. But he held. He held very still while this woman talked to him. Her eyes were wide and alive. Her lips moved. She was hurt, didn't want to hurt him. She just wanted his name. She was happy to see him. The wetness in her eyes was from being happy to see him. And Solo thought—maybe—that he himself was like a shovel or a can opener or any of those rusty things laying about. He was something that could be found. He could be found. And someone had.

Dedicated to Andy Bell, Erin Jump Fry, and Janet Winslow.

You are never alone.

Note to the Reader

This is the final shift, everyone. Next up is DUST, where we'll see how Juliette and Lukas are able to manage Silo 18, what happens to Solo and the kids, and how Donald handles the fate of humanity. Things are breaking down rapidly. It should be a lot of fun.

Just so you know, there's probably not an epilogue this time around. I wouldn't leave the end of this trilogy on a cliffhanger—that would be cruel. So, no point in turning the page, nosiree. Why don't you go outside and play, instead? That's right, resist the urge. Just put the book down and trust me.

Nothing to see here . . .

"But I have promises to keep, and miles to go before I sleep, and miles to go before I sleep."

-Robert Frost

Epilogue

Donald sat in the otherwise empty comm room. He had every station to himself, had sent the others to lunch and ordered those who weren't hungry to take a break anyway. And they listened to him. Donald was in charge.

A blinking light on the neighboring comm station signaled Silo 6 attempting to make a call. They would have to wait. Donald sat and listened to the ringing in his headset as he placed a call of his own.

It rang and rang. He checked the cord, traced it to the jack, made sure it was plugged in correctly. Between two of the comm stations lay an unfinished game of cards, hands set aside from Donald ordering everyone out. There was a discard pile with a queen of spades on top. Finally, a click in his headset.

"Hello?" he said.

He waited. He thought he could hear someone breathing on the other line.

"Lukas?"

"No," the voice said. It was a softer voice. And yet harder, somehow.

"Who is this?" he asked. He was used to talking to Lukas.

"It doesn't matter who this is," the woman said. And Donald knew perfectly well. He looked over his shoulders, made sure he was still alone, then leaned forward in his chair.

"We're not used to hearing from mayors," he said.

"And I'm not used to being one."

Donald could practically hear the woman sneer at him. "I didn't ask for my job," he confided.

"And yet here we are."

"Here we are."

There was a pause.

"You know," Donald said. "If I were any good at my job, I'd press a button right now and shut your silo down."

"Why don't you?"

The mayor's voice was flat. Curious. It sounded like a real question rather than a dare.

"I doubt you'd believe me if I told you."

"Try me," she said. And Donald wished he still had the folder on this woman. He had carried it everywhere his first weeks on shift. And now, when he needed it—

"A long time ago," he told her, "I saved your silo. It would be a shame to end it now."

"You're right. I don't believe you."

There was a noise in the hallway. Donald removed one of the cups from his ears and glanced over his shoulder. His comm engineer stood outside the door with a thermos in one hand, a slice of bread in the other. Donald raised his finger and asked him to wait.

"I know where you've been," Donald told this mayor, this woman sent to clean. "I know what you've seen. And I—"

"You don't know the first thing about what I've seen," she spat, her words sharp as razors.

Donald felt his temperature go up. This was not the conversation he wanted to have with this woman. He wasn't prepared. He cupped his hand over the microphone, could sense that he was both running out of time and losing her.

"Be careful," he said. "That's all I'm saying—"

"Listen to me," she told him. "I'm sitting over here in a roomful of truth. I've seen the books. I'm going to dig until I get to the heart of what you people have done."

Donald could hear her breathing.

"I know the truth you're looking for," he said quietly. "You may not like what you find."

"*You* may not like what I find, you mean."

"Just . . . be careful." Donald lowered his voice. "Be careful where you go digging."

There was a pause. Donald glanced over his shoulder at the engineer, who took a sip from his thermos.

"Oh, we'll be careful where we dig," this Juliette finally answered. "I'd hate for you to hear us coming."